# Our Wraparound Porch

## A Novel

### DIANA DAUB FRENCH

Published by *LifeWorld Publishing*
1713 S. Arlington Avenue
Independence, MO 64052



**Publisher's Note**
This is a work of fiction. Names, characters, incidents either are the product of the author's imagination or are used fictitiously, and any resemblance to actual persons, living or dead, events, or locations is entirely coincidental.

Printed in the United States of America

ISBN 978-0-9976670-1-1

***Cover Art by Alice Oshel***

# DEDICATION

For my delightful mother,
Virginia Johanna Burns Daub,
who encouraged me to go for my dreams
and
for my inspiring husband,
Walter Everett French,
who convinced me I could.

## CHAPTER ONE

Untying the strings was out of the question. I didn't want to use my teeth, so I ran to the kitchen to get the scissors, then back to the front porch where the package sat on the table. Strings off, I ripped through the brown wrapping paper and tore open the enclosed card. It read: *We'll see you at midnight via Skype, don't forget to register. Love, Tina, Henri and Jakie. P.S Forget what we said about you needing a boyfriend.*

That Tina. My daughter—she told me I need a man in my life. She is so bossy and off beam about this boyfriend subject. Now she says, forget it. Thank you, Tina. I'm perfectly content with memories of your father, my work, my friends, spending time with Mom, gardening and reading. Wait till Tina finds out I'm going back to school for a degree in English Literature.

Tina is totally unlike me; I'm the predictable, steady one. She's impulsive, even rebellious. She frequently rebels before she knows all the facts. Jake said she has spunk. I appreciate her spunk, but I'm remembering the adolescent Tina, she has matured, certainly. She lives in France now with her husband, Henri and their five-year-old son, Jakie. So far away, a little town, Grignan, where Henri grew up. From our conversations over the last years, I know she has thrown herself into marriage, motherhood and French cooking. The pictures she sends me of her family are precious. Henri calls her pastry creations exquisite.

Glad FedEx delivered the package on time. This was my Christmas gift from France. Tina told me my gift was delayed, described it, and let me know our New Year's Eve call would be high tech.

I installed the webcam on my computer and registered with Skype to get ready for Tina's call. Done. Now we can visit face-to-face on the internet. I checked to make sure I was still logged into Skype then looked at the clock in the corner of my computer screen. It read 3:35 p.m. I wouldn't have to wait long. Tina and Henri's clock would strike midnight in France in less than half an hour. In my excited state I couldn't sit and watch the numbers turn over on the clock. I threw on a jacket, walked out onto my front porch, leaned over the painted wooden railing, and looked across the street to the U.N. Peace Plaza. I love the sculpture of the child reaching up to the sky, balancing a dove on her fingertip, head thrown back—no cares in the world. Beyond the plaza the Temple shone in the sunlight. The day was clear, the sky blue. I thanked the Lord that Jake and I bought this house before Tina was born. We hoped to have more children, but it wasn't to be. That was okay. Tina filled our lives, from the time we held her in our arms and gazed into the wonder of her dark amber eyes. We vowed to be the best parents we could be.

From my porch I can see not only the Peace Plaza and Temple, but the Auditorium and the Stone Church. I enjoy walking the mile around the Temple and Auditorium whenever weather permits—soaking in the beauty of the blooming Bradford pears in springtime, and in the fall, the gorgeous red leaves of these same trees. They are everywhere on the grounds. This is Zion, I thought, designated as such in 1831 by Joseph Smith Jr., the founder and prophet of the Church. I wonder what he would think of Independence now.

At five minutes to four my cell phone alarm drew me back inside to my computer to wait for Tina's Skype call. Soon my screen alerted me that I had a call, so I clicked to answer it.

Tina's face appeared. I could see her for the first time in a year. This new technology. How mystifying. How wonderful!

"Happy New Year, Mom. I see you. Isn't this great? You are a little wavy, but I'm so glad you received the camera on time."

"Tina, Happy New Year. Henri, I see you. Are you trying to hide behind Tina? Happy New Year to you and to your family. Oh, are they all there? Hi everyone. Thank you for the camera! This is unbelievable, to actually see you, but where is my grandson?"

"I'm sorry, Mom, he fell asleep a little while ago. We tried to keep him awake, but he couldn't hang in. Can you wait to talk to him tomorrow?" asked Tina.

"I guess I'll have to. I sure wish we could do our ritual in person, but it's wonderful to at least see each other on the screen. Are you ready?"

"I am, but Henri only has four. I remind him every year that ten New Year's resolutions are required, but he's not buying it."

"Ah, Henri, Tina and I will go first to give you more time to work on yours."

"But, Mère Marjie, I need more time than that to think about this. I know how serious you and Tina are about it. I don't want to resolve to do something that I know I can't do."

"Remember, Henri, with God all things are possible and if we don't set goals, how will we accomplish anything in this life?"

Tina laughed and said, "We don't take the resolutions that seriously. There's a lot of fun in this and maybe Beelzebub can help us."

Henri hissed, "Tina. Mon Dieu—that is no joking matter."

I wasn't sure what to say, but said, "Tina, please don't speak of the adversary as if he is a helper. And speak for yourself about the seriousness of our New Year's resolutions, Tina. I enjoy the challenge, don't you?"

Tina chimed in again. "Okay, Mom, whatever. You start."

I wanted to read the least important resolution first, but thought—they are all important. I decided to read the one that might be a surprise to Tina last.

"Here I go: Number 10—Eat healthier, Number 9—Exercise five days a week, at least thirty minutes of aerobics, Number 8—Spend more time with Mom, Number 7—Spend one hour per day in private prayer and study of the scriptures, Number 6—Begin a prayer support group that meets once a week, Number 5—Attend Prayer for Peace at the Temple five days a week, Number 4—Become a Youth Friend or foster grandparent, Number 3—Help start a lunch program for the homeless, Number 2—Start a recycling program at the church and learn more about ways to shrink my energy footprint, and Number 1—Go back to school for a degree in English Literature. Okay, your turn, Tina."

"Mother, how will you ever find time to do all of that, work at the senior living home and school, too?"

"I repeat—with God all things are possible, besides I am already doing some of the things on my list and I want to make sure I keep them up."

"I think that's cheating, Mom, but I'll ignore it in the spirit of the season. Here's my list: Number 10—Think before I speak. That will be the hardest one, I know. Number 9—Quit smoking. Maybe that will be the hardest one."

I had to interrupt, "Fantastic, honey. I'm with you all the way. That's the best news I've heard in a long time—the quitting smoking, I mean."

Tina resumed reading her list: Number 8—Read ten books from the list of 100 books recommended by the College Board, Number 7—Read Oprah's top ten novels from the last decade, Number 6—Read to Jakie every night, Number 5—Exercise, Number 4—Lose forty pounds,

Number 3—Improve my pastry skills, Number 2—Move back home with Mom."

I interrupted again. "Wait, wait a minute here. Your resolution is to move in with me! What about Henri and Jakie?"

I thought I detected a slight irritation in Tina's voice. "Do you want to hear my Number 1 resolution or not?" she said.

I could barely contain myself, "By all means. Let me hear it."

"My number one resolution for 2010 is to open a French café in Independence so Henri, Jakie and I can be close to you! What do you think? We have some savings of our own, but you still have the money that Dad left for me, right, and we may need to borrow a little from you, but not much."

My senses brought me to full attention—my voice trembled, "Tina, Henri—you don't know how wonderful this sounds to me. Of course, you can use what he left for you any way you want. It's always been there for you. And I will help, too. Will your family be able to do without you, Henri? When are you coming? I hope it is soon!"

"Don't cry, Mère Marjie. This is good news, oui?" Henri asked.

"The very best news I could ever think of. When are you planning to move back here? Can you come tomorrow? Tina, your grandma will be ecstatic."

"We are planning to come home in April. We don't have an exact time yet. We'll let you know," yelled Tina.

The noise of Henri's family celebration made it almost impossible for me to hear them so we said goodbye, deciding it would be better to talk tomorrow when it was quieter and when Jakie was awake to talk.

I disconnected from Skype and ran upstairs two steps at a time to look at the bedroom Tina occupied while growing up. It still had the matching Laura Ashley pink rose wallpaper, bedspread, curtains, and throw pillows that Tina begged for as a young teen. For some reason she had never tired of it, but I'll bet that they will want something different if they are going to stay here for any length of time.

What a change this will be. It will be like a horde of elephants taking over a monastery, but a wonderful horde. I'll ask them tomorrow if they want me to start redecorating or wait until they get here. Jakie can have the guest room for his bedroom and I can move my sewing room downstairs, so he can have a play room upstairs or maybe we should put the play room downstairs, closer to the main activities of the house. So much to think about. Did they say something about opening a restaurant here? I'm so thrilled that I can't think straight. Too much to take in at one time—Tina's going to quit smoking and sounds like she's planning to do a lot of reading. That girl never leaves enough time for sleep. I wonder who she takes after. It couldn't be me, could it? Maybe we should reduce the number of resolutions, so we could decide what is really important—what we truly value in life.

My gaze landed on the framed picture of Jesus sitting on Tina's night stand. *Lord, why does Tina think she has to tease me about my faith in You? Jake and I raised her in the church. She was fed with love and prayer by us and her grandparents and church family. Why this rebellion against You? When did it start? My only child, this precious daughter of yours, God, and mine. Please give me the wisdom to say the things that will help her to come back to You.*

It was only then that I remembered we didn't give Henri a chance to read his resolutions, reminding me that before she was married this ritual was celebrated by Tina and me alone. Jake didn't want to have anything to do with it. He would say, *You two just tell me what to do and I'll do it. You make enough resolutions for all of us.*

♥

I arrived at Bingham Manor before my regular start time, eager to share Tina's news with the residents and fellow staff members. As I passed the gathering room I heard a loud woman's voice, saying:

"I'll bet my name was written on every men's room wall in Independence—*For a good time call Mildred.*"

Mildred. We never knew what startling utterance would escape her unfettered mouth. Ignoring that interesting tidbit, I stopped at the front desk to quickly share my unbelievable news with Helen, the Manor director, and Joyce, the head nurse. They wanted to give me a play-by-play of yesterday's Chiefs football game. Thankfully, this was one topic they agreed upon. I steered clear of them whenever Obamacare crossed their lips.

Next I went to my office to check the activities schedule for this week and for the whole month. My thoughts drifted back to Tina's news. How will I be able to work full time and go to night school with my family living with me and all the other things I had planned for this year? Some things would have to fall off my to-do list, probably the English lit degree would have to wait. I wanted to help Tina and Henri start their business and spend as much time with Jakie as possible. One day at a time.

After our Wii bowling session, I joined the folks watching the *Who Wants to be a Millionaire?* game show.

"Hi, Marjie. Where have you been? That fool from yesterday just threw away almost $58,000," laughed Mary Florence.

Anna Jean jumped in with, "Can you believe it, Marjie? He had $57,800 and a question about what actress played on 'Buffy, the Vampire Slayer' came up. He had to pick the one who played Buffy. Everyone knows that Sarah Michelle Gellar played her. He picked Mary Tyler Moore. What an idiot. He still had two lifelines left. You know darn well the audience could have answered that question, but, NO, the dang fool picked Mary Tyler Moore even though he wasn't sure. I swear I'm gonna have a heart attack if I keep watching this crazy show." Anna Jean was upset as usual over the contestants making mistakes.

"Anna Jean, Honey, please calm down and think of your blood pressure. They gave him $1000 didn't they?" I asked soothingly.

Her eyes filled with tears. "Sure they did, Marjie, but he could have used his lifeline and still be playing and maybe won the million."

Mary Florence interrupted, "Shush, the commercial's over. Let's see who they bring on now. Oh look, it's a real cute blond. I'll bet she's smarter than that last knucklehead."

I sat on the floral couch between the two venerable women I had come to love, ever since I started working at the senior home. Mary Florence was ninety-two. She moved into Bingham Manor after her son died, leaving no family for her to live with. Her mind was sharp, but her body wasn't keeping up. She required the use of a walker, managing with agility, going up and down stairs, picking things up off the floor. She was a poster child for the elderly with physical impairments. Even though she believed she could still manage alone, Mary Florence didn't particularly like living by herself, so she moved in here and went about bringing joy into the lives of other lonely people, thereby, making her life useful.

She and Anna Jean connected right away. They were the shortest residents in the place, so they saw eye-to-eye, literally. Neither of them had ever reached more than four feet ten inches tall and through the years they had become shorter still.

Anna Jean was only eighty-three years old, but several mini-strokes had taken their toll, her memory being the victim. She remembered her childhood best, and raising her children, but not much of the current day, except for her game shows. If truth be told, she got pretty mixed up with them sometimes, but Mary Florence and I never let on.

Anna Jean's temper soared whenever her memory was questioned. At times, she exhibited some symptoms of paranoia. She accused the laundry staff of switching her bras and panties with Mildred's underwear. The funny part was that Mildred's daughter kept her supplied with underwear from Victoria's Secret. It was such a scandal with the residents and no secret to anyone on the second floor, that an old woman wore Victoria's Secret. The residents chattered about who she was trying to impress.

There comes a time when a push-up bra isn't a good choice. This was one of those times. Mildred had passed the not a good choice about twenty years ago. Well, there were rumors about her and Eugene Sylvester, but Anna Jean didn't believe a word of it.

During the commercial Anna Jean told me, "Don't believe any rumors you hear about Eugene and Mildred. Eugene always sits with me at dinner and always asks me to dance before anyone else. I'll just up and ask Eugene if he has a thing for Mildred. And if he says he does, well, then, he can just sit with Mildred and dance with Mildred from now on. I'll tell him, 'Don't try making up to me anymore, you two-timing sleezeball. I know a rat when I smell one. Your Royal Copenhagen won't serve you well with me anymore.'"

Having decided what to do about Eugene and Mildred, Anna Jean focused her attention back on the show. She yelled at the TV, "Go, girl, go!" After the first five questions, the blond had a total of $42,000 and she hadn't used any lifelines yet.

I clapped my hands and cheered along with Anna Jean and Mary Florence, but my mind never left thinking of Tina and Henri and Jakie.

❤

"Mom, I have something to tell you," said Tina when we finally connected.

I had been unable to reach her all day yesterday and I wanted to talk to Jakie. Naturally, I worried that something was wrong because I'm a born fretter.

"Henri and I decided to keep our move a secret from Jakie and all of Henri's family for a while. We don't want to upset things right now."

"Are you having second thoughts?" I asked.

"I really want to come home. I'm tired of having to speak French to everyone but Henri and Jakie. And I miss you and Grandma and my friends…"

I sensed a *but* coming and here it came.

"But…Henri worries about his father's health. Gregoirie's been tired and irritable lately, totally unlike himself. Henri and I had to take over the cooking classes. And, Mom, after I told you the news I watched Jakie sleeping crossways on his grandparents' king-sized bed with all his cousins. I wondered how Jakie would handle the news that he was to be uprooted from all he had ever known—transported across the ocean to a foreign land, where English would be the primary language, where he has no friends, barely knows his American grandmother and great-grandmother. Worst of all he won't be able to see Mamie and Papi, aunts and uncles, his cousins, his friends, his *country—for he is a Frenchman*. I started asking myself—will he hate us for taking him to the U.S.?"

As I listened to Tina talk, I sat stunned. Even though I knew there would be sacrifices for me, I hadn't really thought through what it meant for them. I mainly knew that I was missing out on their lives, on my only grandchild's life. I felt it was my turn to enjoy Jakie. Henri's family had had him all his five years. He is half American after all. I didn't know what to say, so I said nothing.

"Mom, are you there?" Tina sounded so tired. What could I say to her?

*Lord, help me. Not sure if this is right, but it feels right at this moment.* "Tina, you know I want you here, but I also want what is best for all of you."

"Mom, I know you do. You are the best person in the world. I wish I could be more like you."

Whew. I never thought I would hear those words come out of her mouth. She fought me every step of her growing up. She left home at age eighteen and has only been back to give birth to Jakie and days later, unexpectedly, bury her father. Then she was gone again. Back to her fields of lavender, truffle forests, vineyards and ancient buildings. Back to her French family, Henri's family. I love my daughter and we are as close as we can be living thousands of miles apart. I accept her decision, but I was so looking forward to seeing them all.

Our relationship, always tenuous, seemed better now than when we lived together even though it amounts to nothing more than long distance calls, online chats, now Skype and occasional Hallmark cards. We planned to visit back and forth more often, but it is expensive. I've been there four times, twice with Jake, Tina's first Christmas in France and when she graduated from cooking school. After Jake died I flew over alone for Jakie's second and fourth birthdays.

"Tina, you and Henri have to decide together what you want to do."

I still didn't get to talk to Jakie. I felt like someone jumped off the opposite end of a seesaw plummeting me to the hard earth.

## CHAPTER TWO

The monthly activities meetings with the residents rank alongside
dental cleanings and just above colonoscopies, but it was first Monday at
2:00 p.m. so I sat in the dining room at tables pushed together to make a
large square.

While I waited for all the wheel chairs to be locked in place and
everyone else to take their seats, my conversation with Tina tumbled
through my mind. Each time we talked I grew more convinced that she
and Henri were not on the same page about this move. Better think about
this later. Now, the residents need my attention.

Victoria Secret-wearing, self-proclaimed bathroom wall appearee,
Mildred, said "Marjie, can you please call this meeting to order?"

"Mildred, I am not the chair of this committee, you are, so please,
go ahead and call us to order."

"As usual, they aren't listening to me," she replied in her whiniest
voice.

She was right. All members of the committee chatted gaily, or at
least, unconcernedly. Out of fifteen people present, I guess at least ten
different conversations existed, some residents nattering totally on their
own.

I took the gavel from Mildred's hand, raised my voice to the highest
level possible, the one I would have used to call the children in from
recess had I ever been a school teacher without a bell to ring.

"Hello, let's get the meeting started."

Eugene added his baritone, singing "mañana, mañana—mañana is
soon enough for me."

Half the women pretended to swoon, Anna Jean possessively laid
her head on his shoulder, a couple of men yelled "Ataboy, Eugene", the
rest ignored him. Mary Florence reminded everyone that *Millionaire*

would be on soon. That did it. Now everyone began talking at once. I heard Elvis, the Beatles, Starlight Theatre, the Zoo, Powell Gardens, the Rose Garden at Loose Park, the Nelson Art Gallery, barbershop quartet, bowling, shopping, dancing, the Outback, Red Lobster, and Ruby Tuesday mentioned.

Mildred, Mary Florence and I simultaneously yelled, "Quiet!" getting everyone's attention. After laughter died down, I asked if we could go around the table and get their suggestions one-at-a-time. Thirty minutes later we had our schedule for the following month and some ideas to be worked out, like when can the Elvis and Beatles impersonators come.

♥

I love my Mom. She is fun, perky, and always prepared for every occasion with a trite cliché which she especially loves to use on me. With such a mother, I should be easy-going, but I missed that gene. I have no idea how the worry DNA of seriousness landed in me. Music and laughter filled our home when I was a child. Mom taught music at Noland Elementary and she tried out all the instruments and songs on me first. Dad joined in on the triangle, maracas, tambourine, but his favorite was the cymbals. What fun we had—our little three-man band. I tried to make Tina's life fun growing up and believe I succeeded for the most part with the help of my parents and Jake, my rock. Maybe my serious nature got in the way? I miss Tina so, and Jakie. I have an ache in my heart that can only be cured by holding them close. But I do have Mom and I cherish her more and more as time goes by.

After work I picked Mom up and we drove to the Salon to redeem the gift certificates her friend, Mary, gave her for Christmas. She told me that my gift to her would be to join her for a haircut, a mani and pedi. How could I turn that down? But I did give her a framed picture of Tina, Henri and Jakie with the words *Family—Life's Treasures* written on the mat.

As we drove I broke the news that Tina and Henri were now undecided about moving home. "Now, Marjie, blood is thicker than water, I'm sure Tina will decide to come home," said Mom.

"But I don't want her and Henri to be separated and what about Jakie?"

"How well do you know Tina? She always manages to get her way. She'll talk Henri into moving here. Just give it time. Take it easy for a few, will you?"

Somehow her clichés reassured me, so I took a deep breath. Well, several deep breaths.

As we entered the salon we were welcomed by a young woman with long, sleek black hair, a curvy figure, dressed in something that looked like she was wrapped in a turquoise-colored wide ribbon from her shoulders to her knees.

"Welcome to Casa de Clasico. I am the owner, Adonia. Do you have an appointment?"

Adonia was as beautiful as her name. I couldn't help but wonder how she got into that ribbon wrap get up and what would happen if it started unraveling. I would never be able to wear something like that. I would catch it on something, a nail sticking out of a doorway, the edge of a table, something would grab onto it. I loved the color though. Turquoise is one of my favorites.

Mom smiled and handed our gift certificates to Adonia.

"Bueno, you both have the *Head to Toe* package. We will do your hair, a manicure and pedicure."

Two small young women stood up and claimed us for our manicures and pedicures. These women spoke English well enough to ask how long and what shape we wanted our nails, but didn't seem to want to carry on a conversation.

The girl reached for my foot and began untying my shoe laces. Once the foot massage started, I heard myself moan. "I might be able to get used to this."

"Don't get greedy, Marjie. Christmas comes but once a year," said Mom.

Internal groan. External smile.

Our nails were done—*Fire Engine Red* for Mom and *Bomb Pop Cherry* for me. We both refused the acrylic nails, preferring to keep our nails natural. Both of us like our nails a little short—it makes gardening and typing so much easier. Mom admitted that she was afraid of scratching small babies at church when she let her nails get out of hand.

Adonia reappeared and beckoned us to follow her.

We entered a room with modern looking chairs—all in turquoise, facing a wall of well-lit mirrors. Four turquoise shampoo stations filled one corner of the room. In the opposite corner sat comfy looking loveseats, you guessed it, in turquoise. But there was no time to sit and relax. We were met immediately by Rodolfo and Antonio, who as if choreographed, bent at the waist and kissed our hands. Adonia disappeared. The gentlemen escorted us to their respective styling areas. Mom's sparkling eyes and wide grin showed her excitement, but I bit my lip, then intentionally formed my mouth into an automatic smile.

Rodolfo ran his fingers through my short, mini-Afro, mostly white hair. "May I be blunt with you, Senora Jamison? Your hair makes you look about sixty-five to seventy years old. I know you are not of that age. Your skin is almost wrinkle-free and very supple. We must make a drastic change. It will take time. You must promise to allow me six months to one year to bring your hair back to your youth. We must have some growing time. You are too beautiful a woman to wear this old ladies' hair style. What was your original hair color?" Without waiting for an answer or taking a breath, he announced to the world at large—"It was auburn—a beautiful light auburn with honey gold accents, yes?" This time he waited.

"Well, I always thought of it as reddish blond." I said a bit shyly, "It went gray—then white, very early. I started getting gray hair when I was twelve and by the time I was forty, I was completely gray. My late husband said he liked it that way, so I have never colored it. I started wearing my hair in this style after he died. I wanted something easy, a jump up and go style. My appearance is not really that important to me as long as it's neat and clean and easy to style. I'm not good with hair."

"But Senora, your appearance is *muy importante*. You will have more energy and feel so much better about yourself if you add some color and style to your hair. Leave it to me. Today, I will begin the process of bringing your youth back to you. You are much too young and beautiful to reject all the lonesome men and live alone as a widow. You must have many men who are attentive to you?"

"Actually, no. My life revolves around my family, my job and my church. I don't believe that God cares whether I color my hair or wear a youthful style. Can't you just give me a wash and trim? Style it anyway you think best, but no color. I'm sure the gift certificate doesn't cover that and right now I don't want to pay any extra."

I felt angry that I had to defend my hairstyle, and though I didn't want to seem unappreciative, it was none of his business how I wear my hair or whether I am attracting any men.

"Whatever you desire, Senora. I meant no disrespect."

Here I am, true to my nature, feeling guilty at snipping at Rodolfo, so I softened my tone. "I know that you have my best interest at heart, Rodolfo. Thank you for that. Maybe you can give me a new look without the color?"

At the same time that Rodolfo and I were discussing my hair, I heard Mom and Antonio laughing. I couldn't make out the words they exchanged, but was confident that some platitudes were part of the laughter. I admired my mother's fun-loving spirit and wondered what she would look like when Antonio finished with her.

I had to admit that Rodolfo had transformed me, adding softness, style and femininity. My hair was wavy, with short side-swept bangs, but I worried how Suzie would react the next time I went to her for a haircut. Suzie says she doesn't mind if her customers go to another stylist as long as they worked in her shop. She'll just have to understand and accept.

Mom looked great—a beauty at seventy-nine. Antonio had parted her hair on the side, given her full bangs, combed her hair behind her ears, and into a semi-page boy at the nape of her neck. As Mom and I drove away, she said, "Antonio looked at me and said, 'Think Helen Mirren.' I told him, 'I'm Helen Mirren at seventy-nine.'"

I laughed and said, "Yes, you look beautiful, Mom, more like sixty-nine! And you are lovelier than any actress to me."

Let's see. Helen said it would be easy. Type in www.facebook.com. Okay, computer, do your stuff. Here it is. *Enter first name, Enter email.* What should I use as a password—I know I want a strong one. Upper and lower case, numeral and a symbol—I've got it. FirewifE and Jake's lucky number three and the percent sign. He always tried to figure out percentages on everything—so here goes "FirewifE3%". Great. I have to repeat it. *Sex:* that's an easy one—F. *Birthdate:* 5-1-1958. Can't believe I'll be fifty-three in a few months. Okay, what's this? *Security check.* What in the world? I can't even read those letters. Guess I'll take a chance and try it. Front Magnet. It worked. I'm in. Now I can set up my Profile. *Current city*—Independence, MO. *Hometown*: Independence, MO.

Haven't gone far, but I've had a rich life. Wish Jake were here, but he is no longer in pain and he's with the good Lord. *Thank you, God for loving Jake enough to take him and for loving me enough to give me the faith I need to keep going without him.*

What, they want my sex again? It's still Female. And my birth date again. It's still the same. Am I interested in men or women? I'll leave that blank. I'm interested in all God's children. All are called. All are of worth. *Comments?* What goes in there? Guess I can put my maiden name—Lord. *Employer.* They don't need to know everything about me. I'm leaving the rest blank.

I checked my email real quick. Tina came online and started a chat in Yahoo Messenger.

"Mom, everything's working out. Henri's dad is so much better. I'm confident that we'll be seeing you in April after all."

"Tina, that is good news. I wish I could chat, but I've got to get to Bingham Manor in time to set up Bingo. Can we talk after I get off work?'

She answered, "If I'm still up, if not, let's chat tomorrow. Later Mater. Have a good day at work. Love you."

"Love you, too! Later, Sweetheart."

The roller coaster of emotions that Tina and I had been riding was now in working order—my family would be here soon. I raced out of the house, jumped in my car and headed for work, but halfway there, I realized my timing was off. I still had an hour before I needed to be at Bingham Manor. The news from France created a cause for celebration. I directed my car toward Rosapaloosa, my favorite florist.

♥

I entered the Bingham Manor entry hall with my arms filled with flowers. Helen Reed, my boss, spotted me first.

"Marjie, let me help you with all those beautiful flowers. Who are they for?"

I said, "For everyone! If you will take these I've got more in the car."

I went back out to the car and brought in two more vases and gave them to Helen to distribute as she saw fit. Next I went to find Mary Florence and Anna Jean. I found Mary Florence in the sitting room reading to a lady that I had never met before. Mary Florence introduced her as Irene. She sat in a wheelchair, eyes glued toward the cover of the book. She was tall and thin with dull white hair. She appeared to be much younger than the usual resident. I wondered why she had chosen to live at Bingham Manor, but I never asked direct questions as "Why are you in here?" so I decided to ask what they were reading. It turned out that they were reading the first Harry Potter book, *Harry Potter and the Sorcerer's Stone* by J. K. Rowling. Now I was significantly more interested in knowing more about Irene and about the book. I have never read any of the Potter books, but lately I have been toying with the idea. I wonder if Jakie would be too young to understand them.

Mary Florence said, "Sit down, Marjie, we're getting to a really good part. This J.K. Rowling knows how to tell a story. I sat down as requested and was soon caught up in the mystery and humor of the book. It wasn't long before Anna Jean came into the room and started chattering about the beautiful flowers that someone had brought. Mary Florence stopped reading for a minute to ask about the flowers.

Irene sat quietly for about a minute then she screwed up her face and yelled, "Read Harry Potter. Read Harry Potter."

Mary Florence began reading again and all was well for a minute or two when Anna Jean turned to me and began to tell me about last night's dance. "Eugene kissed me in the arbor after the dance. He wants me to go steady with him. What do you think, Marjie? Should I go steady with him? His Royal Copenhagen scent really turns me on, but I'm not interested in fooling around. You know, having S-E-X with Eugene or anyone else. I wonder what he's up to. If he thinks he's going to get anywhere with me then he's got another think coming. I have my moral principles, you know. No S-E-X out of wedlock!"

Mary Florence had not heard about this kiss or the going steady proposal from her best friend, so she quit reading again to hear the conversation. At this lull Irene started in again, "Read Harry Potter, read Harry Potter."

Mary Florence decided to tend to the needier of her two friends, I suspect she thought Anna Jean would fill her in later, so she wheeled Irene over to another corner of the sitting room. Anna Jean and I now enjoyed semi-privacy.

"Well, Anna Jean, I guess you could ask Eugene what he meant by going steady. Maybe he wants to feel some security in your friendship. He may not even be thinking about sex," I stated.

"Not be thinking about S-E-X, where have you been all your life, Marjie? It's been my experience that S-E-X is all men DO think about. I remember my late husband, Ralph Stokes. He had a fire in him, I want to tell you. Do I miss him. He used to chase me around the house. We had such fun. He was crazy about me and I was crazy about him back. Eugene has been so reserved with me until last night. It's the first time he ever kissed me. My Ralph kissed me the first time we met."

Her eyes took on a far-away look. "We were at a youth picnic on the lawn of the church and he found me alone in the kitchen—I was getting some napkins—our preacher's wife had forgotten to bring them out, so she sent me in to get some. Ralph followed me in there and came up behind me, put his hands over my eyes and said, 'Guess who?'"

"I guessed, Bobby, who was my current beau, but he said, 'It's not, Bobby, guess again.' I guessed, Richard, and he said, 'No, guess again.' I said, Kenny, and that was another 'no'. I said, well, that's the only boys I know here today and he said—'there's one more.' He turned me around and I looked into the most beautiful blue eyes I had ever seen. Well, actually, his eyes and mine were almost the same color—cornflower blue. He planted a big kiss right on my mouth and I was a goner. I never had eyes for anyone else ever again. You know he died five years ago, but I still talk to him a lot."

"I didn't know that's when he died. My husband died five years ago, too, and I still talk to him all the time. It's comforting, isn't it?" I hugged Anna Jean. This was the first time that the two of us had talked by ourselves. Anna Jean always seemed a little childish to me before, but now I discovered a commonality between us.

"What day did Ralph die, Anna Jean?" I asked.

"It was April 24, 2005, why?"

"That's incredible! That's the same day that my husband, Jake, died. No wonder we have such a strong bond between us."

"I'll bet Ralph and Jake are both watching over us," sighed Anna Jean.

"They may very well be, Anna Jean. They may very well be." I hugged her and took her hands in mine, noticing her beautiful pale blue eyes. "Shall we see what's going on with Harry Potter?"

"Okay, Marjie. I haven't decided if I want to steady with Eugene. It will have to depend on what his intentions are. I'm no floozy. And I almost forgot to mention. He has halitosis really bad. Should I tell him to use some darn Listerine?"

♥

I recently bought new phones—land lines for the house. They talk to me. "Call from Deschamps, Christina" announced Tina's call.

"Mom, Henri and I have been doing some research. You can't believe how many wineries are in Missouri and Kansas. We're going to take a wine tour and buy up wine for the café when we get home. And local farmers, we'll need info on them. We want to use local organic food. Will you start doing some preliminary checking on this for us?"

"Oh, you must have told Henri's family and Jakie the news!"

"Not yet, but soon."

"You might want to think about giving Jakie and everyone else some time to adjust," I said.

"We don't think we should tell Jakie until March. We don't want to worry him, but will you please start contacting local farmers?"

"I don't even know what to talk to them about, never mind my paper on *Beowulf* and my creative writing assignments and my job and your grandmother."

"How about if Henri and I come up with a template conversation for you to call farmers with?" My daughter, the clever one, knows me so well.

"Maybe, if you'll do that and if you will at least tell Henri's parents. They need to plan for him being gone, don't you think?"

"I'll talk to Henri about it, okay?"

After our phone call I prayed that God's will be done. I certainly didn't have the answers.

♥

I opened my email and found two friend requests from people on Facebook. One from Director Helen. She said she would send me one. There was another one. From Mark Bryant!

I hadn't heard from him since I saw him at Jake's Celebration of Life. He got me laughing as we talked about all the fun we had in high school, especially the double dates we went on. Mark always was a ladies' man. He dated every pretty girl in school, including my friend Denise for about a year, but I never dated him. He used to tease Jake about wanting to take me out, riling Jake more than a hornet on a hog's bottom—one of Jake's favorite expressions. That almost cost Mark Jake's friendship. They stayed best friends but Jake was very jealous about me before we were married. I don't know why; I never had eyes for anyone but him and his jealousy ended when our marriage began. At least I as far as I knew.

I started to cry. I had been doing so much better about that, after all it has been five years since Jake died, but every now and again I become overwhelmed with horrible grief. I know that is to be expected so I don't spend time worrying about it. I let go until the feelings subsided.

I wiped away my tears and clicked on the underlined thread that would take me to Facebook. I entered my password. A new page came up revealing the *friend* requests. I accepted Helen and Mark.

I wanted to tell Denise that I'm Facebook *friends* with Mark—say, she named one of her children Mark, I wonder, but no, her other sons are Matthew, Luke and her daughter is Johnna—I'm sure they are named for the Four Gospels. She would want to know I connected with Mark for old times' sake. Idea. We need to do lunch.

When I got to my home page there was a stream of comments from Mark. Apparently he likes to let everyone know what he is doing. His picture showed him and three young people—a teenage boy and girl and a younger girl, probably aged ten to twelve. I couldn't remember how old his children were. I wondered why there was no picture of his wife. I was pretty sure he had remarried after his first wife died. One of his comments said Elsa's soccer team had won their game today in spite of his coaching errors. How nice that he is coaching his daughter's team, I thought. This humility is new. The Mark of old would have taken as much self-credit as possible.

I clicked on his picture. It took me straight to Mark's homepage. Wow. He has lots of friends—512. How can anyone have that much time to spend on this—what do they call it? Social networking. I'll never get that caught up in it. Whoops. My fifteen minutes had turned into thirty. Must go.

♥

Another exacting day at work—Anna Jean and Eugene are on the outs again. The drive home through blackened snow-sloppy streets made me eager for shelter in my empty, but warm house.

I decided it was time to take down the meager Christmas decorations I had put up the day after Thanksgiving, according to family tradition. Mom believed and instilled in me that one month out of the year was not enough for the splendid display of snow globes, village houses, candles of every shape and size and the angels and the crèche with the Christ child lying in a manger with Mary and Joseph, the shepherds, the Magi. It took a while to amass the proper amount of decorations. In our first few years of marriage, Jake and I bought a blue spruce in a big pot to use as our Christmas tree. The small spruce was big enough. We only had a few ornaments back then.

I walked to the window and looked out to that once small spruce standing strong in the front yard, now twenty feet tall.

When Tina was born we began buying cut trees from the Boy Scout lot at Crysler Stadium, corner of twenty-third and Crysler. Each year our tree was taller and wider than the year before, until I called a halt when the tree curved over, too tall for our ceiling. The tree we bought stood over twenty feet tall! As a firefighter, Jake knew the dangers of having a real tree, so he took extra precautions and insisted the tree come down the day after Christmas, but all the other decorations stayed put until the end of January or first part of February. When she was little Tina cried when the decorations had to go to the storage room, so I started decorating for all the holidays, getting the Valentine decorations out to replace the Christmas decorations. One year when Tina was thirteen, things were hectic, so we skipped Valentine's and left the Yuletide decorations up until St. Patrick's Day. We had so much fun putting them away in March and even Jake joined in the fun of wrapping the snow globes, angels and houses and putting them to bed for the spring, summer and fall.

The first year Tina didn't come home for Christmas, Jake and I flew to France to be with her, so we didn't bother to decorate for the holidays. The next year Tina brought her new husband home, so I decorated to the hilt, buying new angels for the mantle place, five new houses for the village, snow people to decorate Tina's bedroom and a new wreath for the door.

Carrying all the boxes to the basement storage room wore me out. I climbed the stairs one last time, lit my favorite candle—apple cinnamon spice—and made a cup of tea to enjoy while I recuperated in my recliner with my English Lit assignment, selections from Chaucer's Canterbury Tales. I love that Professor Monk began our class by reciting the Prologue in Middle English, so beautiful the way she spoke it, voicing the ending "e's as "uh's"—*soote, roote.*

*Aprill* and it's *flour's* can't come soon enough for me. April will bring my family home.

❤

Last night the television stations all predicted a blizzard, saying the listening area would receive from nine to twenty-five inches, so when I woke up the first thing I did was pull my bedroom curtains aside to see what happened overnight. A dusting so far, but it's early and it's supposed to snow all day. It is cold and probably slick out there. Glad I don't have to be at work until afternoon, if I can get there then.

I emerged fresh from the shower, quickly dressed in jeans, tee shirt and my old favorite worn denim shirt, grabbed a cup of water, sat down at the kitchen table and opened the gold cover of the Daily Bread from the year 2000. I located today's date and read the scripture at the top of the page. It was from Isaiah 40:31. *But they that wait upon the Lord shall renew their strength; they shall mount up with wings as eagles.*

*Lord, I do wait upon you and need your strength to address the concerns I have this day.*

I continued reading the Daily Bread message. It was written by Barbara Harmon from Louisville, Kentucky about a fifth-grade class assignment to design six-foot-tall hot air balloons out of tissue paper. The students' grades depended on the ability of the balloon to fly. The teacher's criterion was *fly or fail,* but the writer learned as she assisted the students on flight day, that the teacher had a plan. She instructed all the parents who were assisting to look for leaks and repair them with masking tape as the balloons began to fill with air from a propane flame. As a result of the teacher's plan for these timely repairs, every balloon flew.

As I read the next paragraph I felt overcome by God's love for me. Barbara's words comforted me as I read. I know that God is there for me keeping me steady, fixing my faults, helping me to fly.

*Thank you, God, for never giving up on me, for giving me strength to handle each day as it comes. Help me to always remember your love for me and teach me to love others as you love them. Amen.*

*CHAPTER THREE*

The fellowship hall of the church was full of well-wishers for my best friends, the co-pastors' Rob and Eileen McNamara's anniversary celebration. Tonight the hall was full to overflowing. Eileen and Rob's daughters were there with their husbands and families, along with half the congregation, and a host of friends. People took turns sitting down to eat because chairs were at a premium.

I stood chatting with Eileen and Rob as they sat in the guest of honor seats. Their daughters' chosen theme this year was *Our Royal Parents*, so they decorated the chairs like thrones and the grandkids made crowns and scepters.

Eileen turned to Rob and asked, "Why am I sitting here?"

Rob answered, "Because it's chair! Get it. Pun for *because it's there*."

Eileen laughed, "Holy MacAnoli, I mean, your Grace. Your *punnys* aren't so funny. Why aren't we up walking around talking to our guests?"

Rob jumped up, careful of his royal cape, gave her his arm and said, "Your majesty, I presume. Would thou doest me the honor of allowing me to escortest thee around the room to cast thy royal presence upon thy royal subjects?"

Geoffrey Chaucer he was not.

They visited with their guests and were saying goodbye to our oldest congregants, my mentors, Kathleen and Foster, when Rob and Eileen's daughter, Beth, ran by them, almost knocking Kathleen and Foster down.

"Whoa, Beth, watch what you are doing!" yelled her robe-encumbered mother. I was standing at the door, so I took a leap and caught up with Beth outside around the corner of the building. She was leaning against the oak tree, crying.

I held out my arms and she came into them, sobbing onto my shoulder.

"Oh, Marjie, Jerry came home drunk tonight and decided not to come to the party, but now he's here and he's calling me names and telling Susanna that I'm no good. I've got to get out of here!"

I went into consolation mode. "Oh, Beth, I'm so sorry. Where is Susanna now?"

"I don't know. She's probably with her father, that jerk I married," Beth cried.

"Did you drive yourself tonight? Why don't you go sit in your car while I get Susanna? I'll tell your father to go talk to Jerry."

"No, I don't want to ruin Mom and Dad's party. Can't you talk to Jerry? He's always liked you," Beth pleaded.

"I want to make sure that Susanna's all right. How about if you come with me? We'll find her together, if she's with Jerry, I'll corner him while you and Susanna go on home."

"I don't want to go home. I'm afraid. When he gets like this, I can't stand to be around him and I certainly don't want Susanna around him. Can we stay with you tonight? I don't want Mom and Dad to know about what is going on until later. I'll talk to them tomorrow about it, but I don't want to ruin their anniversary."

"Of course, you can stay with me as long as you like." Beth and Tina had been best friends all through school. I hugged her close. "You are like a daughter to me. Let's go on in and see if we can find them."

Beth and I found Jerry and Susanna. Jerry was laughing with Denise's husband, Kenneth, and Susanna was sitting with her cousin, Melea. They were whispering and I could only imagine what they were talking about. They looked serious. Beth sat down with Susanna and Melea. I hoped that Jerry wouldn't make a scene.

I prayed that Jerry would listen to me and go on home without any trouble. I asked the Lord to bless me with the words to say to him. I felt unprepared for a conversation with a drunk person. I had never been around anyone that drank, at least, I didn't know it if I had.

I inhaled and exhaled twice, squared my shoulders and walked up to Jerry. "Jerry, will you please come with me to the children's classroom? I want to talk with you."

"What's going on, Marjie. Am I in trouble? Have I been a bad boy?" Drool crept out of the side of his mouth. His eyes set at half-mast.

"You know exactly what you have done, certainly more than I do, Jerry. You've been drinking and you've upset Beth. I think it would be a good idea if we get someone to drive you home tonight and let you sleep it off," I said as firmly as I could muster.

"No one is going to drive me home. I drove up here. I can drive back home again. I'm going to get Beth and Susanna and go home together. That's what a man is supposed to do. Take care of his family. They are my family and no one is going to get in the middle of it."

I didn't know what to do. For one thing, I couldn't let him drive anywhere, much less take Beth and Susanna with him. Panic set in. I needed help. I tried to take a minute to pray, but Jerry started out of the room and I was sure he was looking for Beth.

I put my hand on his arm. "Wait a minute, Jerry. You've had too much to drink and I can't let you drive. If you try to get in your car, I'm going to call the police," I said, forcing my voice into an authoritative tone.

He pushed my arm down. "You wouldn't do that, Marjie, call the police on me. I'm your friend. I've known you most of my life. You and Jake were my idols when I was a teenager. I wanted to be like Jake. I wanted to join the fire department, but instead ended up selling used cars for my father. I hate selling cars. That's why I drink. That and Beth drives me crazy. She's always gone to this group or that group or going shopping with her sisters or her mother. She never has dinner ready anymore. I have to do my own laundry. We're not a family anymore. Marjie, I don't know what to do. What can I do?"

"For starters, you can stop drinking. Maybe Beth doesn't want to be around you because you've gotten drunk and when you get drunk you are hard to deal with. Have you ever gone to counseling?"

His skin was mottled, his eyes widened, and his nostrils flared. "That bullpuckey—yeah, we went to counseling. The counselor was on Beth's side. They ganged up on me. Said everything that was wrong with our marriage was my fault. Well, there's two sides to every story, Marjie!"

I could see that Jerry was making some sense and seemed to be sobering up somewhat.

"I don't need no crappy know-it-all counselor telling me what to do with my own family. I know I need to make some changes, but so does Beth. She's not miss la-de-da perfect you know."

I asked him to wait while I went to get him some coffee, praying he would be there when I came back. I would get the coffee and stay there with him until he was safe to drive. Then I or someone else would follow him home. At least, that was my intention.

I found Beth, gave her my key and told her to go on over to my house. I explained that Jerry was talking with me and that I planned to stay with him until he was sober enough to drive home. Beth warned me that Jerry could get mean, but I assured her that he wasn't going to get mean with me. I showed her my can of mace and my cell phone. "I'll call 911 if the need arises."

When I got back to the classroom Jerry was gone. It didn't take me long to find him. I followed the yelling. There was fighting in the church for the first time in many years. Rob and his other three sons-in-law had found Jerry. He mouthed off to them. Meg and Jo's husbands were holding onto Jerry and Amy's husband delivered the pummeling blows. Rob was trying to get in between them. Other men arrived. There were shouts and a whole melee broke out.

Eileen found a whistle somewhere and blew it. "Stop, it you idiots! This is a church, our church. There will be no fighting here."

Someone shouted, "Let's take it outside. He'll be sorry he treated our sister that way."

The whistle sounded again and Eileen yelled, "Over my dead body. You fools sit down and listen to me. We are going to pray about this, not fight about it. Do you even know what you are fighting about?"

Everyone sat down while Eileen prayed for peace and wisdom, love and forgiveness. I sat by her and Rob. Jerry cried the loudest, but many tears were shed that night.

I don't know why, because it was totally different, but I was reminded of a fight story my dad used to tell me. It was over a love triangle. He would start the tale with *There was fighting in the church again last night…*He'd always stop there and laugh. Mom would say, *Oh, Frank. Please don't bring up that old story.* But she loved hearing it. When he and mom were little kids he would tease her and tell her they would be married someday. Another boy liked mom too, so they would fight over her. They fought every year at the Fourth of July picnic, from the time they were five until they turned ten or eleven, Dad said.

Pretty soon Rob drove Jerry home, planning to stay with him all night to make sure he didn't try to bother Beth. When I got home Beth and Susanna were there. Susanna was naturally upset so Beth and I tried to soothe her. We watched *The Princess Diaries* with her until she started to fall asleep. I took her to Tina's room where she would sleep for the night. Susanna called it Tina's flower room.

Beth and I stayed up late talking and praying. Before Beth went to bed in the guest room she had decided to ask her mom and dad if she and Susanna could move in with them. I thought it was a good temporary solution. Exhausted, I drifted into a troubled sleep.

♥

The next morning Eileen called me at six o'clock to ask how Beth and Susanna were.

I told her they were still sleeping, that Beth and I talked until about three in the morning. I explained that Beth had decided to leave Jerry. I didn't think Beth would mind if I told her mother. I hoped I wasn't wrong. "Beth is going to ask you and Rob if she and Susanna can move in with you until she can find a place of her own," I said.

"Of course, they can. It will give Rob and me some quality time with Beth and Susanna."

"I think I'll let them sleep until about seven-thirty." A sudden thought hit me. "Oh, my gosh. They don't have any clothes to wear other than what they had on their backs last night. I can probably find something for Beth in my skinny closet, but I don't have anything for Susanna. She's tiny even for a ten-year old. Do you have clothes for them?"

"I don't. I've already talked to Rob and Jerry is sound asleep. I'll bet I could go over there and pack a few things to get them through today without Jerry even waking up. I'll run over there now, get them and bring them to your house."

"Sounds good, Eileen. I'll see you in a bit." I hung up the phone and prayed for Beth, Susanna, Jerry, then added Eileen and Rob. They were all going to need God's blessing.

♥

The phone rang. It was Tina.

"Mom, Henri is starting to drive around saying goodbye to his beloved Drôme Provençale. That's a good sign that he will keep his promise and move to Missouri, right?"

"Have you and Jakie been going with him? I'm sure you need to say goodbye, too."

"Of course, I will miss the south of France and the Alps. You know how I love the mountains. It will be hard to be so far away from mountains and the sea. Why did you and Dad settle in Missouri—so far away from mountains and beaches?"

I drifted into a miniscule reverie. Her question reminded me of days gone by. When she was young we took exciting vacations to the mountains in Colorado, to the beaches in California—all over the country. When she grew up she had a taste for adventure. Now she's a French chef. But surely Tina knew why we lived in Missouri. We were born here. Our families were here. I could have moved to France when Jake died, but Mom didn't want to go and I couldn't leave her and my friends and, after all, I am an American.

"Mom, are you still there?" Tina sounded frustrated.

I answered, "Yes, Tina, I'm here. Just thinking. My trips to France were wonderful. Landing in Paris for your graduation from Le Cordon Bleu—the romance of the city, the spell. I loved the south of France even more, Marseille, the sea, the Mediterranean climate, your home in Grignan with the surrounding truffle forests, lavender fields, only hours from beaches or mountains, it's remarkable. The times I've visited enchanted me, but my heart is in the States, in Missouri as a matter of fact. It's hard to explain."

"You don't have to explain, Mom. I feel it, too. That's why we're coming home. It is my home. You and Grandma are my home. I've been away so long. This is our compromise. Henri understands that we will return to Grignan someday, his home. But now is my time and we do have the Ozarks and lots of countryside. I'm going to talk to him tonight. It's time to tell his family and Jakie."

We signed off. I went out to the back porch to watch the amazing pinks of the sunset over the Kansas City skyline.

♥

When I arrived at Eileen and Rob's for dinner I expected to see Beth and Susanna, as they were living there now. They were there last week for our Friday night dinner, but this time Beth had taken Susanna to her sister Amy's for the evening. I made myself at home by setting the table.

Rob and I watched Eileen wander around the kitchen, muttering somewhat under her breath, but loud enough for us to hear, "One of these days…"

Rob cut in with, "Is that a line from Jackie Gleason's *The Honeymooners*—'One of these days, Alice, one of these days—straight to the moon with you."

Eileen practically shouted, "No, you constant old TV sitcom quotation guy, I was saying—*to myself, by the way*—'One of these days I'll remember why I came into a room!" Eileen sat down at the table frustrated that she couldn't remember what she was looking for.

"Excuse us, for interrupting your private conversation," said Rob.

Eileen laughed and jumping back up, ran over to the oven and pulled out the bubbling casserole. My, she was preoccupied—forgetting dinner.

After we ate Rob went to work on the Message he was to deliver on Sunday. Eileen and I stayed in the kitchen, clearing the dishes and updating each other on the events of the week. When the dishwasher was loaded and running we went into the little room off the kitchen that Eileen liked to call her parlor. There were four comfy overstuffed chairs in a circle with a large ottoman in the middle. Each chair had an end table piled with books sitting next to it. Eileen carried a tray holding two cups and saucers, a teapot and an assortment of dessert teas. I brought in some Splenda for Eileen and a pitcher of skim milk and bowl of sugar for myself. Eileen poured the steaming hot water into our cups. She chose a Cherry Cordial flavored tea bag and I selected Orange Spice.

Eileen sipped her tea then set her cup in its saucer. "I'm so glad I found these teas when Rob and I went to Asheville, North Carolina a few years ago. The Biltmore gift shop was holding a tea tasting that day. I tried these dessert teas and have been ordering them off the internet ever since."

"I am glad too, they are really good and caffeine-free to boot. You know I can't drink anything with caffeine in it after noon? What is the website? I think I'll start ordering them, too, especially, now that Tina and Henri are moving in."

Eileen nodded. "I'll email the website to you."

We drank our tea, quietly sharing a few moments of friendly silence. I was sinking into another reverie, idealizing the wonders of having my family around me when Eileen said, "Marjie, I need to talk to you about JAM."

JAM is our church after school program. It stands for Jesus and Me. Eileen spoke with a bit of caution. This was a clue that she was about to pounce on me for a favor. My wary nature was alerted.

"Sure, what's going on? Everything seems to be going great. Isn't it?" Eileen knows how full my schedule is. Surely she isn't going to ask me to do more, is she?

"Well, you know Beth has been in charge of JAM since we started it. She can't seem to focus on it right now. Can you take it over temporarily? She'll still be there, but she wants to take a minor role—tell a Bible story, or be in charge of the games, but not be in charge of the whole thing. What do you say?"

What could I say? Beth is going through a rough time right now. I should take time to pray about it. *Lord, what should I do? No answer. Sorry to rush You, Lord. Well, when someone is in need...*

"I'll do it, but only until Tina and crew find their way stateside. We should be looking for someone else to take over then. I need to talk to Beth to find out what all she does. It's such a wonderful program. My purpose generally has been to supply hugs or bandage skinned knees. Maybe she and I can get together tomorrow."

"Marjie, you are a lifesaver. Thank you so much." We hugged.

I drove home, wondering if I wasn't taking on more than I should. Then, a familiar scripture washed over me. *You can do all things through Christ who strengthens you.*

♥

Today was Tina's Birthday. I sat down at the computer to call Tina on Skype at the time we agreed upon. It was 6:00 a.m. in Independence and noon in France. She didn't answer. I didn't think much about it because Tina always did like to sleep late on her birthday—it was another of her traditions. I guessed noon was too early for my sleepy-headed daughter.

I opened up Facebook and posted a regards of the day message to Tina on Facebook. There were no other messages from Tina's friends wishing her "Happy Birthday" on her wall, but, it is early, at least here in the States. Maybe she'll get some messages later. I thought at least Henri would post something. I hope everything is all right. I spoke to Tina and Jakie last night so wasn't too worried, only I still don't think Tina and Henri have told Jakie about the move.

Our next scheduled time on Skype was two p.m. Wednesday. Hopefully, we will make that connection. I enjoy saying good night to Jakie twice a week and can't wait for my family to be home so I can see them every day in the flesh. Are they really coming? And when they do, how will it be? Tina and I haven't lived together for eight years. She's bringing home a son-in-law I barely know and a grandson. On most levels I'm as enraptured as an astronaut in space, on another—nervous—how can you really know someone unless you live with them? Even when you do live with them, their thoughts are private, even with myself sometimes I think I don't know who I am. With friends and family you see their actions only when you are with them. I think I've lived alone too long.

The computer screen caught my eye. I noticed a comment thread from Mark Bryant of a video he had posted. I clicked on it and watched in gleeful amusement as I witnessed him and his children (apparently) in a snow ball fight. Lots of snow in Minnesota in February, I suppose! Looked like they were having so much fun.

I clicked *Like* and a pang of jealousy hit me. Then guilt. I was glad that Mark and his children were happy so why was I jealous? I should never feel jealousy. *Guess I'm only human, Lord. I want my family with me. Yes, I know they will be soon, but Lord, I'm worried a little about how we will all get along.* Tina has never been easy to live with. Maybe now that she's a wife and mother? Time will tell. Time will tell. My goodness, I'm becoming my mother—clichés and repetition, both.

It was time for me to face Suzie. I'd been dreading my next appointment with my long-time stylist ever since Rodolfo fixed my hair at Casa de Clasico. I drove into the parking lot of Suzie's Salon Do's, parked my car, grabbed my book, purse and water bottle. I stepped out into the cold. It was windy and raining. The drops pelted me as I ran across the parking lot. As soon as I opened the door to the shop, Suzie began her harangue.

"Why Marjie Jamison, I almost did not recognize you. You went to another stylist, didn't you? I can't believe you let someone else do your hair, especially since I've been trying to talk you into another style than that short curly-permed do that you've had ever since Jake died. I have to admit your hair does look cute. Where did you go? Who fixed your hair?"

Suzie was my age, but dressed like a teenager. Her slim figure allowed her to wear the short skirts and off-the-shoulder tops that were in fashion with the younger set. Her hair was a bright red-orange with jagged pieces framing her oval face, reminding me of a grown-up, real life Pebbles of *Flintstone* fame. Her favorite color was purple so most of her clothes were purple, or a shade of purple. The walls of her shop were silver with painted purple frames of hair styles. Suzie was popular with the men. Her phone rang frequently and I could tell that most of the calls were not for hair appointments. Suzie had never married, but had two grown daughters and two grandsons. She was fun and flirty with her male customers and a great listener with her female customers. I don't believe she ever forgot anything that anyone said to her, but did not repeat gossip. I love Suzie because she has a good heart. She never knows a stranger and always helps those in need when she can.

"Suzie, Mom took me to a salon with her last month. One of her friends gave her a gift certificate and she wanted to share it with me. A stylist named Rodolfo cut it. I'm glad you like it."

I sat down in a chair to wait until Suzie was finished with her current client. My mind began to wander. I thought about how Suzie has a way of getting me to say things I wouldn't say to anyone else. I need to be on guard and not mention anything about Mark.

Why did I think that? What difference does it make if she knows I'm friends with Mark on Facebook? I think she dated him after he broke up with Denise. I still haven't mentioned him to her and I'm much closer with her than I am with Suzie. I'm going to keep my mouth shut and just talk about Tina, Henri and Jakie, oh, and my mom. Those are safe topics. Safe topics. Why wouldn't talking about Mark be a safe topic?"

Confused, I took my British Lit book out and began to read my current assignment, Shakespeare's biography, songs from his plays and his sonnets, enjoying Ben Jonson's quote about the Bard, *He was not of an age, but for all time* when Suzie called me for my shampoo. After washing my hair and towel drying it, Suzie asked how I wanted my hair.

"How about a little trim? Just cut about an inch off all over, that would keep it in the same style, right?" I don't know why she bothered to ask, I knew Suzie would cut it anyway she wanted, it would look okay, maybe not as good as the way Rodolfo fixed it, but passable.

I was proud of myself when I left the shop. I hadn't said anything about Mark, but why was I proud of myself for that? As a bonus Suzie didn't give me a bad time about going to a different hair stylist. What a relief.

## *Chapter Four*

I love being in charge of the Shady Grove Wednesday night prayer meeting. I selected four of my favorite hymns and a few scriptures to share, but prayer meeting was really for all who gathered there, giving everyone an opportunity to ask for prayers for their loved ones, even acquaintances who were in need of special blessings of healing for illnesses, joblessness, accidents, heartbreaks—any needs at all.

And prayers were being answered! Maria Fifel's husband had been in remission from bone cancer for the last eight months, Annie Curry had begun to walk again after her terrible stroke, not to mention Benjamin Happel's son Mike who was in prison for stealing a car at gunpoint—he was leading a Bible study in prison—he who hadn't gone to church since he was fifteen years old. Good things were happening due to the Wednesday night prayer meeting and all the prayers uttered all week long, but Wednesday was a focal point, an evening set aside for prayer and testimony. All could come and share how God was working in their lives right now, today.

I looked out at the friends gathered and asked them to bow their heads while we opened with prayer. We then sang *What a Friend We Have in Jesus.*

When it was time for testimonies to be shared, Beth's husband, Jerry was the first to stand. His head was bowed, so he didn't see his father-in-law bring the microphone to him. When Rob put the microphone into his hand, Jerry looked up into his eyes, and tears began flowing from the eyes of both men—their bond growing closer through the trial of separation between Beth and Jerry. Eileen told me last week that Rob and Jerry met for lunch at least once a week. I wasn't sure if Beth knew about it.

Jerry started to sit down, but changed his mind. He held the mike up to his mouth. "I've made a lot of mistakes and I'm sorry. I want my family back. In front of God and everyone here, I promise to do whatever it takes for Beth to trust me again."

Jerry turned around and saw Beth run from the sanctuary. He started to follow her, but Rob stopped him, saying, "Give her some time, Jerry. It's going to take some more time."

♥

Denise was waiting when I got there to open the door of the church for our Sunday afternoon prayer group. We were both about twenty minutes early, how unusual, how fateful. I decided this was a good time to tell Denise about my new Facebook friend, her high school boyfriend, Mark Bryant. We reminisced about the double dates we shared in our high school days.

"Remember the time we went to Jacomo and rolled down the hill in barrels into the water and the park ranger caught us?" Denise laughed. "Whose idea was that anyway?"

"I believe it was yours, Denise, you were always the little dare devil. It's a wonder we weren't killed. Between you and Jake and Mark, I could always count on exciting times." I laughed.

"And they always interposed *Green-eyed Girls* for Van Morrison's *Brown-eyed Girls* when they sang to us," mused Denise.

"Marjie, they were trying to romance us, but we were strong when we were together. I could say 'no' to Mark when you were around, and even when you weren't there, I was able to fend him off because I knew God wouldn't like it if I had sex out of wedlock. Also, I sure didn't want to have to confess *that* to a priest. Once I did let Mark touch my breast—confessed it that week. We had a visiting priest that told me I had to break up with Mark. Never see him again. I had to say five rosaries, but I did keep seeing Mark—I never let him touch me inappropriately again, but we still did some heavy kissing, couldn't stop that." Denise threw her head back and laughed at the memory.

I remembered Denise telling me about that confession and how glad I was that I didn't have to go through that.

Denise continued, "Mark was really a pretty good guy. I wonder what would have happened if I had married him, instead of Charlie. Course Mark didn't ever ask me to marry him, but I think I would have accepted, if he had. He had dreams of being a writer, remember, went to the MU School of Journalism. What's he doing now?"

"Oh, he's the editor of the *St. Paul Pioneer Press*" I answered.

"Livin' his dream," drawled Denise, "good for him. Maybe I'll *friend* him, too. It would be good to catch up."

When Eileen and Kathleen walked in I was glad to stop talking about Mark with Denise. Why did I feel awkward? Surely I wasn't judging Denise because she is a married woman and Mark had been her boyfriend? Certainly not. Denise has every right to touch base with Mark and it is no business of mine. Still. There was something bothering me about Denise connecting with Mark. Craziness, these unruly emotions.

After the meeting my mind turned to my ecological promise to myself. I went over to the trash container to see what recyclables might be in there.

Eileen and Kathleen were still talking. I heard Eileen say, "What is that noise? It sounds like a small animal in the trash." Turning, she spied me, hands in the trash barrel fishing out plastic cups and water bottles.

"Marjie, what are you doing in the trash?"

"I'm trying to keep my New Year's resolution to start a recycling program here at church and some of these cups are still good enough to reuse. I'm going to take them home and put them in the dishwasher. I'll bring them back for next Sunday's breakfast, but I wish we could just use the church's china and glasses for meals here."

"Let's bring it up at the next leadership meeting. We do have to start taking better care of our planet for our children and grandchildren and you shouldn't have to do it all by yourself."

"I knew I could count on you for support, Eileen, thank you."

Wow, Eileen gets it.

♥

Tina's phone call tonight unsettled me. "Mom, we aren't coming in April after all. When Henri told his parents, they came unglued. Said they couldn't carry on without him. Said he is the genius behind the café and cooking lessons that are keeping the whole family going."

The despair in Tina's voice crushed me.

"Why don't you and Jakie come for a visit then? We haven't seen each other for so long. It would be good for you to get away." I tried not to sound frantic, but my mind was running a mile a minute.

"No, I want to stay here and continue to work on Henri. He's got to see that it isn't fair that we always live in France—with his family and never with mine. Can you come here?"

"I don't have any vacation time right now, but I can see if I can get an advance."

I couldn't sleep stewing over Tina and Henri's inability to decide what they want to do. Indecision can cripple a person and when it's a husband and wife who can't commit to what they want—it's even worse and it's playing havoc with my emotions. First their moving here, then staying there, then here, then there. Can their marriage withstand this unease? Should I try to go over there? Would I make matters better or worse? Their indecision is contagious.

♥

I decided to drop over to Mom's townhouse to tell her all the bad news in person. I told her about Tina. That now Henri won't come.

"Do you think I should go over there?" I asked.

She reminded me that I was in the middle of a semester at school, had no vacation time, and was responsible for the JAM Program. Besides, the way things are going Tina will call tomorrow to tell me they will be here in April as planned.

"Now for the second course of bad news, Mom, our attorney called today to see if our tenants had moved out of the rental house. I told her they haven't moved yet. She will start the proceedings by filing a lawsuit. I know that we have to do this, Mom, but as soon as I hung up the phone with her, I started crying and couldn't seem to stop for a long time. This goes against my nature. I can't believe that we are throwing people out of our house, even if they haven't paid any rent for six months. I wish they hadn't talked nasty to you when you called them last month to ask when they would be able to start paying us."

"I know, Marjie. It's hard for me, too. I keep picturing the sweet faces of their little ones. Where are they going to live now?"

Now both of us were crying.

"Can you afford to let them stay there?"

"No, that's one of the problems, remember, I took out a loan against that house so I could afford to buy this townhouse. I intended to sell the house, but your cousin April needed a place so I rented it to her. Remember how great a tenant she was? She planted all those knock-out roses and laid a brick path to the driveway and built shelves and put in new carpet. Sure wish she hadn't moved out."

"But she did and now we have a mess on our hands. You and I are both crying and picturing little Angie and Malachi out on the street. I can't even get mad at Chuck and Rose."

"Marjie, I feel sorry for them, but when they told me that they didn't have to move out, that they could stay there for another six months, and that they had done this before, well, I had to do something. I don't have a lot of money to live on now. I either need to sell that house and pay off the loan or find someone who will pay the rent and pay it on time."

"And with the housing market the way it is, I doubt you can sell it for enough to pay off your loan." Suddenly, I got this hare-brained idea to lighten our mood. My idiocy caused my eyes to twinkle and my throat to giggle.

"Mom, picture this. You are upside-down on your mortgage. Imagine yourself doing handstands!"

At first Mom stared at me in disbelief, a frown hanging on her mouth. Then we both laughed and hugged for a minute. We needed that relief—that mini-vacation that laughter brings and the peace that a hug between a mother and daughter brings.

After easing the tension we prayed for guidance.

Neither one of us wanted to pursue the eviction proceedings. We had hoped that having the lawyer send Chuck and Rose a letter would cause them to either move out or set up a way to pay us back for past rent and start paying their current rent. The letter had gone out to them on February 1st. At that time they were five months behind on rent. They had their excuses at first. Chuck got hurt on the job in September and he didn't have any insurance because he was an independent contractor. He was able to go back to work in October, but they were behind on their utilities and their truck payment, so he told Mom that he would catch up on the rent in November. November came and went and there was no money from Chuck. Mom called his cell phone, but the number had been changed.

In December we had taken presents over to the children and even some homemade chocolate fruit cake, an old family recipe. We invited the family to come to the children's Christmas party at church and to the Christmas Eve service, which they did. They came all dressed up—little three-year old Angie in a darling white satiny dress with red smocking and tiny red ribbons and five-year-old Malachi in a dark blue suit with a little red bow tie. Chuck and Rose were also dressed to the hilt, Rose wore a red velveteen empire styled A-lined dress with a white collar and a bow in the back and Chuck wore a charcoal-colored sport coat and light grey pants. He had on a white tie decorated with red, yellow, blue and green Christmas lights. I had told them that they didn't need to dress up because Shady Grove was a very casual place, but Rose assured me that they had bought everything at the thrift store because they thought dressing up would make them feel better. I thought to myself at the time that I would feel better if they had used the money as a partial payment on their rent.

Our lawyer, Michele, told us that she would get a court date for them. She would take care of everything. We would not have to face them in court. At court the judge would assign a date for the sheriff to come out to the rental house. At that time, if the renters still hadn't moved out, we would have to get some people to help us move their things out to the street. The sheriff wouldn't help. He would only be there to make sure that the movers were safe—that there was no trouble.

Later that night I knelt beside my bed to pray. My thoughts settled first on Tina, Henri and Jakie, then on Mom and her rental predicament. I worried Tina and Henri's marriage was in trouble. I feel responsible for Rose and Chuck and their children. How can I help them so they will be able to pay, if they do actually have an intention to pay? I can't let Mom suffer like this. I have to put her needs in priority.

*Lord, here is the crux of the matter—I can never get angry with anyone else, I must hold myself to a higher standard, I must hold everything in. When will I learn to let things out? Should I let things out? My God, answer my plea.*

♥

I drove my car to place it in the line of cars in front of the Awesome Day Care facility. Mandy, small, cute as a little neighbor could be, stood with a teacher and a group of children, well, she wasn't standing—she was jumping up and down and pointing to my car. One by one the cars moved forward as soon as the children were belted into their seats. When my car was front and center, Mandy ran up followed by a young woman I supposed was her teacher. I got out and walked around the car to open the back door for her.

Mandy's mother, Nora, had signed a permission slip for me to pick her up on Tuesdays so she could go with me to JAM. Nora and Mike hadn't attended church since moving from Bolivar, Missouri but Nora told me they were looking for a church home. I've invited them to go with me on Sunday morning or Wednesday evening a few times, but they haven't yet.  What a blessing that Nora agreed to let me take Mandy to JAM.

Excitement radiated from Mandy. "Marjie, this is my teacher, Miss Ann. Miss Ann, Marjie is taking me to her church to see Jesus."

Miss Ann looked at me, surely thinking *what kind of crazy person is this, but we do have the note from Mandy's mother.*

I laughed and said, "We have an after-school program at our church called *Jesus and Me* for children to learn more about Jesus. We hope that we represent Him well."

Miss Ann put out her hand to shake mine and smiled. "That sounds perfectly lovely. Have a good time, Mandy. It's nice to meet you, Marjie."

When Mandy and I got to the church several leaders and children were assembled in the gym. Eileen had snacks ready for them. By the time snacks were over, twenty some children, aged five to twelve, had gathered.

I sat down on the floor and all the kids, except Mandy, hurried to sit in front of me on the floor. I patted the floor next to me and Mandy came running over, jelly dripping from her mouth. I asked who wanted to say the first prayer and five hands shot up. I nodded at David first.

"God, please help my grandpa. He's sick in the hospital."

Next, Beth's daughter, Susanna, prayed softly, "Lord, be with our family. Help us to be together again." Beth, Eileen and I worked to hold back tears.

Little Johnny jumped up. "Me next. I want to say a prayer." I quietly asked him to sit back down and then he could pray. Johnny sat and said, "God loves you" then jumped up again. Foster scooted his chair over next to Johnny and held his hand.

"Me, Marjie, what about me", Mandy said, "I know a prayer my gee-ma taught me. Now I lay me down to sleep. I pray the Lord my soul to keep. If I should die before I wake, I pray the Lord my soul to take."

"That's a bedtime prayer, Silly Goof," declared Johnny.

As Mandy's mouth puckered up, Kathleen and I were right there, hugging her. "Mandy, that was beautiful."

I tried to be kind, but direct to Johnny. "Johnny please don't call anyone names. We don't do that here."

"I'm sorry, Marjie," cried Johnny. He turned to face the dejected girl. "I didn't mean to hurt your feelings, Mandy."

Mandy looked Johnny straight in the eyes. "That's ok, boy. I forgive you." The forgiveness found in innocents is an example for me. They are so quick to forgive.

Next I asked if anyone else needed our prayers and the requests submitted included a lost kitten, a sick hamster, a grandma, a brother serving in the Army in Afghanistan, a teacher who is having a baby and a sister, even if she is mean.

Nine members of the congregation, mostly retirees, were there to assist. Kathleen and Foster's duties included hugs and telling the Bible story of the week. Grace managed to sprint from school to be there to lead the games and help with crafts. Beth led the craft this week—gluing shells and sand dollars on picture frames. Rob took Polaroid shots of each child to go in the frames when they were finished.

JAM was over at five-thirty. Mandy helped clean up. When I took her home she bounced in the door saying, "Mommy, I prayed and wiped the tables. Aren't you proud of me?"

I know I was.

♥

It was Henri on the phone—the first time he ever called me. My worst fears engulfed me.

"Henri, is something wrong?"

"No, Mère Marjie, well, maybe un peu, but we will fix it. We have decided to come to America no matter my parents. I called to tell you how sorry I am that we have caused you the turmoil and trouble and to tell you that I will do everything to make it up to you and to Tina. I have been selfish expecting Tina to live here all the rest of her life."

I hoped this came from Henri's heart and not a script that Tina forced on him.

"I understand it is hard for you to leave your family and your country," I said.

"Tina has not been herself lately. Many times I find her crying. This is so unusual for Tina. I have never known her to weep at all."

"No, she rarely cried, even as a teenager," I agreed, thinking shouting, screaming, sarcasm, those were Tina's outlets.

"Anyway, we worked it out. She insisted I call you this time. My brothers and their wives will help more at the café. Things will be tres bien here. Here's Tina."

Tina gushed, "Mom, we are really coming. Gregoirie and Laetitia understand now. They are being supportive even though it means taking their beloved son and grandson. Henri is wonderful—showing excitement about our new adventure in America—in middle America where there are no oceans, no mountains, no Riviera. He told Jakie, stirring him to a level of excitement and fun about our upcoming journey and how great it will be to live with Grandma Marjie and visit with Great-Grandma Karin."

Before I could say anything Jakie was on the line. "Hi, Grandma. Where's Missouri?"

"I can't wait to show you, Jakie. I can't wait!"

I sang to myself and jogged downstairs for a cup of celebratory tea.

My bedtime devotions contained lots of thank you prayers, but I worried about Tina. It isn't like her to cry.

<h1 style="text-align:center">CHAPTER FIVE</h1>

I arrived early at Bingham Manor this morning, feeling urged by the Holy Spirit to get out of the house and go on to work, both energized and concerned by the phone call from France. I arrived soon after their breakfast and looked for Mary Florence and Anna Jean in the Gathering Room, but they weren't there, so I went to Mary Florence's room and knocked on the door. I heard riotous laughter. The door opened and the doorway was filled by a tall woman, crane-like in figure, pasty ivory skin tone, covered in heavy pancake makeup, eyebrows drawn heavily. Her dress, an ivory sheath covered with tiny purple fleur-de-lis. Her hair, dyed blond, a huge backcombed French roll, her eyes a piercing blue, almost violet.

Taken aback at such an unexpected appearance I faltered, trying to overcome my surprise. I looked up at her and smiled, "Hi, I'm looking for Mary Florence. Is she here?"

I was not ready for the cackle that emanated from this formidable personage—for it was a laugh so strange, you could only call it a cackle, but somehow I liked it, especially when I saw the wide grin crease the painted red lips.

"Certainly, she's here. Would I be here if she WEREN'T?" She cackled some more. "Come on in. My name is Adelaide Adler. You must be Marjie. I've heard so much about you. I'm glad we are finally getting to meet."

Mary Florence sat on her sofa of deep navy blue. Anna Jean was sitting next to her. Adelaide sat down in a pink, white and blue floral Queen Anne chair and motioned for me to join her in the matching one.

Mary Florence spoke. "Oh Marjie, I would like you to meet my dear friend, Adelaide. She was one of my star students at Berkeley College in New York. She and her sister, Annabelle, have recently moved here to

Independence. I'm so happy to have them living so close. Adelaide and I are opera buddies. In fact, we're going to see *Carmen* this Friday. We've already got tickets, but we can see if we can get another seat, if you would like to join us?"

"It sounds wonderful, but I'm having dinner with the co-pastors of my church this Friday. Well, every Friday. It's something we started years ago when Jake was still with us. Maybe I could go with you some other time, if it's not on a Friday."

"Oh, yes, you must, we can go any day there is a PERFORMANCE," blurted Adelaide.

"Marjie, Adelaide was just telling us about her sister's dogs," began Mary Florence.

Adelaide cut in with, "Yes, Mikado and Carmen. They are the CUTEST little twin sisters—Lhasa Apso's, they are. Great lap dogs. Do YOU know that breed? Anyway, my sister, Annabelle, and her dogs have lived with me since Annabelle's husband, Deforest DENNIS, not Dennis DEFOREST, like you would think, but his first name was actually Deforest. Anyway, Deforest died about ten years ago.

Several months ago I got this WILD HAIR to move away from New York. Annabelle was against it, but I told her I wanted to slow down a little bit and I have been keeping in touch with Mary Florence via EMAIL and she made Independence SOUND so wonderful, and she told me especially about you, MARJIE, that's why I'm so glad to meet you, so I asked Annabelle if she and Mikado and Carmen wanted to move here to Independence with me, since I found a DARLING LITTLE COTTAGE near the square, big enough for at least six to eight people. I found it on the internet—wanted to get out of New York after my parents DIED. It was about a year ago in a car accident. It was TRAGIC. Of course my father hadn't been able to perform for YEARS.

Maybe you know of my father, Robert Adler, he was a WORLD RENOWNED tenor. He sang in all the GRAND opera houses."

I barely had time to take this in. Surely, she left me no time to respond with her machine gun approach to verbalization. What a fast and loud talker, but interesting, and she was a friend of Mary Florence.

She continued. "Annabelle named her dogs after her two FAVORITE operas. I do like Gilbert and Sullivan, too, but CARMEN is also fun. Anyway, Annabelle taught Mikado and Carmen to sing the *Toreador Song* from *Carmen*. They really SING it. She holds one on each knee and starts singing with them. It's a RIOT. I told her she should take them on David Letterman. You know that "STUPID PET TRICKS" part of his show. They could be FAMOUS, but Annabelle refuses. She says that Mikado and Carmen are NOT stupid pets and she detests David

Letterman anyway, because of the way he made fun of GEORGE W, her favorite president ever. She thinks he's so CUTE. I say, how can any man that drops bombs on innocent people be cute? I'm going to record those dogs and put them on YouTube."

I was caught up in Adelaide's enthusiasm, trying not to flinch at the rapidity and volume of her voice. Interesting character doesn't describe her. I couldn't help myself. I wanted to spend more time with her and get to know her better. I couldn't wait for Mom to meet her.

"I would love to go to the opera sometime with you and I know my mother would, too. Maybe we can all go together next time." I said.

Mary Florence went to the refrigerator and pulled off the list of performances at the Lyric for the rest of the season. "The spring season is almost over. We have tickets for Friday, April 9 to see *Rigoletto,* but we could change them for another night if you like?"

"Oh, I think mother would love *Rigoletto.* Could we go on a Thursday?" I asked.

"Well, I don't have anything else going on," said Mary Florence.

"I'm not going," pouted Anna Jean.

"But you can if you want," urged Mary Florence.

"I hate that high screeching noise. Why can't we go to the American Heartland Theatre where they have such funny shows and good music, when there is music, and you can understand it?"

Mary Florence turned to her friend. "We can go there, too. Do you want me to look on the internet to see what's playing next?" She was always trying to please everyone.

Adelaide exclaimed, "Well, I can't believe that you won't go to see *Rigoletto* with us. The DUKE, being one of Father's favorite ROLES. Oh, well, you can't account for taste."

That last part was muttered, but Anna Jean heard her. She jumped up and stomped out of the room, as much as her petiteness and age would allow.

I think Adelaide felt bad about hurting Anna Jean's feelings. "I'll go apologize to her, even if she is a SPOILED brat," she crowed as she flew out the door.

Mary Florence and I laughed and shook our heads. Mary Florence said, "I don't think Adelaide and Anna Jean will ever be close friends. They are so very different."

"Well, Mary Florence, you are nothing like either one of them and you get along well with both of them," I said.

"You and I, Marjie, we try to see God's Spirit in everyone. We know that all are precious in God's sight. We are like kindred spirits. That's why I loved you the moment I met you. I felt a special bond that very day." Mary Florence reached out and hugged me. I hugged her back, but gently, fearful of hurting my frail friend. Tears filled our eyes and the peace that is found when people connect through the Lord flowed through us.

♥

I parked the car under the canopy of trees in the Temple parking lot and opened the back door for Mom, helping her out, and then went around to the passenger side to assist Kathleen out of the car. Kathleen led the way up the worshipper's path. Even though the three of us walk up this path frequently, we still take time to enjoy the artwork along the path. Kathleen made it to the first bench then sat to catch her breath, just a minute or two, then she caught up with Mom and me again.

"This walk does certainly help to still my mind and gives me a little exercise to boot," laughed Kathleen quietly.

Mom was the first to reach the second bench and Kathleen joined her, both needing to catch their breath. I started to sit down for a minute, but the older ladies rose up and began the rest of the trek. Upon reaching the *Fountain of the Living Water* we stopped to read: *Whoever drinks of the water that I shall give, will never thirst.*

As we entered the sanctuary, the organist played softly. I asked myself for the hundredth time, how can a three-story 5,685 pipe organ be played quietly and why aren't there more people here? Such a small group of worshippers take the time to come to this beautiful, holy place and pray for peace in the temple designated for peace.

We sat near the back of the first block of seats. I sighed and looked upward into the spiral and prayed silently, *Lord, bring peace to your people. Lord, bring peace to this troubled world. Bring peace to Tina, Henri and me. Be with us through the myriad of changes coming our way.*

At exactly one o'clock a woman walked up to the podium and began the service.

♥

I sang *When Irish Eyes Are Smiling* and danced a little jig while walking up the stone path to Mom's condo, thinking, next year Jakie will be with us for the parade!

I sported a green tee shirt with a big white clover leaf on the front with a shiny Kelly green jacket. My pants were polyester and I hate polyester, but they were the only green slacks I could find at the Salvation Army Thrift Store.

Mom opened the front door before I lifted the door knocker. We hugged and kissed as usual, then backed up to take a look at each other. Mom patted the wisps of my errant hair that crept out from under the little white Tam O' Shanter I had found in the back of my closet. Mom wiggled the bright green pom-pom.

"Oh, Marjie, you look darling. What a bonny colleen," gushed Mom.

Mom's blouse was white with a dainty collar where she had pinned a golden shamrock edged in green with a lacey ivory backing.

"Mom, you look great, too. I love that pin. What a glorious day for a parade! It may get up to eighty today, but it's going to be very windy, so better bring a jacket. Do you have a bottle of water to bring along?"

"Yes, Marjie, I do have water and some snacks to bring, some raisins and some granola bars and a jacket, too. It's going to be a wonderful day. Are you sure that the McNamara's want us to ride in their float even though we're not family and not even Irish? Do they have enough room?"

I laughed, "Eileen says the McNamara Clan is open to all people of Celtic origin and you know we are as close as sisters. You know she was born a Baird and her father was definitely Scottish, although he thinks his people originally came from Ireland and immigrated to Scotland. Her mother was Irish—a Murphy. Don't we have a wee bit of Irish in our English blood?"

"Probably, somewhere in your heritage—on your dad's side. I don't think my family, the Sauers, had any Irish blood anywhere in them, but you never know. Besides, I suppose today everyone is Irish who wants to be." Mom chuckled, then, her expression changed. "By the way, what time do we need to be there and how long is the parade? What if I have to go to the bathroom? Maybe I should watch the parade next to a porta-potty."

"Don't worry Mom. Eileen has to go more often than anyone I know. If there isn't a potty on the float, I'm sure there will be a way to get to one. It's time to hit the road. We're meeting at Eileen and Rob's and heading to Browne's Irish Marketplace for breakfast with the rest of the clan. Grab your stuff and let's be off."

I helped her don her bright green blazer pand held her arm as we navigated the flagstone path to my car. Mom hesitated when I held the car door open for her.

"Oh dear, I think I had better go back and go to the bathroom before we leave. How long will it take us to get to the McNamara's?"

Suddenly I realized that I mirrored Mom's discomfort, but we were running late. "Only ten minutes, Mom," wishing I hadn't inherited all these bathroom issues from my mother.

"Oh, I guess I can make it that far."

"Mom, if you can make it, I can make it." We laughed together. What a pair.

During our drive Mom shared some very good news with me. Her tenants, Chuck and Rose and their children moved out of the rental house and into Rose's mother's house without waiting for the sheriff to come. We decided to put the house on the market, the finances would work out. Luckily, we have a friend in the real estate business.

Mom and I enjoyed riding on the McNamara's float, being in one of the largest St. Patrick's Day parades in the country and especially being with friends.

♥

It was Kathleen's precious voice on the phone. "Oh Marjie, spring has sprung! And you know where my thoughts turn. Browning was right. I long to be in *England,* well, Wales, at least, *now that April's there…*"

"Kathleen, so glad you called. Isn't it a beautiful day. It's still March, but April is almost here and brings more than flowers, you know. It brings Tina, Henri and Jakie home to me."

"I'm so happy for you, but Marjie, I had to call you. I walked outside this morning. You know it is the first day of spring. When I went to retrieve *The Examiner* my heart jumped. The sun greeted me joyfully and many of the hyacinths I planted last fall were in bloom. The daffodil faces smiled on me and I forgot all about finding the newspaper. I couldn't contain myself. I was young again and back home in Wales. I walked, a bit stiffly, you know, but fairly erectly, back into the house. I found Foster on the couch in the den. I recited Wordsworth's poem *I Wandered Lonely As a Cloud* to him as I pirouetted as well as an eighty-nine year woman could all around the room. I imagined myself floating as a cloud, over the hills, seeing the daffodils of my youth, next to the lake of my childhood.

Foster applauded me from his reclining position. He said, 'Pretty good for an old dame, Hon.' He then picked up the last verse—apropos as he lie on the couch. Foster get over here and recite that verse for Marjie. Marjie, he's truly not reading this out of a book. Go ahead, Foster, amaze her like you did me."

Foster's scratchy, low voice came on the line. "Here goes, Marjie."

I listened to my dear friend recite and felt the bliss of kinship, my heart filling with pleasure and my mind dancing with the daffodils.

In the background I heard Kathleen say, "Okay, Honey, give me back the phone." Then, "I was so proud of Foster for remembering the whole verse. He is so romantic and I love him so. Marjie, you need someone to recite poetry to you. Have you tried Match.com or eHarmony? I vote for eHarmony. They might be better, according to their own commercial, anyway," she laughed.

"And I'm so glad you called, Kathleen. I hope Robert Browning will forgive me—'So glad to be in *Independence* now that March is here."

Kathleen and I laughed together. How fortunate I am to have had this amazing couple in my life—all my life. They are my idols.

"Marjie, call Eileen and your mother and set up a date for us to go to Powell Gardens. And make it snappy. My soul yearns to be in an immense garden." With that Kathleen hung up. I had a sneaky feeling she and Foster had something of a romantic nature planned.

Mary Florence, Adelaide and I sat on the garden bench admiring the newness of spring and sharing bits and pieces of our lives.

"Marjie I know you are going to UMKC and taking classes, but you haven't told us anything about it. How is it going? What classes are you taking?" asked Mary Florence.

"Going great. English classes are like dreams come true for me—to be able to discuss great works of art and try my skills at creating. I don't know why I waited so long. I'm only taking two classes to start—*Creative Writing* and *British Literature*. It's been so long since I studied anything, I decided it would be best not to take on too much. I am fifty-two you know, the oldest student in the class. Why I'm probably twenty years older than one of my professors. But I love being the oldest student in class. Actually, the kids right out of high school show a lot of respect to me which I find wonderfully refreshing. I thought they would resent me, ignore me or, even worse, make fun of me." I felt my voice quivering a bit with my laugh.

"Are you the only, how should I put it, mature student in your class?" asked Mary Florence.

"Oh, no, there are a few other non-traditional students—that's what they call us. You won't believe this one woman in my class. Our assignment was to write something that had happened to us that made a big impression, something we would be able to describe well—I wrote about Tina's wedding, anyway, this woman in my class, she's almost my age. She read her assignment to the class. She had charts and graphs—it was supposed to be a history of invertebrate paleontology and she tried to make it humorous! It was so confusing and very boring, not funny, thankfully, the professor cut her short since she did not fulfill the assignment."

Adelaide said, "Well, that woman isn't writing something HISTORICAL but she is writing something HYSTERICAL."

Everyone laughed and as it was almost time for *Jeopardy*, we went inside to the TV room.

Eileen and I always joked about going to the hair museum, but when Adelaide told me about it we had to go see for ourselves. We decided to take my Mom and Denise. All of us have lived here our whole lives. We couldn't have a newcomer know more about Independence than we did. It appears that Adelaide is an avid reader of *Ripley's Believe It or Not* and she discovered Leila's Hair Museum listed in the RBION, as she calls it. As soon as Adelaide bought her home on the internet she started looking to see what sights and culture were available in Independence and the Greater Kansas City area. She told me that this museum was a "must see…with tresses of all tresses".

We got there and my, oh my, what sights we did see.

Denise was fascinated with the reliquaries, boxes used to store relics, which according to her were sacred pieces of bone fragments of a saint or something used by or associated with a saint.

Mom and I wandered around looking at all the wreaths hanging on the walls made from hair. There seemed to be hundreds of them.

Eileen headed straight to the jewelry saying, "To think that we have all lived here all our lives and have never been here before."

After meandering from room to room for at least an hour, we decided we could only handle so much hair art at one time so off we went to the coffee shop on the Square for lunch.

Confession Time: I reached my front door after an exhilarating morning walk around the Temple and Auditorium, stirred by the beauty of nature all around me, eager to plan tomorrow's prayer meeting. I stood at the door, pressing the remote, but the door did not open. I heard no sound of unlatching. Then I laughed, for the second time this week I was trying to open my door with my car remote. I don't have a remote for the house. Lordy, lordy, my mind has truly left me for greener pastures.

I unconsciously filled my mug from the tap and stuck it in the microwave, hit two minutes, then pressed start. While the microwave heated the water, I selected a tea I purchased from the new tea shop at the Independence Center, an apricot black tea. My, it smells delicious, I thought, as I put the bag up to my nose. Soon the microwave dinged and I plopped the tea bag into the hot water.

Sitting at my breakfast table I sipped tea and leafed through several books that might have a story or something meaningful to use for tomorrow night's prayer service. I have been in charge numerous times, but planning prayer services still doesn't come easily to me. Hopefully, I picked up *The Hymnal*—the burgundy one that was published in 1980. There are so many beautiful hymns in here. Why is the World Church coming out with a new one? I know they want to include more hymns from around the world. We are a World Church. That's fine, but it will cost the congregations so much to make the change.

I laughed as I remembered that Jake and I said the same thing when the burgundy hymnal replaced the old gray one—and now I can't live without the burgundy songbook. Whatever the hymnal, music fills a place in my heart. Sometimes hymns reach me when sermons cannot, even sometimes when the scriptures cannot. After looking through all the hymns related to prayer, I still wasn't getting anywhere. What is wrong with me? I can't keep my focus. I need to pray about this. I got down on my knees which is rare for me. I often pray sitting in this very kitchen chair and anywhere else for that matter, but today I felt a need to do something different to help me feel the presence of God. I wanted to kneel at the feet of the Lord.

After a few moments of silence, I felt the Holy Spirit come over me. I began weeping and praising the Lord. I looked up through the skylights at the beautiful clouds. I rose and went out on the back side of the porch so I could see more sky and enjoy the plum tree and Bradford pear blossoms and the redbuds, beginning to come into flower. I felt peace. I lifted my hands up to the sky and began to sing *Alleluia, Alleluia, Alleluia, Alleluia*. Suddenly a bluebird flew from the pear tree to the plum tree. Funny how the mind works, the bird reminded me of a book I read about Mary, the mother of Jesus. How Mary must have suffered as she watched her son die torturously on the wooden cross. How unimaginable. I sat down at the patio table and wept. I stared back at the beautiful tree, teary and glassy-eyed, creating an impressionist painting in my vision. The first line of *I Know That My Redeemer Lives*, a treasured hymn of Jesus' resurrection drifted into my mind.

How glorious it must have been for Mary when she saw Jesus after

His resurrection. Now I feel prepared for tonight's service.

♥

On Easter Sunday I awoke thinking, *Lord, how beautiful is your name in all the earth.* I remembered I was going to be in the early morning service today. Every year a sunrise service is held behind the church in the grove. This year we decided to have a pageant and portray the death and resurrection of Jesus. I am playing Mary Magdalene. Many of the congregation are in the cast, but plenty of congregants will be left in the audience and many from other churches will crowd into the grove area and lean against each other and the trees all around.

This year the service was beautiful, as it was every year. "There was not a dry eye in the forest", Kathleen said later. The story was told with as much authenticity as possible. There were soldiers gambling for Christ's robe, the wooden crosses were heavy. It took two men to carry each one. There were three, one for Jesus and one for each of the criminals that had been on each side of Him.

I loved playing Mary Magdalene. I have always felt a connection with her. Mary Magdalene followed Jesus devoutly, loved Him well and spent a lot of time with him. I wanted to do that, too. When I studied for this role in the play I felt Mary's joy when Jesus spoke to her in the garden. According to the *Gospel of John* Mary Magdalene thought he was a gardener, but he spoke to her and asked her why she was weeping, when she told him, he revealed himself to her. She was the first to see him after his resurrection. He warned her that she could not touch him, that he had to go to his Father, but she was to go and prepare the other disciples. What a wonderful assignment to be given. To announce that she had seen the Lord! Several people commented that they felt the Holy Spirit's presence when Mary Magdalene encountered Jesus in the play.

After the pageant everyone was invited into the fellowship hall for a light breakfast of fresh fruit, home-baked muffins, tea bread and quiche. The coffee smelled wonderful, enticing all into the hall. It was crowded this morning. The best turnout ever!

After breakfast we hosted a big Easter egg hunt out in the woods for the older kids and in the clearing for the younger ones. I couldn't wait for Jakie to be there next year, but at least Mandy was with me and her parents had come with us to church this morning.

Later that afternoon Mom and I were invited to have dinner with the residents of Bingham Manor. We were also invited to Eileen and Rob's but chose to go to my workplace and second home. Later we would stop by Eileen and Rob's to visit with their family.

When we approached Bingham Manor, we saw Mary Florence, Anna Jean, Adelaide and her sister, Annabelle, of twin singing dog fame, waiting for us on the front porch. Adelaide and Annabelle had on fancy silk dresses with matching Easter bonnets—Adelaide dressed in purple and Annabelle in yellow. We heard Adelaide's cackle and Annabelle's cock-a-doodle-doo, so like a rooster—lots of er-er-er er-er's.

As we arrived on the porch we spotted four hat boxes sitting on the patio table. The boxes were white, tied with velvet ribbons of pale green, yellow and pink.

Adelaide cackled again and said, "When Mary Florence told me that you were coming today, MARJIE and bringing your MOTHER, Annabelle and I drug out some of our Easter bonnets of yore. I hope you'll enjoy wearing them. I actually brought more, one for each of the ladies here today."

"My goodness, Adelaide, Annabelle, how generous…" I began. Mom started to open her mouth, but Adelaide cut both of us off.

"Well, we aren't really GIVING them to you. They are on LOAN just for today, while you are here with us. You see these are a culmination of many years of collecting, some were  mother's and some are actually from operas that FATHER was in."

When we entered the dining room and saw all the ladies adorned with chapeaus of every ilk, I felt transported back in time. The look on Mom's face told me she had joined me there.

Eugene was there to escort Anna Jean to her seat and several of the other men, some in wheel chairs and others with canes or walkers, lined up to offer their arms to Mary Florence, Annabelle, Adelaide, Mom and me. The ladies took the arms of the gentlemen, sometimes actually assisting the men, except Adelaide who yelled,

"Get away from me, you WHIPPERSNAPPER. I don't need any MAN'S help to get to a table." Adelaide pulled herself into a military stance, straight and tall as a technical sergeant.

Everyone looked shocked until they heard her give a soft chortle. She graciously took his arm. His name was Clyde and he stood about as short as Anna Jean and Mary Florence, with Adelaide towering over him, Clyde looked up into her eyes and laughed,

"Call me a 'whippersnapper' will you, you hussy!" He knew the way to talk to Adelaide. Her cackles could be heard throughout the building.

Lunch was wonderful, especially the company. Mom and I went away satisfied that our friends at Bingham Manor had a great lunch and good fellowship this Easter.

I looked at Mom feeling a goofy grin on my face, "Do you suppose that another romance has budded right here in front of our eyes, first Eugene and Anna Jean and today, Clyde and Adelaide?"

"I predict it won't be long until you are performing a double wedding for these two couples," Mom laughed as I pulled out of the parking space.

Next on our Easter agenda—the McNamara's clan. The children were hunting and re-hunting eggs in the back yard. All the McNamara daughters were there, Meg, Jo, Beth and Amy. Their husbands were also there except for Beth's Jerry. Mom and I joined the circle in the family room and enjoyed Meg's spectacular pineapple upside down cake. Eileen had assigned a cake for each daughter—Meg, the pineapple upside down, Jo, a Lady Baltimore, Beth, who lives with them now, a chocolate caramel cheesecake and Amy, a raw apple cake. I never cease to be amazed at Eileen's managerial skills and sweet tooth.

For once Eileen seemed to be relaxing, sitting in her favorite chair with her feet up. Rob hovered over her, out of character for him. I wondered what was going on. Soon I found out. Eileen had twisted her ankle during the play, not telling anyone, and that explained why she sat earlier during the breakfast, barking out orders to her daughters, Rob and others. I had been so busy and keyed up that I hadn't noticed.

♥

I walked into Suzie's five minutes before my appointment time. Suzie doesn't like it when her clients are late. Although it was perfectly okay for her to get behind with her customers, sometimes up to thirty minutes. I never complained when I had to wait because her shop is so entertaining, full of interesting chatter, the other stylist, Jolene, should have her own reality show.

Jolene rented a station at Suzie's shop about a year ago. I never knew what color or style Jolene's hair would be or what to expect in the continuing saga of her life story. Today's fashion found her hair long and bleached blond with incongruous black-tipped ends. At least it wasn't purple or green. I saw that the other day at the supermarket.

While Suzie finished up with her three o'clock perm customer, I sat in the waiting area and pulled out my nine-ton Norton Anthology, flipped to my assignment of Romantic Poets, hoping to get some reading done, hoping to be transported halfway to Somersetshire, where Coleridge composed *The Eolian Harp*, but it was not to be. I read the first stanza four or five times only gleaning that I craved *the world so hushed, the stilly murmur of the distant Sea* that the poet speaks of.

I gave up and threw myself into the role of eavesdropper. I couldn't help overhearing Jolene as her mouth worked non-stop trying to talk her friend into hitting a bar for a few drinks and then staying all night with her. Jolene has no form of internal editing—anything she thinks comes right out of her mouth.

"Come on, Marissa, it will be so much fun. Like old times before you married that crazy man of yours. We can go to Spike's or wait let's go to Nancy and Mike's or I'll even go to that place in Westport you like. What is it called—Zebra's Little Stripe? Then you can come and stay all night with me. I don't want to be alone. I'll cry if I'm alone."

Marissa's shoulders drooped and she shook her head, but her voice was calm. "No, I'm tired. I've been working all day—a twelve hour shift at the grocery store. I need to go home. I came by to make sure you are okay. Have you been taking your meds and eating? You don't look like you've been eating enough to keep a butterfly alive."

"You are afraid to go out with me. Afraid your old man will beat you up again, aren't you? Come on, Marissa. Let's go to Zebra's. I'll buy you a margarita. I'll buy you two margaritas. Then you can stay all night with me. We'll pop some corn and watch *Titanic*."

"No, Jolene. I want to go home. I'm forty-five years old. I don't stay all night with girlfriends. I want to go home to my husband. Surely you can understand that?"

"I don't understand why you would pick him over me. We would have so much fun! I need to go out and I don't want to go by myself. I know you are afraid of your husband. Why can't you go out with me?" Jolene whined. She walked to the back of the shop and grabbed a brochure from the local home for battered women. "See, it says right here—*Does your spouse call you constantly when you are apart? Does your spouse tell you what to wear?*"

"Jolene, I'm leaving. Fred loves me so much he wants to be with me and I want to be with him and I'm going home right now. He hasn't called me one time and I've been here with you for over an hour. He has never hit me. I don't know what you are talking about. I'll see you later. Go home. Watch a movie and eat something. We'll get together over the weekend when I'm not so tired." Marissa gave Jolene a hug and walked out.

Jolene had a male customer in her chair through all this. She asked him, "What would you do if your wife wanted to spend the night with a friend?"

He replied, "I'd tell her to pack up all her stuff and move in with her friend."

I waited for Jolene's come back, but all I heard was, "Now, Barney, you want a number five on top and a number two on the sides, right?"

Then brightening up she said, "Hey, would you like to go out for a drink after I cut your hair? I've got two more haircuts then I'm done for the day. I've got to get out of this town. I hate this God-forsaken town. All the cops hate me. There are cops at every corner."

"You got it girl." Barney replied. "I'll even buy you three margaritas, but please don't bad mouth the fine Independence police department. My father is a cop. He'd lay his life down on the line to protect you even if you do hate his guts."

"Well, if your father is a cop and you are such a cop lover, I don't want to go out with you after all. As a matter of fact, I don't even want you as a customer anymore. Get outta here right now. If I'd known you were a son of a cop I would have never cut your hair in the first place."

"You are a crazy little number, lady. Believe me. You won't see me in here again. You're a nutcase if I ever met one." With that Barney stood up, threw twenty dollars on the counter and sauntered out.

My life is so interesting. I was thinking how Jolene would be a good character in a novel, then realized this wasn't entertainment, it was real life. I must pray for Jolene. She really is lonely and she probably drinks too much. *Lord, be with her and if there is any way I can help her, prod me into knowing how.*

# CHAPTER SIX

I didn't know what to expect at Adelaide's, but knew we were in for an exciting evening. I picked up Mom and Mary Florence then drove to the address Adelaide had given me, 909 W Waldo Avenue. I was enchanted to find it was the boyhood home of Harry S. Truman. The sign said he lived there until 1904. He would have been about eighteen. The sign also said that there had been *later additions that have greatly altered the appearance of the house.*

"I wonder what it looked like when Truman lived here?" I said.

"Don't look at me, Marjie," laughed Mary Florence. "I'm not that old."

Adelaide described her house as a cottage, but mentioned that there was room for six to eight people. The three of us trooped up the flat walk. There were two red brick steps into the house, a traditional entryway, but off to the right we stepped into the dramatic living room.

Everything was red, black and white: Ceiling-red, two walls white, two red, black lacquer desk and end tables, white coffee table with black inlaid marble, mirrors, art deco paintings, an Andy Warhol print of Marilyn Monroe, white sofa, chairs, two each of solid blacks and reds, floor, black and white tile. I was fascinated with the décor and was soon to find the company left nothing to be desired.

Adelaide and Annabelle had gone all out. It was a wonderful pre-opera party. In the living room we enjoyed conversation and canapés of stuffed mushrooms and bruschetta with goat cheese, with non-alcoholic highballs topping off the appetizers.

For entertainment Annabelle's dogs sang their duet from *Carmen* as promised. Mary Florence, Mom and I were bowled over by their performance. They really did sing the *Toreador Song*! They kept up with Annabelle as she held them upon her enormous lap. I thought they might fall over at some points, but they held their stance. After the applause and treats for Mikado and Carmen. Adelaide ushered us into the dining room.

I felt like I had left the house we were in and gone to another completely different house. This room was decorated like a Victorian tea room. There were shelves of tea cups and tea pots. Everything was lace and florals, pinks, baby blues, backgrounds of ivory everywhere. The antique brass oval-framed photographs on the wall were all in sepia.

Adelaide caught Mom and me admiring the photos and rushed over in her gawkingly effusive way to tell us the history behind the photos. "Here is FATHER in his favorite role as The Duke in *Rigoletto.* And here he is as FERRANDO in *Cosi Fan Tutte.* This one he is Tamino in *The Magic Flute* and here he is playing RODOLFO, *La Bohème,* you know."

"Oh Adelaide, let me show them the rest," begged Annabelle. "Over here is my personal favorite, not because I liked the opera best, because I think you know that I like Gilbert and Sullivan best and he very rarely played in them, not since I was little, I think, or maybe he never did have a G & S role. What do you think Adelaide, did Father ever play Gilbert and Sullivan or did he just take us to watch it? I loved the *Pirates of Penzance.*"

Adelaide arched her enormous drawn-on brows. "SISTER, are you going to show them the REST of Father's photographs?" she snapped.

"Now you're mad at me. I was simply trying to remember if Father ever played a Gilbert and Sullivan role."

Adelaide's face and tone changed. "I'm not MAD at you, Sweetheart, but we need to get on with dinner or we'll be late to the opera." Adelaide said as softly as possible for her, unusual for this loud talking woman.

"Well, let's eat then. They can look at the pictures next time they are here."

Annabelle definitely was one to get her feelings hurt easily. She was a little childish and reminded me of Anna Jean. We are all going to the American Heartland together next month. I wondered how the two of them will get along. Better pray about that.

The main course was made up of Chicken Parmigiana, tossed green salad topped with an Italian olive salad and cheesy garlic bread. The laughter, especially Adelaide's cackling began again as we savored the food.

"Did you hire a caterer for this meal?" Mom asked. "This is fantastic. I've never had a better meal in my life I don't think. Have you Marjie?"

Adelaide answered, "No, heavens, heh, heh, heh, Annabelle LOVES to cook. She's been featured on Martha STEWART'S show a few times. You know Martha throws the best parties. Well, they are ALMOST as good as ours, right Annabelle?"

Annabelle nodded. She was in the process of chewing a bite of the chicken. The sauce was edging out over the corner of her mouth. "Thank you so much. I love to cook. You can tell I love to eat, too." And she laughed patting her soft round tummy. "Er-er-er-er-er-er."

I was on the verge of not being able to contain my laughter because of the sound of Annabelle's laugh so I thought I'd better say something—anything, but I couldn't think of anything to say at that moment.

Unfortunately Mary Florence and I caught each other's gaze and it was over for both of us. We started laughing. Pretty soon Mom lost control and had to go running to the bathroom. She always peed her pants when she laughed. Adelaide's cackle joined her sister's er-er's making this dinner party the personification of a hen party.

When Mom returned from the bathroom everyone else was dabbing their eyes with their napkins or reaching for the Kleenex.

Annabelle waddled out from the kitchen bringing her crowning achievement for the evening—her molded homemade Spumoni, with bits of maraschino cherries, candied orange peel and blanched almonds. We enjoyed the luscious frozen dessert until the stately grandfather clock chimed six times and Adelaide announced that it was time to leave for the opera.

As we got into my car Adelaide said, "Going to the opera is like going to a SWAHILI poetry reading and you KNOW how much I love Swahili. Well, maybe YOU don't, but I do love Swahili, don't I Annabelle?"

Suddenly Adelaide changed the topic and leaned over the seat. "Now, Marjie, you know how to get us there, right? I know you have LIVED HERE in this area all your life, right?"

"I think I can get us there okay. I'll take I-70…"

"I-70! Why child, we don't go on I-70 until we are ALL the way DOWNTOWN. Take Truman Road. MapQuest says that's THE SHORTEST distance and it saves us a minute! We're all about SAVING minutes, a minute saved is a minute more to do something else, right Annabelle?" said Adelaide.

"Right, Adelaide, that's what Papa always said." Annabelle nodded her round head and her opera hat fell off.

"Okay, I'll take Truman Road, but it seems like it would take a lot longer with all those stoplights," I said, as I pulled away from the curb.

We chattered all the way down Truman Road, even I was enjoying the conversation. All of a sudden Adelaide yelled, "STOP! Here's where you TURN to get on I-70.

I turned the wheel for the left turn and took the ramp to the freeway, wishing fervently that I had not driven tonight. Why didn't we hire a cab or taken the bus? Of course, I am not familiar with the bus schedules. I don't even know if any buses run in the evenings from Adelaide's house. I certainly had no idea how bossy Adelaide would be.

Adelaide hoisted her MapQuest again, "Now, Marjie, get over into the LEFT lane."

I was in the right lane and had to cross over three lanes of traffic, but I made it and was getting ready to turn on 13th Street, like I used to when I worked downtown in my youth.

Adelaide yelled, "Good grief, GIRL, I thought you knew THE WAY. Take the Broadway exit. It's a GOOD thing I brought this MapQuest with me."

I was almost in tears. My stomach churned. Frustrated. I wasn't used to anyone yelling at me, but somehow I managed to turn off on the Broadway exit. Then, thankfully, a stop light appeared. I asked in as calm a voice as I could muster, "What do we do now, Adelaide?"

But Adelaide didn't answer. All I could hear was rustling of dresses and some murmuring and fussing between the two sisters in the back seat. It seemed that Adelaide had dropped the MapQuest on the floor and under the long full skirt of her sister who insisted on dressing formally for the opera. With the two of them arguing and Mom and Mary Florence totally silent, I was left to my own devices .

The light turned green so I turned  right on Broadway and drove down to Twelfth Street, where I judged I needed to turn right, remembering the last time I was downtown that Eleventh Street was a one-way going the wrong way. Next, I turned left onto Central and the Lyric Theater was right there. I dropped everyone but Mom at the door.

Adelaide popped out with, "GREAT JOB, Marjie! You didn't need my directions AFTER ALL."

I determined never to ride in a car with Adelaide again. Annabelle held her skirts up as she ascended the stairs, her hat waving in the breeze. Adelaide followed behind Mary Florence as she took to the stairs with her walker. I admired her tenacity, but the view of the three of them together was unusual, I shouldn't say, hilarious, but it was strange.

All I had to do now was find a place to park. I hate to parallel park, but also dislike paying for the privilege of parking, so I drove down the street and found a place wide enough that I could pull straight into. I felt sweat under my armpits and breasts but thanked the Lord we had made it safely with all that yelling going on. Mom thanked me for driving and praised me for my coolness under duress. I told her there was no coolness on my part, I was sweating like a pig, but firmly vowed never to drive with Adelaide in the car again. We got out of the car and walked to the theater.

The others had already picked up our tickets at Will Call when we joined them. The usher gave us each a program and escorted us to our seats which were on the floor, all paying extra so that Mary Florence wouldn't have to climb any more stairs than necessary. Before we sat down, Mom and I excused ourselves and went to the rest room, knowing that an empty bladder would make the performance more enjoyable. As we walked away, we heard Annabelle start to complain about the amount of advertisements in the program and Adelaide cackling, "But that's why you didn't have to PAY for it, Sister."

The performances were excellent. My friends and I were transported to sixteenth century Mantua. I felt emotion running through my body as Gilda sang *Caro Nome,* her soprano simply superb. The hated Duke's tenor was absolutely sublime. I felt tremors up and down my spine during his performance of *La Donna e Mobile*. I found myself hating the villain while admiring his voice tremendously. The Duke and his jester, Rigoletto, scheme and are cursed by Count Monterone. The tragedy plays itself out as Rigoletto discovers his daughter, Gilda, dying.

The audience stood as one, chanting "Bravo! Bravo!" for three encores. On the drive home Adelaide and Annabelle were so busy comparing this performance to the one their father played in, that Mom, Mary Florence and I were able to chat in peace. The ride home was much more enjoyable than our trip downtown.

Today was Mom's appointment with the eye doctor. I dropped her at the door of the professional building, parked the car and met her in front of the elevators.

An elderly man in a wheelchair yelled at me as we waited for the elevator, "What doctor did you come to see?" He didn't look angry, I guessed he was hard of hearing.

I said, "I'm here with my mother. She's going to see Dr. Cross for her annual eye checkup. Who are you going to see?"

"Don't do that," he yelled at the top of his lungs. His caregiver was jerking his wheelchair, forward a few inches, then back.

I could tell that the caregiver was making him uncomfortable, so I quietly suggested that she stop moving his chair, but the woman smiled with an ornery look on her puffy face, and kept jerking his chair.

The man yelled again, "Don't do that!" but his assistant seemed determined to keep it up.

Mom yelled, "Don't do that!" and I yelled with her. Soon other people that had come in and were waiting for the elevator all yelled in a chorus, "Don't do that!"

Shortly, the doors opened on two different elevators. The caregiver shoved the old man on one and everyone else crowded in behind them until the elevator was full.

I asked the caregiver her name and what agency she worked for.

She whirled around and looked at me with eyes of steel and said, "Lady, that is none of your business."

The old man smiled at me and said as plain as day, "Her name is Bonnie Crabapple. The first name's a lie, but the second one tells it like it is. She works for an outfit I'm gonna fire—Peabody's Home Health Care out of Blue Springs. You're darn tootin' I am."

Ms. Crabapple's face blushed a splotchy red and she turned her back on all of us in the elevator. I decided to follow up with Peabody's to make sure they took her off his case, if he didn't fire the whole company, as he said he would.

Mom's appointment went well so we went to the Square Tea Shoppe to celebrate another year of good eyesight for her.

♥

Today Jakie appeared first on the Skype call. "Hi, Grandma! I see you. Do you see me? I'm five!"

I sniffled with happiness as I viewed and heard my small grandson.

"Yes, Jakie. I see you. Happy Birthday! I miss you so much. Did you have a good day today? Did you have a party?"

"Yes, Mamie Titia and Papi Gregoirie, Mams and Papa and everyone in my family were here and my friends were here. My best friend, Julien, and his brother, Alexandre, and their sister, Aurelie were here, and my cousins, Clara and Sarah and Jade. Why don't I have any boy cousins, Grandma? I like to play with boys better. Oh, and my best friend, Enzo and his little brother, Theo came. Everyone gave me presents. Grandma, I got a motorcycle!"

"A motorcycle—Jakie, how big is the motorcycle? Is it a Hot Wheels motorcycle?" I feared that my crazy daughter and her husband lacked judgment as far as my grandson's safety was concerned. I didn't know what Tina and Henri thought appropriate for a five year old.

"No, Grandma. It's big! I can ride on it, but only in the yard. I wish

I could ride it on the road. It's really big. It's bigger than my fire truck and it has a motor on it. It's silver and black, but it's not as big as Papa's motorcycle. Mine is a toy. I want to bring it to Missouri when we come on the plane, but Papa says we have to ship it with the rest of our stuff and I don't know how long it will take to get there. Can you buy me another one, Grandma?"

"Oh, Jakie, I think we will wait until yours gets here from France. It won't take very long. You can ride it all the way around the porch, like your mother used to ride her tricycle."

Tina burst in, "I told him about the porch and how it wraps all the way around the house."

"Jakie, I'm glad you had a good birthday. I miss you so much and can't wait to see you. I want to give you a big hug and never let you go."

"Grandma, you have to let me go sometimes. I have to eat and sleep, you know. Grandma, you are silly."

"Yes, I am a silly grandma and we are going to have lots of fun being silly when you get here. Bye, bye for now. See you soon. May I speak with your silly mother?"

After a few seconds Tina appeared on the screen. "Hi Mom. How are you?"

"I'm great! Can't wait to see you all in person on Monday. I've got your rooms ready."

"Mom, what did you do? I told you…"

I interrupted. "Don't worry. I washed the bedding and curtains, wiped down the walls, vacuumed, dusted—no  redecorating. We'll do it together when you get here. How's the packing going?"

"Well, the packing is fine, but our plans have changed a bit. We won't be able to make it by next Monday. We need some more time to pack and get everything ready for the move."

"You aren't changing your mind, are you?" I felt a sinking in my heart.

"Not at all. Gregoirie needs Henri's help here for a little while longer. His brother hasn't been able to spend as much time as we had hoped. We're looking at the end of May now."

"Well, I guess that's not too bad. I will have to live with it. I miss you all so much."

I felt wilted, but somehow, relieved for this was to be a huge change in my life and theirs. Jakie doesn't know any other home, any other friends, but I know we'll make it work.

"We miss you, too, Mom. Whoops. Gotta go, Jakie's trying to ride his motorcycle in the house again."

And Tina was offline before I could tell her to hug Jakie and Henri for me. I felt bereft. Now I had to wait over a month longer to see my precious family.

I walked out on the porch that Jake and his friends had built, remembering that Mark had helped with the painting when he was in town visiting his mother. There's none like it anywhere—a present for Tina, so she could ride her tricycle all the way around the house safely, and for me so I could drink tea and look at every view that there was to be had from our house. I walked around it now, filled with plants, tables and chairs on the east and west sides. I'll have to move things around so Jakie can ride out here. *Oh, Jake, I wish you were here.*

I prayed silently for my family's welfare and then checked the time. Twelve forty-five. No time for lunch. I grabbed a package of cheese crackers and one of raisins and was off to the Temple for the Prayer for Peace.

When I left the Temple I hurried to my car and drove to the campus at the University of Missouri at Kansas City. While driving I mentally reviewed what I read last night for my Lit class and thought about my writing assignment. There was so much going on in my life right now. I am glad I decided not to go to school this summer. I would never have time to study when Tina and Henri arrive. I want to spend time with them and with Jakie.

Parked, I grabbed my backpack and headed up the hill to Cockefair Hall, anxious to see how my last paper was graded.

I arrived at Mom's condo to take her out for lunch. "Hi, Mom, can't believe how dreary the weather is today. What a downpour. And now they aren't coming until May 26th."

Mom knew who *they* were. I saw the disappointment in her eyes.

I changed the subject. "I wanted to plant my glads. Guess they'll have to wait till the sun comes back around. You are looking springy today."

"Oh, Marjie, thank you. Not too shabby for an eighty year old woman, huh? Just look at the gorgeous dogwood blossoms. Have you ever seen my trees so full? Even the pink one is dressed-up in its fullest Easter bonnet. Do you remember the story about the dogwood blossoms?"

"Of course I do, Mom. It is a beautiful legend and you told it to me every Easter when I was little. I loved looking at the petals –two long and two short reminiscent of the cross on which Jesus died and the brown marks to remind us of the nail holes in His hands. It doesn't matter if the story is true. What matters is that the dogwood tree reminds us of Jesus and His love for us."

"That's right, my wise daughter. I love you. I'm hungry. Let's go to lunch."

"You'll get no argument from me. There's a new salad at Applebee's that I want to try."

Mom and I walked hand in hand to the car. I was so blessed to have my wonderful mother close to me.

♥

I was distracted today. As usual when preparing a sermon I read the scripture from the Church website lectionary, John 20:19-31. My theme was *Peace Be With You*, but I couldn't get a chorus that kept running through my head out of my mind. *Sweet Holy Spirit, Sweet Heavenly Dove, stay right here with us, filling us with your love.*

Where did that come from? I couldn't understand why that particular hymn wouldn't leave me alone. It didn't matter what I was doing, walking, fixing a meal, ironing, driving, even trying to study Tennyson. It was there. This had been going on for about a month. Today I was working on my message and trying to answer the question: *What does it mean to meet the risen Christ?* But *Sweet Holy Spirit* kept on coming. I prayed, *Oh, Lord, I need more from you than 'Sweet Holy Spirit, Sweet Heavenly Dove'. Lord, help me with words for the communion message this coming Sunday. Is this your way of leading me? Is my topic to be the peace of the Holy Spirit?*

I couldn't resist. I felt compelled to go out on the internet to get the rest of the lyrics. I found them and also found an interview of the songwriter, Doris Akers, telling how she was inspired to write this song. I watched a video on youtube.com with Elvis standing there listening to some others sing *Sweet Sweet Spirit*. Elvis just stood and cried and I cried with him.

♥

Monday morning I sat on my front porch reading one of my favorite books, *Hymns of the Saints,* its burgundy cover with gold lettering, so familiar to me now. My thoughts drifted to the beauty of the earth and I got up from the old glider on the porch, and sang one of my favorite hymns, *For the Beauty of the Earth.*

Inspired, I hurried back into the kitchen for the scissors and a basket, I headed for the rows of iris in my cutting garden. I cut yellow and purple and pink, wishing the white and deep purple were blooming. Next I ventured to the side yard where I cut several pale pink peonies and some deep red ones. From my wildflower garden I cut a profusion of daisies. In the garden shed I divided the flowers into five vases, one for Mom, one for Kathleen, two for Bingham Manor and one for myself.

I thought of my loved ones in France. Only twenty-five more days! Great timing. My exams are over about a week before they arrive. Wonderful.

♥

I looked around the fellowship hall eying the gorgeous table decorations that Kathleen had arranged. All the tables were covered with white linen meticulously edged in lace. The decorations were done in ivory-colored baby roses and pale pink tropical lilies, which Kathleen insisted must be fresh. I found Kathleen in the kitchen putting finishing touches on the arrangements for the buffet table. Eileen was setting out all the glass and silver trays she could find. Apparently some of the ladies had brought their baked goods in Tupperware.

"Where are the paper doilies?" Denise yelled from little storage room about twenty feet away.

"Oh, Marjie, how beautiful your Petit Fours are. Mine look a mess compared to yours. Look how uneven the icing is," cried Eileen.

"Eileen, yours are very pretty. I cheated and called Tina for help. She told me to go to a baker's supply store to pick up some flower nails to hold the mini cakes up while icing them. Then put them on the baker's rack to drip. And look at those gorgeous tarts you made. I had trouble fluting the edges of those tiny little things," I laughed. "But you have really outdone yourself. Everything looks so beautiful and dainty. Wish we could leave it like this."

"You know how long that would last with the wild kids we have around here," remarked Eileen.

"And which wild kids are you talking about?" said Grace rather defensively as she walked through the door.

Denise rushed in and interrupted. "I still can't find those doilies anywhere. Any ideas?"

"Oh my goodness, I think they are still in my car. Here are my keys. Can you please get them? They're in the back seat, I think." Eileen answered as she handed Denise the keys.

Eileen turned her attention back to Grace. "Definitely not any of your children. They are always so well behaved. I shouldn't have said that anyway. All children are blessings from God—but some of them really do like to run around the church building a little too fast. It makes me nervous. I worry that one of them will get hurt or run into one of the elderly members and really cause a problem."

"And who are you calling elderly?" laughed Kathleen.

I watched as Eileen hugged Kathleen and Grace, then said, "Certainly not you, Kathleen. You have more energy than I do on any given day. I need all of you to cut me some slack today. I have been on pins and needles about this tea. Everyone has worked so hard—baking and baking and baking and cleaning and decorating the church. I know our guests will have a wonderful time and our fund raiser will be a success, but Lord, please give me peace. I'm all-a-goggle."

"What time is it? It's two thirty-two." I asked and then answered my own question as I pulled my cell phone out of my pocket to check the time. "Even though the invitation said three o'clock our guests may start arriving any minute. You know how over-prompt some of them are."

Eileen waved her hands in the air, then brought them down knocking the napkins askew. She quickly rearranged them. "And some of our helpers haven't arrived yet. I wonder where my daughters and granddaughters are."

Just then her daughters Meg, Jo, Amy, and Beth walked in with their daughters and one lonesome little boy.

"Hi Marmee, sorry we're late, but you told us to only bring one car so we wouldn't take up all the parking spaces and it takes time to pick everyone up." Amy hugged her mother, then me.

"I thought you would all meet at our house and ride together from there, but no matter. You're here now. Let's get to work." Eileen looked at her to-do list and soon was issuing orders like a sergeant, albeit a sweet-voiced sergeant.

I walked over to the drink table in time to see little Teddy leveling off the glasses of poured milk by slurping each one of them.

After the tea was over and all the clean-up done and money counted, Eileen gave her report. "You will be glad to know that the tea raised over five hundred dollars for the homeless. That is only a drop in the proverbial bucket. I know we need more, but it's a start.

I had been looking forward to dinner at the McNamara's all week. I let myself in and heard Rob grumble—"What do you mean there won't be any life insurance on me if you die first? We have that federal policy that you kept when you retired. Remember, the family part. We kept it at the maximum because it was so cheap. You said there is $25,000 on me.

What happened to that?"

"That's right. If you die before I do, I get the money, but no one else can be the beneficiary, only me. That's because the main policy is on me, but at least we can name anyone as beneficiary in case of my death."

"So there will be no money to bury me if you die first, right?"

"That's what I'm saying. I totally forgot about that when we cancelled the policy we had on you from the teacher's union."

"Well, let the wolves, worms or whales have me then. I won't care anyway."

"Don't worry. You are a veteran. You can probably be buried in a veteran's cemetery. I'll look into it."

They finally noticed me standing there. I said, "I walk in on the most interesting conversations at your house. I hope when Tina and her family move in that we will be as fascinating as you two are."

Rob gave me a brotherly nudge, "Even if they are fascinating beyond belief—you'll probably all speak in French and we won't understand a word, so if you want to dazzle us, speak English, *por favor*."

"Uh, Rob, that's Spanish for please. If you want to say it in French, it would be *s'il vous plait*," I laughed.

Eileen said, "Let's eat before the wolves, worms and whales find this beautiful roast."

After Eileen said grace the three of us enjoyed another wonderful evening filled with conversation, laughter and melt in your mouth food.

Only seven more days till they get here, until my life changes forever. I parked my car in front of Suzie's shop, barely closing the door behind me when Jolene approached.

"Marjie, how do I look? Do I look fat in these shorts?"

I didn't know what to say. Jolene had on cut-off short shorts that were ripped up the sides. The skin that showed looked pretty good to me. She's at least ten years younger than I am and I spend every day with senior citizens, but she didn't give me time to talk anyway.

"Does my cellulite show too bad? My old boyfriend, he's a millionaire you know. He's coming by the shop today. I have to look good. He's married and we haven't been together for fourteen years, but he called and is coming by. I'm so excited. I'm going to ask him for twenty dollars. We would have never made it together. He's so boring, but we had something. We can't be left in a room alone. There's too much spark between us. He's so boring. Only listens to talk radio and he's a Republican. I could never live with a Republican. We don't get along, but there is something about him. He's like a magnet to me. Do I look fat?"

Jolene stopped talking for a mini-second and I opened my mouth, but she was off again.

"Oh here is the olive oil. I thought I had left it at home. My hair has to be shiny. I have to look good. I hope he drives one of his new cars. I hope he doesn't drive one of his pick-up trucks. I would love to go for a ride in his sports car. I don't know what kind he has, but I know he has one." Jolene squealed and ran outside to the curb.

I glanced out the window in time to see Jolene's spray-glittered body hanging over the side of a cherry red Corvette convertible, hugging the driver.

While Suzie shampooed and cut my hair we talked about our children and grandchildren, the weather, anything, trying not to listen as Jolene flirted with her former boyfriend. They were now inside the shop.

I cringed when Jolene said, "You need to leave that wife of yours. I'm the only one who loves you enough to change your diapers when you're seventy."

I was uncomfortable being around such behavior but hoped the boyfriend had enough sense to leave by himself and go back to his wife. I didn't want to be judgmental and I knew nothing about the boyfriend or his wife, but I did know that Jolene was a bit off-balanced and had a problem with alcohol.

When I left the shop Jolene was out in the street passing out flyers to cars driving by, at least, she was handing them to anyone who would stop and roll down their window for her. Her opened car trunk held a sign advertising ten dollar haircuts. I sat in my car waiting for traffic to clear so that I could pull out of my parking spot. No wonder the police are always after her to stop passing out flyers. She's creating a traffic jam right here on the square.

❤

So much to do. They'll be here the day after tomorrow. I can't wait! Wish I were as organized as Eileen, I thought as I backed my car out of the garage, Coca-Cola in the cup holder, unwrapped crackers with cheese on a napkin in the passenger's seat, my frequent lunch on Meals-on-Wheels delivery days. I munched on the crackers at traffic lights between deliveries, loving the camaraderie I felt with the people I delivered meals to.

First was Meri Phillips, who lives down the block from me. Meri is only sixty-five, but homebound due to knee replacements gone afoul three years ago. She greeted me from her front porch. Meri loved the outdoors so we sat and chatted on the porch for about fifteen minutes. That was all the time I could spare if I wanted to get everyone's lunch delivered by eleven.

Next, I drove to Sully's. Jonathan Fitzgerald Sullivan. He is so fascinating. We talked about his days as a pilot, especially when he served Truman during the air lift.   Today I listened as Sully talked about his first drop.

"I was in the first C-54 to land at Tempelhof. It was June of '48. The first thing we did is drop candy bars for the children. Those Berliners were on the ground waiting for us."

I had heard his tales many times, but always took as much time as I could with him, knowing that he didn't have many visitors.

My third stop was the home of Margaret and Fred Ulsterhausen. Margaret is ninety-four and Fred eighty-nine. They have been married for sixty-nine years. Fred was a college student when they met, living at home attending a local business college. Margaret moved next door. Fred took one look and he was smitten, followed her around like a lost puppy for three months. Then he started picking flowers out of his mother's garden and taking them to her. They went out for a soda at Woolworth's, back when you could actually get a soda at Woolworth's. That's where she fell in love with him. Margaret could still get around pretty well, but she had no stamina. Couldn't stand long enough to fix a decent meal and Fred was in a scooter, so when their daughter suggested Meals-on-Wheels for the umpteenth time, they gave in. I enjoy getting to know all about them and their children and grandchildren and talking politics. Their TV is usually set to MSNBC. They are staunch Democrats. Fred and Margaret loved getting their blood pressure going, so every once in a while they tuned in to FOX to see what they were saying. They'd get mad and then laugh their heads off at what they called "the stupidity of the GOP talking heads."

After I left the Ulsterhausen's I went to my last stop and it was a happy one. The lady of the manor, Genevieve Bonnet, was almost 104. She had round the clock care, but was signed up to receive one meal a week.

Genevieve was still alert and enjoyed visitors immensely. She carried on a great conversation. With her wonderful memory, Genevieve regaled me of many events that had happened in her lifetime. She talked about growing up on a farm, horses and cows, buggies and plows, barn dances and infrequent trips to town, churning butter, World War I, when she lost her favorite brother to the fields of Belgium, the Great

Depression, World War II, her loves and woes.

I left Genevieve's feeling uplifted as always after spending time with this special woman.

That evening I put finishing touches on the house before the Kids' arrival. They are really coming tomorrow.  Home to stay—I hoped, my only daughter—only child, Christina Jane, who went to school in Paris to become a chef and came home two years later with her husband-to-be, the twinkling blue-eyed, tall, dark and wonderful Henri Gregoirie Deschamps. He had put a smile on Tina's face that I hadn't seen for a long time and when I watched Jake walk Tina down the aisle to her waiting Henri, I knew through my tears that Tina had found someone who would love her and care for her, someone she would laugh and cry with. I prayed that they would be as happy as Jake and I were. I picked up a picture of Jakie and thought, this little guy, so much a picture of his grandfather, will be living with me now. My house would hear laughter again. I won't be alone anymore.

### *CHAPTER SEVEN*

I turned to the woman in blue standing next to me. "Are you waiting for someone coming from Paris, too?"

The woman looked at me. She must have noticed my eager state. I hoped I looked all right. She answered, "No, my sister is coming for a visit. She lives in Marietta, Georgia. I think her flight originated in Paris. Ah, Paris, how I have longed to visit the capitals of Europe—Paris and Rome and London. And you must be waiting for someone coming from France."

I turned to my new friend and grinned from ear to ear. "My daughter and her husband AND my five-year-old grandson! We haven't seen each other for over a year. Thank heaven for Skype. But it's not the same."

I started rambling. "Thank goodness I found a decent parking spot. I hope their flight is on time. They will be exhausted, I know, but I can't wait to see my little grandson."

My airport chum said, "AF8582 is listed as on time at five thirty-two p.m. I checked the monitor as I came in. My name is Carol, by the way."

"I'm Marjie."

Soon people were coming out of Gate 14. I watched as Carol ran to a woman who looked like her twin, only shorter. They hugged and I waved goodbye to them. People flowed through the doors, searching, waving, finally hugging their loved ones and friends. I began to worry that Tina and Henri had missed their flight when I caught sight of Tina's flaming red hair flowing half-way down her back and my tall, dark and handsome son-in-law, Henri. First, I felt weightless, my fingers tingled. I couldn't wait to get my arms around them, Then, I panicked. My legs froze. I didn't see Jakie. Where was my grandson?

Tina reached me first. We hugged, but I was distracted. "Tina,

Henri. Where is Jakie?" I said, my voice quiet.

"Here I am, Grandma!" He laughed as he jumped out from behind his father.

I picked him up and swung him around and around. "Oh, Jakie, you scared your Grandma. I thought your Mommy and Daddy had left you in Paris or maybe you were riding in the baggage compartment. I'm so glad to have you all here. I have missed you terribly. You have grown, Jakie. I'm going to put you down for a little while."

I was overjoyed to see my family after so long a time. I couldn't stop looking at the three of them. My family. Home to stay.

We chattered, talking over each other. I heard Tina say, "Luggage" just as the same word slipped from my mouth. We laughed and hugged again.

"Let's go get your bags, then we can go home and, Jakie, you can see your new room!"

"But I'm hungry and I'm a growing boy," he complained.

"So am I, son," said his father. "Hungry that is."

Tina chimed in, "I'll bet Grandma has something tasty waiting for us. Don't you, Grandma? Let me guess. Lasagne? Spaghetti and meatballs? Or my favorite—beef stroganoff with cherry pie ala mode for dessert."

"You'll see when we get there," I said, trying to make my voice sound mysterious. "I can promise you a salad and some whole-grained rolls."

"Oh, Henri, here we go. Mom's on a health kick again," Tina groaned.

"Hush, Tina. We can stand some healthy food to put in our tummies, besides I can eat salad and rolls and still have room for stroganoff, is it?" teased Henri.

"I don't want stroganoff—whatever that is. I want ice cream, Grandma. Can I have ice cream?" Jakie chimed in.

"You can have whatever you want, Jakie, as long as I have it at home. Let me think, do I have ice cream? Guess we'll have to wait until we get there."

I grabbed Jakie's hand and clasped it inside my own. Then, I giggled, and started skipping, not caring what other travelers thought. My family was home and I wanted to sing, skip and shout. Jakie, then Henri, and finally, Tina, skipped arm in arm with me down the wide corridor toward the baggage carrel.

All bags were in the car, barely. Tina climbed into the front seat of my Camry while I attempted to instruct Henri how to strap Jakie into the new child seat I bought. Henri didn't really need my help, but politely listened to me. All the way home we chatted about how wonderful it was to be together, to be working together, how successful we would be.

"Mom, it will be so grand. There aren't any French restaurants in Independence—from what I found on the internet there are only one or two true French restaurants in the whole metro area," said Tina.

Jakie fell asleep. I could see him in the rear view mirror sitting in his car seat—his father leaning against him.

♥

We left the bags in the car. Henri carried Jakie up the porch steps. I went around him to unlock the front door. He took Jakie in and laid him on the sofa. Tina lagged behind. I heard a muted cry from the porch, so I went out to see and found Tina, looking glazed, standing by the porch swing.

"Dad. No, this isn't right. Dad should be here. I wanted to explain, tell him I'm sorry. I didn't mean it," said Tina. I ran to her.

She crumpled out of my grasp, elbows and head onto the swing, knees on the wooden porch slats. Henri appeared from inside, he knelt beside her, holding her up. She began wailing. I have only witnessed this level of weeping from an adult a few times in my life. Every time has been at the sudden loss of loved one. The sounds came from deep within her, primal sobs.

"Henri, what is she talking about, explain what?" I asked.

He said he didn't know, that she has been moody since around November, but it got worse after New Year's when she announced they were coming here, but he had never seen her like this. He asked me to make sure Jakie was still sleeping, so he could stay outside with Tina. He pulled her up so she was sitting on the swing and sat next to her, trying to comfort her.

I felt helpless and confused. Could she still be grieving this hard so long after her father's death? I hadn't ever lost it the way she is doing. Is this why she would never come home for a visit after he died?

I went inside and found Jakie awake, sitting on the sofa, looking around curiously. He had found what Tina always called the shrine walls, one filled with pictures of Tina—Tina at every stage of life—as a baby and in her band uniform, jazz dance costumes, cheerleader uniforms, chef pictures, bride and groom, pictures as a mother, the other wall filled with as many pictures of Jakie I could squeeze on the wall, the latest additions showed him on his little motorcycle and on a pony.

"Grandma, is this a museum of Mams and me?"

He is clever for his age. The idea. A museum.

"Well, there are also some pictures of your papa and you and Grandpa Jake and your Great-Grandma Karin. You'll see her soon."

"Oui, Grandma, I'm hungry. Can we eat now?"

I took him to the kitchen to fix him some dinner and allow Tina some time. I hoped Henri could comfort her. I prayed he could.

Jakie became restless after he ate and wanted his parents. I felt I should stall a little longer before going out to the porch, not knowing Tina's condition. Maybe the flight had completely worn her out. Maybe she wasn't rested when they left. Hopefully, we'll be able to talk this out. She truly seemed glad to be here when they landed and all the way home in the car. Seeing the house with all the memories of her father must have been too much for her.

I told Jakie that his mother was not feeling well and convinced him to go see his new bedroom where I showed him his bed and his bookcase full of books that used to be his mother's. We looked at a few and he was enchanted with some of the titles, *The Goat in the Moat, The Bat in the Bunkhouse* and *No Spinning on the Ceiling*. I had to help him sound out some of the words, but he impressed me by his familiarity with written English. Tina must be keeping her resolution to read to him every night, not to mention he must be a genius.

As much as I enjoyed being with Jakie in my own home, ours now, my thoughts overwhelmingly turned to Tina.  I left him to look over the treasures in the toy box, most of them from friends whose children had outgrown them, but I had bought a few new ones, too. I told him I would be back in a few minutes and he seemed content exploring all his new possessions.

As I walked out on the front porch, Henri was climbing the stairs with suitcases in both hands. He looked exhausted. Tina was nowhere to be seen.

"Henri, where's Tina? Is she okay?"

"She's in her old room, a bit calmer, but still crying a little, not talking much, repeating, she's sorry. She won't tell me what about."

"Do you think she would eat or drink anything? I did make her favorites, the beef stroganoff and cherry pie." Is this all I could offer my troubled daughter?

Henri, sadness and worry on his face, said, "I'm sorry. I know you worked so hard to make everything nice for us, but I don't think either of us could eat anything that heavy right now. Do you have some strong coffee and perhaps some bread and cheese, some fruit? Oh, Tina might like some water with lemon."

Later, while Tina slept, Henri and I began a ritual. We sat at the kitchen table, he with strong coffee, me with my milky sweet hot tea, and talked.

He filled me in on the last several months, telling me that Tina became obsessed with coming home to Independence, but she wasn't herself. She was sad and irritable.

"At work she was fine and around my family and Jakie, but whenever we were alone…I must tell you she's been lying to you and I'm her accomplice. My family never tried to hold us back. They were supportive from the first time Tina mentioned our leaving. They understood she missed her home, and you. My father wasn't sick. She used that as an excuse. I think that while we were in France she could pretend that her father was alive. All these years she wouldn't come home. He is a Fire Chief in Independence, Missouri she would tell people. She never talked about him in the past tense. Then all of a sudden this year this yearning to be home came over her."

"My darling daughter. I should have been there for her, but during my visits and on the phone she seemed okay."

"She did go to a therapist once and he gave her some pills for depression. They have helped. You will be amazed at her ability to function. Tonight, coming to the house…she had to face the fact that her father is not here and he won't ever be. I made sure she took her pills before I left her upstairs."

Knowing that nothing would be solved tonight, Henri and I hugged, prayed together and went to our beds.

I believed there was more to it than grief over her father's death or why all the *I'm sorry's* and needing to explain? Why can't she explain to me? What in the world does she think she did to hurt her father? Does it have anything to do with Jakie's birth being the day before Jake died? I think I'll call Eileen tomorrow. She and Rob went to a grief counseling class a while back to help with their ministry.

All I could do was pray that God would help Tina and all of us.

♥

I awoke after a mostly sleepless night. I kept rehearsing things to say to Tina. Nothing felt right.

When I went into the kitchen I was amazed to see Tina, Henri and Jakie feasting on a breakfast of beef stroganoff and cherry pie. Didn't they know I would want to enjoy this with them? They probably thought I needed more rest. Why didn't I hear them out here? Oh, yes, the radio. I was trying to take my mind off them so I could sleep. Guess I slept more than I thought. Might as well put on a happy face and join them.

Tina rushed to give me a hug. "Mom, I'm so sorry about last night. I think I was tired and it is the first time I've been here since Dad…" She started to tear up, but caught herself.

I repeated the mantra I'd been practicing throughout the night. "Your dad had suffered so much with the cancer. He was tired of fighting. He waited for Jakie's birth, then let go."

"I know," she said. I tried to forget all that. Always remembering him as healthy, as he always was before. Why didn't you make me come home sooner? To have more time with him."

"Honey, you were pregnant with Jakie. We thought he'd get better, but then he didn't, and you came and spent the last three months with him. He was so happy to have you with him and so happy to hold his namesake, even if it was only that one time."

"I can't believe he's gone," Tina cried. We hugged some more.

"Honey, I understand. You want your dad to be here. So do I, but cancer was eating him up. It took him faster than we expected. He was tired and ready to go."

She nodded her head. We hugged again. "Mom, you must be starved."

To prove her point, I stuck a fork in the serving dish and grabbed a mushroom. Henri handed me a plateful with lots of gravy, mushrooms and meat. It looked like they ate all the noodles.

The rest of the day Tina and I pulled out old family photos and reminisced. We cried a lot, but it was good. We made a list of all the things we wanted to remember about Jake. It was a long list.

I was able to relax a bit about Tina, but I still tossed and turned that night, finally falling asleep at dawn. We were together. That's all that mattered.

♥

The next day we needed to get down to business. I knew Tina's feelings were fragile, but I couldn't seem to stop myself. My fear of failure drove me. I've always been afraid to take financial risks. My doubts came pouring out, exhaustion allowing unfiltered words to tumble from my mouth. "You already know, of course, that profit margins are notoriously low in the restaurant business."

Henri looked hurt and Tina's eyes flashed with anger.

Thankfully, Henri spoke first. "Mère Marjie, Tina and I have come up with a budget and a business plan. We are both French trained chefs and I have worked in my family's café since I was a boy. We know what we are doing."

Tina smiled at her husband, but turned to me defiantly. I thought she was ready to say something, but I beat her to it.

"Henri, Tina, I know you are both wonderful with food—but I'm not sure how a French restaurant will be received in Independence. Did you work that out in your business plan? What about the cost of your staff and the cost of goods? If I'm going to invest in your business I need to see your business plan and budget."

Tina grabbed her purse and Henri sniffed with impatience. Why was I bringing this up now? I knew why they were moving in with me.

"But of course. They are right here." Henri put the papers in my hands. "Take all the time you need to look them over."

Tina bristled, then sweetened. "Mom, while you are doing that, I think Henri and I will take a drive to look at potential properties. Can we borrow your car? I can't wait until we can buy one of our own."

"What about Jakie? Are you taking him with you?"

"Don't you want him to stay here with you?" Tina replied.

"Not if I want to study these papers," I said.

Henri agreed that Jakie should go with them so I was left by myself to read papers I wouldn't be able to understand and feel guilt that I hadn't been more encouraging, more enthusiastic about their plans. Plans that I had agreed to invest in when they first told me about their ideas. Now I had to face reality. I promised to help them with their business and I would do so even if it took all my savings. I started reading their business plan first. I don't know anything about business, why I thought that reading these would allay my fears, I don't know.

As I read I thought to myself how Henri seems more mature than I remembered him. Maybe becoming a father has changed him. I'm not sure if becoming a mother has changed Tina all that much. I sighed and fell back to studying the papers. I was still apprehensive about investing so much in a restaurant—a French restaurant in Independence. Of course, the Italian restaurants have always done well here and the Mexican and Chinese, why not the French? I think I'll ask them for a sample menu to run it by my friends and see what they think and talk to my financial advisor. Why didn't I think of that sooner?

I got up early to listen to the birds and spend a few quiet moments in the garden before church—my family still sleeping. They were not used to the time change yet, so I would go to church without them this Sunday, but looked forward to next week when in my imagination they would accompany me to Shady Grove.

I sat down on the porch glider, enjoying the birds, admiring the statue across the street and the Temple beyond. My family had only been here a few days, but I was already learning to cherish my alone time. Have I always been this way, needing to have my space, or is this something that developed since Jake died leaving me alone for the first time in my life?

I heard the owl call. I wonder why he isn't asleep after being out hunting all night. What is he saying? Who is he talking to? I remember one time when Jake and I were at the lake, he said that the owls were bragging about what they caught the night before.

*Oh, Jake. I miss you. I am glad that Tina, Henri and Jakie are here, but I wish you could share them with me. You would be so proud of Jakie. He is so smart and really athletic. He had his first T-ball practice yesterday. The other boys have been playing for about a month, but Jakie hit the ball farther than any of them. Tina says he's the fastest runner on his soccer team in France…and he looks like you did when you were a little boy.*

*Tina's moodiness comes and goes, but she seems to have accepted that you aren't with us anymore. That's a big step. Tomorrow is Memorial Day and we are going to the cemetery. Tina believes this ritual of cleaning and decorating your gravesite will further her healing. I pray it's so.*

♥

While Henri cleaned up the breakfast dishes, I gathered up some old rags, cleaning spray and scrapers and put them in a plastic bag. Earlier Tina, Jakie and I went through the garden looking for any remaining peonies, iris and daisies to cut for decorating the graves, but decided to wait and take them to Bingham Manor instead. We agreed silk flowers would last longer and be better for the grave sites, but Tina cut one perfect peony bloom for her father.

We picked up Mom and loaded the water bottles, chips, fruit and sandwiches she had prepared. We stopped at a Catholic church to purchase silk flowers. Mom, Tina and Henri carried armfuls of flowers to the trunk of my car while Jakie supervised.

Both Jake and my dad were buried at Woodlawn Cemetery. We went to Jake's grave first because Tina insisted. She sprayed her father's marker with the cleaning spray and started wiping it with a rag. Her hair fell onto the stone as she worked, scraping all the mud off that had accumulated since I cleaned it last fall. In my mind I pictured Mary Magdalene washing the feet of Jesus. I don't know why. I was impressed that Tina held herself together so well. After it was clean and the flowers placed we all knelt down, praying silently. Then Tina began to cry softly.

Henri and I hugged her then left her by herself for a while, walking several feet away to where Dad was buried. This time Mom insisted on doing the cleaning. She said it was her way of showing her love to her husband, my father, who had passed so many years ago. After his marker was cleaned and flowers placed we loaded the cleaning supplies back in the car. Jakie sat down by his great-grandfather's stone and said, "Let's eat with great-grandpa and grandpa."

I was surprised because earlier he seemed excited about going to the park. I said, "Jakie, don't you want to go to the park so you can play on the jungle gym and swings?"

Mom's eyes sparkled. She said, "Jakie, that's a great idea. When I was a girl the gypsies used to always stay all day and eat a picnic lunch in the cemetery with their loved ones."

I went over to get Tina. She stood, her face streaked with dirt and tears. I sprayed a clean towel with water and wiped her face. We hugged and I felt closer to her than I had in years. We didn't seem to need to speak.

After a few minutes I heard Mom say, "Marjie, Tina, get the food and drinks. I'll pour a glass of lemonade for great-grandpa. He'd love it."

It was settled. We ate and toasted our loved ones, hoping their heavenly spirits were enjoying this special time with us.

The next day after a breakfast of pancakes, eggs and sausage, my clan and I piled in the car to go look at potential properties together. Tina and Henri's trip around the square the other day hadn't turned anything up, so they broaden their internet search to include the Kansas City Metro Area. Actually there was one place on the Square, but they hadn't been able to reach anyone to show it to them, so they decided to keep looking while waiting for a call back from the Square property owner. We had an appointment in the old Englewood shopping district in Independence and some in historic Westport in Kansas City's mid-town.

"Where to? Your chauffeur awaits directions," I quipped.

"Mom, run us up to the Square first. We want to show you the place we found, even though we can't go inside," said Tina.

I decided to take the opportunity to drop off some dry cleaning first. It was only a few blocks out of the way.

"Mom, are we going the wrong way?" Tina's voice expressed irritation.

"I need to drop off these clothes. I want to wear this suit on Sunday so it needs to go this morning. It will just take a minute."

"Please don't get into a conversation with the clerk. I know how you are."

How can she go from cheerful to seething in ten seconds? It is my car. I didn't want this to turn into a tit for tat day of bickering, so I kept my mouth shut, praying that today would be a good day and that God would give me the right words to say to Tina.

We dropped off the cleaning in relative silence, well, Henri kept Jakie involved in a conversation in French. That bothers me. It shouldn't because I want Jakie to stay bi-lingual, so I better think about learning French—maybe use a computer program and practice with the kids.

As we drove past the Truman home on the way to the Square, Jakie proudly said, "That's where the President used to live. Mams said we can go look inside it someday! That would be fun, wouldn't it, Grandma?"

"Yes, it would, Jakie. We'll have to do that. You know your Grandpa Jake met President Truman several times," I said.

Jakie's presence reminded me how thankful I was to have my family home at last even though at times Tina was still hard to deal with. I vowed to try never to take them for granted. We would live each day as richly as possible.

My grandson brought me back from my thoughts. "How did he meet him? Mams said this is a dead President's house."

"Let's go to Clinton's Soda Fountain for a treat and I'll tell you all about it." I exclaimed, since I was driving at the moment and it was difficult to talk to Jakie in the backseat. I can walk and chew gum, but not give full attention to my grandson while driving.

"Mom, we're supposed to be looking for a restaurant space." complained Tina.

"Okay, well, I'll just pull over to the curb across from the Truman home for a minute, then," I answered and proceeded to do.

"Oh, all right, see if we let you drive again, but don't' forget we have some scheduled appointment times," muttered Tina.

I checked the clock on the dashboard. We had plenty of time before the first appointment. I, wisely I thought, decided not to argue that I felt it important to answer Jakie's questions when he asked them. I wanted to encourage his curiosity. Besides, this was a history lesson.

"When your grandpa was about ten years old he first met the President. He was playing with a friend out on the lawn next to the Truman Library when President Truman walked by. He was known to take his daily constitutional, walking all over Independence with his cane. That's why the signs have him pictured with his cane. Anyway, just as the President walked by your grandpa and his friend jumped out of a tree, barely missing Mr. Truman, the breeze of their landing, knocking off his hat!"

"What happened next, Grandma?" asked Jakie. "I want know more about Grandpa almost jumping on top of a dead president."

"Well, the President wasn't dead then, Jakie. He picked up his hat and looked at the boys, saying, 'You'll have to try harder than that to knock me down, you know Dewey tried and failed, and lots of others have tried to whip me and I've not been beaten yet.'"

"What did Grandpa say?" Jakie asked, looking mesmerized by the story about his grandpa.

"Grandpa apologized to President Truman, told him they didn't see him coming. He felt badly that he had almost hurt the President." Then I laughed, "He told the boys they didn't have to call him Mr. President anymore, he had thankfully given up that title. He said, 'Just call me Mr. Citizen, boys, and don't try to waylay me anymore. I might have been knocked senseless and I always pride myself on my common sense.' Your grandpa said the former President laughed and walked off, swinging his cane and whistling."

"Now can we go look at the property?" Tina never had much patience when she was prevented from doing what she wanted to do. Jakie knew his mother's tone and kept quiet.

I smiled at my daughter, pulled the car back out onto Delaware Street and drove up to the Square. Tina and Henri directed me to the available property, catty corner from the Courthouse Exchange restaurant, buttressed on one side by a beauty salon and the other side by an antique shop. I saw the potential in this location.

"Looks like a good option, don't you think Mom?" Tina said.

"A good one, yes, what do you think, Henri?" I asked.

"If we can ever make contact with the landlord, oui," replied Henri. "This was a restaurant before from the looks of it. There's even a small courtyard in front and look at that sweet balcony. It looks perfect, but it's the only one we've looked at."

"Are there any more properties available on the Square?" I asked.

"The only ones we saw are too small or have never been fitted out as a restaurant. This is perfect!" answered Tina.

"Well, you have some appointments to look at places in Englewood and in Westport you said. Do you still want to check them out?"

"Yes, we need to get cracking," Tina replied. "Our first appointment is in Englewood in ten minutes."

"Guess, we'll put off the soda fountain for later, Jakie. Tell you what. I'll take you tomorrow, okay?"

"Sure, Grandma. I like sodas." Jakie licked his lips and said, "Yum."

On the way to the next property, Jakie saw the historical sign about the Battle of Railroad Cut and asked about it. I told him it was a Civil War battle right here in Independence. Jakie knew nothing of the Civil War and wanted to know all about it.

I knew Tina didn't want me getting off the track again, so I told Jakie I would tell him about it at bedtime. I wondered if telling a five-year-old about a battle and war right before sending him to sleep was a good idea. I thought again that living together was wonderful, but wondered how much I would be able to keep my mouth shut and let Tina and Henri parent their child. *Lord, give me wisdom.*

We pulled into the center diagonal parking space in front of the prospective property, an interesting looking building. I remembered it formerly was an interior decorating business. The building was beautiful, a two-story brick, about a block west of the Englewood Theater. The windows were covered so we couldn't see inside. We had barely stepped up to the door when it opened. A tall, slim, silver-haired man welcomed us into the building, introducing himself as "Al". He was dressed impeccably in dark trousers, and a beautiful Hawaiian shirt, black, silver, and burgundy hibiscus flowers. Introductions were made all around. I saw Al look at me like no man had for some time, at least, not that I had noticed.

I flushed, somehow glad that I dressed in my new fitted short-sleeved summer sweater of sapphire blue and matching Capri pants.

Al winked at Jakie and said, "Your grandma is very pretty, don't you think?"

Jakie became embarrassed and hid behind me.

Henri winked back at Al. "You're right, Al, she is lovely."

Tina walked farther into the building. I wondered if she was embarrassed that her mother received this attention from an attractive male. She turned and asked, "Is there a kitchen in here?"

"A little galley," Al said. "I'll show you. Please follow me."

We followed Al into a small room that contained a double stainless steel sink, a small refrigerator, a microwave, and a freestanding electric range. It was rather nice for a decorating store, but would not work for a restaurant. It would have to be gutted and walls knocked out. We talked to Al about what our needs were and talked renovation and lease price for about a half an hour. Henri was starting to talk about the possibility of buying the building, when Tina realized we needed to leave right then to be on time for our next appointment. Al handed his card to Henri and told us he would have to talk to his ex-wife who was the co-owner and to some remodeling contractors for bids and expertise on the possibility of building a kitchen that would work for our restaurant. He took my hand and kissed it.

Jakie started pulling on me to get me away from Al.

When we drove away, Henri laughed "Mon ami, Mère Marjie, you made an impression on Al. He couldn't keep his eyes off of you."

"Really, Mother, you shouldn't encourage him. He seemed so, so *oogly*." remarked Tina.

"Grandma, I didn't like him very much, did you?" said Jakie in a decided voice.

"Well, Jakie and Tina and Henri. Oh my. But he was very nice and attentive. It doesn't hurt to be appreciated by someone of the opposite sex occasionally, does it?"

Henri answered me, "Certainly not. You are a very beautiful woman. I'm sure that many people think that you are Tina's sister, not her mother."

He turned quickly to Tina. "But always remember, my coquette, you are the most beautiful woman to me and you look much younger than your mother. I don't know how anyone could say that you look like sisters."

"Talking out of both sides of your mouth, aren't you Mr. French Romantic. You'd better believe I'm the most beautiful," Tina batted her eyes at her husband and laughed. "Let's get going. I'll drive. We've got to make up for lost time."

♥

Tina held out her hand for my keys and I dropped them in, but not before a warning, "No more than five miles over the speed limit. You know the rules."

Tina fairly flew after she hit the fifty-five mile per hour speed limit sign, I knew she was going over sixty, so I said somewhat calmly, "Tina, you're exceeding the speed limit and our family rule, either slow down or pull over and I'll drive."

She slowed down to sixty, hitting the brakes as we descended the hill. The speed limit changed to forty-five right before the red stoplight. She skidded to a stop. The light turned green and she sailed through that light in time to make the next one, only to be stopped by the turn signal at the freeway entrance. Once on I-435 Tina cruised along at seventy, slowing down a bit for the exit onto I-70 then back up to speed.

I held on to my armrest, saying, "Watch it, watch it…oh, Tina, watch that car over there. Your precious son is in the back seat. Your husband and your mother are in the car with you."

"Mom, please I've been driving for a few years now."

Yes, on French autoroutes, I thought.

Tina begged me to stop back seat driving, negotiated the exit, slowing down to the actual speed limit of forty-five miles per hour.

I think she finally looked at the clock on the dashboard and realized we had plenty of time to get to the next appointment in Westport, so she slowed down, probably to prevent me from having a heart attack.

We arrived in Westport. The first thing Jakie pointed out was another historical sign about the Civil War. I answered his questions as well as I could. I understood that I was going to have to brush up on local history for my very inquisitive grandson. Isn't it grand! I love history.

We pulled into Westport Landing. The owner of the vacant spot showed us around, but Tina and Henri were disappointed. There wasn't any pizzazz. No place for a courtyard, no balcony. They could deal with creating the ambiance, but this didn't work for them, so we went to the next place. It was a little more difficult to get to because of the traffic which was insane for a Tuesday morning, we thought, but as Henri said, "Hey, traffic is a good thing."

We passed so many restaurants. They were everywhere.

"Look, there's the Bistro and there's the Westport Café and Bar. They both showed up on urbanspoon.com as French restaurants. Maybe we should stick with Independence. There aren't any French restaurants there," said Tina.

I thought, probably there aren't any French restaurants in Independence for a reason—no customer base, but I kept my thoughts to myself. And, why am I so negative about the people of my own city? There are a lot of people that appreciate good food and the culinary arts in my hometown, aren't there?

"Where is the place we are going to see?" asked Tina.

"It's down on Broadway, used to be called the Batcave. I wonder if you can make a left hand turn here?" I answered.

"We're going to legal or not," huffed Tina, as she turned the corner.

I didn't hear any sirens. We made it.

We met with the leasing agent at this property, but were unhappy with it, especially the fact that there was not enough parking. After that meeting we drove down to the Plaza. There were no appointments there, but we wanted to get out and stretch our legs and let Jakie have some fun at the J.C. Nichols Fountain. Jakie was in awe of the horses and their riders and the huge amount of water spewing out of the several spigots.

As Grandma and self-appointed historical tour guide, I explained, "Jakie, the equestrian riders…"

I noticed Jakie's questioning face, so I added, "the horseback riders represent four great rivers of the world: the Rhine, the Seine, the Volga and the Mississippi. The fountain was created in Paris…"

Jakie's eyes perked up. "My Paris, Grandma, the one in France?"

"Your Paris, my little love, and the Seine goes right through it. This fountain was created in Paris for a rich man in New York and was brought to Kansas City when I was a little girl. I remember coming here with my parents. We used to come on warm Sunday afternoons and walk all over the Plaza."

"Can we walk all over the Plaza now, Grandma?" asked Jakie in his sweetest voice.

"That will be up to your parents, Jakie. What do you think, Tina, Henri?"

Henri answered first, "I want to go to that Cheesecake Factory across the street."

Tina scoffed, "Henri, that's a chain restaurant."

"Well, I don't care. If it has cheesecake in its name, can it be bad?" said Henri.

"I'm hungry, too, Mams, and cheesecake is good," agreed Jakie in his most persuasive voice.

The two men won out, so we walked to the Cheesecake Factory. Tina and I ordered salads, for me, the French Country salad with mixed greens and the thing that I could not resist—candied pecans. Tina ordered the Boston House salad changing the dressing choice to Bleu cheese, which she ordered as Roquefort.

"Is this bleu cheese actually Roquefort from the caves near the Combalou Plateau?" asked Tina of the youngish waitress, who, I am sure she knew, would have absolutely no idea where the cheese came from.

The waitress said she would have to ask the chef, but did she want the blue cheese even if it wasn't from the caves?

Tina laughed. "Yes, don't bother about asking. I was just showing off."

The waitress laughed, too, and turned to Henri to see what he wanted. Actually, I was watching her. She was eyeing him. He did look like a movie or TV star; I'll have to admit. When he opened his mouth and his French accent came pouring out, the waitress almost lost her balance, she dropped her order pad, knocking into Tina with her tiny rear end as she stooped to pick it up. I furtively glanced at Tina to see her reaction. There was none. I guess she was used to women falling all over themselves in the presence of her handsome husband.

Henri ordered for Jakie first. "This little man will have the tomato, basil and cheese pizza and a strawberry lemonade." I watched as Henri looked her in the eyes, then saw his gaze drop down to her nametag. "Cherie, why that's a French name, it means *darling* in French."

Tina glared at Henri. So much for what she was used to. He straightened up and ordered the California omelet.

He smiled at Cherie, but when she left the table he turned right back to Tina and taking her hand, said, "You are the only one for me, Tina. You know that, right?"

The waitress turned back to take another look at him and saw him kissing his wife's hand. I became a mind reader. She was thinking, *Oolala, why can't I find someone like him?*

Tina eyed her husband and for a moment. I think she forgot that Jakie and I were sitting there with them, much less the waitress that was obviously smitten with this handsome Frenchman.

The food came and we ate. We were waiting for Cherie to bring the check and the cheesecake we had ordered to-go when Tina's cell phone rang. Her ringtone was *La Vie en Rose*. It was the first time I heard Tina's phone ring and I wondered how in the world Tina had gotten that tune. I decided to try to remember to ask her later.

I listened to Tina's side of the conversation. "Of course, we can meet you. Did you say your name was *Mel*? Right, short for Melanie. In about half an hour. Can we make it forty-five minutes? We are at the Plaza right now, still waiting for our check and have to walk to our car. An hour. That might be better. See you at two then. Yes, we know where it is. Thank you for calling."

Tina turned her attention to Henri and me. "Guess what, guys. That was Melanie from the rental agency for the place on the Square." Tina's eyes widened. A grin spread across her face as she high-fived Henri. "That's really the place we want, if the inside looks as good as the outside. Although the Englewood property was bigger and very nice, they would have to put in a totally new kitchen. Of course, Al would probably do it for Mom."

"I don't know what in the world you are talking about, but the one on the Square will be better, I think, except that the Englewood area has recently been designated an Arts District so you might get more traffic there," I said.

"That is something to definitely consider." Henri's facial expression turned from gleeful to quizzical.

Tina jumped up and hugged him. "I think we want the one on the Square. If it's as good as we think it will be, it's perfect."

"That settles that." Henri hugged Tina back, catching Cherie's attention. She brought the check and the cheesecake at the same time.

As we were leaving the restaurant Jakie said, "When do I get to eat my cheesecake?"

His father, mother and I all laughed. "We haven't been paying any attention to you, have we little man?" Henri said as he put his arm around his small son's shoulders.

"I don't care about that, Papa, only when do I get to eat my cheesecake?" grumbled Jakie.

I sensed Jakie was getting tired. I reassured him that we only had one more stop to make and then we would be home. Tina chimed in that he could have his cheesecake for dessert that night if he ate a good dinner.

"Aw, Mams, can't I have it as soon as we get home?" whined Jakie.

"After dinner, toi," reiterated his father.

I drove back to the Independence Square, thankfully no argument from Tina. We were early, but so was Melanie. The premises were Spartan, the wooden floors atrocious, but Tina and Henri were charmed by the possibilities. As we entered the building we were greeted by an atrium through which we saw a long black bar, with a huge wine shelf over it. There were seating areas to the left and to the right of the bar and an indoor balcony above the area to the left of the entrance

After we toured the upstairs, Henri got out his measuring tape and I wondered why he hadn't measured any of the other locations we had looked at. I guessed Henri was seriously thinking this was the place, even though the location in Englewood might be a little better. The Square still had a movie theatre, an updated bowling alley, lots of shops and a handful of restaurants—with nothing like they were planning. I could see why he was excited.

Henri judged the place would seat seventy-eight inside, not counting six seats at the bar and sixteen outside on the patio. "An exact one hundred," he announced.

"This will be better than my family's café at home. Don't you think, Tina?"

I heard Tina even though she whispered in his ear. "Yes, Mon Cherie, but let's not show our enthusiasm too much in front of Mel."

Henri tried to calm his eagerness, but it was hard and Mel had already taken notice.

"Are you interested in a two or three-year lease?" Mel smiled, looking from Henri to Tina to me. I'm sure she wondered who the decision-maker really was, man or wife, or mother?

"We'll have to talk it over," Tina said.

"You can certainly do that, but we do have several others that are interested right now. In fact, I'm expecting a call sometime this afternoon from an out of town restauranteur."

Mel smirked as she said *out of town*. "My owner prefers to lease to a local business. He wants to keep everything unique here on the Square, no chains whatsoever, but who knows, if he gets the right offer."

"How much does this lease for and can we get a year's lease?" asked Tina.

Melanie gave them the figures for a one, two or three-year lease written on a monogramed sheet she tore from a periwinkle blue pad of paper.

"What an unusual monogram. It spells MOM." My curiosity aroused, I had to ask. "What is your full name if you don't mind my asking?"

"It is unusual and I'm not even a mom, except by initials," laughed Mel. "My given name is Melanie Ophelia Montgomery. I asked my parents, when I was a teenager and everyone teased me about my initials, what they were thinking, giving me that name. My mom said, 'you know why honey, you are named after both your grandmothers, would you rather be called OMM.' Maybe not. I told her. My friends would be rhyming it with bomb, bomb, bomb, bomb, bomb Iran, or worse yet, they would be going into chant mode, omm, omm, omm, whenever I walked into a room."

We all laughed and we shook hands. Melanie complimented Jakie on his businesslike manner. Tina assured Melanie that one of us would call her by five o'clock that evening.

We drove back over to Englewood and sat where we could see the building we had looked at earlier. Henri wondered if we should talk to Al again to see if he could give us a ball park price on the lease, knowing that he wouldn't have time to get estimates on the kitchen remodeling yet. "What do you think, Tina, Mère Marjie? I'm leaning toward the one on the Square," stated Henri.

"The price for the Square property seems fair, but we really get a break if we go for a two-year lease. What do you think, Mom?" Tina turned to me. I was sitting with Jakie's head on my shoulder; he was unable to make it through a day of real estate searching.

"I don't know. I like the one on the Square best, too, but should we look at other areas?" I asked. We all became quiet, lost in our thoughts.

Henri, looking from Tina to me, broke the silence. "I've actually been surveying the market in this area for some time, you know, via the internet and this is really a pretty good price. I think the two-year lease would be best, because of the price break and we won't know if we're going to make it until after two years. I also want a firm right to renew in the lease."

I sat thoughtfully for a few minutes, then made up my mind. "I agree. Take the two-year lease. I like the location better. It's less than a mile, you can walk there from our house on nice days and to drive it will only take a few minutes. Think of the gasoline fumes we'll keep out of the atmosphere! Let's do it."

With our elevated voices, Jakie awoke. "Can I have cheesecake now?"

Almost in unison, we three adults shouted, "Yes, let's go have cheesecake to celebrate."

Tina called Melanie and arranged to meet her back at the restaurant in an hour. We went home, had our cheesecake, then back to meet the broker at the restaurant that would soon be named *La Vie en Rose*.

That night as I washed and moisturized my face, I remembered the compliments from Al and the way he had looked at me. I remembered the hair stylist's comments, what was his name, Rodolfo? I checked myself out in my three-way mirror—thank God for making me attractive enough to get along easily in this life, but not so beautiful that it goes to my head. It did feel good to have a man look at me as if I am desirable again. It's been a long time or maybe they have been looking, but I haven't been noticing?

# CHAPTER EIGHT

It was such a beautiful day today. Jakie and I walked hand-in-hand across the street from our house to the Temple. Jakie was impressed with the building's large spire in the shape of a sea shell from the first time he saw it. He called it a spiral. How cute.

"Grandma, can we watch popcorn while we eat a movie?" said Jakie as we walked up the sidewalk to the Temple entrance.

Confused, I laughed and sat down on a stone bench outside the entrance and lifted Jakie up beside me.

"Jakie, what are you talking about? We're not going to eat a movie. How can we *eat a movie?* Are you teasing me?"

"Oh, Grandma, you know I meant to say eat *popcorn* and watch a *movie*," Jakie laughed.

"Yes, I know. It's good to have a little fun though, right?" I was still in awe that Jakie was here with me and not talking to me on the phone or on Skype.

"I told you last night when I tucked you in that we were going to the Prayer for Peace today. Our church, Community of Christ, has a temple here in Independence. Every day, 365 days a year, at one o'clock there is a Prayer for Peace service held in the sanctuary. Every day a different country is held up in prayer. We ask God to bless this particular country. Church members all over the world pray at the same time for this country. Today we will pray for Zimbabwe. We hope to bring peace to the earth by praying for all countries of the world."

"I remember, Grandma, but Mams told me you were taking me to see a movie."

"After the service we'll see if there is a movie that we can watch to learn more about the Temple and we'll take a tour. How would that be?"

"That sounds okay. Will there be popcorn—not to watch, but to eat?"

"No popcorn here, Buddy, but we can pop some when we get back home. Okay?"

"Okay, Grandma. Let's go make peace for the world." He looked so earnest. What a wonderful grandson.

Even though my house faces the west entrance to the Temple, I walked Jakie to the main entrance on the east side so he would be close to the Worshipper's Path as soon as we entered. I guided him through the carved glass doorway depicting the grove of trees in New York State where Joseph Smith, Jr. had first encountered the Divine. When we came to the textile of the burning bush, I explained this was an artist's idea of the bush that God used to call to Moses. I was more than a little surprised to know that Jakie had never heard of Moses so I told him I would read him a story about Moses that night before bed. I wondered what happened to the children's bible story book that I sent him for his first birthday. I decided not to ask Tina about it, but just buy him a new book.

Next, Jakie stood before the black granite carving of the Prodigal Son. "Who's this, Grandma?"

Good thing I realized there would be so many things for Jakie to see and do in the Temple, and had gotten here early. I related a quick explanation of the Prodigal Son parable. Jakie liked that story very much. He loved that the father welcomed his long lost son home with a big party.

Then Jakie and I passed through the shadow of the empty cross. "What's that, Grandma?"

"That is to remind us that Jesus loves us. I'll tell you more about it later."

I'll start reading Bible stories to him every night at bedtime unless Tina has a real objection to it and he can go to Sunday school at Shady Grove.

I told Jakie that the cross symbolized the victory of life over death. "Jesus died for all of us. He took all of the bad things we have done and erased them. Because Jesus died on the cross and rose again from death, we know that we will rise again and be with Jesus when we die."

"Why did Jesus have to die? Tell me more about Jesus."

"Jakie, there is so much to tell. I can't tell you everything in one day. You and I will start reading together and you will learn gradually. I am fifty-three years old and I'm still learning about Jesus. We can learn together."

"Grandma, you are really old. You don't look that old." Jakie said seriously.

I giggled. "Jakie, fifty-three isn't really old. In a few days I'll take you to meet some people that are older than I am, but you have to promise not to tell them that they are old or that they look old. It would hurt their feelings."

"Oh, I won't. I hope I didn't hurt your feelings. I love you, Grandma."

"You didn't hurt my feelings. I love you too, Jakie. I'm so glad you and your Mom and Dad came to live with me."

As we passed the Tree of Life sculpture, Jakie exclaimed, "I like this tree better than the other one—that cross."

"Yes, it is more beautiful—but we couldn't have its beauty without the empty cross."

"Look, Grandma, it has different colored metals. Trees aren't made from metal. They are made from wood, but this is pretty. I like it. See the buds on the tree branches. We had an orchard at home in France. The trees were so beautiful in the spring. There were blossoms. Papa held me up to pick apples in the fall and Mams made apple tarts from the apples. Yummy."

"You are so smart to know that trees are made of wood, not metal. This one is an artist's idea about new life, good fruit and spiritual growth. See how the leaves move. Isn't that neat?"

"I am smart, but I don't know what spiritual growth is. Can you tell me, Grandma?"

"Spiritual growth is learning more about God, Jesus and the Holy Spirit. You and I will read together and pray together. We will both learn more about God. How does that sound?"

"Great. I love God. I used to go to Mass with my Mamie Titia. I miss her and Papi and my aunts and uncles and cousins."

"I know you do, Jakie. Maybe you can talk to them on the webcam when we get back home."

"That would be good, but we're going to eat popcorn first, remember, Grandma Marjie?"

"Certainly, popcorn first. Now let's see what else we will find on this Worshipper's Path."

*The leaves of the tree are for the healing of the nations.—*
Revelation 22:2

"Here is the Ikebana."

"Those are pretty flowers," said Jakie.

"These are flower arrangements like the people in Japan make. That's a country that is far away from here—far away like France only we have to travel to the west to get there. These flowers are here to set a mood for harmony—a feeling that everything is as it should be so that we can think about God and how much He loves us and the whole wide world."

I read the scriptures aloud as we passed them.

*For as the earth brings forth her bud, and as the garden causes the things that are sown in it to spring forth; so the Lord God will cause righteousness and praise to spring forth before all the nations.*—Isaiah 61:11.

As Jakie and I turned away from the flower arrangements we reached three dark sculptures. Jakie saw the first one and asked, "Why is the man so sad? Doesn't he know that God loves him?"

"Jakie, these are what an artist thought of. You see the first man is very sad. He is looking down. He has forgotten that God loves him and would never leave him alone. Then the next one is searching for God. He is looking up to the heavens, but he has his hands on his chest. He is still living without the full knowledge of the love of God. The third man has found God and has given himself to God and opened himself up to God. He knows God loves him."

"These first two bodies kind of make me feel sad, Grandma. Oh look, up there at the top of the walk. There is a wall and water is coming down it." Jakie pulled me up the rest of the walk. "This is really cool."

I whispered, "It's called the Fountain of Living Water. It stands for the wonderful life that God has given to us. We know water quenches our thirst and God quenches our spiritual thirst and makes us feel loved."

I read: *"The water that I will give will become in them a spring of water gushing up to eternal life."*

John 4:14

"I like it here Grandma."

What a joy it is to have Jakie here with me.

♥

Surprisingly, after such a wonderful day with Jakie, I couldn't sleep and was up before Henri for a change.

My dreams had turned into nightmares. I fought a kitchen sink that was spewing water all over an unfamiliar room. The walls clouded over with mist. I was floating on top of a barstool, going round and round. I saw Tina and Henri through a doorway or was it a keyhole? Jakie floated by on a large plastic toy, was it a rubber duck or a swan? Jake was hanging from a ladder fully outfitted in his Fire Chief uniform. He was trying to reach me but he couldn't. I tried to reach Jakie, but he floated out of sight. Then Jake was gone, the ladder hanging empty. I heard Tina and Henri laughing, laughing...

I awoke in a sweat and lie there for a few minutes. I felt out of breath. I reached for the glass of water on my night stand and knocked it over.

"Darn, what a mess!" I jumped out of bed the nightmare fading. Good. I didn't want to remember that one. I soaked the water up with a washcloth and dried my nightstand with a paper towel. I'll have to remember to polish it later.

Today was to be a really fun day. No time to be upset over nightmares or spilt water. We were going to the National Trails Museum—Tina, Henri, Jakie, Mom, our little neighbor, Mandy, and me. None of us had ever been there before. I was sure Jakie and Mandy would enjoy it, especially the covered wagon ride and the picnic on the old pioneer campground.

I took Jakie next door with me to get Mandy. He and Mandy hadn't met yet, although they had eyed each other a few times when out in their respective yards. We went before breakfast, planning to keep Mandy all day so her parents wouldn't have to take her to her day care before going to work. Mandy was ready, waiting at the door. She and Jakie took a long look at each other when I introduced them.

"Jakie, that's a baby name," said Mandy.

"So is Mandy, Mandy Pandy, Mandy Pandy," said Jakie.

With those words my fears of rivalry between the two of them were realized. Down deep from my memory came the words "Marjie Parjie". That's what Mark called me in high school and even recently in his Facebook texts, he was still calling me that. I laughed and the little ones looked up at me. Their little faces skewed misunderstanding that I would laugh at them.

"Guess what Mandy and Jakie, Grandpa's best friend used to call me 'Marjie Parjie' and still does. We are great friends. I'm sure the two of you will be, too. Now let's go see what your papa made for breakfast."

When we opened the door, Jakie yelled, "Crepes. I can smell them! You'll like them, Mandy. My papa made them."

Henri made a big fuss over Mandy, kissing her hand and Jakie's jealousy seemed to dissipate almost as quickly as it appeared. I remembered hearing Henri telling Jakie always to be nice to females. It pays. I don't think Jakie understood the rationale for this yet, but knew he could trust his papa.

We had a choice of blueberry or strawberry and Henri had whipped some cream to adorn the fabulous crepes. I chose blueberry and left off the cream, trying to keep my healthy diet in the wake of living with two French chefs. I believed once the café opened I would be cooking at home and making sure my cholesterol intake remained controlled. I poured papaya juice for the children and myself. Henri drank nothing but strong coffee in the mornings. I was already learning his habits after only one week.

Everyone had finished eating when Tina strolled into the kitchen, still in her pajamas, hair covering half her face. "Coffee, Henri, s'il vous plait and one of each of those crepes." Tina started to sit in her chair, but luckily noticed Mandy sitting there before she sat on top of her, so she grabbed a chair from the corner breakfast nook, dragging it over to the larger kitchen table.

The phone rang. "That will be your Grandma wondering what time we are picking her up," I said to Tina. "How long will it take you to get ready?" I picked up the phone before it went to voice mail, checking caller ID to be certain. "Hi, Mom."

"I did want to eat and take a shower and wash my hair," Tina said as stretched both arms over her head, then rubbed the back of her neck.

Henri and I shot her disapproving glances and looked at the children, then back at Tina.

"Okay, if you can stand to be with me, I'll just eat and dress. Be ready in half an hour," Tina responded.

I spoke into the phone. "Mom, we'll be at your place about nine o'clock. Love you, too. See you in a few."

While Tina got ready and the kids looked at the children's books I piled on the table, I helped Henri clear and load the dishes into the dishwasher. We were a good team, so it took only minutes, especially since Henri was really good at cleaning up while he cooked.

As we finished up I sat down to relax a moment. A conversation that Tina and I had before she and Henri were married came to mind. She had said, *Henri is more like the child you always wanted. He is sweet and does dishes.* Of course I assured her that she was the child I always wanted.

The phone rang again. I didn't recognize the number but answered anyway. It was Al. "Hi, Marjie, it's Al from the property in Englewood, Al Schmidt. We met the other day. I wanted to tell you how much I enjoyed meeting you and to tell you that I was looking at my bucket list today and found that Numero Uno on my bucket list is going out on a date with a beautiful woman named Marjie, a petite, lovely woman named Marjie. So what do you say? Want to throw caution to the wind and go out to dinner with me? Don't say no. It's simply dinner."

I could not talk. I needed time to think about this. A hot flash ran through my body. How did he get my number? I had no interest in dating Al, no interest in dating anyone. I loved Jake. Our relationship wasn't perfect, but it was near to it, and I suspect I have romanticized him in the five years since his death, but... Finally, I spoke. "Thank you for thinking of me, Al, but I need to say *no*. My family has recently arrived from France and we are just getting to know each other again. We have so many plans. I am busy at church and I have my mother to consider…"

He interrupted. "Marjie, I'm not proposing marriage, purely dinner."

With that, I calmed down a bit. What would it hurt? Then, no, I'm not interested. Then, why not?

While I sorted through every scenario of why I should or shouldn't go out with this stranger, Al said, "Why don't you sleep on it and I'll call you tomorrow? But remember you are on my bucket list and it would be fun besides we can talk about your ideas for the restaurant," he laughed as he hung up the phone.

That night I said my thank you prayers—for such a wonderful day to remember, my family all together, Mom, Tina, Henri, Jakie and, as a bonus, Mandy. The children loved the movies they saw in the trails museum, Henri devoured the exhibit information, reading each quotation from a pioneer's journal with relish, Tina and Mom loved the art work and I loved being with my entire family. I looked forward to many experiences with them and, of course, I wished Jake had been with us. He was in spirit, I knew.

*Family and friends are what makes life worthwhile, Lord, thank you so much.* What was it that I read this morning in my journal that Mother Teresa said? *If we have no peace it is because we have forgotten that we belong to each other.* We do belong to each other, I thought as I nodded off to sleep, having totally forgotten about Al and his bucket list.

Tonight there would be no nightmares.

♥

When we arrived at the McNamara's, dinner was already on the table, a first, because Eileen always wanted everything to be at its peak when eaten. Tonight she had prepared a cold meal, leafy green salad with a mix of summer berries, creamy gorgonzola cheese and walnuts, with chilled chicken and herb potato salad, five bean salad, Jell-O salad with Mandarin oranges, and Hawaiian sweet rolls with creamy butter. Tina made pecan apple tart for dessert, this being the new tradition she insisted on, wanting to try out desserts for the café.

I was surprised that Rob managed not to offend anyone at dinner, although I'm sure he wanted to find out what was going on with the restaurant idea, he held his tongue. Eileen and I had talked a week or so ago about Rob. We both felt that as pastor, Rob was growing in sensitivity, not improving fast enough for his wife sometimes, but she used their code whenever necessary and that was certainly helping. The code was *All things math.* Whenever Rob heard her say this he knew he was dangerously near sticking his foot into his mouth, which really wasn't good for a pastor to do. All of their close friends and most of the congregation knew about the code, but acted like they didn't hear a thing whenever Eileen said it. We all love Rob for his good heartedness, which goes a long way to excuse a few unintentional faux pas.

I am so glad that Henri likes Rob. He told me that he appreciated Rob's sense of humor and knew that whatever Rob said, he meant it in the best possible way. They spent the next couple of hours playing pool with Jakie, who was ecstatic to get to play with his papa and his newly adopted Grandpa. That's what Rob said to call him, but then, that's what all the kids at JAM and church called him.

My good night thank you prayers were filled to the brim. Everything was working out so well for Tina and Henri, they had found the restaurant space they wanted, Tina and Beth were together again, Henri and Rob had adopted each other. What a wonderful evening.

♥

Al phoned with his apologies for not calling yesterday as he had said, wanting to give me more time to think about it. Also, he wanted to talk to Henri or Tina to see if they wanted to get together to go over offers on the remodeling job for the restaurant.

I felt embarrassed that we forgot to call him and tell him that we were going to lease a property on the Square. That weakened my resolve not to go out with him.

I sensed he knew me better than I knew myself. He seemed to know from meeting me one time and our brief phone conversations that I was a woman who would never want to hurt anyone's feelings. I have no idea why, but he seemed genuinely attracted to me and wanted to get to know me better.

"How about lunch on Wednesday at someplace either on the Square or close to it?" I can't believe that came out of my mouth, but I did read somewhere that the safest date is a lunch. It's short and we'll both have to get back to work.

My heart was in my throat when I hung up the phone. I was glad that Tina and Henri didn't know about my lunch date. I didn't want anyone to know. I almost felt ashamed, like I was cheating on Jake. I probably wouldn't sleep tonight, maybe not at all until Wednesday. Al is attractive, but I don't need a man, now of all times. Couldn't I meet someone when my life is not so full, then remembered that my life had always been full. I made it that way.

♥

Tina didn't want to get out of bed for church, but Henri, Jakie and Mandy went with me. As we drove past the Vaile Mansion on Liberty Street, Henri and the children took notice. No wonder, the mansion towers above anything around it and it is shaped like a wedding cake, a red-brick, iced with stone trim.

"Who lives there, Grandma?" asked Jakie.

"Oh, no one lives there now, but a long time ago a very rich man and his wife lived there. It's kind of a sad story, but the home is beautiful. There are marble fireplace mantles and chandeliers…" I began.

"Have you been there, Grandma?" asked Jakie.

"Yes, Marjie, have you been there?" Mandy asked in an awed voice.

"Oh, yes, I've been there several times. I like going during the Christmas season when it's all decorated, but it's beautiful anytime. Would you like to go there someday?" I asked.

Henri said, "Oui, Mère Margie, I would."

I knew that French landmarks are much grander than the Vaile, but reasoned that Henri was thinking of the children, and, of course, me. Even his hometown of Grignan featured a castle from the seventeenth century.

"Then we will go. We'll put it on the calendar," I promised.

Today was Communion Sunday. I explained to Henri that he was welcome to participate in the Sacrament of the Lord's Supper with the congregation. That all who had been baptized and wanted to remember the love, sacrifice and resurrection of our Lord Jesus Christ and who want to recommit themselves to following Him were welcome to take the bread and wine.

Henri reminded me that he had taken communion at his wedding service and when they were here for Jakie's birth.

And for Jake's death, I thought—the two events ever linked in my memory.

"Of course, Henri, I remember now. I believe that all Christian churches should be one family. We are all in the family of God," I said.

"And I believe that all God's people whether Christian or not, should be one family. All are created by God," answered Henri.

"Henri, you are right there. I misspoke. I believe God wants all of his creation to love one another. That's why I'm so glad that our church is a church of Peace."

"But what does that mean, Mère Marjie, a church of Peace?" questioned Henri as we parked in the shaded lot.

"Ah, I see I am going to have to spend some time researching before I ever bring anything up with you," I laughed. Maybe we can discuss that in our Church School class today. See what the rest of the class has to say about it. I know the teacher pretty well. It's Samuel."

"This is turning into an interesting day already. I only wish Tina were here," said Henri.

"So do I, Henri, so do I."

Mandy took Jakie to their Sunday school classroom and introduced him to their teacher, Miss Patty, who I am certain made a big fuss over him. She loved the children in her class and made sure that every one of them felt her love. After class he couldn't wait to show his papa and me the little giraffe that he had chosen from Miss Patty's famous big brown bag. The giraffe was riding on a stuffed motorcycle—another reminder that we needed to send for the one he had left in France. I was thrilled that he had a good time.

We entered the sanctuary and walked toward the front on the left side, where I usually sat alone or with Mandy. We were greeted by smiles, hugs, and handshakes as I introduced my son-in-law and grandson to my friends who hadn't met them at breakfast or in class. After announcements were made and the first hymn sung, Eileen stood at the podium, her wavy red-blond hair forming a halo in the light shining from the stained glass window behind her. I knew her well enough to know that she was taking in the aura of the gathered congregation.

She began: "Our theme today is *Share All Things*. Jesus, the ultimate Sharer— gave his life that we may live forever with him in eternity. What can we do for HIM? Let us begin with an exercise in sharing with God and with each other. I am now going to read the words of a hymn that I believe God asked me to bring to you. Please find someone to hold hands with as we share this together. I changed the words slightly to make it a group unity prayer. Please repeat after me and breathe in the Holy Spirit after each phrase."

The hymn we repeated was *Breathe on Me Breath of God*. I proudly held Henri's hand and with the other hand, clutched Jakie's stubby fingers. I could barely contain my happiness. I was overwhelmed with joy having my family with me at church. Then Jakie offered his hand to Mandy who was sitting next to him. I was glad that he and Mandy were becoming friends. God's Spirit truly filled me with life anew.

❤

I was bursting to tell someone about my upcoming date with Al so I headed for Bingham Manor early. As I drove, I wondered if I should confide in Mary Florence or Anna Jean or both. Mary Florence was the more logical of the two, but did I want logic or just someone to share with? I would play it by ear. I may not even have a chance to share my news. The girls were always so full of their own tidbits, their children's escapades, stories about Adelaide and Annabelle, clever food combinations from the Manor's chef.

When I got there, a van from *The Examiner* and a couple of local news stations were parked outside.

The first person I saw when I entered the building was Anna Jean, who stood away from the crowd in the gathering room.

"Marjie, you'll never guess." gushed Anna Jean, dying to tell me the latest and greatest news from Bingham Manor.

Suddenly Mildred rushed over to greet me. "Mary Florence won the Ms. Missouri Nursing Home Pageant! Our own Mary Florence."

Anna Jean's eyes flared at Mildred for beating her to the announcement, but I have to give her credit, she didn't make a scene—this time. I guessed she was proud of her friend and didn't' want to spoil her big day.

It seemed that all the residents had assembled to celebrate Mary Florence's newfound fame. *The Examiner* photographer and TV reporters were gathering their equipment together, getting ready to leave.

"She's going to be on the five o'clock news and her picture's going to be in the paper on Thursday this week. On the front page they said! The tenth of June. Ain't that special!" piped up, Jack, one of the male residents.

After the news crews dissipated I went to the guest of honor. "Why Mary Florence I didn't know anything about this. When did you enter the pageant?" I asked.

Anna Jean drew herself up to her full height. "I'm the one who nominated her. Didn't even tell her I did it."

Eugene was there too and said, "She didn't even have to do the swim suit competition. What a rip-off."

"Eugene," Anna Jean warned sternly, "I told you that joke isn't funny."

The director, Helen Reed, brought over a cake and sat it in front of Mary Florence, so she could cut it.

This didn't seem like the time to discuss my date with Al, so I joined in the fun and celebrated with my very special friends.

Soon we adjourned to play Bingo.

## CHAPTER NINE

This had to be one of the stupidest things I'd gotten myself into—meeting up with someone I barely know, now glad I hadn't told anyone about it. I knew he was divorced, so that didn't say a lot for him, but I didn't want to judge him on that, since one of my best friends, Denise, is on her third marriage and I know a lot of people who married too young or who made the wrong choice, or maybe didn't try hard enough—being divorced doesn't make you a bad person.

I stood looking in my closet, wondering what to wear for my lunch date. Not the same thing I wore when we met, although what difference would that make. Maybe I should wear my Lion and Lamb polo shirt—let him know right away who I belong to, oh darn, that had a spot on it. I thought I had washed it. Well, try again—I tossed it into the hamper, reminding myself to spray it with spot remover before washing it again. I spotted my Outreach International tee shirt, but thought, no, I should wear something dressier than a tee shirt. Maybe that cropped-top that Tina gave me with the matching slacks.  I decided to wear that. At least it didn't have to be ironed.

Tina, Henri and Jakie were out looking at tile samples for the café, so I had the morning to myself. I dressed, did my hair and make-up with a little more care than usual, actually put mascara on, which I hate doing, but I knew I looked better with it. All the while wondering why I cared what this stranger thought about me. Thank heavens it's a lunch and I will be going straight back to work from there, so if I get frazzled, I will shortly be able to pull myself together. I thought of Jake. I know he would want me to be happy. And, it's just lunch, I probably won't ever see this guy again. No big deal.

I ambled down the front steps of the house, admiring the profusion of dark pink knock out roses growing on either side of the front walk.

They are no *Mister Lincoln* or *Midas Touch* like Jake planted in our rose garden in back, but the knock outs do last all summer and into the late fall.

I hesitated before getting into my car. I had Al's cell phone number. I could still call and cancel. But why? A lunch. It's only lunch. He seemed to be a fun person. I like fun, but usually with women and children—not with men, oh there's Rob, we're like brother and sister. I could be a sister to Al. This could be fun.

Whew. I had about worn myself out by the time I finally drove to Antonio's, found a parking spot and walked to the entrance of the restaurant. Al was waiting for me in the doorway. He took my arm and escorted me to a booth in the back behind the curtains.

When I am nervous I either don't talk at all or can't stop talking. This time I couldn't keep words from pouring out of my mouth. Before the waitress came to take our drink order, I told Al about Mary Florence's honor of being Ms. Missouri Nursing Home, about Jakie's first T-ball game, the trip to the Frontier Trails Museum and how I love my flower gardens, especially the roses.

Al was a handsome character—like Cary Grant with his silver wavy hair and his smile, his suave manners, his impeccable clothing. Today he wore another Hawaiian shirt, this one flaunting bright red-orange bird of paradise. He listened to me babble away, barely taking his puppy soft brown eyes off my face. The waitress came back to take our lunch order, but neither of us had looked at the menu—me blah, blah, blahing and Al contentedly listening to my inane chatter.

I ordered a half chicken salad sandwich and a house salad. For an appetizer to share Al selected the live cheese-free nachos with bean pate, guacamole, and salsa. For his meal he ordered the spinach and black bean enchilada. I had never heard of live nachos or any nachos without cheese, but I felt adventurous today and decided to try it, a little worried about my irritable bowel syndrome and the salsa. I would only take a tiny bit of that.

After we ordered I became mute, so Al started trying to bring me back out. He asked me how Tina ended up marrying someone from France, had I ever been to France, where did I grow up, what my hobbies were, did I have a bucket list?

I answered his questions one by one as if they were on an exam:

- "Tina went to culinary school in France, met Henri in school, they were both chefs, Tina leaning more toward pastries, Henri to main courses. He was also an expert on wines.

- Tina came home to have Jakie, spending three months with us, my husband died the day after Jakie was born. I went to France for a while with Tina so we could grieve and care for Jakie together. It was a strange time.

- I grew up in Independence.
- My hobbies were gardening, music, writing, grandson, reading.
- No, I don't have a bucket list, but I have Resolutions—New Year's Resolutions. Tina and I and Henri, (although, he cheats, by not having the required ten), all read our resolutions to each other every New Year right after midnight."

By the time the food came I started feeling more like myself. Al was very nice, courteous, and acted interested in me. He had weird food choices, though, I have to admit. I smiled and between bites began to try to find out a little about him. "So you have a bucket list?"

"I do. Thank you so much for meeting me today, so I could cross one off." He was so smooth, but I liked him, in spite of my doubts and determination to keep this platonic. Here I was already assuming a relationship—that he would actually ask me out again.

"What is your next item, if you don't mind my asking?" I finished a bite of sandwich, chicken salad falling out of the toasted bread, thankfully onto my plate. I've always been cognizant of others who were messy eaters and try diligently to follow all rules of etiquette.

"Saturday after next a group of my friends and I are going up in a hot air balloon. Would you like to join us? I'd love to have you experience the fun with us and there happens to be room for one more person." His grin spread from ear to ear, showing gorgeous white teeth and making him look almost boyish and, additionally, so charming. I had never seen that smile from him before, of course, this is only the second time we had met.

I bit my lip, took another bite of my sandwich, chewing slowly while my mind traveled back several years. A hot air balloon ride. It was one of things that Jake had always wanted to do and I had put him off. The cost seemed ridiculously high for the time we would be up in the air. I told Jake that when he retired we would go to New Mexico for the Albuquerque International Balloon Fiesta and ride a balloon, but he hadn't retired. He died instead. If I went up in one now, I would feel guilty.

"Marjie, where did you go?" asked Al sweetly.

I couldn't believe it, but I teared up, waved my napkin at him and said, "My late husband, Jake, always wanted to do that, but I wouldn't go with him and didn't even want him to go…"

"Ah, so you are afraid of heights?" he asked.

"No, that's not it. I didn't want to spend the money."

I practically yelled *money* as I burst into full-fledged wailing, feeling mortified, but unable to stop. This was unbelievable. I hadn't cried like this over Jake for a long time. This—this balloon ride invitation turned me into a pitiful, sappy, melodramatic mess.

Al moved over to my side of the booth and put his arm around me. "It's okay, Marjie. It's okay. I caught you off guard. Take all the time you need."

I wiped my eyes and tried to smile. I looked at my napkin and saw mascara all over it. That's why I never wear this stuff, I thought. I excused myself and went to the ladies' room to try to repair my face and my dignity. I guess I'm not ready for dating. What a disaster. He probably won't even want to be my friend after this. But he does seem nice. Actually, I thought he was kind of a wolf, but I'm glad I gave him a chance. I was too embarrassed to think about seeing him again so I slipped out the back door, vowing never to try anything like that again, grateful that I hadn't told anyone about my lunch date.

I was dusting my collection of angel plates, covering them with bubble wrap and packing them in a cardboard box when Tina wandered into the dining room. "Mom, what are you doing with your plates?" Tina asked.

"Oh, we're having a silent auction at the church on Saturday after the talent show fund raiser. I'm donating these and anything else I can find around here that someone might want."

"Mother, you can't give those away. Dad and I gave you most of them. Don't they mean anything to you?

I stopped packing and looked at her. "The memory of your dad and you giving them to me means a lot to me, Tina, and if you want to keep them for me, I'll give them to you. I am tired of taking care of things when people are so much more important. Taking care of possessions takes too much time. I want to start giving things away. This fund-raiser is for the homeless. There are so many children who are homeless right now. It's really mind-boggling. How can I enjoy mere possessions when children are hungry?"

"I guess you are right, but I thought you would never give away your angel plates. They meant so much to you when I was a little girl and Dad and I would buy you one for your birthday and Christmas and Mother's Day. If you give them away, it's like Dad and I don't mean anything to you or maybe I'm afraid I'll lose you like I lost Dad. It's complicated. Can we please hold on to the plates, at least?"

"Sure, Honey, if you want them. You can have them. Where do you want to keep them?"

"I want them right here in your hutch, like always."

"But who's going to take care of them. I don't' have time to dust them anymore. Do you?"

"Oh, a little dust never hurt anything." Tina laughed.

We unpacked the plates and put them back where they came from.

I sighed. "How about my crystal, can I give that away? We seldom use it and I bought it myself for my hope chest.

"Not on your life are you giving that away. Henri and I will use it at the restaurant."

"You mean all six stems?"

"Darn right, all six." That ended my packing for the day. I'll have to find things to donate when Tina is not around, but not the angel plates, never the angel plates.

❤

*Lord, please help me to spend my time at the computer wisely. If there is someone I can help, please help me to have the words that You would have me say. Let me be a light shining on a hill for someone today. Amen.*

Goodness, look at all these messages in my email box. I have no idea who all of them are, but they are responding to a message that Mark posted. I deleted all of the messages then went to Mark's Facebook page. I read his profile discovering that he is interested in *women*. Same old Mark, I chuckled, then, the thought of Al came to mind—that terrible fiasco at lunch. So glad he hasn't called me.

I clicked on Mark's Employment and Education section. I had forgotten that he went to the University of Missouri School of Journalism and he now works at the *St. Paul Pioneer Press*. I remembered that he was on the Chrisman school newspaper. I couldn't remember what the paper was called and decided to send Mark a message to ask him.

I typed, *Hi Mark, Great being your Facebook friend. What was Chrisman's newspaper called? I've been racking my brain, but can't remember.*

I was startled when the little box showed up with Mark's answer. Apparently he was online. *It was the Envoy—the William Chrisman Envoy. How are you doing Marjie? Sorry I haven't kept up with you. It seems like yesterday when I was in Independence at Jake's funeral talking with you about old times. Say, I'm going to visit my mom in July. She turns eighty on July 12th. I know she would love to see you. Why don't you come to the party? I'll send you a formal invite by snail mail.*

*My sister and I are throwing a big shindig on the Saturday before her big day. I think it's on July 10th at 1:00 p.m. at Mom's clubhouse. She lives in the new retirement village east of town. You have to come! You can meet my kids! They are the most wonderful kids ever born! And I do say so myself. Look who raised them.*

A party—that would be fun. I hesitated a few minutes before responding. Then wrote, *Mark, how good to connect with you this way. I'm doing fine. My daughter, Tina, her husband and their little boy live with me now. There is never a dull moment with a five-year-old. Tina and Henri are planning to open a French restaurant on the Square. I would love to come to your mother's party. I remember her as a wonderful, carefree spirit—like someone else that I won't name, who now lives in St. Paul. What do you do at the Pioneer Press?*

After a short delay, while I sat looking at my nails, thinking that I need to give myself a manicure, Mark answered. *I've recently been demoted from reporter to editor, such is the luck.*

I laughed and typed: *Wow. An editor. You're the boss. Does management know what they have gotten themselves into?*

Another delay. I wondered if he was chatting with other *friends* at the same time.

He came back with, *I'll let you know when I figure it out. Better go. Got to go work out with Mark Jr. We lift weights. He's trying to stay fit for football next fall and I'm trying to be a He-man. Nice chatting with you, Marjie Pargie. Hope to talk to you soon.*

And as fast as that—he was gone leaving me feeling let down for a few seconds. I shook my head, jumped up and went looking for a small boy to play with.

❤

Tina and Henri grabbed me as I was coming home from work. It was time to go sign the lease on the building for the café.

Excitement, nervousness, jumpiness described us as Tina, Henri and I put pen to the legal document. Henri told Mel the café would be called *La Vie en Rose*. Tina and Henri were excited, but I, who signed the check, was plain scared.

I reminded myself that it was Tina's money, too, after all, it came from Jake's insurance policy. Tina refused to take any when her father died, but this café was something she really wanted and it had brought her and my grandson, home to me. Tina always said Henri's family was wonderful, took her in as family. But she shared with me that living together in a compound was getting to her and she was homesick. She had made few friends in France, except for Henri and his family. He was her best friend.

I missed the times when Tina and I were best friends, but everything should change when children get married. I know Tina loves me. She doesn't often show it, but I know she loves me deeply. She loved her father and still can't believe he is gone. Her grief was possibly more excruciating than mine because her faith in God is not secure. I said a sentence prayer for her.

Before bed I looked at my calendar. There had been so much excitement today that I forgot Denise's birthday. Dear, Dear, Oh Darn! I'll call her tomorrow to see if we can go for lunch on Wednesday. It was her Fiftieth. Surely her family did something to celebrate for her, but I didn't hear anything about it. I'd better write it down so I don't forget again. My, oh my, my life has gotten busier and busier. Thank heaven I decided not to go to school this summer. Who knows if I'll ever go back to school?

As I began my thank you prayers, I was interrupted by negative thoughts. Tina completely ignored Jakie today. He tried to get her attention, but she cut him short, telling him that this was grown-up business. All he wanted was to be involved in the excitement of the new café.

I don't know why Tina's first response to everything seems to be sarcastic and sometimes even cutting. I try to be patient with her, so does Henri. Why is Tina the way she is? She can't even be nice to Jakie all the time. She is too self-centered. She worries that Jakie is closer to his father and to me. I've barely been in his life up to now but I can see that he loves his mother.

Tina said today that she is happier than she has been in years. She and Henri will open their very own café. They are the chefs, the owners, the everything, and don't have to consult Henri's family if they wanted to rearrange the furniture or add salmon to the menu. This would be heaven and she would be in charge.

*I think I'm too tired to sort all of this out, Lord. The emotions of today wore me out. I want to thank you for everything, my blessings, my family, my friends and your love.*

♥

I checked my email to see if Joyce sent the list of planners, presiders and speakers for next month so I can call people to participate in the worship services.

I found another posting on Mark's Facebook page. His daughter's soccer team won again. I commented with a hearty *Congratulations!*

There were no other messages of importance. Just junk emails. I deleted them and got up to check to see if the regular mail had arrived yet. It had. Gas bill. Bank statement, ad, ad, ad. Here's something from St. Paul, MN. It was the invitation to Mark's mother's party, addressed to Marjorie Jamison and Family. Wonderful. I can take Jakie with me. Maybe Tina and Henri will come too. That would be fun. We haven't been to any parties since they've been here, unless we count dinners at the McNamara's.

♥

I chatted with this summer's Vacation Bible School volunteers while waiting for Denise to start the meeting. She stood at the front of the church and described what we could expect. The theme this year would be *Jesus is Our Friend*. The children would get to learn about all the disciples, especially Peter, James, John and about Mary, Martha and their brother Lazarus. They would get to roleplay the various people of Jesus' time and Jesus himself. They would each be in a group of adults and all ages of children and would travel the roads that Jesus traveled.

Beth and I were glad that we would be teamed together, each leading a separate group, but when it came time for crafts, snack time and game time our groups would be together.

After the meeting Denise and I talked about where to go for her birthday lunch tomorrow—Denise excited to tell me about the surprise her husband and children pulled on her.

We walked out together carrying the packets of materials needed for our groups in July when Bible School would take place.

Denise still hadn't decided where she wanted to go for lunch the next day. She wanted to go to Stephenson's Old Apple Farm Restaurant, but it was now closed. We reminisced about how we had enjoyed celebrating there through the years.

"I know, Marjie, let's go to the new Stephenson's in Raytown and check it out. They are supposed to have a lot of our favorites," said Denise, her light green eyes dancing with excitement.

"Do you suppose they will have the pork chops, apple fritters and their famous green rice casserole?" I asked, as eager as Denise. "Let's have a meal like we never eat anymore. We'll satisfy our guilty pleasures for once. I'll call and make reservations, pick you up at eleven?"

"Sounds good! Kenneth will be jealous, but, hey, I'm the one who turned fifty, not him. Or should we take him and our moms?" asked Denise.

I debated myself for one half second, then said, "No, you and I haven't done anything together, just the two of us, for ages. It'll be fun. We can pretend we're playing hooky from high school," We giggled like school girls.

Denise went on and on about how wonderful I am, making me start listing all my faults to myself. It's so hard for me to take a compliment. We parted and I began day dreaming of apple fritters, homemade hot rolls, and that luscious green rice casserole. Years ago I tried to make it at home with the packaged seasoning that Stephenson's sold, but it wasn't the same. In fact, it was lousy.

♥

Sitting in the booth at the J.L. Stephenson's Santa Fe Restaurant, Denise and I laughed so hard remembering Prom night of junior year when we double-dated—Jake and I, Denise and Mark. The memories tumbled out. Mark wearing Denise's stole for the last fast dance, Jake trying to compete and one-up Mark by jumping on the stage and singing *Da Doo Ron Ron* along with the band.

"He never could carry a tune," I laughed, tears running down my face, "but he did love to sing."

Denise said, "Mark couldn't carry a tune to save his bacon, but you know how he used to sing when we'd drive in the car and at the picnics at Jacomo."

"Remember when Mark got that Mustang convertible? He must have gotten it before our Junior Prom because we had it that night, so he got it in '74 probably. What year car was it?" I asked.

Denise replied, "It was a 1969 Ford Mustang—candy apple red with black interior. I loved that car. Sometimes we drove for hours, never really going anywhere, feeling the wind in our hair, stereo turned up, listening to *Tonight's the Night* by Rod Stewart and Sly and the Family Stone's *Dance to the Music*. Remember?"

As if planned Denise and I broke into the chorus, singing "Dance to the Music."

We reminisced, oblivious to everyone around us, but, I later realized, garnering attention from everyone in the restaurant. When the waiter brought our food we calmed down to relish the flavors from our past, letting the music go and the food take over.

I finished my second apple fritter, then looked up and into the brown eyes of Al Schmidt. I had hoped never to see him again, but there he was and seeing the look of amusement on his face, I blushed crimson and wondered what in the world he was thinking.

Denise spoke up. "Marjie, do you know this gentleman?"

"Why, yes, I do. Al Schmidt, meet Denise Day. I mean Denise Davis. Denise, meet Al Schmidt." I was a little nervous. I couldn't remember my friend's last name, resorting first to her maiden name of Day and then to the name of her first husband.

Denise corrected me. "Hi, my name is Denise Nelson. Marjie and I have been conjuring up memories from the past so she logically harkened back to my former names. It's nice to meet you Al. How do you two know each other?" Denise looked at Al, then me, then back to Al, her smile as mischievous as the Cat in the Hat.

I gave her a look which let her know she shouldn't have asked.

"May I join you ladies for a moment?" spoke Al suavely.

I noticed a hint of a southern accent, which I didn't remember him having before.

I nodded ascent. Denise said, "Sure".

I suddenly experienced an upset stomach, all that laughing and rich food, what was I thinking eating foods like this all at the same time? I can spread them out, but can't eat them all at once. I can't excuse myself right now, can I? Al will think all I do is go to the rest room. But what do I care what Al thinks?

I got up and went to the rest room, thoroughly worried about leaving the two of them alone to tell each other secrets about me. Who am I to have secrets? I have nothing to be ashamed of, do I?

When I came back Al stood to let me back in the booth and said, "I told Denise that we met in Englewood when your daughter and son-in-law were looking for restaurant space. I'm glad to see you again," he said as he turned to me. "I have an appointment right now or I would stay longer, but I suspect that you ladies would rather get back to talking about your high school days, anyway. Good to meet you Denise, good to see you again Marjie. Would it be all right if I call you sometime?"

Al, such a gentleman, he didn't even say call you *again*, in case I didn't want Denise to know that he had already called me. And I don't. I especially don't want her to know that I met him for lunch and made a total fool out of myself. I felt Denise and Al both watching me, waiting for me to say something, yes, no, maybe, go fly a kite. I didn't know what to say, but heard words come out of my mouth.

"Sure, I guess you can call sometime, but we are firm on that other restaurant location. We signed the lease yesterday."

"Well, I wondered if you would care to go to a movie or out to dinner or dancing," he said, again with that southern accent. How odd. I know he didn't have one before.

Denise interrupted, "Well, if you get Marjie Lord Jamison out dancing, I want to be there! She never dances. She didn't even dance when we were in high school."

I shot Denise a sizzling stare, turned to Al and said, "Sure, give me a call, we can at least talk."

After he left, I told Denise the whole grizzly tale of my disastrous lunch date with Al. Denise sympathized with my embarrassment, but encouraged me to give Al a chance and my*self* a chance. "You are a young woman, Marjie, and you deserve to enjoy life. Jake would want you to," Denise smiled her biggest smile with no mischief showing and squeezed my hand.

"As are you, Denise, a young, beautiful woman and a wonderful friend."

"We're fifty and we love it, let's drink to that," said Denise, holding up her peach-flavored iced tea for a toast.

I'm over fifty, but who's counting. A handsome man asked me for a second date. Go figure?

# Chapter Ten

After my morning prayers I checked my email and found a Facebook message from Mark. I clicked on the link so I could answer him. He wanted to know how things were going with my daughter, son-in-law and grandson moving in.

How considerate. Mark didn't use to be considerate. Guess he has changed. I noticed a green dot next to his name on the right side of the screen, meaning that he was online and in Facebook right now.

I clicked on his name and typed, *Hi, are you there?*

I didn't have to wait long until Mark responded, *Hey, Marjie Parjie, how're things?*

I typed, *Couldn't be better. Tina, Henri and Jakie are settling in. They signed a lease for a space on the Square. It'll be a French café called La Vie En Rose. We're really excited. Jakie's playing T-ball. All's right with the world.*

He responded, *Sounds great, can't wait to see you at Mom's party. You're still...*

The phone rang. I looked away from Mark's message. My talking phone announced that it was Al Schmidt.

I wonder why he is calling so early? It's not even eight o'clock yet. I thought as I answered the phone.

There was that drawl again. I had to ask.

"Say Al, what's with the drawl? You didn't have it when we met or when we went to lunch."

"A confession, sweetness. I am trying to woo you in any way that works—trying to get your attention," laughed Al. "What do you think? Is it working?"

"Well, I answered the phone and I have caller ID, so maybe," I admitted to him and to myself.

I didn't want to have a relationship with anyone, but he seemed fun, so what was the harm. We could be friends. I'm a fifty-three-year-old widow, not an innocent school girl, but…he does make me feel rather like a school girl.

"Good, that's the answer I wanted, so do I keep the drawl?"

"That's totally up to you, Kind Sir," I laughed.

"Well, Ma'am, I kinda like being called 'Kind Sir', so I'll keep it for now. Just don't expect me to start speaking with a French accent. That ain't gonna happen. Let's see this is Thursday, how about lunch?" drawled Al, making it extra syrupy.

"I'm sorry, I can't do lunch today. I'm eating at my mother's."

"Well then, how about dinner tomorrow night?"

"Actually, I have a standing date every Friday night with my friends and family." I thought I was going to have to tell him my entire schedule if he kept asking for times that were set in stone.

"Saturday night then," he said.

"I can do dinner on Saturday, but it has to be an early evening because I have preparations to make for Sunday's service at church. I'm preaching this Sunday." He might as well know what he was getting into with me. My family, friends, and church always come first, after God, certainly.

"Preaching!" This in his unaccented voice. "I'm going out with a lady preacher. Well, hog tie me and call me Tex!" I think he was going for a Texan drawl this time.

We agreed that he would *call for me* at six p.m. on Saturday. Those were the words this southern gentleman chose to use. I gave him my address and hung up.

I went back to my Facebook chat with Mark. I'd forgotten about him while I was on the phone with Al.

He had asked, *You are still coming, aren't you?* referring to his mother's birthday party. Then he had written, *Where did you go?*

I keyed, I'm back. *Had a phone call. See you at the party. Looking forward to it.*

I smelled Henri's coffee and went to share breakfast with my family. How wonderful. I can eat breakfast in my own home with my own family I am truly blessed.

❤

Saturday morning I put the finishing touches on my sermon. True to my love for literature, I managed to work in Langston Hughes' *Mother to Son*. Tomorrow's theme was *Encourage One Another*. As soon as I knew the theme, that poem came to mind. The imagery so telling—*tacks* and *splinters* and *boards torn up*. The mother in the poem tells her son her life hasn't been a *crystal stair*. It's been hard, but she keeps *climbin' on*. She tells him not to turn back, but to endure when obstacles confront him.

God doesn't want us to give up because things aren't easy. Life is hard, but it's also wonderful—full of love, hope, peace and joy.

I was glad to have my message finished in time to get ready for my date. Yes, my date with Al Schmidt. Henri said he was going to ask Al about his intentions. Tina surprised me by encouraging me to have a good time, not to stay out too late or do anything to get in trouble with the law. She didn't want to have to bail me out of jail. Jakie was used to his parents and their teasing, so he joined in.

"Yes, Grandma, we don't want to have to bail you out of jail. What's bail mean? What's jail?" he asked.

"Don't worry, Jakie, I won't do anything to get in trouble. I'm going to a restaurant to eat dinner with Al. Remember him? We met him in Englewood when we were looking for property."

"Yuck! I remember him. Mama called him *oogly*. You don't want to go anywhere with him, do you Grandma?" Jakie seemed stricken at the thought of me going out with that *oogly* man. I reassured him that Al was a very nice man. A new friend.

Soon Al was at the door, greeted by the whole family.

"Well, it's so nice to see you all again," said Al.

"Come in. You remember my daughter, Tina, her husband, Henri and my grandson, Little Jake?"

"Grandma! You promised you wouldn't call me Little Jake. I'm Jakie or just Jake," he announced.

"Well, I'll call you 'Just Jake', how would that be," laughed Al.

Luckily Jakie had taken a little nap earlier, so he was in a pretty good mood. He laughed back, "That's pretty good. Just Jake. I guess you can take my Grandma out if you don't put her in jail."

Al looked surprised and for a moment didn't seem to have a comeback.

I was glad to have my family support and their sense of humor. I laughed and told Al, "It's a private joke, but I'll tell you later. Maybe we should go, did you make reservations somewhere?"

Al escorted me out of the house leaving my family standing on the front porch, Henri's arm around Tina and Jakie jumping around like a five-year-old, saying, "I'm hungry. When are we going to eat?"

♥

Dinner with Al was wonderful, his closeness sending old familiar feelings through my veins. He walked me up on my porch and drew me to him. I thought he was going to kiss me when he stepped back and looked me in the eyes.

"Marjie, a woman like you should be dancing!" Al raised his hands over his head, snapped his fingers like a calypso dancer, and smiled that contagious smile of his.

I wondered what he meant, a woman like me, but I kept my mouth shut, afraid of what his response would be. "I've always been clumsy. I never learned to dance, unless you count the folk dancing we did in junior high school or was it high school or both. Anyway. I can't dance."

Al clasped both my hands and whirled me around. "See, you can dance. All you need is someone to teach you. I believe I am that someone. I promise it will be fun."

My goodness. Al was so charming and persuasive. How could I tell him no? What harm could it do? I grew up in a church that frowned on dancing—thought it could lead to immoral behavior, worse than playing cards, but now the tide has shifted. My own congregation sponsored a Valentine's Day dance this year. I know students dance at Graceland University now. This boils down to whether I want to allow myself to get closer to this magnetic man.

"Marjie, you jumped into your private think tank again. Do you want to go dancing with me, or not?"

His smile so contagious, his body so near, how could I turn him down? I said, "Maybe someday." I told him my family and I would be gone for a week-long family camp in Excelsior Springs, back on Saturday. He said he would give me a call when I returned. His kiss was soft and sweet, not lingering, but very nice.

That night in my prayers, I thanked God for all the many blessings I have, especially my family, friends, old dear friends and new exciting friends. I didn't forget to tell Jake good night and wondered if he knew that I had a date tonight—a date that had actually gone well. No upset stomach, no fears, just the fun of getting to know a new friend, a kissable new friend. And I do want to be whirled and twirled and dipped, someday.

As I stood before the people of Shady Grove, I saw my special friends Kathleen, Foster, Denise, Eileen and Rob and my family's faces glowing with expectancy. I prayed silently that God's Spirit would help me to say what He would have me say. I began:

"Grace to you and peace.  I give thanks to God for all of you here at Shady Grove, for all you do, for your faith and labor of love and steadfastness of hope in our Lord Jesus Christ. I know, brothers and sisters, that you are loved by God. He has chosen you. For God's message of hope in Jesus did not come to you by words only—it came in the Power of the Holy Spirit. Look in our bulletin and you will see only a trifle of what goes on here as we come together often to worship together, to work together, to fellowship together, to help each other and, yes, to encourage each other."

Suffice it to say that I was blessed today and, if I can believe what others said as they came to greet me after the service, God blessed others through my words today. What more can I ask?

I was tired after the emotional ride of delivering the spoken word and of the emotion-filled night with Al, so I took a nap before my group meeting. I can't remember needing a nap in years.

"Where are we going, Grandma?" asked Jakie as he climbed into the back seat of the car and buckled his seat belt.

I turned around to look at my little grandson. I was so proud of him. I couldn't wait to show him off to my Bingham Manor friends. "We're going to meet some of my friends. We won't stay long. We've got to start packing for Reunion."

"What's Reunion?" asked Jakie.

"Reunion is a gathering of our church family. You, your mom and dad, Great-Grandma Karin, me and some people you know from church and lots of people you have never met will be there. Remember, I told you that we'll go swimming and fishing and learn new things and do crafts and eat lots of good food."

"Oh, I remember," answered Jakie. "Mams calls it 'Torture Camp.'"

"What! Oh your mother is teasing you. She loves going to Lake Doniphan for Reunion. She went every year from the time she can remember until she left home to go to France. You'll have a good time, I'm sure."

"Well, Papa did say we would go fishing. I've never been fishing. It will be fun." Jakie reassured himself. "You and Papa would never lie to me. Mams does like to tease me. Well, so does Papa, but not the same way. It's like Mams tries to scare me and Papa just wants to have fun."

Oh, that Tina. I need to have a talk with her, I thought. I don't know why she would try to scare her own son, a defenseless five-year-old.

"Here we are, Jakie, Bingham Manor," I said as I pulled into the huge parking lot.

"Wow, Grandma, this is a big place! Do people live here?" Jakie asked, looking with awe at the high rise.

"Oh, yes, Jakie, people live here. Let's go meet some of them." I held Jakie's hand as we crossed the parking lot. We stopped at the front entrance. I flashed my key card to open the doors.

I could see that to Jakie's eyes the atrium was huge. I led him to the sign-in book and let him print his name after mine. I looked at my watch and told him to write 10:15 a.m. in the Arrival column. We had been working on how to write time the other day and he wrote it perfectly. As I praised him, Helen Reed peeked out of her office to say 'Hi' to me and when she saw the little tyke with me, she came all the way out.

I introduced them, telling Helen that Jakie was going to meet Mary Florence, Anna Jean and their friends for the first time.

I wasn't sure where to look for Mary Florence, who I wanted to see first, so I took Jakie to the TV room where we found Eugene, Mildred and Irene. I guessed that Anna Jean and Eugene must be on the fritz again.

Everyone was anxious to find out who this little boy was. Eugene called out, "Marjie, bring the big guy over here."

I complied. "This is my grandson, Jakie. Jakie this is Eugene. Shake hands, Jakie. This is Irene and Mildred and the rest of the gang." Mildred smiled at Jakie and asked how old he was. Some of the residents waved from the corner of the room where they were putting a puzzle together.

Irene wheeled herself closer to Jakie, looked him up and down and asked him if he had any candy for her? I told her 'no' that he didn't have any candy. I knew that Irene was not supposed to have candy as she was a diabetic, but she tried to get it from everyone anyway. It's too bad when the mind goes before the person.

Jakie looked at Irene, staring at her face. "Why do you have a mustache? Aren't you a woman?"

"What did you say, young man?" yelled the irate Irene.

I told Jakie to tell Irene he was sorry for being rude, took his hand again, firmly this time, and headed for Mary Florence's room. On the way there I explained to Jakie why he couldn't ask a lady why she has a mustache. That it was rude.

"But why, Grandma? She does have a mustache and yellow teeth too, but I didn't say anything about her teeth. My Mamie Titia has yellow teeth. Why aren't your teeth yellow, Grandma? You are pretty old. Mamie says hers are yellow because she's old."

I thanked my lucky stars that he hadn't mentioned the teeth, wondered if bringing him was such a good idea, but then realized he needed to learn how to get along with people of all generations.

We reached Mary Florence's apartment and knocked on the door, but no one was there, so we tried Anna Jean's, but they weren't there either.

I remembered Mary Florence liked to be outside. Jakie and I went out to the back patio and there among the potted plants stood Mary Florence, watering the plants while Anna Jean sat on the wicker chaise lounge chattering away to her friend. The watering can sat securely on the tray of Mary Florence's walker as she moved about the patio. I decided to bring another plant the next time I worked. Jakie could help me pick one out!

Anna Jean spotted me first. "Hi Marjie, who is that you've got there?"

Introductions were made. Jakie being the object of hugs, kisses and so much love from the two ladies. Jakie mainly kept his mouth closed except when spoken to, which made a huge impression on Mary Florence and Anna Jean.

I reminded them that I was going on vacation. I told them about our upcoming trip to Lake Doniphan and that I would be back at work the following week.

We didn't stay long, as we still needed to pack. I'm sure that night at supper Mary Florence and Anna Jean heard a totally different version of my grandson's manners from Irene, Mildred and Eugene, but I am glad he made a good impression on my special friends.

I awoke raring to go as a teenager. Every summer since I was a child our family attended Reunion, the church name for a family camp. It was a week of reconnecting with friends we only saw at Doniphan, or at Mission Center or World Conferences. It was a week of fun in the sun (or rain), of nature walks, fishing and canoeing. The food was pretty good too. In years past families signed up to cook the meals, but now

Doniphan hired paid cooks. The campers still helped with getting drinks, serving the food and cleaning the tables, but many missed the camaraderie of working in the kitchen together, cooking, doing the dishes, laughing, sharing. The laughing and sharing wasn't missing, we could do that anywhere, but there was something about working together that brought everyone closer, that was what we missed.

"C'mon Tina, Henri. Let's get loaded up. Jakie's so excited," I yelled, but I believe I was even more enthusiastic than he was.

Tina and Henri drug their suitcase out to the car. Henri opened the trunk and put it in along with Jakie's duffel bag and my suitcase that I had set next to the car in the driveway. I made sure everyone had a water bottle, filled with distilled water from the three-gallon jug that sat on its stand in the kitchen. I never buy individual bottles of water, that wouldn't be good for the planet. I also bought gallon jugs from the water store and refilled them each week.

We climbed into the car, fastened seat belts and off we went.

I started singing, "On the road again…" Tina joined me with "just can't wait to get back on the road again." Henri and Jakie joined in as we headed out to pick up Mom.

Mom was ready when we arrived at her condo. The trunk was pretty full, but Henri managed to wedge his grandmother-in-law's case in. Soon we were on our way to Lake Doniphan which is a few miles outside Excelsior Springs, Missouri.

When his great-grandma got in the car and we drove off again, Jakie started the singing… "On the road again…"

We all laughed and joined in. On the forty-five-minute trip to the reunion grounds we sang every camp song Tina and I could remember, including *Poor Little Bug on the Wall* in every version ever concocted— robot, underwater, operatic, typewriter—you name it.

When I turned down the gravel lane leading to the camp, joy filled my heart. I said, "How wonderful to share this experience with our family of four generations."

My heart was in my throat; happiness tears ran down my cheeks.

I drove on down the lane and Jakie saw the lake.

He was so eager, calling, "Grandma, can I go fishing?"

"We'll have to check the schedule, Jakie, but as soon as we can, we'll fish." I assured him.

I had registered early so we would be staying in the main lodge. I pulled the Toyota around to the front entrance. There was a line of cars ahead of me, so I asked my family if they wanted to get out and start looking around.

Then I changed my mind. "Oh, Henri, can you stay with me, so you can help me unload?"

Of course, obliging Henri said 'yes.'

Mom, Tina and Jakie got out and went to check-in. Soon they were back with two manila envelopes—one for Mom and me and one for Tina, Henri and Jakie.

The envelope included our room assignments, name tags and the schedule for each day. Soon our car found its way to the front of the line and we unloaded. With five of us unloading took only minutes. Henri went to park the car in the upper parking lot.

Rob and Eileen fairly ran out the door as Henri pulled away. They hugged Tina and Jakie profusely. Then Rob stepped in it. "Where is your master going?" he asked Tina.

"My MASTER, what the hell. Okay, Mom I see your glare of concern for my little son's ears, I mean, what the heck are you talking about Rob? Henri is my husband, not my master!"

Eileen and I exchanged looks. Rob had stuck his foot in it again.

Eileen got between Rob and Tina and speaking to Rob, said, "Honey, were you trying to say something in French that turned out to sound like Master?"

"Well, yes, I was trying to say the word that means *mister* in French. Had no idea that it was going to come out and sound like *Master*. I realize that no man would ever be, could ever be, in fact, no woman or child, or animal or something from the plant family could ever be, Tina's master, whew."

I felt Rob's embarrassment after his goof up. He loved Tina and I knew he was thrilled to see her after all these years. After all, not only had he practically helped raise her, well, that was an exaggeration, but he had watched her grow up at church and as a guest in his own home and he had been her high school math teacher. He was trying to impress her by using a French word. Whoops!

By then Henri was back. He took in the scene. Rob, red-faced, Eileen and me laughing, Tina, looking, well like Tina does whenever she feels like someone offends her, angry, Jakie and Mom looking uncomfortable, but starting to laugh. Henri stood there waiting for someone to say something, looking back and forth at all the players of the moment. He had missed something. That was certain.

Eileen began to explain to Henri, but Tina walked over to him and said, "Hey, Master, it's about time you got back here. You are missing all the fun."

Eileen, being Eileen, had to make sure that everyone was okay, said,

"Henri, Rob was trying to call you 'monsieur' and it came out 'master'. Everyone's okay now, right Tina?" and in a wifely tone to her husband, "Rob, stick with English. They both speak English."

"I know, I know. All things math," laughed Rob.

"All things math," agreed Eileen. "I love you, you Holy MacAnoli, you," Eileen said as she gave him a playful hug.

The Rob and Eileen self-appointed welcoming committee went on to inflict themselves on other unwary new arrivals, rather, to bestow their wonderful presence on expectant new arrivals.

My family and I carted our suitcases to our adjoining rooms which were on the upper level of the lodge located near the dining hall. Tina and I picked up towels and sheets from the table by the front door then went to make our beds. Jakie loved that we had adjoining rooms. He ran back and forth between the rooms, circling through the entry doors and the adjoining door. Soon I noticed another little boy following him, running behind Jakie, then a little girl joined in, soon there were four children running through the rooms, so I thought I should do something before someone got hurt. I grabbed Jakie as he ran by and all the other children stopped in a row behind him.

"Let's find your parents to see if you can go with us for a walk around the lake. We'll even go take a look at the swimming pool. What do you think?"

The kids scattered and soon were back with their parents. They were members of the Haven Heights congregation and I knew them by name and by sight, but had never put the faces and names together. Soon all the parents, another grandmother, the children, Mom and I began a hike around the lake.

♥

The next morning I sat on a bench by the lily pad-topped lake I had loved since childhood, enjoying the solitude and coolness of the early morning, praying for peace in the world, especially the Middle East and Afghanistan. Suddenly and very unexpectedly (since Tina was not usually an early riser), I was jolted out of my communion with my heavenly parent when Tina plopped down on the bench beside me and began to rail.

"Mother, I don't know why I let you talk us into coming here. I don't fit in. Everyone here is saccharine sweet, kind of like you, Mom. I'm grating, sarcastic and angry. I'm not ready to be around church people. I want to be able to be grouchy when I want to be grouchy."

I was hurt that Tina thought I was faking being sweet, like my cousins who gave me the name Marjie Goody-Two Shoes when we were little, but what concerned me more was Tina's well-being, so I said a silent prayer that I would say the right thing to Tina. It meant so much to Mom and me that we all have a good time at Reunion.

"Tina, I thought it would be a fun vacation. You and Henri can fish and swim and walk in the woods. You don't have to cook or even find a restaurant. No worries. Plus, Grandma wanted you to come so all four generations could be here together. She wanted to show you off. You can surely understand that. Why don't you and Henri go for a walk around the lake for a while?"

"Because, Mother, there are lily-white, sin-free church people walking around the lake. These people are abusive in their holiness. I don't feel comfortable here."

My face must have shown my disappointment.

Tina changed her tone. She quit whining and put on her sales pitch voice—the one she used as a teenager to talk me into whatever she wanted at the moment.

She put her arm around me. "And, Mommy, here's another reason that you will probably find more palatable. There is no privacy here at Lake Doniphan—nowhere to go to be by ourselves. Maybe you have forgotten. Henri and I have lived with his family since we got married. Now we're living with you. Just once I'd like to see what it feels like to spend some time alone together."

"Well, when you put it that way, I do understand and I have a great idea. Why don't you and Henri go back home and spend the week alone. Grandma and I will keep Jakie here. What do you think of that?"

"That might be okay, actually, but I was thinking of somewhere more romantic than Independence." Tina curled her long hair around her fingers and smiled at me.

"What are you saying—Independence not romantic? Well, Kansas City is right next door? Are you forgetting about the carriage rides around the Plaza and your beautiful Laura Ashley bedroom?" I laughed. "Where would you like to go instead?"

"I'd like to show Henri the Ozarks and check out some wineries. Show him the Missouri lavender fields. Maybe we could find a little cabin, hopefully rather isolated—rent a motorboat when we want to get out a bit," Tina grinned the grin that never failed.

"Is that okay, Mom? I'm sorry to be such a grouch, but this reunion was really a bad idea. I don't want to hurt Grandma's feelings, or yours, for that matter, but I'll make it up to you somehow. Maybe we can take a little family trip and stay in a bed and breakfast in a little town somewhere, but for now I want to escape this den of holiness and be alone with my husband. I'll talk to Henri and see if he wants to go away with his sexy bride." Tina pulled in her stomach and pushed out her ample chest and winked at me.

"What do you think he'll say? What if he doesn't want to go with me?" She went from sexy to crushed in one nanosecond.

She went on. "He's already signed up to help with the fishing derby and the croquet games and who knows what else. He seems to be having a wonderful time. He's so much like Dad, not in looks, of course, but in energy and his love of people. I'm really lucky to have lured him into my web, aren't I, Mom? Maybe he would have more fun here that alone with me."

Tina, being Tina, was up one minute and down the next. I smoothed my daughter's unruly thick and fiery red hair.

"Tina, Tina, Tina. You are lovely. You are fun and you are sexy. I'm sure Henri will want to go away with you. He loves you so much. I see it in his eyes every time he looks at you. He always does everything he can to make you happy. I'm sure you know that."

Tina and I got off the bench and headed back to the lodge to find Henri, Jakie and Mom. We found them in line waiting for breakfast. The gathered Saints made room for Tina and me so we could join our family.

Tina smiled at me and whispered, "See how sweet these people are? They don't even ask us to go to the back of the line. I'm not used to this goody-goody treatment."

I whispered back, "You should be use to people treating you wonderfully. You've been treated that way all your life."

Tina laughed and said out loud, "Henri, we're not in France anymore."

Henri had no idea what Tina was talking about but smiled at her and took her hand and kissed it.

The crowd around us said, "OO LA LA" and then everyone shushed as the blessing over the food was given.

While we were eating Jakie said, "What does OO LA LA" mean?"

Tina, Henri and I looked at each other. Tina looked Jakie in the eyes and said, "It means Papa and I love each other."

That satisfied him and I breathed a sigh of relief.

After breakfast Tina got Henri alone and he agreed to go to the Ozarks with her. His only request was that they leave after the fishing derby which was to be held that morning from ten o'clock to noon. He had already promised to help some of the little ones bait their hooks and take any caught fish off, measure and record the lengths, and throw the fish back in the lake.

Jakie was hot to trot for the derby. He didn't remember ever going fishing before. His parents assured him that they had taken him when he was two, but he didn't remember, so as far as he was concerned this was his first time. Tina understood Jakie's enthusiasm and agreed to wait to leave after the fishing contest. This turned out to be a very good thing because Jakie actually won the derby and received a nice trophy for his efforts. Mom and I took lots of pictures of him and the fish, which measured fourteen inches. At first, Jakie was upset that his fish had to be released back to the lake. It was his fish. He wanted to take it home and put in it a tank in his room, but we grownups prevailed, explaining that he could come out to the lake every day that week and talk to his fish and his fish would die if he tried to take him home. He needed lots of water and other fish friends to live a long and happy life. Jakie named him Derby Boy and helped his father gently put him back into the water. He promised to visit Derby Boy every year while he lived in Missouri.

The word got out that Tina and Henri planned to leave for a rendezvous in the Ozarks. One of the young men who knew Tina from Zion's League offered to let them use his laptop to find and make reservations somewhere. But Eileen and Rob suggested their family cabin, adding that they would take Mom, Jakie and me back to Independence after Reunion. I agreed to let Tina and Henri take my car. Everything fell into place. Tina and Henri jumped at the offer.

Tina had spent many summers at the McNamara cabin. She gushed her thanks to Rob and Eileen, then described it to Henri. "It's a nice-sized cabin with huge picture windows to enjoy scenic views of the lake. There is also a stone fireplace, wood floors and cathedral ceilings. Henri, you'll love it. So rustic."

Tina and Henri packed up their stuff while Rob sketched a map and penciled the route. Eileen said they would need to stop in Osage Beach to pick up some groceries, so Rob added directions for that.

A send-off committee escorted Tina and Henri to my car. Someone had written in shaving cream on the windows, *Honeymoon bound* and *Ozarks or bust*. There were tin cans strung from the bumper of my Camry.

Jakie grabbed his father's hand, "I'll miss you, Papa." He wrapped his small arms around his mother. "Go have fun with Papa. OO LA LA!"

Everyone in the send-off committee echoed, "OO LA LA!"

Tina hugged Jakie, her grandmother and me, then Rob and Eileen, then Jakie again. Henri hugged everyone, too. Then he swept Tina up in his arms and placed her in the driver's seat, letting everyone know that he didn't mind being the navigator for the first leg of the trip. *"Au revoir et je vous remercie tous les.* Thank you all."

Henri yelled to me, "We'll get the car washed in Excelsior Springs, Mère Marjie."

Tina stuck her head all the way out of the car window, getting shaving cream on the side of her hair, "Thank you everyone. I hope you understand why we are leaving."

To this Rob yelled, "Yeah, you love birds want to be alone. We get it—have a good time!"

Eileen added, "Don't forget the sunscreen. We love you!"

The send-off committee and I waved and watched as Tina and Henri pulled out of the parking lot, wipers spewing shaving cream all over the car.

Mom, Jakie and I followed the rest of the well-wishers into the lodge. It was lunchtime and our tummies were rumbling.

The rest of the week was eventful—swimming, canoeing, campfires, craft classes, preaching services and study sessions. Jakie kept me running from one thing to another. Luckily classes were provided for the children for two hours each day so I got a break during his class times. I usually found Mom visiting with friends in a sewing circle in the gathering room of the main lodge. I didn't have any handwork to work on so I relaxed and enjoyed the conversations.

On Wednesday, half-way through the week-long retreat, I took my camera, the old Minolta 35 millimeter that still required manual focusing, and took close-ups of Mom and the other ladies gathered in the sewing circle. I tried to catch them unaware, intending to get as many candid shots as possible, but most of them stopped what they were doing when as I focused in on their lovely faces, lined and care-worn most of them, but some of the girls in their thirties and forties enjoyed the circle as much as the older ladies did, so I photographed them as well. Eileen's girls were there: Meg, Jo, Amy and Beth, the daughters she so graciously shared with me over the years, as I shared Tina with her. I planned to make a little book for each lady I photographed. When it was time for this session to end so everyone could get refreshed for the evening meal, I took a group shot. Eileen asked me to give her the camera so she could take one with me in it. I jumped at the opportunity to be included.

As I walked up the hill to Jakie's classroom I wished Tina and Henri had stayed. They would have enjoyed it if Tina weren't so stubborn. I do understand their need—at least Tina's need to be away. I knew that Lake Doniphan reminded Tina of her girlhood and all the summer reunions spent here with her dad. I missed Jake, too, surely more than Tina missed him, but I was certain that Jake was with his heavenly Father and I feared that Tina did not share that certainty. I'll have to put her in the Lord's hands. I can't make her believe as I do.

♥

Saturday came and it was time to pack up for home. Mom, Jakie and I said goodbye to our friends and got into Rob and Eileen's van.

As we drove by the lake Jakie yelled, "Stop, Grandma, make Rob stop! I have to say goodbye to Derby Boy!"

Rob pulled over to the side as far as he could on the one lane road. Jakie jumped out and ran over to bid adieu to his friend the fish. He climbed back into the car and fastened his seatbelt. "Okay, Grandma, let's go home. Can we stop at McDonald's on the way? I'm hungry."

We had eaten breakfast so I didn't want to ask Rob and Eileen to stop. It was only a forty-five-minute drive home, but I also didn't want to listen to Jakie's pleas all the way, so we stopped at McDonald's for a drink and a cookie. Rob confessed that he wanted a cookie, too. He's such a wonderful friend.

We sat down at a table to split the cookies between us, when Mom asked, "Where are Tina and Henri? Why didn't they come with us?"

My stomach tightened, but I calmly, I think, answered, "They are at the Ozarks at Eileen and Rob's cabin. Remember, we all went up to Reunion together, but Tina wanted to get away with Henri to be alone, so they left and went to the Ozarks on Monday. Are you okay, Mom?"

"I think I'm okay, now I remember them leaving, but did we just come from Doniphan? I don't remember leaving there." She looked around, her face showing confusion. "I believe we are at a McDonald's now. Which one? Exactly where are we? This doesn't look like the McDonald's on Noland Road or the one on 40 Hiway by Costco. I feel kind of funny, not sick, but somewhat dizzy and I don't remember leaving camp. Also my vision is kind of blurry—a little doubled."

"We are still in Excelsior Springs, Mom. Let's take our cookies and go," I said. "I'm going to ask where the closest hospital is. You all please wait here one minute while I find out where the hospital is."

I felt scared, but knew that Mom needed to be seen by a doctor—the sooner the better. We got directions and Rob drove to the Excelsior Springs Medical Center and parked in the Emergency Room lot.

Mom argued with us, wanting to go to see her own doctor and not wanting to bother Rob and Eileen any more than we already had.

"Mom, it's Saturday and your doctor won't be available until Monday. This can't wait. Hopefully, a doctor will see you right away." My mother can be stubborn when she wants to be.

We checked in with the triage nurse and sat down to wait. While we waited, I asked Mom if we could pray. Given the okay, I held hands with her and so did Jakie. Rob and Eileen each put their hands on Mom's head.

I prayed the doctors would know what to do and that Mom would be blessed. No sooner had I finished the short prayer than a nurse called Mom's name. She and I went to give the nurse information regarding the medical problem and hand over insurance cards. Mom was covered by Medicare and a secondary benefit company through AARP. When the nurse discovered that the patient was eighty years old, she said, "I'm going to fast-track you. The doctor will see you asap."

After taking care of the paper work, Mom was taken back to a room. The nurse kindly let me keep Jakie with us while Rob and Eileen stayed in the waiting room. We waited about twenty minutes for the doctor, giving Mom time to change into a hospital gown. Jakie and I stepped out for a few minutes while she changed.

This was really a nice hospital, even the emergency room had a private bathroom, so convenient and novel an experience that Jakie felt compelled to check it out, which he did, several times. I was grateful I didn't have to leave Mom alone to take Jakie to the bathroom.

When the doctor came in he asked more questions. He was pretty certain that the culprit was a clot that had travelled to the brain and only momentarily blocked the blood supply to part of the brain. He called it a transient ischemic attack or TIA, the most common type of stroke.

"This TIA," he said, "is like a mini-stroke. There shouldn't be any permanent damage, but you should take this as a warning. These are caused by a buildup of cholesterol—fatty deposits called plaques. Let's get some blood and check your cholesterol. Have you or anyone in your family ever had a stroke?"

I knew Mom was very tired. She couldn't remember anyone having a stroke. Cancer had taken her father, brother and sister. Her mother died from a ruptured brain aneurysm.

I sensed that Mom was too tired to answer. I told the doctor the family history I was aware of.

The doctor wanted to order a CT scan of Mom's head. He told us that he might be able to detect narrowing or clotting of the carotid arteries by seeing a 3-D of her brain.

Mom wanted to go home. "Doctor, I appreciate all that you've done, but I have decided to go home and rest up until Monday. I'll go to see my own doctor as soon as I can get an appointment."

"Uh, Mrs. Lord, we at least need to do a blood test. Your blood pressure seems to be fine now, but I really think we should run some preliminary tests and keep you here tonight.  A TIA is a warning not to be taken lightly." I could tell he was concerned, but my mother can be very hard-headed, especially about her health.

"I believe you, doctor, but I feel fine now. If anything happens, I can call 911 and get to the hospital in Independence. I live really close to Centerpoint." She crossed her arms over her chest and stared right in the blue eyes of the young doctor.

"Okay, Mrs. Lord, if you insist, but I don't want you to be alone. Will you have someone to stay with you?"

I assured him that I would not leave her alone until her doctor felt comfortable that she would be all right. We would make an appointment first thing Monday morning and call 911 if any more stroke symptoms appeared.

I couldn't argue with Mom's logic. She was doing fine now, except for the fatigue, there was no droopiness or any other effects from the probable TIA. The McNamara's would drop us at Mom's home. Jakie and I would stay there with her. We could sleep in the guest room, where Mom had put twin beds, very intuitive of her. I knew she would rest more comfortably in her own bed than at my house so I didn't suggest it. Luckily, we still had clean clothes and I had all my other necessities, such as deodorant and skin cream.

It was like we were on the same wave-length—Mom said, "I don't want to go to your house, I want my own bed. I'll sleep so much better there. You and Jakie can have my guest room."

Jakie was so good through the wait at the hospital and the ride back to his great-grandmother's house. I had brought some books and puzzles for him to read and play with at Reunion. I also had a package of raisins and some nuts that kept him from claiming starvation.

It was about three in the afternoon when Rob and Eileen dropped us at Mom's condo. Eileen was concerned because we wouldn't have a car, so she decided to bring her car over for us to use if we needed it.

I got Mom settled and comfortable then made Jakie a quick peanut butter and jelly sandwich and some Campbell's chicken noodle soup. Mom and I ate crackers and cheese and finished off the soup. We drank milk, ours white, Jakie's—chocolate.

After the small meal Mom napped in her room. Jakie and I drew pictures.

I knew I needed to try to contact Tina, but I wanted to keep Jakie busy while I called her. I found some old *Better Homes and Gardens* magazines Mom had in her recycling bin that he could tear up and make a collage on some construction paper. I put an old plastic tablecloth on the kitchen table, gave him the glue and let him have at it.

I called Tina's cell phone, but got no answer. I left a message on her voice mail, not knowing if they had reception at the cabin. I called Eileen and found out that there weren't any towers close by. Eileen reminded me Tina and Henri were planning to be back in Independence tomorrow. She assured me that Tina would have reception when they reached the highway. Eileen had already called the prayer chain for Mom. Before we hung up Eileen and I prayed together over the phone.

Al called to see how my week went. I told him about Mom. His concern seemed genuine. He said he was leaving town for a while to take care of business in California, but would keep in touch.

♥

I was dreaming. I wasn't sure where I was, but when I heard my cell phone ringing, I sat straight up and recognized Mom's guest room. I saw Jakie asleep on the matching twin bed on the other side of the nightstand. I picked up my flip phone, opened it, relieved to hear Tina's voice.

"Mom," Tina said, "We got your message and we're on our way back to the cabin to pack and come on home. I'm so scared about Grandma. Is she all right?"

"She's doing fine. What do you mean you are on your way back to the cabin? Where are you and where have you been? You don't need to come back tonight. It's one o'clock in the morning! Why don't you wait until daylight? I don't want you two having an accident driving those winding Ozark roads in the dark." My imagination ran wild. Why were they up so late? Were they okay?

"We'll be fine. We went out to get a couple of drinks in Osage Beach, met some really great people. It was a hoot! Can't wait to tell you about them. I checked to see if my phone would work and it did. Got your message. We miss you and Jakie and want to see Grandma."

Tina's speech was a little slurred and if Henri had been drinking too, I definitely did not want them driving the four-hour trip tonight.

"If you leave now, Grandma, Jakie and I won't be awake when you get back. Get some sleep. Come back tomorrow when you are fresh. I don't need to worry about you driving unfamiliar roads when you have been drinking."

"Oh, Henri, only had two drinks. He's fine to drive. He's driving now, but maybe it would be better if we came in the morning."

"What do you think, Henri?" I heard Tina ask.

"Mom, Henri says to tell you we're praying for Grandma and we will leave early in the morning. At first light. Be home around nine or ten. I'll call you when we are on the road. Okay."

"Sounds good, Honey. I can't wait to see you. Grandma's doing fine. She had a little mini-stroke, a TIA. It's a warning and I'm taking her to her own doctor on Monday. We'll see what he has to say. Jakie has been a champ through all this. He's sleeping quietly now. We'll see you tomorrow. Don't know if we'll go to church or not. Depends on Grandma. Call me when you get on the road in the morning. Be safe. Love you, Sweetheart. Love, Henri, too."

"Love you back, Mom. See you in the morning."

We hung up. I laid my head back on the pillow and soon was back to sleep—exhaustion enveloping me.

Tina and Henri arrived at Mom's this morning without episode. They took Jakie home and I stayed with Mom.

That night I lay in bed praying. *Lord, thank you so much. Mom seems her old self today. A little tired, but that is to be expected.*

## *Chapter Eleven*

Mom's doctor gave her a thorough check-up including all the tests the doctor in Excelsior Springs wanted done. He found no trace of the TIA. We went out to lunch to celebrate. After we ordered I checked my calendar and found that I had a hair appointment tomorrow. I didn't want to leave Mom yet and she needed her hair done, too. So I made the call.

"Hello, Suzie, how are you doing? Are you busy? I know I have an appointment tomorrow, but I was wondering if you could fit my mother in, too. Yes, her regular stylist quit on her and she's looking for someone new. Right, I know you usually are scheduled pretty tightly, but thought I'd ask. Mom had a mini-stroke a few days ago. She was supposed to have her hair done yesterday, but her Lulu quit. Sure, I guess she could go to Jolene. I'd much rather you do it, but Jolene will be okay. See you at nine o'clock."

Jolene is good with hair, better than Suzie, but unpredictable in attitude and always interesting.

Hanging up the phone, I smelled the aroma—Kona, I guessed. Wonderful, Mom is up and has made coffee. She must be feeling good today.

I dressed, praying all the while for everyone on my prayer list, my special prayer group friends, but especially concentrating on Mom, Tina and Henri, Jakie, Beth and Jerry.

I decided not to prepare Mom for her upcoming experience with Jolene. After all, maybe Jolene would act fairly normal today. I've seen miracles before.

When we entered the shop, Suzie looked up from the head of the person whose hair she was cutting and said, "Hi, I'm Suzie. You must be Marjie's mother."

I introduced Mom to Suzie and looked around but saw no sign of Jolene. "Where's Jolene?" I  asked.

"She's in the back reading a book," Suzie pointed with her thumb. Then she hollered, "Jolene, your nine o'clock is here."

I stood stock still as Jolene rounded the corner, hair all one color, a natural brown, cut in a cute short conservative style. She looked wonderful, what's the word—wholesome. Pleased to see the changes in Jolene, I introduced her to Mom. Jolene escorted Mom to her chair, talking in muted tones.

Soon it was my turn in Suzie's chair. I relaxed, hearing nothing but friendly, normal conversation between my mother and Jolene. They were talking about books. Will wonders never cease?

♥

After lunch and the Prayer for Peace, I needed to get back to work. I asked Mom if she wanted to go to Bingham Manor with me. She did. Mom met Mary Florence the night we went to the opera, but she had never met the other residents.

In the back of my mind and maybe Mom's, although neither of us mentioned it to the other, was the possibility that Mom could look the place over to see if she might be interested in living there someday. Not now, of course, she was getting along very well living alone in her condo, but the TIA had scared both of us a bit, so this seemed to be a perfect time to check the place out.

We arrived before the afternoon sing-a-long, so glad that Helen agreed to take over a few of my duties so I could work part time for the summer, at least. I was delighted to see many of the residents sitting in a circle, some in wheel chairs and some in dining room chairs, in the Main Floor Recreation Hall, happily awaiting, for most, and impatiently waiting for some, the arrival of the song leaders and the piano player. I introduced Mom to Anna Jean and Eugene first, noticing that Mildred sat on the other side of the room with Jack. I took Mom over to meet Mary Florence, who welcomed Mom warmly and we took our seats just as the singing group arrived. Today was a special treat. It was a quartet that volunteered their time going around to various assisted living and nursing homes to involve the residents in an hour of music and fun. They wore matching vests, deep purple in color with gold lamé lapels, over lavender shirts and matching gold lamé trousers.  They passed out songbooks to each resident, introduced themselves and the piano player and asked each resident and guest to introduce themselves one at a time and select a song from the songbook. There were about thirty people in the circle and each song took about two minutes, so it should have lasted about an hour, but they forgot to figure in the time for introductions and song decisions, so the song fest lasted over ninety minutes. That was fine for many of the residents, but not for all. Some were sticklers for time and when the hour was up, they left the circle and went back to their rooms or to the TV room or wherever.

It was interesting to watch the demeanor of the residents. Some who would never speak to me sang up a storm, one pretended he was an orchestra conductor, standing in the middle of the circle waving his arms around. He reminded me of Leonard Bernstein, but he couldn't have been as Mr. Bernstein had been gone for at least twenty years. The event was so stimulating. We sang songs from the 1940's, including *Bewitched, Bothered and Bewildered* and *I Could Write a Book* by Rogers and Hart; *Day by Day* by Sammy Cahn; *I Don't Want to Walk Without You* by Loesser and Styne and so many others.

I couldn't imagine a better time to bring Mom to visit, even though, technically, we weren't visiting with the residents, but Mom loved music and singing the old songs. After all, she taught music at an elementary school for many years.

After the song fest, we went to Mary Florence's room. Anna Jean joined us to get better acquainted with Mom, who had become so popular with the men during the singing, even Eugene couldn't keep his eyes off her. Anna Jean liked to know her competition. Mom charmed her as well and since she was visiting for the day only, Anna Jean forgave her for being so attractive. "I can sure see where Marjie gets her good looks," she told Mom. I heard the compliment and gave Anna Jean a big hug.

After a wonderful day with Mom she convinced me that she could live alone again. She knew how to call 911, she said, so I moved back home. I entered my house to a grumbling duet. Tina and Henri were grousing about something.

Tina greeted me as I dropped my purse on the hall table. "Mom, Melanie called. The repairs to the plumbing aren't done, the tile hasn't come in yet and the painters are only half finished. They need another month to get things ready for us. She wants to meet with us today to sign an amended lease."

We went to the Square. After we met with Melanie, Henri was happy. They would have another month to relax a little and work on some more entrees and appetizers for the café. Tina was impatient and wanted to get the business going. I remained silent, trying to think of something to say and failing. We arrived home and sat down on the porch. Suddenly I thought of something to say. I assured them that everything would work for the best, saying, "God is in control."

Tina said, "Mom, if you say that one more time. I'm going to gag."

My first impulse was to say, *then gag away. I will probably say it again*, but I stopped myself. I took a breath, looked at my daughter, walked over to her and hugged her. We both laughed. Maybe I do need to be more careful around Tina. I don't want to totally turn her away from God. I need to let the Spirit work with her since everything I say seems to be wrong.

After dinner that night I thought of something that Al said. He reminded me that Tina and Henri needed a business license, including a liquor license from the city. He offered to help them with the paperwork if they needed it. I sought Tina and Henri in the den and told them what he said.

Tina seemed offended. "I think Henri and I can figure out how to fill out forms for the city," she said. "Who does he think we are, morons?"

I walked out of the room, grabbed the doorsill and peeked around the corner, "Better go to city hall tomorrow, Kids." I didn't wait for any of Tina's sharp-tongued remarks. I went to find Jakie to teach him some songs from the Forties.

♥

After church, Jakie and I went home to change for the Fourth of July festivities. My friends, Bob and Jeanine Freeman had invited us over for a picnic and fireworks display to celebrate. Bob was a former fireman friend of Jake's. They lived in Buckner on fourteen acres. Henri and Jakie wanted to add to the stash that the Freemans had, so yesterday Henri and Jakie had gone to the fireworks tent. Jakie picked out sparklers, snakes and ladyfingers. Henri chose Roman candles, cones and cakes.

I was afraid of fireworks, like my mother, who refused to attend any fireworks demonstration, especially homemade ones, but Jake always talked me in to spending Independence Day with his firefighter friends. He would always say, *"Who better than firemen to be around when people are blowing thing up?"* Tina wanted to go to Buckner where all her childhood memories of the Fourth of July rested, hoping that these memories would help her keep her father alive.

Tina and Henri had the picnic basket and the cooler full of Tina's goodies: tarts, blueberry and lemon, pear and almond and a strawberry-rhubarb pie. Henri squeezed oodles of lemons and limes to add to the watermelon puree, making his special watermelon lemonade. I couldn't wait to try it, so he filled a small juice glass with ice, turned the tap on the jug and handed me a glass. It was wonderful. We loaded up the car, driving U.S. 24 Highway out to Buckner. It was less than thirty minutes to the Freeman's farm.

Today was also Henri's birthday. He was eager to celebrate his birthday with fireworks, especially now that he had chosen to live in America, at least for the foreseeable future. I was thankful to Henri for bringing Tina back to me, thankful to have my family close to me. I wondered if the French used fireworks. I had never thought about it, so I asked Henri as we drove along. He told me that the people of his country used fireworks to celebrate La Fête Nationale on the Fourteenth of July.

He said, "You Americans think of it as Bastille Day. It commemorates the storming of the Bastille on July 14, 1789. You should come to Paris someday to see the largest military parade in all of Europe."

"Oh, yes, Grandma," cried Jakie, "We should all go to Paris for La Fête Nationale. We went last year; it was so awesome! Can we go this year, Papa?"

"My son, we got here only a month ago. We can't fly back and forth for parades," Henri responded.

"Ahhh, darn."

Luckily Jakie found lots of children to play with at the Farm, shooting off firecrackers and lighting snakes, under total Grandma supervision, of course.

It wasn't really a farm, but the Freemans had both been raised in the city, so it felt like a farm to them. They had a small vegetable garden, but mostly flowers and greenery planted everywhere. Jeanine, Bob's wife, was a master gardener and the property showed it. Their water gardens had been on the national tour for several years. There were stone bridges, waterfalls, fountainscapes and ecosystem ponds—the ponds a virtual fairyland of lily pads, butterfly ferns, water hyacinths, fairy moss and water lettuce.

After all the hot dogs, hamburgers, watermelon, and Tina's luscious desserts were eaten, darkness fell. Parents and grandparents gathered their children onto blankets. The firemen, with the addition of a French chef, began to light the fireworks, lighting the starlit sky with vivid pinks and purples, red and blue and white, casting reflections over the water gardens and a spell on the happy crowd of onlookers celebrating

Independence Day, more than two hundred and thirty years after the Declaration of Independence and the bloody war fought to free this nation from the British.

Tina, Henri, Jakie and I went home contented that night. Jakie fell asleep in the car on the way home. His dad carried him to his secure bed in his new house in America. It is a new house for Jakie, a familiar and welcoming home for Tina, and a comfortable and happy one for me, with memories of my Jake, a home now more precious because my family is here with me.

♥

It was hot. I fretted over what to wear to my high school librarian's party, trying on several outfits. I finally dug out a soft blue and white striped cotton dress with spaghetti straps and white sandals. Tina didn't like the summer dresses she had brought so she wore a pants suit that was a little snug on her, wishing she could just wear her usual shorts and a tee shirt. She complained all the way to the party. Henri and I ignored her complaints by singing songs with Jakie.

We arrived at the new senior living complex, Blue Ribbon Estates, following signs and balloons directing the way to the clubhouse where the Bryant party was being held. The road curved around the edges of the golf course but we finally made it.  By the time we arrived, Tina wanted to turn around and go home, but I gave her a look that silenced her, adding, "Tina, I haven't seen these people since your father's funeral. I would like to spend a little time here. If you are so uncomfortable why don't you run back home and change?"

"Sure you don't mind. I'm sorry I put this wretched thing on." She looked down at her mustard yellow pants suit in dismay. "I'll be back in a flash. Henri, coming with?"

Henri looked around the festooned patio and inside the clubhouse, seeing tables filled with fresh fruits and vegetables, a bar with iced drinks, punches and teas, a gorgeous cake, people laughing and joking.

"I'll stay here with Mère Marjie and Jakie, my little coquette." Henri smiled and kissed his petulant wife on the cheek.

I watched Tina tromp off to the car and sighed. I turned to find Mark and there he was. He bear-hugged me and held me tight for a few seconds. Our eyes locked, he picked me up and whirled me around a few times before letting me go.

"Marjie Pargie. You came! Mother will be so glad to see you."

As soon as I regained my balance, but not fully my composure, I looked around to find Henri and Jakie so I could introduce them, but they were nowhere to be seen, so I took Mark's offered arm and went to greet his mother.

Rosalie Bryant sat in the chair of honor, with her family standing next to her. She was dressed in a lovely peach colored short-sleeved suit, with a calf-length skirt. I reminisced at seeing her twinkling blue-green eyes, remembering how much fun she was. Mrs. Bryant was the cool librarian at William Chrisman High. She made everyone feel they were the most important person on earth. She was a great role model, especially for us girls. She sponsored a book club that met every two weeks and always recommended books that I loved. I remembered the lively discussions she facilitated lasting for hours.

Mrs. Bryant looked up and seeing me on Mark's arm, let out a squeal of delight. "Oh Marjie, I haven't seen you in such a long time. How have you been?"

"I am good, fine, actually, wonderful, Mrs. Bryant. It is so good to see you looking well. I'm so glad that Mark invited me. I will introduce you to my son-in-law and grandson as soon as I find them. They seem to have wandered off somewhere. My daughter, Tina, will be glad to meet you as well. She'll be here soon. She remembers me talking about you and how you inspired me to go back to school. That talk you had with me about doing what I had wanted to do all my life finally sunk in."

Mrs. Bryant jumped up and hugged me, exclaiming, "You went back to school. Isn't that wonderful. Where are you going and what are you studying?"

"I'm attending UMKC, but have taken the summer off. I am majoring in English with an emphasis in literature. You know my love of reading. You certainly encouraged that when I was in high school. This summer I'm not taking any classes because my daughter and her family are living with me now, temporarily. They are opening a French restaurant on the Square. Tina and her husband and son have been living in France. My grandson is a Frenchman, but thank heaven he is bi-lingual or I wouldn't be able to talk to him. Henri also speaks excellent English. He was a foreign exchange student to the US when he was in high school and he lived in London for a while. Oh, here they are now, Henri and Jakie."

Henri practically ran into me. He looked distraught and there were tears in his eyes. He grabbed me and hugged me. Jakie stood there looking lost. Mark tried to talk to the little boy, but Jakie's eyes were glued to his father's face.

"Oh, Mère  Marjie, mon père est à l'article de la mort. I mean he is at death's door; close to death. I must go home now," cried Henri.

I was shaken, but knew I needed to be strong for Henri and Jakie.

I asked, "What happened. Your father was fine when you spoke to him last night, wasn't he? He had been working in the garden you said?"

"He had a heart attack. They don't expect him to live. We must go now! I need to make reservations. Where is Tina? I tried to call her, but she didn't answer."

I prayed silently and tried to keep my voice calm. "She should be back here by now. Did you try her cell phone?"

Henri was getting frantic. "I tried her cell and your home number, both." He was pacing and tearing his fingers through his hair.

Jakie, seeing his father so upset, stood stoically by his side, his face pale and drawn.

Thank Heaven for Mark. He heard everything that was going on. He guided Henri to a chair by his mother and drew Jakie and me close.

Mark's sister and her family scattered. His children that he hadn't even had a chance to introduce to us also left the immediate area so Henri could have some privacy. As soon as the five of us were gathered in a circle—Henri, Jakie, Mark, Mrs. Bryant, and me—I asked Henri if I could offer a short prayer before trying to call Tina again. Henri nodded his consent. We bowed our heads and I began to pray, hoping that my words would give Henri and Jakie some peace.

"Dear God in Heaven, merciful God, be with Henri's father and mother at this time. Send your angels to minister to them. We know that You can perform miracles of healing. We ask that of You right now. We ask You, Lord, to heal him in body and in spirit and to be with his loving family. We also know that your plan for him is best, so we ask that if it is your will to heal him, let it be so. In Jesus' holy name we pray. Amen."

As we opened our eyes and looked up, Tina appeared. She smiled curiously, "What's up, Guys?"

We waited for Henri to speak. And so he did. "Tina, mon père is dying. We must go home now."

Tina was stricken. She collapsed against Henri.

I drug her aside for a minute. "Tina, you have got to be strong for Henri and Jakie right now. They need to believe that Gregoirie will recover. Give them that hope. If he doesn't you'll have to show strong faith that he is in Heaven, that he no longer suffers. Do you understand?"

Tina looked at me through tears. Didn't speak for once, merely nodded her head.

As Tina, Henri and Jakie headed for the car, I hugged Mrs. Bryant and Mark, "I'll see you soon. Sorry we have to leave this way."

I felt Mark's eyes watching me as I ran to catch up with my family.

❤

I picked Jakie up at Mom's where he stayed while I attended my prayer group. The phone rang as Jakie and I walked through our front door.

I answered, "Hello, Jamison Residence."

It was Mark. "Hi, Marjie. Have you heard anything about your son-in-law's father?"

"Not yet. I don't think Tina and Henri would have gotten to his hometown yet. I took them to the airport last night because Henri insisted, but there wasn't a flight to New York until this morning. They had to fly to Marseille and drive to the hospital in Nyons. They promised to call me as soon as they landed, so I guess they haven't made it that far yet. Jakie wanted to go with them, but we thought they could move faster without him."

"I'm sorry about Henri's father. I hope he will be okay." Mark said.

"Thank you, Mark. That means a lot."

Jakie ran up the stairs to his room to take the new coloring book and colors that his Great-Grandma Karin had given him.

"Marjie, I know this isn't the best of circumstances and kind of late notice, but I would like to invite you to dinner. How about tonight? I'm leaving for St. Paul in the morning."

I waited a moment, thinking about my fatigue, about Gregoirie, and my stomach issues. I knew I would be embarrassed if I had to spend a lot of time in the rest room, Mark and his family waiting while I sat on the pot. I should say no, but thought it would be fun to be with Mark...

As if in slow motion, I said, "Oh, Mark, I don't know. I've got Jakie here..."

Mark interrupted. "That's great! He'll love it. How about pizza at the old Fun House on 40 Highway? It's still there, isn't it? I'll bring my kids, too. It'll be like old times, only we're thirty or forty years older and we'll have kids in tow."

"Oh, I don't know, Mark. Jakie's a little out of sorts with his parents taking off so quickly."

I thought again...And pizza sometimes doesn't agree with me, but I wanted to go.

"Even better reason to take him to the Fun House. He can play games with my kids. They love little ones. I'll pick you up at six. Be ready."

I knew Mark was right—Jakie would have a ball playing the games and being the center of attention of older kids.

I laughed, "You always have been bossy and impetuous. Okay. We'll be ready."

"That's what the ladies love about me. See you soon, Marjie Parjie." Click.

I sat in stunned silence for a moment. That Mark! He always did talk everyone into doing what he wanted to do. I would like to meet his children. Maybe this will take Jakie's mind off his grandfather. I climbed the stairs to Jakie's room to tell him about our new adventure—pizza at the Fun House.

At six o'clock sharp the doorbell rang. Jakie raced to the door and recognizing Mark from the birthday party, unlocked the door and let him in. I was right behind him, hoping I looked okay, and not like I was trying to look girlish or anything, in pale pink wide-legged pants with matching shirt, baby pink roses embroidered across the bodice.

Mark eyes ran over me appreciatively. I blushed.

He whistled, then said, "Marjie, you look like you did when we went for pizza in high school."

I laughed, "Hardly, but thank you for making this old grandma feel younger anyway. You smooth talker, you."

We hugged—this time briefly. Mark escorted Jakie and me to his Buick Enclave. Luckily he owned a vehicle that seated eight people, because when his mother found out that he was taking me and the kids out for pizza, she wanted to go along.

As Mark and I stood at the counter placing our order, Mark held me by the waist, tightly. I felt a spark of heat go through me, so I pulled away in time to see his daughter, Greta, give me a disgusted look. Greta rolled her eyes and walked back to the game center.

Everyone had different tastes it seemed. Jakie and Elsa both wanted Hawaiian, Mark's mother and I wanted plain cheese, Greta wanted pepperoni and Mark and Mark Jr. wanted any and all of it, but especially the barbeque chicken and supreme. There was a lot of back and forth about the bacon cheeseburger and barbeque chicken, but Mark finally decided. He was the one who couldn't make up his mind. He wanted to have what he used to eat in high school—supreme and meat-eaters, but had to try the barbecue chicken. After all, he stated for everyone to hear, "When in KC, do as the KCer's do—eat BBQ!"

Mark brought pitchers of coke, root beer and diet Dr. Pepper to the table where his mother and I sat on benches, carved benches that looked the same as they did when we were in high school. I asked him what was in the pitchers. When I found out everything was caffeinated, I asked him to get some water for me and Sprite for Jakie. I was a little embarrassed to send him back after he had already ordered, but he should have asked what I wanted.

Mark said, "I thought you'd be impressed that I remembered that you always drank coke, Dr. Pepper or root beer."

"I am impressed, but, Mark, that was over thirty years ago. Something happened to me when I turned fifty—if I drink caffeine after one p.m. I can't sleep and Jakie seems to have inherited this from me, poor boy."

"You know, Mark," said his mother, Rosalie, "I should probably stick with water myself."

"Wow, the ladies in my life are not only teetotalers, but tee-non-caffeiners. I'd better get the water and Sprite. I wouldn't want to cause either one of you, or Jakie either, a bad night's sleep. Good thing none of you are in the newspaper business."

As soon as Mark's name was called over the loudspeaker, he retrieved the pizzas while I went after the kids. Everyone left their games (as soon as they hit "game over"), except Greta who stared rudely at me and proceeded to put more tokens in the cash box.

What had I done to her? This was the first time we'd ever met.

Mark decided to leave Greta alone for a while. "She'll come over when she gets hungry," he said. But when almost all the pizza was gone, even Greta's special ordered pepperoni, he went to the game room to get her. He, his mother and I had been keeping an eye on Greta, making sure she was safe.

He came back and said Greta told him she didn't want any pizza or anything to drink. She wanted to go back to Grandma's and on home as soon as possible. She said missed her friends and her cats, Twinkybelle and Blinkybeau.

Thank heaven for Mark and Rosalie. It seemed so strange to call her that instead of Mrs. Bryant, but Rosalie insisted. They kept the conversation going all the way home. Poor Greta, I can understand that she has been through a lot, losing her mother, then having an immature step-mother. I learned this from Rosalie when we sat alone at the table while Mark and all the kids played video games.

Hopefully, Rosalie could reach Greta and make her understand that I was not a threat. I was not interested in marrying her father. I was just an old friend from high school and that was a long time ago. Then I remembered, our thirty-fifth reunion is coming up next year. I didn't want to think about it. Besides, wasn't I a college student? Well, maybe,

I thought, but I'm out for the summer and who knows if I'll be able to go next fall, with the restaurant and all, but I didn't mind. I would give up everything to have my family with me. I prayed that Tina and Henri will be home again soon.

*Lord, be with them and Henri's family.*

♥

Jakie bounded out of the car anxious to see Mary Florence. She had made a big impression on him, telling him stories about herself when she was a little girl. I reminded him to wait for me before walking across the parking lot, well, I walked. Jakie marched.

When we got to the entrance, I handed Jakie my key card. He reached up and barely managed to swipe it in front of the keypad. I had spoken to Mary Florence ahead of time and found out that Adelaide would be visiting this morning. Adelaide was already there when we arrived.

"Hello, young MAN," said Adelaide, "I know your grandmother calls you 'JAKIE', but what is your GIVEN name?"

Jakie stared in awe of the strange looking woman, who towered above him. She also towered above me and way above Anna Jean and Mary Florence, who were so short for grown-ups.

He pulled me aside.

"Look, Grandma, that woman is taller than my papa! She reminds me of the vulture in a Disney movie, The Jungle Book. Remember, there are four vultures, and she reminds me of Flaps the blond vulture. Her hair is golden blond, like Flaps."

He hushed his voice to a whisper. "She looks funnier than anyone I've ever seen. Her dress has a big white collar, like Flap's feathers, and a gray dress with huge black sleeves that wave in the wind as she struts around and moves her arms up and down, up and down."

Adelaide cackled at us. "Marjie, bring THAT BOY over here and make it SNAPPY."

Jakie couldn't contain himself, "You look like Flaps and you sound like Flaps."

"Well, I have no idea who this Flaps is, but she must be GORGEOUS if she looks like me," she cackled again. "You still didn't tell me your given name, Sonny, WHAT is it?"

By now, Jakie seemed curiously attracted to what apparently seemed to him like an old hag of a woman that looked like a vulture from The Jungle Book, so he smiled at her, then looking at me, said,

"Grandma, what is my given name and what is a given name anyway."

"Your given name is your first name, Jacob. Your middle name is Gregoirie, and your last name or your family name is Deschamps," I answered.

"Oh, THAT given name" said Jakie, laughing, "I thought it was a name I never heard of. I know all those names. I was named after Grandpa Jake and Papi Gregoirie"

"So who is this 'FLAPS' that I look like? Dare I ask?" said Adelaide as she swooped down with her huge sleeves and stuck her big red Flaps nose in Jakie's face.

"In my movie, The Jungle Book, Flaps and the other vultures kept Shere Khan away from Mowgli. They were good vultures."

" A VULTURE am I? So glad to be a GOOD vulture," cackled Adelaide, "if I have to BE a VULTURE. Heh, heh, heh."

Jakie went away charmed with his new friend Adelaide, who invited him to come to her house and it was the very house that President Truman lived in as a boy. He couldn't wait to tell his papa about meeting a girl Flaps. He hoped they could Skype today, but most of all he wished his Papi Gregoirie would get well and come to see him in America.

Mark called me when he got back to St. Paul. Jakie was down for the night and I was getting ready for bed. Our conversation seemed a little stilted, formal. He asked about Tina and her family. I asked about his mother and children. We didn't seem to have very much to say to each other. That was strange; Mark and I never had difficulty talking to each other. Guess we were both tired. I was unusually tired. I chalked it up to the strain of worrying about Tina and Gregoirie and his family. I prayed my thank you list and nodded off.

# CHAPTER TWELVE

The phone rang, waking me. I turned over and stretched my right arm to reach the phone, noticing the time on the digital clock, 11:22 p.m.

Tina sobbed on the line, "Mom, Gregoirie is dead. I can't believe that he is dead. They tried so hard to save him. That triple by-pass yesterday. Henri was certain his father would be all right. I even prayed, went to Mass with Henri's family. Why does God keep taking people from us, Mom? Gregoirie was like a father to me. Treated me like his daughter. I already lost one father and didn't need to lose another one."

In my sleepy state, I began to ramble. "Tina, I'm so sorry for your loss. I want to be there for you, to hug you. Do you want me to bring Jakie over there? Please tell Henri and his family how sorry I am. I'll pray that the Lord will give them peace. It will take a long time, though, Tina. I still miss your dad so much, but with time and the Lord, it is getting easier. I wish I could be there with you..."

Tina cut me off.

"No, stay there with Jakie. He doesn't need to be around this—this scene of death and despair and depression."

I heard sobbing, then she said quietly, tiredly, "Thanks, Mom. I wish you could be here, too, but I need to go now. Henri needs me. Please take good care of Jakie. Will you tell him about his *papi?*" Tina's voice broke into a wail.

What could I say from this distance to console her? "Of course I will, Honey. You and Henri hug each other for me. Maybe we can Skype tomorrow? I know Jakie wants to talk to you, see you."

I could still hear the anguish in her voice, but she brought herself under control enough to say, "Sure, I'll try to call you in the morning on Skype about eleven your time. Will that work?"

"That would be perfect. We'll talk to you and see you tomorrow.

Bye, Tina. I love you. Give my love to Henri. And please give my condolences to his family, especially to his mother."

"I'll tell them. Talk and see you tomorrow. *Au revoir*. Love you."

I felt myself grieving. I was grieving for the loss of Henri's father, but also the distance between Tina and me. I felt the need to lean on someone. I went to my computer to message Mark but he wasn't online. I typed a message to tell him about Gregoirie's death and then called Eileen.

♥

When I woke Wednesday morning, my first thoughts were of Tina and Henri and his family. I prayed for them and Mom and Jakie, then added my prayer group and the rest of the congregation and all the needs of the world, feeling overwhelmed, but the Spirit wrapped me with strength, so I thanked God and added, *Lord, please help me to be a blessing to others today.*

My next thoughts were of Mark and his family and then Al popped into my head. It's been a month since we went out to dinner. I wonder why he hasn't called. He said he would, especially since he knew about Mom's TIA.

The Skype call came at ten minutes after eleven. Jakie talked to his parents and Mamie Titia. They cried together,

I sat with him on my lap in the computer chair, hugging him close. He would miss his Papi Gregoirie. He begged Mamie Titia to come to America when his parents came home, then he wanted to know when his parents would be back. They were still unsure, but promised to talk to him every day until they were home.

Home—they do think of our house as home. That is very comforting, but am I being selfish? Henri's family home is their home, as well.

After the call, Jakie was still upset, missing his parents and his Deschamps family. I decided we needed a diversion. We would skip the Prayer for Peace at the Temple and go to a movie. I found the paper and discovered that *Toy Story 3* headed the playbill at the Pharaoh Theatre on the Square. We ate a quick lunch of fruit and chicken sandwiches and off we went to get reacquainted with Buzz Lightyear, Jakie's favorite, and Woody, his other favorite. In fact, Jakie liked all the characters. He had watched them in French before, but now would enjoy them in English.

I checked my Facebook page and found a message from Mark. He expressed his condolences to Henri and his family. His kids' teams won again.

Later that night I logged onto the computer there was a Facebook message from Mark asking how everyone was doing. I replied about as good as can be expected.

♥

"Jakie, it's time to go," I said. "Put away your toys and go wash your face and hands, please."

"Aw, Grandma, I am having fun with these new gizmos you bought me.  What did you call it? We are always going somewhere. I wish we could stay home for a change," balked Jakie.

"It's an erector set. You can leave the pieces together that are already joined, just put the loose ones away, please. Did you forget that I am taking you and Mandy to Vacation Bible School and we are going to stop to see Mary Florence and Anna Jean before we go to the church?"

"Oh, right. I did forget. I can play with this anytime. Let's go get Mandy right now." He jumped up and was nearly out the door when I caught him. I pantomimed washing of the face and hands.

Jakie laughed, "Okay Grandma, I'm going to wash real fast so we can hurry up. I know Bible School will be really fun!"

Soon Mandy and Jakie were buckled in to the Toyota and we were driving to Bingham Manor. Even though I was on a leave of absence while Tina and Henri were gone I still wanted to visit my friends at the Manor.

I couldn't wait to see the residents' eyes light up when I walked in with two little ones. I was right. Everyone made a fuss over the children, making leaving in time to be at the church for Bible School somewhat difficult.

Surprisingly, we made it with time to spare. When we walked into the Fellowship Hall, it had been transformed. I felt as though we had been transported to a foreign place. Huge backdrops covered the walls with scenes of Nazareth, Bethany, a mountain and Jerusalem.

Mandy spoke first. "Marjie, this reminds me of a page in the Bible storybook you gave me."

"It reminds me, too, Mandy." I said as I hugged her and Jakie.

"Why does it look like this?" asked Jakie.

Rob came up to them at that precise moment and answered his question. "We've gone back in time, Jakie." He pointed to one area of the hall and said, "This is Nazareth. Over there is Bethany, there is a mountain, and there, Jerusalem."

"Who did the decorating?" I asked. "Someone is really talented."

"The youth group did it. The teenagers. Isn't it wonderful?" said Eileen as she joined us and noticing my disbelief, she continued, "Who knew they just needed something to do that would be fun and creative to get them involved with church."

"Your class did this?" I was blown away.

"My class gets an A for this and guess what, they will be helping throughout Bible School. I've assigned two to each group, so you get two helpers and the rest of them are helping with crafts, snacks and playtime," said Eileen proudly.

Jakie and Mandy were among the first children to receive their name tags and costumes. Everyone was dressed in Biblical era attire. They were both in the green group, so they had green head coverings and sashes. All the children's robes were beige with ivory stripes, but their head coverings and sashes were color coded to help the leaders identify their groups.

Eileen knelt in front of Jakie and Mandy. "You are in my group. I'm so happy to have you both. We are going to have lots of fun. Let's go to our meeting place. It's over in the corner on the green blanket. See Rob over there waiting for you?"

Rob waved them over and I went to find my group. I looked for the children with blue head coverings and sashes.

My group included five children, aged ten to eleven. I knew two of them, Susana and Melea, extremely well, both were Eileen and Rob's granddaughters. Grace's daughter, Jessika, was also in my group. I had watched her grow up, but only knew her at church.

Rounding out our group was a neighborhood boy named Michael and his friend, Gabriel. Michael had been coming to Sunday breakfast almost every week with his mother and little sisters. They had never stayed for Sunday school or church, but had occasionally come to the other activities, like Jesus and Me, Halloween and Christmas parties, so I was slightly acquainted with Michael and his family, but didn't know them well.

I corralled my group of ten and eleven-year-olds and guided them to the dining area. Teen-aged helpers served a meal of hot dogs, chips, corn, green beans, celery and carrot sticks and applesauce. The planners knew that many of the children didn't get to eat before coming, so when we switched to evening Bible School we started serving a light meal before the activities. We tried to make the meals as healthy as possible, keeping in mind what children will eat. The hot dogs and chips were a hit and some of the kids even ate the carrot and celery sticks.

The light supper was over at five-thirty. I gathered my flock and headed for the first activity, which was drama time. We climbed the stairs to the largest classroom where we found Samuel, Grace's husband, dressed in shepherds' clothing complete with a staff. I was anxious to see how the activities would work with only twenty minutes for each one. How would that give the children time to get into their roles? This year Denise, as director of VBS, decided children learn best by doing, so she got a team together to create five different scenarios of Jesus' life in short scenes. The scripts were written large enough for the children to read them easily. Someone read the lines to the younger children and they repeated them.

Yesterday, Beth and I prayed together over the phone for God's Spirit to send us the right words and actions so our charges would feel loved and welcomed.

Samuel selected Michael, the neighborhood boy, to play the part of Jesus, Gabriel to be Simon Peter, Susanna to be James, and Melea to be John. Jessika, Samuel's step-daughter asked, "And who can I be, Papa?"

He answered, "Someone very special. You will be the leper."

Samuel handed out the scripts for each member of the cast, also giving Jessika several strips of white cloth to wrap around her face. I assisted her in making the transformation.

Michael, playing Jesus, called Simon, James and John from fishing the lake to become fishers of men. They followed him. Jessika, as the leper, stepped out and fell on her face saying, "Lord, if you will, you can make me clean."

Michael put his hand on Jessika and said, "I will do this, be clean."

Jessika jumped up, the strips of cloth falling from her face. She ran to show herself to the priests, played by our two teenage helpers and me.

Singing, crafts, and snacks filled the rest of the evening, but for me, nothing matched the beautiful spirit of watching the neighborhood boy, Michael, heal Jessika of leprosy. All the kids seemed to have a good time. They were excited to come back again tomorrow.

We sang the final songs in the sanctuary gathering. After parents claimed their children I collected my two little ones, Jakie and Mandy. I couldn't believe it was almost nine o'clock. The time had flown by. Bible school was supposed to be over by eight-thirty, but had run over the first night. The kids were tired and so was I. I drove home, all of us singing *What a Friend We Have in Jesus*, our main theme song for the week.

Mandy couldn't wait to tell her parents all about Bible School. She ran faster than Jakie and I, reaching her front door before we could catch up. Her mother let her in and seeing me huffing and puffing to catch Mandy, waved at me and yelled "Thank you for taking Mandy tonight. See you tomorrow." With that she shut the door. Jakie and I turned and walked back to our own front door.

I asked Jakie what part he got to play in the story about Jesus calling his disciples and healing the sick man. Jakie puffed his chest way out. "I got to be Jesus, Grandma. Can I call Mams and Papa and tell them?"

"You'll have to wait until tomorrow, Jakie. It's still dark in France. It's only five o'clock in the morning."

"It's dark here, Grandma. See the sun is gone. Why can't we call them now?"

"We'll call them at our usual time, at eleven tomorrow. That's the best time for all of us."

"Well, it might be the best time for you grown-ups, but NOW is always the best time for me," said Jakie in his most authoritative old voice, crossing his arms and looking me square in the eyes.

"I understand, Jakie, but it's time for us to get ready for bed and your mams and papa are already in bed."

He can be a handful sometimes. My weariness caused this negativity, I'm sure.

"Okay, Grandma. I guess I can wait for tomorrow to Skype them, but can I have some ice cream now?"

"Jakie, you had dinner and a snack at Bible School."

"Yes, only a snack. I didn't have dessert." He nodded his head emphatically. What could I do? His reasoning was correct. I dished ice cream for both of us. Butterfinger, yum.

Bible School week exhausted everyone but it was worth it. Attendance soared to sixty-two children, many parents, lots of teenagers and most of the congregation. All of us felt the value of VBS. The timing turned out to be good for Jakie and me. It kept him busy and not dwelling on the death of his Papi Gregoirie. I suspect he didn't understand death at his young age, but I explained that his Papi was in Heaven and that he would get to see him again, but it would be a long, long, long time when he was an old man. That seemed crazy to Jakie. He said he would ever be an old man. I told him his Papi Gregoirie and Grandpa Jake were watching over him together now.

He looked up at the ceiling and waved.

♥

"Hey, Sweet Thing, have you missed me?"

Al's mock southern drawl. I felt strangely excited. Shouldn't I feel anger, miffery, ignoration?

What am I doing? Thinking in Rob's language, making up words as I went along.

"Oh, hi Al. How are you?" I twirled my hair around and around, something I hadn't done since my teen years, or at least young motherhood, unsure of myself.

"You didn't answer my question. Did you miss me?" he asked again.

What should I say? Had I missed him? I did think about him once in a while and wondered why he hadn't called, but then with everything going on with Mom, Gregoirie dying, full charge of Jakie and all my usual activities and Bible School, I really haven't thought about him much at all. I think I'll tell him the truth. That's always best. Besides I'm not a flirt and not really interested in any so-called relationship. If he can't handle the truth, then that's his problem. I've got enough on my plate now without worrying about any male ego.

"Awfully long pause, there, young lady. Guess you didn't miss me after all…"

I cut him off. "I have to tell you I did wonder why you didn't call me, but then I've been so busy, I haven't had a lot of time to brood over it."

"Well, I called to see if you would be interested in going to see a movie or a play or something with me," said Al, dropping his southern drawl.

"Well, right now I have Jakie to think about, Henri's father died about ten days ago, so Tina and Henri went to France and left Jakie here with me, plus, remember, my mother had a mini stroke so I'm spending more time with her. How about giving me a rain check?"

"Well, how is your mother? I've been out of town for the last month or I would have called sooner. I want to see you very much. Couldn't Jakie go with us…and your mother, too? I would love to meet her. I'm sure she is as wonderful as you are." His accent still gone, maybe he had given it up.

"That is really nice of you. When do you want to go out? I'll call Mom and see if she is available."

"How does next Saturday night at five o'clock sound?" suggested Al.

"I'll talk to Mom to see if she has anything going on and let you know. Where are you taking us? Guess I said yes," I laughed.

"I'll have to think about that. Where does Jakie like to go?" asked

Al.

"Let's try to broaden his horizons. His favorites are Chuckie Cheese and McDonald's. Oh, he does love the Cheesecake Factory and French restaurants, of course."

"When Tina and Henri get back we'll check out some French restaurants around town, so they can judge the competition. I'll come up with something that everyone will like. I'll call you tomorrow night to find out if your mother will be joining us, okay?" said Al.

"Sounds good to me. Talk to you tomorrow then." I hung up the phone and walked into the kitchen to fix myself a cup of tea. I poured hot water over the tea bag to the tune of the ringing phone.

It was Mark.

"Hi Marjie Parjie, how's tricks?" said Mark. We bantered for a few minutes and he said, "I'm coming in town next Saturday to visit my mother. Want to get together?"

I was in shock. Two men, both handsome, intelligent, to my knowledge at least, and fun to be with, had asked me out for next Saturday within the last ten minutes. Has my world gone upside down? Rodolfo, the hair stylist at the spa, must have ESP.

I heard myself say and could hardly believe my own ears, "Saturday morning Jakie has a T-ball game, want to come and watch with me? And bring your mother. Mine will be there too. It'll be fun."

When I hit my bed that night I prayed my usual thank you prayers, then added: *Thank you for bringing an old friend and a new friend into my life at the same time. You'll have to help me with this, Lord. This is totally new territory.*

♥

At prayer group today I announced Tina and Henri's planned arrival home in one week. "Jakie and I will be so glad to have them home again."

I didn't mention anything about my upcoming Saturday dates with two men. I rationalized that Saturday morning with Mark was an outing to watch Jakie's T-ball game. That's not really a date. We are old friends, just hanging out as the young people would say. At least I think that is what they would say.

Eileen got my attention with her next comment. "I have a praise report. Beth and Jerry are going to start counseling again. Jerry says he hasn't had a drink since Beth left him. She is starting to believe him. You know he's coming to prayer meeting every Wednesday night and church every Sunday and helping at JAM. He's here whenever the church doors are open."

We all looked at each other, smiling. Denise said, "He helped at Bible School, too. I am happy for them."

Eileen leaned in, turning her gaze to rest on each of us in the group. "Susanna wants them to reconcile. It's been so hard for her going back and forth between her parents. At first, Beth wouldn't even allow Susanna to see her dad, but Rob arranged to go with her whenever she went with Jerry until he was convinced that Jerry really had quit drinking and we felt secure that Susanna would tell us if anything was amiss."

Kathleen nodded, "That was a good idea. I'm proud of the way you and Rob have handled this situation."

Eileen continued, "Beth talked to Susanna before she allowed visits alone with her dad, coached her, that if she saw any signs of drinking or felt uncomfortable in any way that she should call her mother and she would come and get her, but that hasn't been necessary. It's been working beautifully. Beth and Jerry went out to dinner and a movie last week. Beth is softening. I knew that if Jerry quit drinking Beth's heart would change toward him. They were such a loving couple when they were first married."

"Wonderful news!" said Denise.

"The Lord be praised!" said Grace.

"The effectual fervent prayer of a righteous man (or in this case, *women*) availeth much. James 5:16" said Kathleen, who knew her Bible better than anyone else in our group. Kathleen, my teacher, my mentor forever, taught me that verse when I was a teenager.

I was thrilled. "That is what this group is all about—tell each other your troubles and confess your faults, and pray for one another that ye may be healed. That includes broken marriages. I'm so happy for them. I feel certain that they will be able to work out their problems and fall back in love again. Heaven knows, Jake and I had to take stock every once in a while."

"This is great news, Eileen, and after hearing the scriptures from Kathleen and Marjie, I feel like we've already begun our Bible study and we haven't even finished our prayer section. Since I'm in charge of that today, let us pray for everything we are thankful for," said Cindy, a teacher friend of Grace's, the only Catholic in our group and we were blessed to have her with us.

❤

*Thank you, Lord, for this wonderful week. This wonderful day,* I prayed as I awoke on a bright and sunny Saturday morning. The week began with news that Beth was willing to go to counseling with Jerry. Mom is doing well—keeping busy with her gardening and friends. Mary Florence and Anna Jean are both in good health and spirits—Anna Jean and Eugene back together again. Jakie loves going with me on all my activities. He's growing fond of the good people on my Meals-on-Wheels route, especially Sully, who tells exciting tales about his adventures as a pilot in World War II, but he loves Meri and Genevieve too, and thinks Margaret and Fred are great fun. Of course, they always give him candy or a doughnut and that is a big draw for Jakie, but not necessarily good for his health. I am especially thankful that he loves going to the Temple every day for the Prayer for Peace and of course, visiting his great-grandmother, which also always includes food, since we lunch together three times a week. That child does love to eat.

*Lord, I fear I am neglecting my scripture study a bit. Thank heaven for my group on Sunday and Mom taking care of Jakie.*

I promised myself I would hit the scriptures later. I needed to get Jakie's T-Ball uniform out of the dryer and get us both ready. I shouldn't have left it in there last night, but we stayed at Rob and Eileen's so late that, truthfully, I forgot all about his uniform. It was incredibly wrinkled so I dampened one of his socks and threw it in the dryer for a few minutes while I got ready. I decided to wait until after the game to shower. I had one yesterday, checked under my armpits—they weren't too bad. I used some wipes and deodorant. I couldn't remember if Mark was going to pick us up or meet us at the field? I decided to call Mark after we ate. As I came out of my room headed to wake Jakie, I hummed a song from the Forties that the sing-a-long at Bingham Manor had brought to mind, thinking how fun it would be to see Mrs. Bryant, I mean Rosalie, again, and Mark, too.

The doorbell chimed to the tune of, *Oh, How We Danced On the Night We Were Wed.* That Jake, he thought that it was such a hoot to have that tune for our doorbell—even though we never danced on our wedding night, never danced much at all except at the Prom and we were both terrible.

I hurried to the front door. Thankfully, I was dressed, but barefoot in tee shirt and jeans. I answered the door, thinking it would be Mandy wanting to go to Jakie's game with us, but it was Mark, his mother and his youngest daughter who stood front and center. They all greeted me with big smiles.

"Goodness, I mean, hello, come in, come in. I was about to wake

Jakie and fix breakfast, well, pour it out of a cereal box. Have you eaten? Let me get the coffee on." I gushed, embarrassed, wondering if dried drool was on my face as I hadn't washed it yet.

I hugged Rosalie and Elsa, her name finally coming to me.

Mark laughed as he hugged me. "Caught you off guard, did we Marjie? Sorry about that. I couldn't remember what time I was supposed to pick you up or even if we were supposed to meet at the field...so we came on over."

But he could have called, I thought, then remembered all the times Jake and Mark had shown up unannounced on my doorstep when we were in high school. I laughed. "I couldn't remember either. This is great as long as you don't mind waiting for us to get ready."

As I escorted them in I noticed Jakie's toys strewn through the entryway and all the way into the kitchen. Oh, well. I should have had Jakie pick them up, but what does it matter in the scheme of things? I kicked some of the toys to the side wall, to give Rosalie a clear path. It's not like the house is dirty, it's not a pig sty.

"Sorry about the mess. I'd better go get Jakie up. That doorbell should have awakened him, but he sleeps like a hibernating bear sometimes.

Mark said, "We've already eaten, stopped at Mickey D's on the way over. That's what Elsa wanted. She likes their breakfast burritos."

"Yeah, I do." echoed Elsa.

"Please have a seat everyone. Where are your teenagers, Mark?" I asked, feeling bad that I couldn't remember their names.

"Oh, they both had plans with friends this weekend. Greta is staying with her friend next door. Mark Jr. has to work, and at age seventeen he's almost an adult, so I let him stay by himself once in a while. The neighbors keep an eye on him."

Rosalie said, "I wish they had come with you, but Mark Jr. is a very responsible young man and I'm going to get to see them on your birthday, which is only ten days away. You are still coming home for your birthday, right? You want that cherry chocolate cake that only I can make, right?" she said, laughing.

Rosalie's squealy laugh, seemingly uncharacteristic of this very proper lady, took me back to my high school book club days. I loved Rosalie's delightful laugh. Today was going to be fun.

I remembered that Jakie's uniform lay in the dryer, probably more wrinkled than ever. Excusing myself, I ran down to the basement, took his things out of the dryer, grabbed a bottle of spray de-wrinkler that Tina used and gave the uniform a once over. I shook it a few times as hard as I could, snapping the shirt and pants in the air. Next I laid them over the ironing board and hand pressed them. Holding them up again, I thought, not bad, not bad. This will do.

Jakie and I finished our cereal. Mark helped Jakie load his gear and put his car seat in and we all piled into Mark's fire engine red Enclave, Mark and I sat in front, Jakie claimed the whole back row for himself, so he could pretend he was hanging on the back of a fire engine, he said. Rosalie and Elsa took the middle seats.

When we got to the game Mark helped his mother up on the bleachers, then gave me his hand. I sat beside her, but he climbed up and eased his way between us. Elsa sat on the other side of her grandmother. We laughed so hard at the game, I feared we would be thrown out, but how could we help ourselves? One of the little girls sat down on third base and played with the dandelions, a little boy in left field whirled himself around and around until he was dizzy, and the coaches were being overly serious. They weren't angrily yelling at any of the kids, because that would not have been funny, but they were trying hard to get the kids to follow the rules albeit in vain. Apparently some of the kids didn't want to play ball, but their parents wanted them to, or possibly, they did want to *play*, but not T-Ball.

Jakie was an exception, impressing Mark with his serious demeanor at the young age of five. His eyes rarely left the game on the field. I told him and Rosalie that Jakie practiced at home in the back yard with a tee and his ball and bat, spending hours, even when his mother, father and grandma wore out, he stuck to it. Putting the ball on the tee, knocking it as far as he could, sometimes the ball landed in my flower garden, but he was careful not to trample anything. He was a good boy. He ran the bases he had made with some old roofing shingles I found. He would retrieve the ball, run back to the tee, beginning the process all over again. Henri, Tina and I took turns watching him from the kitchen window when we weren't outside with him. He cracked us up, so determined, but we were proud of him.

After Jakie's game we sat and watched another team play, just for the fun of it. Mark told Jakie and Elsa we were going to Chuckie Cheese for lunch.

"Mark, you are spoiling him, every time he sees you he gets pizza."

Mark responded, "He's not the only one I want to spoil, Marjie Parjie."

I was taken aback, then, seeing his sea-blue eyes twinkle as the old high school Mark, realized he was still my old teasing friend.

Rosalie was listening. Her face lit up and she squealed with delight.

She climbed around Mark, getting between her son and me, pushing me over and away from him, whose attention was back on the game. Rosalie put her arm around me and whispered, "Marjie, I've always dreamed of you and Mark getting together, prayed for it except when you were both married to others, of course. You are such a treasure. I've known it since the two of you were in high school. You were made for each other. Now Mark is starting to realize it, too. I am so happy for you." She hugged me, side-to-side, so we didn't fall off the bleachers.

This admission caught me totally off guard and now wasn't any time to confront her, but I needed to let her know that Mark and I are friends, nothing more. I have no desire for a romantic relationship with him, especially him. He was Jake's best friend. Our relationship can never be more than friendship.

I wandered away from Mark, his mother and Elsa for a few minutes to talk to Jakie, who was playing with his teammates, and to help one of the team mothers get the snacks ready. On my short walk from the bleachers to the dugout area I thought about a few weeks ago when Tina and I were talking about Jakie.

*Tina had asked me, "Where does he get that determination, that stick-to-itiveness from, Mom? Not from me, maybe a little from Henri's side and a little from you."*

*"He gets it from your father, Tina. Your father, who is still watching over you and me and Jakie, and always will."*

*Tina had looked thoughtful…maybe she was considering the possibility.*

*Then Tina's face hardened, "He may have gotten some genetics from Dad, but how can he be watching over us? He's dead, Mom. Face it." She walked away.*

*My heart was broken for my daughter.*

*Lord, be with Tina. Help her to know YOU again, Lord. Help her to believe that her father is alive, close, on the other side of the veil.*

I took a minute to compose myself and get back into fun mode before looking for Mark, Rosalie and Elsa who I found loading the car— Jakie was giving directions about where to put his gear. After lunch I thought they would just drop us off at my house, but Mark got out of the car, opened the doors for all the ladies, let Jakie jump out like a fireman, yelling "Geronimo", then followed me up my walk. Everyone came inside. Mark made himself at home, finding iced tea in the fridge and tumblers in the cabinet. I brought out some cookies I baked a few days ago while Mark and his mother made themselves comfortable in the family room. Jakie asked Elsa if she wanted to see his play room. I suggested that he and Elsa take the toys that he had left lying around the hall and the family room back to the playroom and they complied.

I began to worry that I wouldn't have time to get Jakie and myself ready, pick up Mom and get back home before Al arrived at five for our dinner date. When Mark and his family were still here at three o'clock, I thought I would have to say something, but just in time....

Rosalie seemed to sense my nervousness. She went to find Elsa and drug her oaf of a son, his flowing, wavy hair, touched with a little grey, complaining, out of the house. I stood on the porch waving at them until they pulled out of the driveway.

♥

Dashing inside, I hurriedly filled Jakie's bath, assured that he got in and out quickly, and sent him into his room to dress for dinner in his best slacks and shirt.

I showered faster than I believed possible, washing my hair, rinsing, toweling off, skipping the lotion, but not the deodorant. I ran a comb through my hair, glad my hair style was a wash and comb do and thanking God for my naturally wavy hair. I dressed in my favorite pink dress, put on make-up and was out the door, Jakie in tow, on the way to get Mom.

Traffic was bad for a Saturday afternoon. What was everybody doing out on the road? Couldn't some of them stay home? As always, I drove carefully, but I'll admit, more impatiently than usual. Having men in my life was bringing out some bad qualities in me. Jakie chattered away in the back seat, but I barely listened to him. Another bad sign. This may be the last time I go on a date with anyone, even if he is willing to take my mother and grandson along.

When we got to Mom's Jakie and I scurried up the flagstone path to her door. Wouldn't you know Mom *had* to show Jakie some new books and a movie she bought to have on hand whenever he visited. I took a deep breath and sat down a minute to share the new resources with Jakie and his great-grandmother.

At four thirty I jumped up. "We've got to go now or we won't be there when Al arrives to pick us up."

"Okay, Jakie, we'll have to look at these later," Mom said, looking at me like she wondered what had happened to her usually calm daughter.

"Ah, Great-Grandma, I wanted to watch a movie with you and Grandma," griped Jakie.

"Let's go eat a nice dinner with Al first. You can watch a movie at home tonight, if we don't stay out too late and Great-Grandma doesn't mind loaning it to you," I said to my darling, but complaining, grandson, who was holding onto a copy of *Alvin and the Chipmunks: The Squeakquel* with a Spiderman-like grip.

Mom said, "You can take it with you as long as you bring it back tomorrow. We can watch it while your Grandma is at her Group. How will that be?"

On the way back to my house I filled Mom in on the T-ball game and our day with Mark, Rosalie and Elsa. "Mom, do you think I'm crazy, making plans with two different men on the same day? Of course, Mark wasn't a date. He's an old friend, but I feel like everything is going bonkers around me. I've got Jakie, Tina and Henri now. I don't need any more complications in my life, do I? I hope I'm not fouling things up by enlarging my social life, adding all these men,"

She raised her eyebrows and laughed. "I thought you said there were two men, Mark and Al. Are there more I should know about? But, seriously, Honey, you are much better at fixing things than you are at fouling them up." My mother ended on a thoughtful note.

"Mom, you always know the right thing to say. I wish I could be more like you."

"Well, thanks for the compliment, but I learn from you every day. You are the one who works at Bingham Manor, delivers meals-on-wheels, heads up the Jesus and Me program, leads a weekly prayer group, visits your old mother almost every day, takes care of your grandson and Mandy and I don't know who all. You really are a saint in my eyes. I'm so proud of you." Mom's eyes misted over and her voice caught.

"Aw, shucks, Mom, don't get me crying and make my mascara run before my date even starts."

"What's this, 'aw shucks' Marjie? I've never heard you say that before," asked Mom. She tried to sound shocked, but her chuckle gave her away.

"That's because you haven't met Al," I laughed.

Al was in my driveway, getting ready to walk up the porch steps, when we pulled in. He immediately went to the passenger side of my car to assist Mom. He was dressed, as usual, in a Hawaiian shirt. This one deep midnight blue on cream with aquamarine accents, his pants perfectly creased, the same midnight blue.

Jakie jumped out of the car and I stepped out before Al could make it around to my side of the car, but he tried.

Mom apologized for me. "Marjie has been independent so long, she has forgotten how to be treated by a gentleman."

"Too true," I sighed, standing back, I handed my house key to him. He gave a little bow and opened the front door.

Jakie took his Chipmunk DVD to his room. I went to my room to grab a jacket in case it was cold in the restaurant.

Soon we settled in Al's car. I asked him where we were going for dinner and to my silent dismay found that Al planned an outing to a little Italian place so Jakie could have pizza.

"Yea, pizza again, Grandma," yelled a happy Jakie.

"Pizza again?" Al questioned.

"Yes, we went to Chuckie Cheese for lunch after my T-ball game with Grandma's friend, Mark," said Jakie.

"Well, this place has pizza and a lot of other things, Jakie. Lots of vegan dishes and I'm sure that your grandmother and your great-grandmother will find many menu items that will suit them," stated the all-confident Al.

Why are men more confident than most women I know? Better not get started on that track right now. Besides, Tina takes the cake in confidence—when she's not being unsure of herself.

We drove across town to hit I-70 and headed west. I asked Al where the little Italian place was located and was told it was in the River Market area. "Their Vegan dishes exceed most Kansas City Italian fare," he said.

Dinner was wonderful. Mom and I found several appealing menu items, taking a while to make up our minds. Jakie knew what he wanted—pepperoni pizza, Al ordered black bean cakes with spicy sweet potato sauce. He added a side of broccoli, red pepper and almond couscous. Mom selected Italian Wedding Soup and I chose baked chicken with pastina and a house salad.

During the meal Al skillfully directed the conversation, keeping a nice easy flow between all of us. We talked of Jakie's T-ball game, Mom's and my gardens and my Jesus and Me program.

Al was good at getting information from people, but he didn't reciprocate. I realized I knew little about this man except that he was charming, handsome, owned at least four Hawaiian shirts and a building in Englewood. He had a bucket list, an ex-wife and a dislike of meat.

The maitre'd and the waitresses all seemed to know and like him. No man could be as good with children, my Jakie; with septuagenarians, my mother; and widowed-women, me; as Al, and so good with other people, or could they? I thought about Mark and Jake and Henri for that matter. They were all great with people, maybe it's something in male genes. Women are supposed to be the nurturers and they are, but some men seemed to be adept at making people feel at ease. Al certainly headed this group. Eyes of people in the restaurant followed him as we walked in. He had a certain something, a *je ne sais qua*, Henri would say. I thought, a magnetism, charisma. I never remember feeling this drawn to a person before.

Mom and I laughingly refused dessert. I personally worried my dress would split out. Al and Jakie each had an Italian ice—Al the gelato di limone and Jakie the spumoni.

When their desserts were delivered to the table, Mom and I caved in on our determination not to eat dessert and decided to split a tiramisu, but I only ate three spoonsful. After dessert there was coffee for Al, milk for Jakie, and tea for Mom and me.

After dinner we dropped Mom off then Al brought Jakie and me home. We didn't linger on the porch. Al came in with us for a few minutes, probably waiting for a chance for us to be alone, but Jakie made sure that didn't happen, so Al just kissed my hand and left, not mentioning when he would call again. He likes to retain his mysterious quality, I guessed.

That night when I said my thank you prayers, I thanked God for my family, each by name, my friends, mostly by name, and tonight I added, *Lord, help me to know if Al is a person I should be spending time with.*

# CHAPTER THIRTEEN

Amy, Rob and I walked out of the small room used for administration and stood before the congregation, looking side to side, the three of us sat down simultaneously. Thank Heaven the sanctuary was cool. It was ninety-nine degrees outside. As I looked out at the congregation, I saw all the familiar faces, Kathleen and Foster, Denise and her family, Grace and hers, the McNamara clan, Al, my mother and Jakie.

*Al*, what was Al doing here and sitting with Mom and Jakie. That man never ceases to amaze me. He did ask where we went to church, but I never thought he would come here. I guess I should have invited him. I hadn't thought of him as religious, but then again. I barely know him. This Hawaiian shirt is nice, black on white, but they all are nice. This makes number five, I think. I've got to ask him someday if he has 365 of them.

I tried to focus on the service and stop thinking about Al. The gathering hymns were over and it was time for me to offer the opening prayer. I opened my mouth to speak, striving to concentrate, to choose my words carefully, seeking to be in tune with the Holy Spirit.

Rob was in charge of the service. He told a little joke as always, having studied several books about conducting a service, and believing that God has a sense of humor, he tried to inject it whenever he could possibly get away with it. He then introduced Amy to the congregation as the speaker for today.

"For most of you, Amy needs no introduction, but for the very few that don't know her well," he said, "You are in for a treat. Amy is Eileen's and my middle daughter. You've all heard about middle children. How they don't get enough attention from their parents. Well, this middle child is an exception. She made sure she got our attention not by acting out in a bad way, but by being sweet, precocious, beautiful, loving…oh, wait, I'm describing all my daughters. They are all wonderful and so are my wife, my mother, and my mother-in-law. Did I miss anyone? All of you women here in the congregation and my second grade schoolteacher." Rob turned around to see a red faced daughter, but she was laughing along with the rest of the congregation.

"Amy, I love you and I'm so proud of the woman you have become. You are educated, teaching math at my alma mater, Central Missouri State, which most of us call simply, Warrensburg. Amy holds the Office of Priest and this is the first time she has been our speaker here at Shady Grove, but we finally talked her into it. Okay, Amy did I take up enough of your time?" he laughed.

If Amy wasn't nervous before this, and she shared with me before the service that she was, I bet she was twice as nervous now. Rob finally introduced the next hymn.

The theme was *Lord, Lift Me Up*. We sang the popular hymn *Higher Ground.*

When Amy got to the rostrum, she read the words of the chorus.

Then, she spoke with a sarcastic tone, "Wouldn't it be great to be lifted up and placed on higher ground—on heaven's table land? Lifted above the fray, above worrying about our national security, threats from Al Qaeda, ISIS, the wars in Afghanistan and Iraq, a nuclear Iran and Korea, tsunamis, earthquakes, tornados, downgraded credit ratings, Wall Street, influenza pandemics, shootings in shopping malls. We *want* a higher plane. We *want* peace. We *want* justice. Face it folks, we live in a broken world. It's all doom and gloom—we read it in the papers, see it on TV, on our computers, now we get news on our Smartphones. Twenty-four seven, news at our fingertips and usually, it's bad news."

Amy's words riveted me. How was she going to turn this around to a message that would uplift the congregation, or would she? I believed in Amy's ability. I watched her grow from an infant. I feel close to all of Eileen and Rob's daughters, closest to Beth, since she is Tina's age. Amy is three years older than Beth and Tina. I sought Eileen's face to see how she was handling her daughter's message. Eileen looked composed. I'll bet she heard Amy's talk or at least read it sometime before the service. I knew they were close and Amy trusted her mother's judgment. I surveyed the congregation, noticing some unhappy faces, but also, some trusting ones, some with eyes closed, maybe they were napping? Mom seemed a bit disturbed, uncomfortable, probably Amy's plan was to get everyone feeling nervous and then bring them back. My eyes met Al's. He was looking at me, smiling, taking everything in stride.

I missed some of Amy's words by worrying about them. When I began focusing on Amy's message, I heard, "We have to live in this world, and as Gandhi said, 'We must *be* the change we seek in this world.' We can't be complacent when we see the bad stuff. Jesus taught us to love God first of all, to care for our neighbors, to bind up the bruised and brokenhearted, to love and forgive others as we would be forgiven. When we do this, when we really love one another, we are lifted up on a higher plane. When we are the hands and feet of Jesus, we are lifted up to Heaven's Tableland. Let us go and lift each other up. Amen."

Amy sat down. I knew I had missed a lot of the message.  She was animated, her voice lilting at times, never monotone. I'll ask her for a copy of her notes, by the looks of the congregation, she did a good job.

I found Mom, Jakie and Al talking with others around them, Al being welcomed and asked to come back again next week; I was certain. That's how this congregation is, welcoming, inviting, making everyone feel at home. I joined them, Mom and I both blushing when people thought Al was Mom's friend, which he was but only through me. I didn't know how I felt—other than awkward, and I definitely didn't know what to say—to Al or anyone.

I was glad to see him in church, but certainly wished I had known he would be there beforehand. No one but Denise knew about him until today. Now there would be no keeping secrets from anyone. Rob would make my life miserable in his jovial way. I hoped he would wait until we were in the privacy of his home at the Friday night dinner.

Al, Mom and I made our way down the aisle, Al charming everyone he met. Jakie had disappeared to find his friends. Mom explained that Al was my special friend. I was in between agony and delight. Denise came up and introduced her husband, Kenneth, to Al, whispering in my ear like she was a teenager, "Why didn't you tell me you were still seeing Al and it must be getting serious if you invited him to church."

I shushed Denise and told her we would talk later. I was still worried about running the gauntlet with Rob and Eileen. Amy stood by the outer door of the sanctuary as is the custom, her parents by her side. The congregation flowed by to congratulate her on a "lovely service", "good message", "really got us to thinking there, Amy" and to Rob and Eileen, "you must be so proud." It was the habit of church members to hug or shake the hand of the speaker and the presider. We told Amy how much we appreciated her message. Al held Amy's hand a little too long for her father's liking, I guessed. I was surprised to see Rob in his most formal pastoral persona. For once, he didn't try to play the role of a joker. He looked dead serious.

Jakie appeared as we walked out the door. He reached and grabbed Al's hand. Oh my. What have I done? I shouldn't be getting Jakie close to people that may not be in our lives very long.

I thought we'd escaped further probing and wondering looks when we reached the parking lot, but Kathleen and Foster caught us and invited us out for lunch, Al included.

Al relieved my anxiety by saying he had to take off, but asked for a rain check. I couldn't handle an escalation to whatever relationship we had and worried that eating out with him two days in a row with family, and now friends, would definitely increase the pressure on both of us.

Al explained, as if he needed to, that he had an appointment at his building, another person that might be interested, but he asked me if we could have a few minutes alone. Assenting, I steered him back into the building where it was cool. We found a corner alone in the gym.

"Marjie, this was a wonderful service. Nice people. I hope you didn't mind that I came here today without warning you." There was a question in his voice, sweet, humble, boyish. He reminded me for a minute of Jake. I told him that he was welcome at Shady Grove anytime the doors were open.

He took off, saying he would talk to me soon and that he had enjoyed the service very much. I was glad he didn't try to hug me in church. Me, being glad someone didn't try to hug me. This did not compute.

♥

I found Mom and Jakie talking to Kathleen and Foster. "Where to for lunch," asked Foster.

Jakie said, "McDonalds!" His great-grandmother and I groaned. It was going to take more than McDonald's to restore my equilibrium after Al's unexpected visit to church and Mom hates McDonald's. She likes to be waited on.

"I know, let's go to Backyard Burgers and get a milk shake," said Kathleen and Foster added his approval.

I said, "Sounds good. We'll meet you there." Mom, Jakie and I piled into the Camry.

"Are you sure this is okay, Mom? I know you like to be waited on."

"Oh, you can place my order at the counter and they have staff bring it to the table, so it will be fine. I love the company I'm with, no matter where we are."

Jakie had never been to Backyard Burgers, but he never met a burger or milk shake that he didn't like.

As we received our order, my cell phone alarm rang.

"What's that for?" asked Mom.

"I don't know," I answered slowly. "I do remember setting it yesterday, but that was before our dinner last night and church this morning. What was I supposed to do at one o'clock?"

"Oh, I remember, Marjie, you told me that today you were meeting someone at the café that Tina and Henri are leasing, to pick up the keys."

Mom's memory is fantastic. Even after she had that mini-stroke, she remembers things better than I do.

"Mom, you are a lifesaver. I set the alarm early, so if we were at lunch we would still have time to get there by two o'clock. Guess I had a brain yesterday before Mr. Hawaiian Shirt showed up."

"He is very handsome, sort of reminds me of Cary Grant," said Kathleen. "How long have you been seeing him, Marjie?"

"Not long. He's an acquaintance. Tell you what, Kathleen, I'll tell you all about it later. We've got to eat and go," and with that I shoved a big bite of cheeseburger in my mouth. Mom, Foster and Kathleen kept up the conversation during the rest of the meal, Mom telling Kathleen that she agreed with her about Al looking like Cary Grant.

♥

We met with Mel at the soon-to-be café. She thanked me for meeting with her and offered her condolences to Henri and his family.

Mom was impressed with the place, looking into all the cubbyholes and cabinets, under the sinks. The only think she found disfavor with was the bar and the wine racks and the bathrooms.

"Bathrooms have to be nice or customers will go elsewhere," she said, rubbing her hands together.

"They are going to be remodeled, Mrs. Lord," said Melanie. "Tina and Henri have already picked out the tile, fixtures, and lavatories."

"When are the remodelers supposed to be here?" I asked.

"On Tuesday, this week," answered Melanie.

"Oh good, Tina and Henri will be back from France. They are so anxious to get started. They get home tomorrow, so they'll be tired, but I'm sure they will want to be here when the contractors arrive."

"Did they get their liquor license yet?" asked Melanie.

"Not yet, but they applied for it and their city occupational license the same day. They also have to go through a background check. I hope that isn't a problem with Henri. Do you think it will be?"

"I've never had any experience with non-citizens getting business or liquor licenses, but if I were you, I would keep it in yours and Tina's names," advised Melanie.

"Maybe we did. I can't remember anything right now. Thank heaven, they will be home tomorrow and we can get back to working on this," I responded.

Melanie showed me the location of all the light switches and how to get the tricky key to work in the old lock. We left the café. I felt overwhelmed, Mom was tired and ready to go home to relax but Jakie was ready and excited to go to Great-Grandma's to watch a movie.

As I drove off to my group meeting I worried whether or not my mother was up to taking care of Jakie. I thanked God that Tina and Henri would be home tomorrow.

♥

Their flight was delayed six hours due to a storm in New York where they changed planes for the flight to Atlanta, then home to Kansas City. Tina called to let me know, thank heaven. She suggested I check the flight information on the internet before coming to the airport.

Jakie and I were at Mom's when I received Tina's call. "That was thoughtful of her, wasn't it, Mom?" I said to Mom. She was sometimes critical of her granddaughter, so I always tried to build Tina up in her eyes.

"Do you want to go to the airport with Jakie and me?"

Mom said, "No", it is getting late and I feel a summer cold coming on."

"Well, get some rest. Drink lots of fluids. I'll call you later." I said as I hugged her goodbye, feeling like I needed to stay with her, but I had to go.

I took Jakie with me to the airport. He was anxious to see his parents, had missed them so badly, even though he loved me and his great-grandma a lot, we weren't his papa and mams.

Jakie struggled to stay awake on the bench outside the arrival gate. He had almost given out, but not quite. I patted his arm when his parents' flight began to unload. He stood up on the bench and was the first to spot his papa, couldn't quite see Mams yet, but Papa was there, so he knew Mams was too.

Soon he was in Henri's arms and then in Tina's, next I managed to winnow my way into their group hug. We all cried. They were glad to be home, but worn out and still grieving for Gregoirie.

At home we drank hot chocolate and ate graham crackers, tucked Jakie in with a bedtime story and went to bed ourselves.

In bed I said my thank you prayers. *Mainly, thank you, God, for Tina and Henri's safe arrival home again.*

♥

Tina and Henri went early to the café to be there when the contractors arrived. I stayed home with Jakie, over his protests. He just got his parents back. He didn't want them to go anywhere without him, so as soon as we ate a quick breakfast of scrambled eggs and toast, we joined Tina and Henri. The workmen were not there yet. It was eight-thirty. They were supposed to be there at eight. Nine o'clock came and went. The usually patient Henri was tired from their long flight and was about to lose his temper when his son arrived and livened up his mood. Even Tina cheered up when we got there.

At nine-thirty Tina called Melanie to see what was going on with the workmen. Melanie said she would call her back. She did. It turned out that she had forgotten to get the building permit. It was her fault, but she would take care of it. She apologized profusely and offered to give them a break on their next month's rent. Tina lost it. She yelled at Melanie and told her that they were going to break the lease if they weren't able to open on schedule, Labor Day Weekend, during Santa-Cali-Gon.

Melanie made the mistake of saying that they didn't even have their liquor license yet, so how did they plan to open the first weekend of September anyway. Tina curtly told Melanie, "You had better get that building permit tomorrow."

Tina handed the phone to Henri and began to sob. He held her in his arms, and spoke softly to Melanie. "Please do what you need to do."

Henri, exhausted, hung up the phone without any more comment.

We locked up and went home so they could rest, planning to go to city hall again tomorrow.

A distraught Tina managed to yell at Henri about the liquor license, Jakie about his toys, and me because I was there, before Henri urged her upstairs for sleep.

Jakie went crying to his room. I followed him and we watched his favorite movie, *Toy Story*. Henri stayed with Tina.

That night in bed I knew I needed to thank God for everything. I thanked him for my family and asked that through this experience we be made stronger and more closely knit.

♥

"Good Morning, Henri," I said as I entered the kitchen and saw him there making his usual stiff coffee. I was sure Tina and Jakie were still in bed.

I put the tea kettle on and then gave him a hug. "You know, I haven't had the opportunity in person to tell you how very sorry I am for the loss of your father."

"Thank you, Mère Marjie, I appreciate that. You know I'm the one who lost my father, but Tina is taking his death much harder than I am. When we were in France and even now, she is the one who is falling apart. She is angry with everyone, she even yelled at the morticians for the way they combed his hair and the funeral home staff for closing the casket too early. You would have thought that she was his wife, not his daughter-in-law."

"Oh, my goodness. How awful for you and your family. How did your mother take Tina's actions?" I asked.

"My sainted mother is a lot like you, Mère Marjie. She, though grieving herself, tried to be understanding. We all know that Tina has never recovered fully from the death of her father," replied Henri while sipping his steaming coffee. "Ma mère loves Tina as her own daughter, as did my father. We were very happy together in France. Maybe we should have stayed there."

Henri broke down for the first time since he had been back in Independence. I stood behind him, hugging his broad shoulders, crying with him. I barely knew Gregoirie, but he was a good man who loved my daughter and the grandson we shared. I grieved for the pain that his death caused my daughter and son-in-law.

I stayed behind Henri, praying silently as he cried, mainly praying for wisdom. I wished Tina had stayed home after her father's funeral instead of going back to France so soon. If only we had been able to go through it together instead of oceans apart, just talking on the phone and sending an occasional email. Tina has changed so much from the fun-loving girl I once knew. She has always been a little selfish, probably due to being an only child, but she had lots of friends. People were drawn to her sometimes outrageous behavior, having to be the center of attention, but she has a good heart and loves people more than she realizes. She loves people deeply. I've got to talk to Eileen about the grief counseling she went to. Maybe she could talk to Tina?

Henri and I were broken out of our individual and corporate reveries by Jakie bouncing into the kitchen, "I'm hungry. What's for breakfast, Grandma?"

Henri's grief abated at the presence of his famished man-child. "Ah, what's for breakfast–Grandma! Have I been gone so long, my son? Don't you remember it is I that usually prepares your breakfast? And doesn't your Grandma deserve a break?"

"Okay, Papa, what's for breakfast? I don't really care who fixes it, but, please, can one of you? I'm hungry." Jakie climbed up on his wooden stool and plopped his elbows on the table.

After breakfast was eaten, the kitchen straightened and dishes put in the dishwasher, I noticed the time. It was ten o'clock. Tina still wasn't out of bed. At least, we hadn't heard a peep from her.

Henri went to check on her. He came back and told me he peeked in their bedroom and Tina was lying there awake, staring at the ceiling, silent tears running down her face. He went in and handed her a tissue and asked her if she would like something to eat.

"Mère Marjie, she growled at me, saying 'No, leave me alone. I am tired and I want to sleep.'  She put the pillow over her face and turned her back on me. What should we do about Tina? She's been taking her pills, maybe too much or maybe she needs another kind?"

Seeing Henri's face so forlorn, I was at a loss of what to do. I was about to mention grief counseling when my thoughts were interrupted by a call from the prayer chain. Foster Grant was in the hospital. They didn't know what was wrong with him, he was having trouble walking. Possibly he had a stroke.

I called Eileen to see if she knew any more about Foster, but got her voice mail. I guessed Eileen and Rob were probably at the hospital with Foster and Kathleen.

I felt torn. I wanted to be home when Tina got up. I thought, maybe I should go into her room to see if there was anything I could do. I longed to be with Foster and Kathleen, my most cherished friends and mentors, from childhood to today. I prayed and felt led to go to Tina first to see if she would be receptive to me.

Tina, back toward the door, was sobbing. I went to my daughter to hold her, comfort her. Tina lashed out, pushing me away.

"Why can't you people leave me alone? Is that too much to ask? I'll get out of the blooming bed when I feel like it. I don't feel like getting up yet. I have jet lag. Just leave me be."

I softly said, "I love you, Tina. I want you to know that. Henri loves you, too, and Jakie."

"Well, if you love me so freaking much will you please leave me alone so I can get some rest?" yelled Tina.

"We will let you sleep a while longer, but I will be back to check on you and so will Henri. You are not alone in your grief."

"What are you talking about, grief. I told you *I have jet lag*. WHAT PART OF THAT DON'T YOU UNDERSTAND?"

I closed the door softly. Back downstairs I asked Henri if he minded me leaving Jakie with him while I went to the hospital to see Kathleen and Foster. He snappily reminded me that Jakie was his son, after all.

His tone softened and I realized he was also on edge. He said they would go outside and play T-ball for a while.

"I won't be gone long. I want to be here for Tina when she needs me. Call me if she gets up. You've got my cell number, right?" I said as I hurried out the door.

♥

I drove to Centerpoint Medical Center even though I hadn't asked where Foster was, but they lived closer to it than any other hospital since both the San, or Independence Regional, as it was renamed, and the Medical Center of Independence had been closed when Centerpoint was built. Now it was the only hospital in the city limits, built on the east side of town, irritating Independence residents to no end, especially the ones who lived on the northwest side of town.

Centerpoint was touted to be up to date. The older hospitals could never be the standard bearer for such a modern age as ours. All the rooms are private rooms. Concerned citizens asked about the people whose insurance would only pay for wards or semi-private rooms. Hospital promoters stated that, if that's all there is, Medicare and Medicaid would pay for it, but would they, or would they send the poor people to Truman East? All of this ran through my mind as I drove to Centerpoint, my brain keeping me from worrying about Tina and Foster.

Arriving at the hospital, I stopped at the information desk and found that Foster was there, in the intensive care unit. "Are you a relative?" asked the receptionist.

"No, but very close, very close to the family." I responded.

"You'll have to wait in the waiting room, but you'll be able to see his family members as they take turns in the ICU. They can only stay ten or fifteen minutes and only two people at a time can be in there with him."

She sounded like she had repeated these same words thousands of times, which she probably had. I felt cold.

I found my way to the ICU, following signs and asking directions when needed. When I rounded the corner and came into the hallway where the waiting room was, I saw Rob, Eileen and Kathleen's granddaughter, Carrie, who lived in Overland Park, Kansas, a short thirty-minute drive from Centerpoint. I asked Carrie how her grandfather was doing.

Carrie told me her grandpa had a heart attack, not a stroke. He was being well taken care of by the doctors and nurses.

"You know Grandpa is ninety years old, so the prognosis is not real good, but he is strong. You know how strong he is, Marjie," Carrie stated emphatically as she broke out crying.

I helped her to a seat in the waiting room and Carrie got herself under control. Pretty soon her husband arrived with their three children. He had picked them up from school and come on over. Kathleen came out of the ICU, smiling when she saw her granddaughter's family there and me, too. She hugged all of us.

"He's calling me 'Katy.' You know he's the only one I ever let call me that," she said brightly, ever the proper Welsh lady, perfectly groomed even under these circumstances. "He's doing well. Carrie, do you want to take the children in to see their great-grandpa? I think he would like to see them."

"Are you sure it's okay, Grandma?" asked Carrie.

"Sure, why don't you and Kathy go in, then I'll take Mike and Barry."

"We don't want to wear him out, Grandma," said Carrie.

"Oh, he'll be fine. Eileen and Rob administered to him a little while ago. He is feeling much stronger and he would want to see all of you. Marjie, as soon as all the kids have had a chance to see Foster, I'll take you in with me. No nurse will say a word to try to stop me, besides, you are like family and an elder, so that's it." Kathleen spoke softly, as always. Such angels, both she and Foster. I wanted to talk to her about Tina's anger and depression, but not now, not now.

While Carrie was in the room with Kathy, I found out that Kathleen had called their two daughters, one in Minneapolis and one in Oklahoma City. She had also called her daughter-in-law, wife of her son, Christopher who had died when he was forty-four, over ten years ago. He died of a heart attack. So suddenly. A massive heart attack. Not like Foster's. Foster was going to be okay… Kathleen knew it. He wouldn't leave her yet. They had another spring, at least one more spring…for her to listen to him recite Wordsworth once again.

Their daughters did not hesitate, making plans to come immediately. Would this be the last time they would see him alive?

Their dad was ninety years old, a heart attack was bound to weaken him. Still he was strong, kept himself in the best shape possible for an old man, he always said, laughing as he pushed the broom to sweep the fellowship hall or picked up trash, leaning over holding on to his walker.

As we sat in the waiting room, Kathleen reminisced with Eileen, Rob and me, Carrie taking her children in one by one to see their great-grandpa. He was in great spirits and everyone started feeling much better. He was eating and joking with the kids.

Sitting in the waiting room Kathleen talked about the love of her life. We all knew most of the history of Foster and Kathleen, having known them for many years, but if Kathleen wanted to talk, we wanted to listen.

"We met at Graceland College over seventy years ago," she said. "I came over from Wales to attend school there. I met Foster and that was that. He was so handsome, tall and thin with nice brown hair. Yes, he had hair back then," she stopped for a minute and smiled, her eyes far away.

"He graduated in 1940 and I left school without finishing my degree at that time. He got a job teaching math at William Chrisman High School. He enlisted in the Navy after Pearl Harbor and served until just after the end of the War. He used to joke about all the *cruises* he had been on. Those years were hard for me. Jeannette was born during the war. She didn't get to see her father until she was three years old. My family was all in Wales. My in-laws lived in Pennsylvania. I was alone except for my church family. I don't know what I would have done without them." Kathleen looked at all of us, smiling with her eyes, quiet for a moment.

She began again. "Our children wanted to send us on a cruise to Alaska for our fiftieth wedding anniversary, but Foster never wanted to get on a ship again after the War. He did satisfy their longing for us to do something spectacular for our fiftieth by agreeing to fly with me to Alaska where we took land trips to see the sights. We've had a wonderful life together."

My turn finally came. I went in to see Foster. He looked a little gray in the face, but other than that, same old Foster, joking around. Asking me how my love life was going? That darn Al had to come to church before I was ready for anyone to know about him.

After visiting with Foster I excused myself, telling Eileen about Tina and wondering if she could spend some time with her. Do some grief counseling, maybe? Eileen told me she would be honored if Tina wanted her to. She said, "The main thing is to let Tina grieve. Keep her talking about Jake and Gregoirie." We hugged.

I knew that their family and Eileen and Rob would take care of Foster and Kathleen. I was happy to see Foster looking as well as he did.

♥

I arrived home about eight o'clock in the evening, hungry. I remembered eating lunch, but that was hours ago. I grabbed a handful of grapes from the frig to tide me over until I checked in with my family. I wanted to find Henri and Jakie to see how their day had gone. I found them in the basement playing pool. Jakie was a little too short, but he loved playing the game. His papa helped him aim the cue stick and even let Jakie help him with some of his shots. They kept no score, just had fun.

"How's Tina" I asked.

"She's still in bed," answered Henri. "What are we going to do?"

"I talked to Eileen about spending some time with Tina. She and Rob have been through grief counseling classes. Other than that I don't know, I just don't know, besides praying, that's all I've got," I said. "But Eileen did say that we need to get Tina to talk about your father and hers."

We knelt on the basement carpet with Jakie between us and prayed for Tina.

After helping me up off the floor, Henri remembered a phone call. "Mère Marjie, your friend Mark called you today. He said he would try again tomorrow and he would send you a Facebook message tonight. I think he said he's coming in town next week."

I didn't feel like checking my email or Facebook account right then. I wanted the comfort of Jakie. I helped him get ready for bed.

He said, "Grandma, I don't need help. I can do it myself, but will you run my bath water and stand outside the door while I wash and brush my teeth?"

I stood listening to the sounds of splashing water and mouth rinsing, so grateful my wonderful grandson, my only grandchild, wanted me close while he washed.

After Jakie's bath he read his favorite book to me, Dr. Seuss' *Green Eggs and Ham*. Ah, grandchildren give us the opportunity to be what we wished we had been to our children—full attention givers.

That night I ended my thank you prayers, praying mightily for Tina and thanking the Lord for my grandson, who, everyday looked more like his grandpa Jake.

♥

This morning I decided to tackle Tina head on. Henri thought it best if I talked to her. I knocked on her bedroom door and hearing nothing, walked on in.

"Tina, we need to talk," I began, "I think Eileen would be a good person for you to talk to. She's been to grief counseling classes."

Tina was sprawled on top of the bed covers, face down, her hair splayed, matted, tangled, reminding me of her teen age years, the moodiness, the crying. Her dad was always the best one to reach her. He used to sing to her, *Hey Mambo, Mambo Italiano*. I'm sure that if I tried that now, it would not be a good thing—only remind her of her dad, but she needs to remember all the good times with him and with Gregoirie and with me and with Henri and Jakie.

"Tina, honey, you need to pull yourself together, for Jakie's sake. He is confused. Doesn't understand why you won't come out of your room."

"Tell him I'm sick."

She sounded sick, I thought. She is sick, but it's emotional. I could deal with the flu or a cold.

"He wants to see you, Honey. He lost his grandpa. He needs all of us right now."

"Well, I'm no good for him. I can't quit crying or if I do I start yelling. I know you and Henri are taking good care of him. He's all right. I made it all right with just one parent."

"Tina, you were a grown woman with a husband and a baby when your father died." I had learned not to use euphemisms for death with Tina, who disliked the word passed, which almost slipped out of my mouth.

"Jakie is five years old. He needs his mother." I could hardly believe my firmness, but somehow felt it necessary. I knew she was hurting, but kindness hadn't helped and I was at a loss.

Tina fired back. "Well, maybe if I hadn't gone off to France and met Henri and left Daddy here, he wouldn't have died. Maybe I would have taken better care of him than you did. And then just as soon as I leave Gregoirie he up and dies. I'm not good for fathers."

Oh, my God. Tina blames herself and me for her father's death.

"Tina, you were here in this house when your father died. Neither you nor I could have stopped the cancer. And Gregoirie had a heart attack. You couldn't have stopped it, Honey. Death is a part of life. It happens to everyone at some point. Your dad and Gregoirie are both in a better place…"

"Stop it Mom. They are dead in the ground, rotting. They are not in a better place and when you die and when I die we will *not* be in a *better place*. You make me so mad when you say that." Tina turned to me, her face filled with anger—anger at me, her mother.

The energy flowed out of me. "Tina, all I can say is what I believe. Just try to hope that what I believe is true. Just hope it. Wish it. It will help you move on with your life."

"Move on with my life. My life is in a mess. The café isn't ready. We're not ready. Jakie loves you and Henri and everyone else more than he loves me. I'm not sure that Henri still loves me at all. Why would he?"

"Will you at least talk to Eileen?"

"Are you crazy? I've known Eileen all my life, but I don't want to bear my soul to her. I'll be all right. Just leave me alone!"

I was in over my head. How could I help my daughter? I didn't go through anger or depression when Jake died. I got busy. Cried sometimes sure, but all in all, seemed to get through the grieving process much easier than one would think. What was wrong with me? No time to think about myself right now. Need to figure out a way to help Tina.

I went downstairs to find Henri. Patient Henri. He just lost his father and now his wife is grieving more than he is, not seeming to care how he feels.

I hugged my son-in-law. "We will keep on praying. I know Tina will be okay. She needs time and love. We can give that to her."

Henri cried. He was too tall to cry on my shoulder. He cried on top of my head.

♥

I called Eileen to tell her Tina didn't want to talk to her about grief, but maybe we can still find a way. I asked her about Foster and found that he was doing well. They were keeping him in the hospital, but he was out of ICU. Rob and Eileen had visited with him this afternoon, enjoying Foster's humor, Kathleen's peacefulness and love and their whole family.

I ran to the store to pick up a few things for dinner. When I arrived home Mark had called again. I decided to return his call and see what was going on.

"Marjie Parjie, so good to hear your voice. Say, my kids and I are coming to town next week for a vacation. One of the items on the list of things to do that made me think of you is a picnic at Jacomo. Are you up for it? Henri told me you have a friend in the hospital. My mother is coming too and I thought you might bring your mother and your daughter, Tina, isn't it and her family. What do you say? It's my birthday. You can't say no to a birthday boy."

I had no idea what to say. Tina's depression affected the whole family. But Tuesday, was clear except for lunch with Mom and she's invited to the picnic, too. I told Mark I would call my mother and ask her if she wanted to come. I didn't mention Tina, but prayed that by Tuesday Tina would feel well enough to join us. She's bounced back before. I called him after talking to Mom and Henri to tell him we were delighted to come to his birthday picnic.

"Do you want to meet at Jacomo, if so, where?" I asked.

Mark said he would try to reserve our favorite shelter house from high school days, Number Five. He would call me back and let me know if he was able to reserve it. If so, we could meet out there, if not, we could caravan. His car wouldn't hold everyone unless Tina and Henri didn't come and he wanted them to, very much. He said he wanted to get to know them better.

I hung up, eager to get everyone together, strangely hopeful that Tina would want to go. Mark and his mother were two of my favorite people and my family hadn't been on a picnic since the Fourth of July. Oh no, Jakie will be expecting fireworks. I'll tell him this is a daytime picnic, there will be food and games. He'll love it. Should I mention fishing to Mark? Wouldn't Jakie love that. I'll send Mark a Facebook message.

Lying in bed it was time for thank you prayers and sleep. Tomorrow will be a great day. Wonder if Al will be at church again on Sunday.

# CHAPTER FOURTEEN

Henri, Jakie and I were at the breakfast table, mid meal, when Tina came downstairs and into the kitchen. She was dressed in jeans and a red and white tee shirt with an E.B. White quotation on it. He posed the question, is it better to improve the world or enjoy it.

"What's cooking, Mama?" asked Tina.

"Good morning, Tina," so glad to see you looking so well."

Jakie ran and put his arms around his mother's legs. "I'm having pancakes, Mams. Do you want some?"

Henri was also up and out of his chair, hugging his wife and murmuring, "My little coquette" into her hair.

"You chose an interesting shirt this morning. Looks like a good conversation starter," I said.

"I thought I would let the three of you decide whether we should improve the world or enjoy it. Sorry I've been such a lump," Tina said with tears beginning to brim around her eyes.

I spoke first. "I think it is possible to both improve and enjoy at the same time. I do it all the time, Oh, did that sound pompous? I didn't mean it that way."

'It's okay, Mom, you are among friends, well, family, and yes, you do so much to improve the world and I know you enjoy all the good you do for mankind," said Tina, not even rolling her eyes.

Henri said, "We had better check with city hall to see where we are on our building permit and liquor license. Then we need to work on our menu."

"Henri, my very wise husband, you are right. We've got to get this show on the road. Should we all go to city hall?" asked Tina.

"We might as well. Everything is in your mother's name and yours, but I want to go with you anyway," said Henri.

"Me too," said Jakie.

"Of course, you are going. You are the man" said Tina to her little son whose eyes lit up at the attention from his mother. Tina's eyes filled with tears, but she wiped them away, grabbed Jakie and swung him around.

I silently thanked God for this miracle, thinking I should still try to get her together with Eileen.

At city hall we found out that the liquor license has to be approved by the City Council. It could take several months. This was not good news.

"Mom, don't you know anyone on the City Council?" asked Tina.

"Well, yes, I do know one council member. He goes to our church. You know him, too, Tina. It's Denise's husband, Kenneth."

"I don't think I've met him or if I did I don't remember him. Which husband is that for her, number four?" asked Tina.

"Not quite, Kenneth is her third husband. A very good man. Loves her, loves her children and they love him back. I'm so happy for Denise. I've never seen her so settled in life. You probably haven't met him. You have been in France the whole while they have been married. Wait, yes you have, he was at reunion—the tall thin guy that fished next to Henri and Jakie in the fishing derby."

"I want to go see Derby Boy! I'll bet he has really grown and maybe even forgotten about me." Jakie started to pout a little, but Henri assured him that they would take a drive up to Lake Doniphan as soon as they could, maybe Sunday.

"Just thought of something, when is our car going to get here? Mom needs her car on Sunday. She has group," said Tina.

What a change in Tina. For three days she wouldn't get out of bed and now she's even remembering that I have group on Sunday, being considerate. Well, good for her. *And thank you, God! You make all good things possible.*

"Jakie, guess what? Mark invited all of us to celebrate his birthday this Tuesday, at Lake Jacomo. You can fish there. Mark said he would bring enough rods and his tackle box," I said.

"Do you think Derby Boy will be there?" Jakie said as he bounced from foot to foot.

"If not Derby Boy, certainly his brother," said his father. Jakie was pacified and started pantomiming a fisherman.

♥

On Friday night my family and I piled in our car and headed for Rob and Eileen's house. When we arrived Eileen opened the door. "Come in. Come in. So glad you could come. Seems like forever since we've seen you."

I pointed toward the blackboard where Eileen's menus could always be found. Tonight we would feast on grilled salmon, a green bean, grape and pasta salad, with crusty rolls, and Tina's dessert.

Eileen's kitchen was bright as a sunny day, with apple green walls and starched white curtains, pulled back to let in the light. The cabinets were painted white, several with etched glass fronts lit to display her mother's neatly stacked bone china.

Henri and Rob disappeared into the study. Jakie followed.

Eileen, Tina and I set the food on the table, Tina joking around with Eileen the way she used to when she was a teenager. Eileen and my eyes met with an understanding that passes between close friends who also happen to be mothers.

During dinner Rob, the unthinking, brought up Al's name.

Eileen said, "All things math, Rob. All things math."

Jakie said, "Yeah, Grandma, where's Al? He promised to take me for pizza again sometime."

I flushed and grinned. "I'm starting to think Al is living two lives. Maybe he's in the CIA. Anyway, I haven't seen or heard from him. Maybe he will turn up in church again tomorrow, but I'm not counting on it. Besides, we're barely acquainted. It really doesn't matter to me if I ever see him again."

Whoops, that sounded like I did care if I see him again, and I didn't, did I?

Tonight lying in bed I thanked God for my wonderful day, especially Tina's elevated mood. She was really fun to be around today—so good for Jakie, and for Henri, and for *Tina*.

❤

I woke at 6:00 a.m. Before my feet hit the floor I prayed, *O God, thank you for this day. Help me to make a difference in someone's life today — a difference for the good, help me choose my words wisely, to uplift and strengthen everyone I meet. Lord, let me begin my day cherishing those I love most, my mother, my Tina, Henri and Jakie and all my church family.*

Still in pajamas I went to start the coffee, beating Henri to the punch today, a rare occasion. For myself, I filled the teapot, set it on the stove and went to select a tea from the tea caddy.

I will treat myself to some Ashby's apricot tea this morning, I thought, as I picked up the tea bag. I decided to use my grandmother's Royal Doulton bone china tea set. It's light as a feather, pastel blue, with creamy ivory and gold, with a design of crests and florals. I felt like celebrating.

Henri walked in as I took the delicate china cup out of the cabinet. He came to me, picked me up, saucer in one hand, cup in the other, and whirled me around, saying, "How is my favorite mother-in-law this beautiful Sunday morning?"

He set me down. "Oh, Henri, I still can't get over how blessed I am to be able to sip my tea while you enjoy your coffee each morning. This is a fabulous habit we have gotten into," I said as I hugged my tall son-in-law. "You are unusually happy this morning, right."

"I am. Tina started taking her pills again and she has agreed to start meeting with Eileen. I wish she would take them the way she is supposed to. She miraculously has pulled out of her doldrums and plans to come to church today, although she asked if I could come back and get her for the eleven o'clock service." Henri put down his cup and crossed himself. "Thank you, God, for giving me my wife back"

"Amen to that and thank you, God, for giving me my daughter back."

Henri went to get Jakie before beginning breakfast of cantaloupe, honeydew melon, and grapes with blueberry crepes.

I went to my bedroom to dress for church. Knowing it would be hot today, over one hundred degrees again, I selected a sleeveless pale blue sheath, with a light-weight cream-colored jacket in case the air conditioning was too cool. I laughed when I looked in the mirror, realizing as I fingered the bright gold buttons on the jacket, I had dressed in the colors of grandmother's china. In keeping with that color scheme I slipped on strappy gold sandals then went to the kitchen to hug Jakie.

Tina was awake when Henri, Jakie and I left to go pick up Mom. She surprised us by appearing in the hallway as we were leaving. She was fully dressed, in jeans and a tee shirt that read:

*Touche pas à la cuisson, elle est à moi.*

It was signed *Henri Gregoirie Deschamps.*
I had to ask. "What does it mean in English?"
"It means, 'Hands off the cook, she's mine,'" answered Henri.
He turned to Tina, "Tina, I didn't know that you still had that shirt.

You haven't worn it for ages. Look Mère Marjie, I made this for Tina when we were in cooking school, when I first fell in love with her and wanted all those other Frenchmen to leave her alone." Henri smiled at his wife and me then gave Tina a big hug.

"I love this shirt, Henri. I would never part with it. It is the first gift you ever gave me," said Tina still in his embrace. She kissed him on the neck, just a little peck, but the look when their eyes met were flaming hot.

Jakie wiggled his way between his parents, so glad to see them happy with each other.

I hated to ruin this tender moment, but I happen to be a stickler about being on time. "We'd better go or we'll be late for Sunday school. See you in a bit, Tina." It was a statement, but I questioned if Tina would make it to church.

"Yeah, Mom. I'll see you in church, if you don't think the building will catch on fire when I walk in." said Tina.

"Only afire with the Holy Spirit, my darling daughter. Everyone will be so glad to see you, especially me." I hugged Tina and walked out the door with my two favorite men, Jakie and Henri, one on each side.

The heat hit us as we stepped out the door. Another hot one. Well it is August. *Thank heaven for air conditioning. Lord, be with those less fortunate that don't have it.*

Tina came to church, wearing her tee shirt and jeans, but that was okay with me, glad to have her there, besides half the congregation dressed in jeans nowadays. My emotions brimmed to overflowing having my family all together and in church. After the service Tina was mobbed by the congregation. All the people who had known her while she was growing up wanted a piece of her and everyone that was new wanted to get to know my daughter. They had already come to love Henri and Jakie and now Tina was their *object d'arte*.

Tina's being here signaled the possibility that she truly wants to hope, wants to believe in God. I pray it is so.

After church we went out to lunch, trying out a new Mexican place with Rob and Eileen and some of their family. The food was good and the fellowship heaven sent, but something gnawed at me. This should have been one of the happiest days of my life, and it was, but there was something that I couldn't put my finger on.

After we dropped Mom at her condo and were home, Tina and Henri announced they were going to take a nap. Jakie went to play with Mandy next door and I went to change into something more comfortable. While disrobing something came to mind.

Al was not at church today. I felt relief, then stopped myself, what kind of a Christian am I, not wanting someone to come to church?  I guessed my at my reasoning—my life is too complicated right now to add a relationship or even a new friendship. That seemed kind of stupid, too. Why shouldn't I add new friends into my life? I'm must be tired.

Today our prayer group prayed mightily for Foster and Kathleen who was still by his side in the hospital. They thought he would be able to go home tomorrow. His daughters and daughter-in-law had left for their homes this afternoon. We prayed for their safety.

I broke down and told them about Tina's depression, unsure why I mentioned it now after all this time and now that Tina seemed to be coming out of it. We prayed for Tina and Henri, for Grace and her family, for Denise and her family, and for Cindy, a single parent who had challenges with her children and for Beth and Jerry, who were still in the counseling and dating phase, but it was going well.

Tina, Henri, Jakie and I piled in the car with all the paraphernalia required for a picnic, well not all, because Mark and his family were providing a lot of the important stuff—to Jakie that meant fishing equipment and bait.

"Oh, Grandma, will Mark bring worms? We have to have worms to feed the fish," said Jakie, so tickled that he was going to get to fish again and maybe find Derby Boy's brother.

We picked up Mom, who was ready with sunscreen, a sombrero, blankets and a strawberry pie.

When we arrived at Shelter House Five, Mark and his family were unloading. You would have thought we were going to be there for a week.

Mom and Rosalie seemed to take to each other like Lucy Ricardo and Ethel Mertz, chatting away in the lawn chairs Mark had thoughtfully brought for them.

Mark's blue-green eyes danced with eagerness. "Marjie, do you remember my favorite musical artist of the 70s?" he asked as we spread blankets on the picnic table and benches, knowing the chiggers would eat us up if we sat on the grass.

I answered, "No, I don't think I do," as I watched his youngest daughter, Elsa, placing Citronella candles around the perimeter of the table.

"Dad, these darn candles never work and Elsa you can't put them around the edges of the table. That's where our plates go. We'll be knocking them over trying to get to the food," complained Mark's eldest daughter, Greta.

"Oh, Greta" I said, "I brought some bug spray with me. Do you want me to spray you?"

Greta rolled her eyes. It seemed to be her favorite way of communicating with me. I turned away.

"It's Van Morrison," answered Mark, Jr, "Your favorite song—*Moondance,* right, Dad?"

"You know it, Son." He began to sing, off key, as always. Granted it is a very difficult song to sing.

I laughed and finished the verse, noticing Greta's dagger-like eyes. I thought, oh, oh, must be stepping on dangerous ground here. I must let Greta know that I am not looking for romance with her father. That we are just old friends. I'll have to pray about how to do that.

Mark and Greta set up the croquet set while Mark Jr., Elsa and I finished unloading the picnic basket and cooler. I found a diet drink in the cooler that I actually like—a grapefruit splash. Elsa selected the same one. Mark Jr. picked a cola, popped the top and downed it all in what looked to me like one gulp.

The rest of the day we enjoyed fried chicken, potato salad, baked beans and chips, Mom's strawberry pie and my chocolate cake. We also fished, played croquet and badminton.

Mark and his children competed fiercely. You would have thought they were trying out for the Olympics or something. Mark Jr. and Elsa tried to include me in the competition by giving me pointers, but Greta either wouldn't look at me, or else she glared at me with her enormous blue eyes. When caught looking at me, Greta looked away.

Mom and Rosalie had their heads together, laughing and talking, stopping to swing croquet mallets and to be the judges whenever any of the kids, and they meant everyone else there, cried foul during the game.

Jakie couldn't wait to fish. He dragged his parents to the lake as soon as we finished eating. His enthusiasm rewarded with five fish to catch and release. One was surely Derby Boy's brother, the others his father, mother and two sisters.

Mark and I laughed about old times at William Chrisman. How he and Jake always had to beat each other in basketball stats and track records. I noticed how free and easy Mark's children were with him and how his son teased his sisters, especially Greta. Greta gave it right back to him and seemed to enjoy the banter. They were close in age, he seventeen and Greta, sixteen. Elsa was only eleven, but she tried her best to beat them at croquet and badminton. I played croquet with them, but couldn't even keep up with Elsa.

After the croquet game, the kids went down to the lake, Mark Jr. assuring his dad that he would watch after the girls. Tina and Henri were fishing with Jakie, while Rosalie and Mom cheered them on. They were close enough that I heard Tina hush them, saying they would scare away the fish.

Mark spread the blanket on the ground for us to sit on. Pretty soon I climbed back up on the bench. Being on the ground was hurting my back. I didn't want to complain about my aches and pains so I explained, "the ground is a little wet", and "oh, those chiggers".

Mark stayed on the blanket leaning against the bench, not minding the chiggers. *He* had let me spray him with bug spray.

We talked about the weather, the stock market, the upcoming elections for Congress. Soon our conversation turned back to high school days—the junior play, both having landed leading roles in *The Sound of Music* and the school newspaper—he had been editor, I an occasional reporter or feature article writer.

Mark took my barefoot heel in his hand, just holding it. I liked the feel of his hand on my foot. It was comforting and felt so natural. I have no idea how long we sat like that, our conversation slowing, stopping. We were gazing at the view, lost in thought, at least I was, but not really thought, lost in being. Elsa and Greta came running up the hill from the lake with Mark Jr. chasing them. Greta stopped with a jerk when she saw her father holding my foot.

"Oh, Daddy. That's what you used to do with *Mama*," cried Greta. She turned and ran away. Mark jumped up and caught her about fifty yards away. He was huffing and puffing, but he was still faster than she was.

That night my thank you prayers were very confused.

Mom and I arrived at Suzie's Do's about fifteen minutes before our appointments, so I leafed through some hair style books, while Mom flipped through the assortment of magazines until she found a *Reader's Digest*. It was three years old, but if Mom had read it before, she wouldn't remember it anyway. She turned to the *Laughter is the Best*

*Medicine* page and started reading aloud to me.

Most of them were corny, but she did find some pretty good ones.

I looked at all the hair styles for older women, then found a section on short styles, one reminded me of the cut Rodolfo gave me in January. The model's hair was reddish-blond, or strawberry blond as Jake used to call my hair. In an instant I decided that I wanted my hair colored the way it used to be. Rodolfo was right, I am still young. I need to look my best for me, not for anyone else.

Certainly not Mark or Al—even though I hadn't heard from Al for ten days, but who's counting, I guess he finds me attractive and, Mark, what is going on there? My husband's best friend, Denise's old boyfriend, and a good friend of mine back in high school. I feel so natural with him, but as friends, like brother and sister. We are going out to dinner on Saturday by ourselves. Mark said it was so we could talk without family members jumping to conclusions. Well, anyway, he deserves to see a young looking Marjie Pargie. And this may make me feel better when I look in the mirror. That was really the main reason I wanted to color my hair, wasn't it?

Suzie was inspired. She had been dying to color my hair for ten years. Suzie looked at the picture I showed her then went to get some color samples from her stash, her purple earrings swinging as she scurried across the floor. She held the natural hair samples up to my face while Mom, Jolene and a few other customers looked on.

When I picked the one I wanted, Mom said, "That's it, Honey. That's the color you were born with!" I saw Mom's eyes mist as she remembered me as her red-headed baby girl.

♥

I met Mark on my front porch.

"Wow," he said, "your hair—just like it used to be. I love it. Now you won't want to go out with an old gray-haired man like me."

Mark laughed and ran his fingers through his dark blond, silver only at the temples, wavy, thick, little bit longish, hair that reminded me of that MU basketball coach who resigned before going on to the National Basketball League, what was his name, Quin Snyder? I have always been a sucker for long wavy hair on men, even though Jake wore his short, said he didn't want to take a chance on it catching fire under his helmet.

*Oh, Jake, I miss you so. It is nice getting to be with Mark. Being with him just makes me feel close to you. I didn't mean it about the hair.*

Mark brought a corsage, pale pink baby roses with baby's breath.

As he pinned it on I was amazed, "You didn't prick me. You must have had a lot of practice with this."

"True, I wear one whenever I go to a newspaper reporter's convention," he said with his meticulous dead pan voice, as he smiled his silly goofball smile that reminded me of the many double dates we shared with Jake and Denise during high school, when he and Jake tried to outdo each other with their Alfred E. Neuman facial expressions.

We sat on the porch swing, swinging back and forth, laughing. Henri, Jakie and Tina came out to sit with us for a few minutes.

Jakie stood before us. "Are you going to take my Grandma out to dinner? Her friend, Al, took me and Great-Grandma Karin out when Mams and Papa were in France." The little imp turned to me, questioning, "Why can't we go this time, Grandma?"

"Her friend, Al, who is Al?" asked Mark, looking overly inquisitive, his brow wrinkled, his jaw set.

Inexplicably, I blushed and a tiny giggle escaped from my throat, as I turned to hug Jakie. "Al Schmidt. I don't think you know him. He's not from here. He owns some property in Englewood that Tina and Henri looked at before they leased the building on the Square. I don't know him very well, but he seems to be quite nice."

"And very handsome," inserted Tina. "Grandma Karin thinks he looks like Cary Grant. One weird thing though, he always wears Hawaiian shirts and his pants are so carefully pressed you would think there was cardboard in them. He looks like a male model, albeit a Senior Citizen model. He's got to be at least sixty-five. How old do you think Al is, Henri?"

This was getting to be too much for me and probably for Mark, so we said our goodbyes and headed down the steps.

"This corsage is so beautiful, Mark, thank you. Did you remember that pink roses are my favorite or was it a lucky guess?" I asked, feeling coquettish in my frothy pink dress with double Peter Pan collar and full skirt.

"I think it was a lucky guess, but I asked Tina, so she was the lucky guesser," he admitted.

I laughed. "No, Tina does know my favorite flowers. That was no guess for her, but a good move on your part."

"Well, I figured it was the least I could do since you are taking me out to dinner, even if it was at my invitation,"

We went to Buca De Beppo's on the Country Club Plaza. The hostess seated us in the Pope's Room. Hundreds of photos on the walls of Italian-American movie stars, pop singers and lots of group pictures everywhere increased the fun eclectic atmosphere. The food was served family-style so Mark and I decided to share the veal parmigiana. It was so good we had sauce running down our chins, but I didn't care and Mark didn't seem to. I thought about Al and what he would have ordered, in fact, I told Mark I was glad he was my date tonight, because Al would have ordered a salad with no cheese and the eggplant parmigiana with no cheese. Mark quizzed me about Al, but I couldn't tell him much.

"He is an enigma, just an acquaintance. I may never see him again unless, as I suspect, he is an agent for the CIA like me and we get put on an assignment together."

Mark said, "I would like to be put on an assignment with you, one where we have to pretend to be married."

"Mark, you haven't changed a bit, still the same old Romeo."

We laughed so hard about being spies we could barely eat dessert, chocolate chip cannoli for him and Italian crème cake for me. I hadn't had this much fun in years. It seemed as if Father Time had gotten lost during the years we had been apart.

He loved my hair, said the color reminded him of spun copper. I didn't think it looked coppery, but held my tongue, even with a friend like Mark, compliments should not be corrected like an English paper. They should be enjoyed and he did mean it as a compliment, I was certain of that.

Mark insisted on picking up the check even though I was supposedly taking him out.

I said, "Okay, but next time you are in town, I'm cooking you a meal. What's your favorite home cooked meal?"

He answered, "Anything that doesn't come out of a box."

When we pulled into my driveway I asked him to come in, but he declined, saying that he knew his mother would want a full report, and the kids were waiting for him, too.

"I do have a confession, Marjie Pargie."

"A confession, Mark, what do you have on your mind?"

"My mother wants us to marry each other. Your mother told her about Al at the picnic the other day. Mom couldn't wait to tell me. She doesn't want some other guy to come along and spoil my chance for happiness. She believes and has for a long time, apparently, that you and I belong together. When she saw me holding your foot the other day at the picnic, that sealed it for her, she urged me to act quickly. She knows I care for you, Marjie, but I didn't call you just because my mother told me to. Then I heard this Al has already been to your church for Heaven's sake...."

"Mark, I can't believe this. You and I are friends..."

He interrupted, "Marjie, hear me out. Friendships make the best marriages. You got your hair colored. Was that for Al or for me? Things are changing so fast. I couldn't wait to see you again. That's why I came to town and arranged the picnic and convinced you to take me out for my birthday. I knew you couldn't refuse after you didn't pull away when I held your foot."

"Mark, let me clear a few things up. I had my hair colored for *me*, not for Al *or* for *you*. I wanted to feel younger. I don't know why, but I like it. You are wrong about Al. We are just friends. There is no romance there—as far as you and me—you were Jake's best friend, my friend. I never thought about you romantically. Can't we keep things as they are? My life is messy right now with Tina, Henri and Jakie and the new restaurant coming up."

"I'll let you off the hook for now, Marjie Pargie, but I can't forget how I felt when I held your dainty heel in my hand and you didn't pull away. At least, not until my teen-aged keeper, Greta, barged in."

"Forget the foot thing, Mark. We enjoy each other's company. We are friends. Let's keep it that way. I'm not looking for romance."

"Sure you don't want to play CIA with me?" he grinned.

"I'm sure. Aren't your mother and kids waiting for a report?"

"They are. Mom is not going to be happy. She wanted me to propose tonight." He laughed again, a little sheepishly.

He walked me up to the door and put his arms around me. I hugged him quickly and gave him a peck on the cheek, promising to email him soon.

He said he would let me know when he would be back in town. He would try for mid-September.

"Great, Mark, it's been so much fun. I'll talk to you soon." I went into the house and he went back to his car and drove off.

I sought out Tina and Henri. They were relaxing in the family room watching a French action film. Jakie was in bed sound asleep. I sat down to finish watching the movie with them even though I could only pick out a word here and there, at least we were together. They even paused the movie while I fixed myself some chamomile tea, hoping to settle my nerves after the evening with Mark turned a little more serious than I expected.

In bed I tossed and turned unable to fall asleep. My feelings for Mark were complicated—friend, companion, fun, more than that? Romance? I wondered if Mark was really serious. I hated to ruin our friendship. Were his feelings for me so strong? What are my feelings? We laughed about his mother's plans for us, but was it funny? And what about Al?

I just need to move into a nunnery and then I won't have to worry about men, I thought drifting off to sleep, actually forgetting to say my night time prayers for the first time in years.

♥

After group, Eileen, who knew about my dinner date with Mark, grilled me for details. I told her we had a great time, laughed a lot, reminisced a little more, talked about our families. I told them about the corsage, but not about Mark's confession or our joking about being CIA agents. That would remain between Mark and me.

"Marjie, I am happy for you. So glad you are having a good time," said Eileen.

Kathleen winked at me. "I'm glad to see you are stepping out there, Marjie, and I love your hair. You look fabulous."

Denise was also there. She hadn't said a word during Eileen's grilling, so unusual for her, but she finally hugged me and whispered, "I'm happy for you, too."

I wished I hadn't told anyone about my date. I just wanted to go home and play with Jakie.

I had barely stepped in the door when the phone rang.

I heard Tina answer and start to tell whoever that her mother wasn't home, but I made my presence known so Tina handed me the phone, laughing, "It's one of your boyfriends, Mom. Then she whispered, "Mark is my favorite. My bet's on him. Al is too oogly."

This time I rolled my eyes at her. I took the phone into my office for a little privacy.

It was Mark.

"Marjie, I can't tell you how much last night meant to me. I want to see you again before I leave in the morning."

"Mark, wait…let me talk first…"

"No, I made the call. We're on my dime now. I just want you to know….I feel like a lovelorn kid—a Romeo—a Valentino—a Cary Grant."

Had he heard that Mom thought Al looked like Cary?

"I want to carry you away to New Orleans like Rhett carried Scarlett, to Rome like Antony and Cleopatra. Our love is like Lancelot and Guinevere, Tristan and Isolde, Paris and Helena…"

I interrupted, laughing, "Mark, those are all tragedies…"

"How about to the White House like Barack took Michelle or New York like Meg Ryan and Tom Hanks…"

"Mark, Mark. Listen to me. You can joke all you want, but the timing and distance is all wrong. I've got Tina, Henri and Jakie. You've got a young family and a job in St. Paul. And Greta. She resents me. Think about Greta. We've got to consider our families. Maybe in a few years when your children have graduated and Tina and Henri are on their own. Right now is just not a good time for us to be thinking about anything other than a long-distance friendship."

"Marjie, you are wrong! *We matter*. We both have lost loved ones. We can't afford to throw away another chance for love. I love you, Marjie."

I was definitely not ready for his proclamation of love. I stayed silent for a moment, not knowing what to say.

Mark let the silence rule for a few minutes, then he said, "I don't mean to make you uncomfortable, but I had to let you know how I feel. I know you are dating this Al guy, who by the way is much too old for you, also, what do you know about him?"

I had to stop him there. He was going too far and way too fast.

"Mark, I value you as a friend, one who I enjoy being around very much. We have a good relationship now and I do care about you as a friend. Let's leave it at that. Don't put pressure on me. I am not a school girl anymore. I am fifty-three years old and you should respect me enough to let me choose my friends. I think we should end this conversation for now. Goodbye."

I sat in my office staring out the window over my desk, looking at the Temple. My gaze fell to the African violets on the window sill, then to the desktop picture of Tina, Henri and Jakie, then to the picture of Jake and myself on our twenty-fifth wedding anniversary.

*Oh, Jake, what have I gotten myself into?* Wait, I didn't do anything, but accept friendship from Mark. I didn't lead him to believe that I was interested in romance, certainly not love. What should I do? I don't want to hurt him. When he and I are together, I laugh more than I have in years and laughter is important. I know I don't do enough of it.

I decided to pray about it. *Lord, I value Mark's friendship, but I can't think of it as more than that right now. My life is so full and I enjoy being with Al, too. I'm not ready for a serious relationship. It scares me. I loved Jake with all my heart. We had twenty-seven years together and he left me. I can't put myself in a position to be abandoned again. Can I, Lord? Please let me know Your will in this matter. Can I serve You better*

*in harness with another servant? Lord, guide me to know what is best.
All I want to do right now is run away and hide from Mark and Al, too.
From all men, please help me.*

After my prayer, I felt better, safe in the knowledge that keeping my mind on God would lead me in the right direction.

I found Tina and Henri in the kitchen working on a new dish for the café. They were frying up eggplant, zucchinis, onion, capsicums, tomatoes, garlic, each in a different skillet. I appreciated the fact that they would be doing the clean-up.

"Yum. That looks good. What's it called and why are you using so many pans? Can't you cook it all in one pot?"

"Mom, Henri prefers the traditional French preparation where everything is cooked separately to keep the flavors more distinct. This dish is called Ratatouille, a vegetable stew containing all these veggies, cooked with Provencal herbs in olive oil. We're going to serve it with roasted red potatoes and French bread, as a Vegan dish. Won't Al be proud of us?" smiled Tina.

"He probably won't eat the bread if it has whey in it," I said.

"Oh for goodness sake! Now we've got to find vegan bread, Henri. This just never ends," griped Tina.

"It will be worth it, mon petite. Don't you think, Mère Marjie? We decided to feature some vegetarian choices and even some vegan ones. Of course, we can fix things as Vegan, add cheese, Voila—it's vegetarian, add meat and cheese and it's full blown American. Ha Ha," said Henri.

"I say, keep up the good work. Where's Jakie?" I asked.

"He's in the back yard playing T-ball with Mandy. Can you get him and have him wash up for dinner, please, Mom?" asked Tina.

After dinner I headed upstairs to put clean sheets and towels in the linen closet, rounding the landing of the stairwell, I looked out my window and directly into my neighbor's house. Claude and Nancy were kissing on their stairs. I looked away feeling like an intruder. I had never seen them on their stairs before and now I catch this personal moment— in their own house, but couldn't they do it behind a curtain or somewhere else? I laughed, it was just a kiss, happy they still have each other and the desire for a stolen kiss on the staircase at their ages.

But, I didn't want to see love portrayed. I wanted to block out the memory of my last conversation with Mark. I didn't want to think about love.

### *CHAPTER FIFTEEN*

The day Jakie had waited for all summer, the first day of school, arrived. Kindergarten. The Big K, Henri called it. All of us were excited, then Jakie announced:

"I can't go to school Grandma, Mary Florence, Anna Jean, and Great-Grandma Karin will miss me too much. I need to go with you. And I can't miss the Prayer for Peace. The countries need my prayers. And I can't go to school on Mondays because the Meals-on-wheels people will miss me.

"Yes, Jakie, everyone will miss you. Your parents and I will miss you most of all, but we want the best for you and your job right now it to go to school and learn a lot. Learn so many things to teach us when you get home."

"Mandy said I have to play with her when I get home, but I will tell her that I have to teach you first." Jakie stood with his feet spread wide and nodded his head, reminding me so much of Jake.

"We'll see. Maybe you can play first then teach us after dinner. We will work it out. Playing is very important for your body."

"What if we play Old Maid, that isn't very good for my body, is it?"

"Jakie, you are so smart. What am I going to do with you?"

"Just love me, Grandma. Just love me."

I choked up with the wisdom of my young grandson. All I could do was hug him.

Mom's doctor ordered a sleep study for her and I wanted to take her. We checked to make sure she had all the essentials she would need for the overnight sleep study— her robe, toothbrush and toothpaste, floss,

189

Listerine, her nighttime pills, including eye drops and nose spray, slippers, her three pillows, two for her head and one for between her knees, pajamas—she never slept with the bottoms on—just panties, so hoped she wouldn't have to tonight. She decided to just wear the same clothes home that she wore in, so she didn't pack a change of clothes. She also packed some books—an Agatha Christie Miss Marple mystery—to entertain her until about ten o'clock and *War and Peace* to put her to sleep. We loaded everything into the car and drove to Centerpoint.

I helped Mom carry everything to the elevator. We got off at the Fourth floor and followed the signs to the Sleep Lab.

"I don't know why my doctor wanted me to have this study done. He doesn't know if I quit breathing during the night," Mom complained.

"Mom, your doctor ordered this study to find out if you have sleep apnea. You told him that you are so tired in the morning, even after nine hours of sleep, that you never really feel rested, that you fall asleep almost every time you sit down," I explained.

"I should learn to keep my big mouth shut, but he just keeps asking me questions every time I go see him and I believe it is just common courtesy to answer his questions, don't you think? I'm going to start eating more apples. You know 'an apple a day keeps the doctor away.'"

"He's just trying to take good care of you. You've been going to Dr. Scott for twenty years and he's well respected by all of our friends. I go to him myself. He doesn't order tests unnecessarily. You'll have the study, he'll assess it and we'll go from there." I wanted to relieve Mom concerns and mine. We were both nervous about this study.

"I bet I won't sleep at all and then they won't be able to assess anything," Mom claimed, chin lifted in defiance.

"Mom, this is for your own good. Don't try to stay awake. Do everything you can to relax and fall asleep. You usually fall right off to sleep, right?"

"Well, it usually takes me about fifteen or thirty minutes, I think. I pray and sometimes that keeps me awake, praying for you and Tina and Jakie."

"Well, let's have a word of prayer when we get to your room, okay?" I said as calmly as possible.

"Okay, Marjie. You are such a wonderful daughter to put up with an old complainer like me."

We hugged and opened the door to the Sleep Lab.

A nurse greeted us. She introduced herself as Mary, leading us to a nice room, painted pale green, a seafoam color, just like my bedroom.

There was a double bed with a night stand on one side and a small chest of drawers on the other side. The TV was on the wall—up high. I knew Mom would hurt her neck if she looked up at it. Glad she brought her books. There was a private bathroom with a shower, toilet and sink.

Mary left for a few minutes so Mom could get settled, returning before we had time to pray. She turned to me, saying, "You'll have to leave now. I need to spend some time with your mother and then she'll need to get ready for bed."

"May we have a minute for prayer before she goes? Mom asked, then added, "You are welcome to join us,"

"I'll give you some privacy. Just let me know when you are ready for me," Mary said as she closed the door.

My mother and I sat on the edge of the bed while we prayed.

I spoke aloud, "Lord God, our provider and comforter, please be with Mom tonight. Help her to fall asleep and get the rest she needs. Help those who are analyzing this study to be proficient in their jobs so that their report to the doctor will be accurate. I pray that Mom can begin to get good sleep and have the energy she needs to do your will. In Jesus' name we pray. Amen"

I said goodbye and kissed Mom on the cheek. "Call me in the morning as soon as you get up. I'll be over to pick you up in a flash."

Mary was waiting when I opened the door. "We'll take good care of your mother. And, in the morning, we'll get a wheel chair to take her down if she's very tired."

"Thanks, Mary. We can probably use the wheelchair to carry her stuff down. Those pillows of hers are bulky and a little hard to carry," I laughed, but meant it.

Mary laughed with me. "Well, you can use two wheelchairs if you need them."

❤

We did use two wheelchairs when I picked Mom up.

She chattered all the way home. I didn't even have to ask her how it went.

"Marjie, you'll never believe it. After you left Mary proceeded to wire me up and left me to read or watch TV for a while. She told me she would be back about nine-thirty to turn out the lights. I thought to myself, this is crazy. What am I, a child? Go to sleep at nine-thirty! I can't even get into a half-comfortable position to read in that bed and watching a TV that's up high on the wall is out of the question. My neck would never forgive me."

Mom scrunched her shoulders up, then back down, then continued, talking at teen-aged speed level.

"I was wired all over, with every color imaginable—even peach and lime. I felt like a sherbet. It was cold in there to boot. I had bands around my chest and abdomen, wires out my head, attached to a big receptacle I had to carry around when I used the bathroom. Good thing she let me brush my teeth before she put all this gobble-de-gook on me. I might have electrocuted myself. Marjie, I thought, how am I ever going to sleep like this? She wanted me to sleep on my back. I had those pajama bottoms on so they could watch me all night, so I would be covered up in case I got up to go potty. I never sleep with the bottoms—just panties and top, and they must be all cotton."

She took a deep breath and I breathed with her, realizing my body was tensing along with Mom's.

Her voice slowed for a half-second, "Remember, your dad used to call me his *Princess and the Pea*. Everything has to be perfect for my delicate skin."

Mom turned and fired at me, the totally innocent daughter. "Why don't they use cotton blankets at these places? They had acrylic. I hate acrylic. At least the sheets were comfortable. Well, my doctor wanted to put me through this for my own good, you said."

Mom stopped talking for a minute and I thought I would try to say something comforting, but I was driving and couldn't seem to talk and maneuver traffic at the same time, so before I could open my mouth, she said, her voice resigned, "I decided to try to go to sleep. That's all I could do. I prayed, 'Lord, help me.' I recited the Twenty-third Psalm. Got as far as *He restoreth my soul* and I was out. Mary must have come in noiselessly to turn out the lights, I never heard her. She told me I was asleep at nine-thirty."

I was glad that Mom had a good night's sleep and glad to have her home. Now we'll wait for the results.

At Bingham Manor I found Mary Florence and Anna Jean pacing the patio walkways, distracted. They didn't notice me until I spoke.

"Hi, Ladies, what's going on?"

Mary Florence turned to look at me. Her face distraught.

"Marjie, you won't believe it. Annabelle, you remember, she's Adelaide's sister, that nut. She just called me and asked me to plan a birthday party for Adelaide. Annabelle insisted that it has to be a surprise and it has to be right on the actual date of her birth, September tenth. 'Adelaide will only turn sixty-five once and she loves surprises', Annabelle said. She asked me to make all the plans, invite the guests, reserve the room, order the cake, get someone to play the piano, for there must be a piano, and singers—opera singers, preferably a tenor and a soprano, too. Oh, and it has to be somewhere that will let her bring those singing twin dogs!"

"Oh my, Goodness, what did you tell her?" I asked, putting my arm around her.

"I wanted to tell her to go take a flying leap into one of her boyfriends' arms and plan the party herself. I don't mind helping, but why can't she do anything? But of course, I'm not smart enough for that. I asked her if she couldn't do some of the planning, like ordering the cake and getting the singers. Where she thinks we are going to get opera singers, I don't know."

"I would have told her to put one of her sexy, tight dresses onto her *pleasingly plump* body and jump into the orchestra pit," announced Anna Jean.

"Well, I didn't," stated Mary Florence. "Adelaide is my most treasured student and I want to honor her and if her purple-headed, man-crazy sister won't do it, I will. I'm just not sure about a place for dogs and opera singers," She ran her fingers through her hair, tightened her mouth and closed her eyes.

I pictured the dogs and opera singers warming up with do-re-mi's but contained my laughter, sensing Mary Florence close to tears. I had never seen her upset like this.

"I would be glad to help," I offered. "What do you want me to do?"

"Oh, Marjie, you are a life saver. Bless you. Bless you," said Mary Florence as she sagged against her walker and me. Anna Jean and I assisted her to a patio chair and sat down with her.

"Well, I think you are both crazy, that Annabelle should do something. What were her excuses?" asked Anna Jean.

"She is afraid if she does any of the planning that Adelaide will find out," answered Mary Florence.

"She is such a knuckle head. That's probably true," said Anna Jean, "but she needs to at least give us some names of people to invite."

"Oh, she has, but they are all her own boyfriends, bless that kooky woman. Too bad her husband died so young, Adelaide says he kept her more stable. Anyway, Annabelle said she would try to sneak a peek at Adelaide's address book and copy the names of people that live close enough."

The three of us put our heads together and came up with a division of labors. I would ask Tina to bake the cake, but needed to know how many to plan for, talk to Eileen to see if we could bring the dogs to the church and, if so, call Kathleen to see if we could reserve the church fellowship hall for that night.

"You know, our World Church has many opera-trained singers, several of the Center Place Singers perform classically and live in this area. I'll talk to our music director to see if she can get us a tenor and a soprano." I was getting excited about Adelaide's party, having forgiven her for her backseat driving the night we went to the opera.

"Whew, Marjie, you aren't leaving much for me to do," grinned Mary Florence.

"She is an Activities Director, you know," said Anna Jean, smiling at me.

"You and Anna Jean get to write the wording, order the invitations and make a list of refreshments and decorations you want. As far as decorations are concerned, we have some lovely things at the church. Why don't we go over there on Friday afternoon and check things out?" I asked.

"As long as we are back here at Bingham Manor in time to watch *Millionaire* and *Jeopardy* sounds good to me," said Anna Jean. "Can we go out to lunch, too? I haven't escaped this coop for a while."

This startled me. I have been neglecting my duties here, working part time has been good for me and my family, but not for the Manor residents. I'll schedule some outings right away.

"We sure can. We can go anywhere you want, as long as it's within twenty minutes driving distance, if you want to be back here by four o'clock," I said.

♥

Mom called, she went to the doctor today. The sleep study showed no signs of sleep apnea. She was so glad she wouldn't have to use that CPAP machine. The doctor suggested she begin exercising more to see if that would help. She was fine with that. Her condo community has a great walking trail and groups that walk together. She promised to start tomorrow. That will be good for her.

At the computer that evening I connected with Mark. Thankfully he had cooled the pressure to escalate our relationship. I did not want to lose his friendship. It had become our habit to instant message every Sunday evening and I enjoyed this special time with him, talking about our kids, how Jakie likes Kindergarten, how things were going with the café.

I was pleased to chat online with Mark tonight, to get his weekly update and read his lame jokes. We kept things light, no romantic talk. I was more comfortable that way. I started to tell him about Adelaide's party when my phone rang, announcing *Al Schmidt*. Wasn't I on Facebook with Mark the last time he called?

I picked up the phone, wondering what in the world he wanted. "Hey, Marjie, you are a hard lady to track down. Glad I caught you," said Al in his natural voice.

"What do you mean, I'm a hard lady to track down?" I asked. "I haven't left town. Where have you been looking?" What kind of line am I going to get this time?

"Well, I went to your church this morning and met some folks who thought you were at the Santa-Cali-Gon booth, so I went there, facing the huge mass of people, but no Marjie. I was so looking forward to seeing you selling deep fried corn dogs or kettle korn or funnel cake, or seeing you up to your elbows in fritter batter, whatever it is that your booth sells."

I was still reading Mark's message and trying to respond to him by typing with one hand. It slowed me down a bit, but I didn't want him to know I was talking with Al, although why I should keep it from him, I wasn't sure.

I explained to Al that I was scrubbing walls at the café part of the day, working at Bingham Manor and getting ready for Adelaide's birthday party the rest of the time.

"I am leaving town in the morning. I hoped I could see you tonight," said Al in his most charming tone.

I hit a few more letters in my chat with Mark, so he wouldn't think I'd forgotten about him. Handling two men is tricky. I wouldn't mind Al's company as long as he left by nine, so that's what I told him.

As soon my phone hit the cradle ending my conversation with Al, I hit send on Mark's goodnight message. Doubt of my sanity crept into my psyche. What was I thinking, letting Al come over on a moment's notice? I darted to my bathroom mirror to freshen my makeup, noticing the fatigue lines around my eyes. Oh well, he either likes me when I'm tired-looking or he doesn't. Can't worry about that.

There was no need to worry. Our evening was calming and pleasant. Al and I watched a movie with Jakie, while Tina and Henri planned their work schedule for tomorrow and Tina baked the cake for Adelaide's party. Not only was Tina doing the cake, but she and Henri were preparing entrees for the birthday party.

I learned a bit more about this Hawaiian-shirted mystery man as we chatted during the movie. Jakie shushed us at the beginning, but then lost interest in us when Peter Pan flew into the Darling children's nursery.

Al explained why he called and showed up infrequently. He owned property on the west coast—quite a bit of property, all up and down the California coast. Al kept the conversation going, discussing his holdings, prime objectives, and hobbies, my tiredness holding my usual vivacity at bay. Although I was eager to learn more about him and I was relaxed and enjoying myself, I booted him off the porch around ten o'clock after enjoying some of his delicious kisses.

I tried to fall asleep, wondering why I wanted Al to come over tonight, moreover what does Al want from me? Maybe all he wants is friendship, but his kisses suggest more. At least to me they do. What do I want from my friendship with him? I found out tonight that his full name is Aldo Frederick Schmidt. According to Al, Aldo is an Old German name meaning old. Aldo was an eighth century saint. Frederick means peaceful ruler. He told me that his mother wanted him to live to be an old, peaceful ruler.

Al seems to like being with me and chatting, teasing with his pseudo Southern accent. That's nice. Tonight I think I relaxed with him as much as with Mark—with Mark before he said he loved me, because now I can't imagine seeing Mark. Chatting online is okay, but talking on the phone is extremely uncomfortable for me and for him too, I think.

Soon my body's need for rest took over. I worked physically hard today. I said my thank you prayers, tossed for a few more minutes, then conked out like an overworked, over-aged postal carrier.

I picked up Mary Florence and Anna Jean early so we could be at the church to complete last minute touches for Adelaide's surprise party.

When we walked in Mary Florence squeezed my hand. "Oh, Marjie, this looks wonderful. I can't believe how you have managed to get everything done. Everything is red and black, just the colors that Annabelle asked for. Where did you find that red and black china?"

"You'd better look closer, that's not china, more like plasticina," I laughed, thinking how fun it is to make up words. I should have started doing it years ago.

"Well, that is more practical. The cleanup will be a lot easier if we can just throw everything away," said Mary Florence.

"Not exactly, Mary Florence, I will collect all of it, wash it, reuse anything that is salvageable and recycle anything that is not. I'm working to improve my ecological footprint. I really wanted to use the church's white china, a much more elegant setting, with our embroidered white table linens," I mused.

"That wouldn't be Adelaide. You did just right; she'll love the plastic red and black. It's dramatic, like her," said Mary Florence. "And I'm proud of you, Marjie, for your care of the earth. Somebody better do something—our oceans are filling up with plastic bottles and rising with the melting of the ice caps. Too bad that Al Gore didn't get elected in 2000. Our country would be making more of a difference right now."

"Oh, don't get me started, Mary Florence, or we'll never be ready for our guests," I grumbled as I set up the punch bowl. It was clear glass, but the punch would be bright red, mostly cranberry, grape and apple juice, with some ginger ale thrown in for sparkle.

Tina and Henri sidled in carrying the enormous cake—big enough for one hundred people, the exact number invited. Decorated with vivid red frosting reading, *Happy Birthday, Adelaide* on an ivory background. Tina refused to make the background black, though she reluctantly added some black roses, very real looking floribunda. The red velvet cake was stunning. Tina had used two bottles of red food coloring to make it bright enough for Adelaide's liking.

By ten minutes to seven, the piano was in place, the opera singers standing by, the guests hiding in the Sunday school class rooms, all scrunched up. The tables were decorated with black table cloths, adorned with red oriental lilies, mums, and Japanese anemones.

All the food was laid out, various cheeses and crackers, meats, relishes, veggie trays, lots of bread that Henri had baked, rolls of all types, Kathleen's famous cranberry tarts, Denise's famous home-made mints. Mom brought a pâté with black olives.

At seven o'clock Adelaide's sister, Annabelle, and her beau of the day drove into the parking lot. Henri, the appointed watchdog, gave the signal and all the guests scurried to be in place for the surprise. As the door to the Fellowship Hall opened, Henri gave the second signal and everyone jumped out, yelling, "Surprise."

But there was no Adelaide. Annabelle cried, "I can't find Adelaide anywhere. What are we going to do?" She looked around, seeing all the people, all the food, the decorations, the piano and piano player, the opera singers and cried some more. Her escort tried to soothe her.

Anna Jean, who never had an ounce of tact, well, maybe an ounce, bustled out of the classroom with the rest of the guests, stepped right up to face Annabelle and said, "Didn't you have a ruse to get her here? People always use a ruse for a surprise party." Anna Jean's face scowled and Annabelle cried into the sleeve of her male companion.

I heard people talking: "No guest of honor." "What are we to do?" "I hope we get to eat soon. Did you see that food?" "I hope Adelaide is all right."

"Annabelle, did you try her cell phone," asked Mary Florence, flustered, but trying to appear calm in front of the befuddled masses.

"Her cell phone? Why I never thought of that. I wonder what her number is," said Annabelle, with an incredulous look on her perfectly made up face. She was wearing the tightest, most unflattering, low cut, bright red dress, that I could imagine, (showing off her wrinkled breasts), but one look at her newest boyfriend's face, made me aware that maybe Annabelle knew something about men—something I would never understand.

I watched as Mary Florence got her cell phone out and pushed on the phone book button, finding Adelaide's number at the top of the list. She reached her voice mail, left a message, and turning to the assembled crowd said, "Let's give her thirty minutes before we dive into the food, but let's not wait on the drinks."

Tina and I poured iced tea, punch, and naturally flavored water into glass cups. People lined up to get them then found places at the tables, some grumbling at the ridiculousness of trying to surprise anybody these days, everybody so mobile.

"She might be in Louisiana or California, for all we know," huffed Anna Jean.

Adelaide's customers were the majority of the guests. I visited with them while we waited, finding she was a very popular accountant with local small business owners not only because of her bookkeeping adeptness, but also her entertaining manner, unusual for accountants.

I knew she prided herself on being on time, usually showing up at least half an hour early. What was her sister thinking, not telling Adelaide that they were meeting friends here at the church and then going out to dinner to celebrate her birth? That's all she had to do.

Annabelle and her male guest sat with Denise and Kenneth, Mom and Jakie, Eileen and Rob, Kathleen and Foster, who was doing much better, though he tired easier than he used to. Tina, Henri and I floated among the guests.

At seven-thirty we uncovered the food. Half of the people flocked to the food tables, someone said, "Wow, this brisket looks and smells great." Then the rest of the guests got in line, hoping there would be enough brisket for all. They found plenty of brisket, and also cut-up barbequed chicken, Roussillon meatballs and glazed ham.

I actually heard someone say, "I don't care if Adelaide shows up. This food is enough reason to get me out of the house on a Friday night."

At eight-fifteen some of the guests came to tell Mary Florence and I how much they enjoyed the party.

They were preparing to leave, when Mary Florence's cell phone rang to the tune of *Strangers in the Night*. She barely heard it over the chattering guests, but luckily she did hear it. She flashed her iPhone at me, showing Adelaide's name on the screen. She answered, "Adelaide, where are you?"

Mary Florence's phone was on the speaker setting so I heard Adelaide say, "Your MESSAGE sounded URGENT. I'm just leaving the Pharaoh Theater. Just saw *Diary of a Wimpy Kid*. What a HOOT. Remember I asked you if you wanted to go out with me on my BIRTHDAY and you said, 'NO'. In fact, everyone I ASKED had SOMETHING to do, so I decided to TREAT myself to a night on the TOWN. I'm headed to Clinton's SODA Fountain for a strawberry SODA, want to MEET me?"

"No, well, I would rather you come to me. We have a lot of people here at Marjie's church wanting to wish you a happy birthday. Remember we came here to a tea back in May—a fundraiser for the homeless. Do you remember where the church is?" asked Mary Florence.

I hoped Adelaide would come right away and we could convince her guests to stay.

Mary Florence handed her iPhone to me just as Adelaide said: "It's out there on Liberty, NORTH of 24 Highway, right? So who is WAITING for ME? Why didn't anyone tell ME about it?"

"Adelaide, it's me, Marjie. It's a surprise party for you. You are right. The church is on Liberty, just north of 24. Please come quickly before all your guests leave. There is still plenty of food and we haven't cut the cake yet, although my grandson and a few other little ones have tasted the frosting a bit. I'll go guard the door to keep your well-wishers from leaving."

When everyone heard that Adelaide was on her way and that Tina, a very special pastry/dessert chef from France had baked the cake, well, not a soul left the church.

*CHAPTER SIXTEEN*

I entered the kitchen to find Tina and Henri pouring over newspapers and magazines, other papers scattered about—I started to sit in my chair when I discovered a pile of papers covering the seat. Tina quickly reacted by tossing them on the floor.

"Come on and join us, Mère Marjie. We are trying to decide where to put our advertising dollars. I'm sure you'll have some good ideas," said Henri.

"I don't want to get in the way. It looks like you are really getting into it."

I picked up the stack Tina had thrown on the floor and saw the business plan and budget they had shown me when they first got back from France. I started reading through the business plan until I found the advertising category. "Here's the advertising list you have already made in your business plan. Have you looked at this recently?"

"Are you kidding?" Tina huffed sarcastically. "Nah, we thought we'd just start over from scratch."

"Honey, do you want my help?" I felt irritated, but tried to keep it out of my voice.

"Yes, Mom, I'm sorry. I'm just frazzled right now. Do you mind making a list of places to advertise from the plan? Here's a tablet. Henri and I will start working on the wording for the press release."

I started a list from the plan, turning the legal sized pad sideways and writing headings across the top of the page: *Hotels, TV, Radio, Magazines, Newspapers*. Retrieving the Yellow Pages for the Greater KC metro area from my office, I concentrated on Eastern Jackson County, the casinos and nicer downtown KC and Westport areas, listing specifics under each category.

"How many hotels and motels do you want me to list?" I asked.

Tina and Henri both spoke at once, faces focused on their business plan. "Use your own judgment," Henri adding, "Mère Marjie, s'il vous plait."

Tina said, "Whatever you think, Mom. We're going to take menus around to some of the best hotels in the area and mail the rest. What do you think?"

Tina's unusual politeness did not go unnoticed and was appreciated. I knew I was interrupting them as they worked on the press release. I went to my office, created a spreadsheet and entered the data, making it easier to manipulate the information by location, thereby cutting down the delivery time and saving gas as well.

Next I tackled magazines to advertise in. I chose *Gourmet, Bon Appétit, Food & Wine* and an assortment of travel magazines, my excitement for *La Vie en Rose* building. The café was going to be an actuality, but my research would have to wait. It was time for my Group at church.

Driving home from church I tuned into 89.3 KCUR, the local public radio station. It was the end of their semi-annual fund drive. I had already signed up online to be a sustaining member, so I started to change the station, but stopped when they played "Have a banana, Hannah, Try the salami, Tommy…"—the theme song for the *Walt Bodine* food critics show. The proverbial light bulb lit my brain. We've got to get *La Vie en Rose* featured on Walt's radio show and others, like *Central Standard*. And morning local TV stations. We could be picked up by national programs—the Food Network. Ideas rolled through my head. This could be fun. I could be like a press agent for Tina and Henri. They will be so proud of me.

But when I arrived home full of ideas for making the café into a world renowned eatery, Henri's news trumped my lofty plans and brought my feet back to ground floor.

That evening on Henri's regular Skype call with his family, his mother dropped a bombshell, telling him that she couldn't stop crying with so many reminders of her beloved husband, Gregoirie and she missed her son and grandson so much.

"She wants to come to America to stay with us for a while." Henri looked at me with a question mark plastered on his face.

The first words out of my mouth, I'm rather ashamed to say, were: "How long is a while?"

Henri didn't know.

I was apprehensive, but what could I say? "I would love to have Laetitia here with us."

I lay awake in bed that night until after midnight—my mind awhirl. What room will we put her in? The rec room was the only answer. Jakie would have to share his playroom with Laetitia. What would it be like having three adult women in one house? With Henri using the kitchen as much as Tina and I, all four of us will have to share. And Jakie, I'll have to share Jakie with another Grandma. She doesn't speak English and I don't speak French. Anxiety began to build. *Think good thoughts.* She'll be able to help with the café. She's owned one all her life. She'll help with Jakie. We'll form a common bond—two widows who both love our families. She will be here in two weeks. *Lord, please help us all.*

❤

I greeted Adelaide at the door of the café. She arrived early, brief case in her right hand, left hand patting her dyed blond French roll into place. The frisky autumn wind had played havoc with the high backcombing, but her thick makeup held its own. Every time I saw her with those thickly drawn eyebrows over her piercing violet eyes, I was drawn in. And I knew those eyes never missed a thing.

"It's so good to see you again, Madame Adler. We enjoyed so much meeting you at your birthday party," said Henri as he welcomed Adelaide into the café's small office.

"And I enjoyed your food last night. Thank you SO much. By the way, I'm not a *Madame*, but a *MADEMOISELLE*, Monsieur. I decided never to marry, but I didn't want to be an old maid SCHOOLTEACHER, but an old maid BOOKKEEPER," she cackled. "Please CALL me ADELAIDE."

She smiled and Tina and Henri caught my eyes. I'll bet they were agreeing with Jakie that she really did resemble Flaps, the blond vulture from Jungle Book.

"Do you have references, Mademoiselle Adler?" Henri asked the tall, thin woman with a slight hump in her shoulders. Tina and I sat around the table while Henri interviewed the prospective bookkeeper for the café.

She looked slighted surprised, but acted swiftly.

"Yes, of course I have REFERENCES. Here is a list of ALL my clients. You can call any of them. They'll all SWEAR that I keep books better than a LIBRARIAN, heh, heh. Besides, I thought HUEY over at the office supply store across the street RECOMMENDED me, and your MOTHER and I are OPERA buffs and great friends, but here is a LIST of references if you really MUST check me out." Adelaide looked at the two young people and then me.

"Ah, yes, I see you have quite a list. Merci. Tina and I will talk it over and give you a call."

Adelaide ignored Henri. "Don't you WORRY, you two, I'll keep your books straight for you. My fees are FAIR. I charge by the month. Let's say you have about four hundred transactions a month, for that and the FINANCIAL statements, I'll charge you three hundred dollars per month. That will take a LOAD off your plate. PLATE—heh, heh, get it? Plate—you own a RESTAURANT. I said "take a load off your plate," she hooted.

Tina and Henri laughed at her joke and I joined in. It's hard not to laugh when she starts all that cackling.

"Well, I see I've taken up ENOUGH of your time and you MUST know your mother and grandmother, Mary Florence and I are going to the OPERA tomorrow night and I still need to go to the RETRO shop to pick up a new gown, well, a NEW gown for ME. What color should I wear for Carmen?" She didn't hesitate long enough for anyone to answer her. "You're RIGHT. RED IT IS." Her long lanky arms smoothed her skirt over her thin frame as she stood. "How will I EVER keep my girlish figure working for the two BEST chefs in Greater KC?"

Adelaide stopped at the door to hug me and looking over my shoulder where Tina and Henri were standing, said, "OH, by the way, I'll be back at the end of the week to install a COMPUTER program that I insist you use. It'll make my job EASIER and SAVE you a LOT of money, if you get my drift. *La Vie en Rose*..." She hummed a few bars of the French standard. "I LOVE that song. Annabelle and I will be your FIRST customers. Do you have a copy of your MENU that I can take with me?"

Tina handed her a sample menu on plain bond paper. Adelaide chirped, "I'll get out of your soup so the proverbial BROTH won't be spoiled. TA TA for now," she said as she hooted her way out the door.

After she left Tina and Henri looked at each other in disbelief, I laughed and said, "I told you she would be fun. If you don't hire her as your bookkeeper, you can always hire her to perform a stand-up routine. Have you ever heard anyone cackle like that? I've heard of cackling, but I never knew what it sounded like."

"Henri, what do you think?" Tina looked at her husband quizzically.

"I think she's a *bouffée d'air frais* (a breath of fresh air). We can certainly use a few laughs around here and if she works for all the businesses on her resume and Huey vouches for her. Let's call her tonight. Not right now. My stomach hurts from all the laughing. What's next on the agenda?"

"I'm off to be home when Jakie gets there," I said.

"I'm off to pick up the fancy-smancy menus we ordered," Tina said as she flounced out the door.

♥

The next morning I knocked on Tina's door to tell her I was leaving for work.

"Mother, you are doing it again." Tina sat up in bed, sleepy-eyed, her matted red hair hung in clumps covering her chest, tee shirt stretched tightly over her plump body.

"Doing what again, honey?" I asked innocently.

"You're putting other people before your own family. You know I need you today!"

Oh my. This daughter of mine. Try as I might, I couldn't help putting my hands on my hips.

"Tina, we talked before you moved in with me. Remember, you said, I should just go ahead with my life as usual. That you and Henri and Jakie would not take over my life. Of course, you all *are* my life, but I still have to work."

A scowl crossed her face. "Look, Mom, I've got to be at the café early this morning. You know the men are coming to lay the tile and Henri is interviewing waiters and waitresses. We're supposed to open in six weeks, for God's sake! I can't get Jakie ready for school, fix breakfast, and get myself ready and be there on time. Can't you just once think about my needs?"

I sat at the edge of Tina's bed. The same bed she slept in as child. This loved, yet selfish, only child of mine had no idea that Jakie was already up, dressed and breakfasting with his father on oatmeal with fresh blueberries and hot muffins. I couldn't help but chuckle.

"Jakie's dressed and eating now. I'll stay here until his bus picks him up. Your needs are already taken care of, Sweetie—unless you want me to bathe and dress you."

I ducked as Tina threw her pillow at me. "Better hurry if you want to walk over with Henri. He's the one who sent me to wake you."

"Yikes, what time is it? Eight! Tell Henri I'll be ready in two shakes of a *sucre tamiser*. I thought you were going to help Henri with the interviews?"

"It's better if you help him. After all, it's yours and Henri's café. I'm just the occasional hostess *and* the full-time nanny."

Tina grinned, finally out of her morning blahs. "And our press agent AND major funding source. Thank you, Mama. What would I do without you? Give me a hug."

I would never turn down the opportunity to hug my Tina. I started back down the stairs to spend a few minutes with my adorable freckle-faced imp of a grandson before his bus came to whisk him off to kindergarten.

I stopped to reflect mid-staircase. Oh, Jake, I miss you so. I know you are watching over all of us. I feel your presence here on this staircase mingled with the love of God. The thought hit me that if not for my faith in God and Jakie's birth the day before Jake's death, how would I have escaped the deep pit of depression?

*God, be with us all today and keep us safe. Watch over Tina, Henri and Jakie and help me, Lord to be a blessing to everyone I meet today. May I remember to think before I speak, so that my words will be soft and kind. In Jesus name. Amen.*

Entering the kitchen I heard Jakie exclaim in his most defensive tone: "Papa, I might eat glass—but not cellophane! Besides it wasn't really glass—it was a broken Christmas ornament and the doctor said just give me bread and mashed potatoes and I'd be fine and I was."

Henri's laughter filled the kitchen.

"Grandma!" Jakie ran to me, his protector—his one and only Grandma, at least for a little while longer. "Papa's teasing me again. He says he is hiding the raisin packages so I won't eat the cellophane."

I good-humoredly scolded Henri and hugged Jakie as I scooted him out onto the wraparound porch while we waited for his bus. He ran around the circular porch three times before the bus came. Oh, to have his energy.

♥

I awoke to the familiar voice of Steve Inskeep on NPR's Morning Edition:

*Today, September Twenty-ninth, Western Christians celebrate Michaelmas, the Feast of Saint Michael the Archangel, sometimes called the Feast of Saint Michael and All Angels. This day is especially noted in England and Ireland as the conclusion of the husbandman's year, the end of harvest time. It is close to the autumnal equinox. Days will begin to grow shorter until December, when they begin to lengthen again...*

I hit snooze on the radio alarm, laid back down and snuggled under the warm sheets. My mouth dry as a bone, tongue stuck to the side of my teeth. I forced my tongue to move around, moistening my gums and the inside of my cheeks, tongue cooperating, but mouth still parched.

Darn. My water cup is clear across the room on the dresser. I struggled out of bed, wobbling to and fro, crossing the floor to retrieve the cup gone astray.

It's not fair. It's still dark outside. I want to stay in bed.

Where are these thoughts coming from? I always get up at six a.m. It's dark most of the year when I get up. Why can't it stay June and July? There comes that negativity again. *Lord, be with me, light or dark, warm or cold. I'm having a tough morning. These allergies are getting to me. Give me energy, give me strength. Good morning, Lord. I love You. Thank You for all my blessings, especially my family, my friends and your love. Help me to be a servant for You today. Help me to bring joy, love, hope and peace to all that I come in contact with.*

Picking up the Scriptures from the nightstand I began to read from Doctrine and Covenants 163:10 a: *Collectively and individually, you are loved with an everlasting love that delights in each faithful step taken. God yearns to draw you close so that wounds may be healed, emptiness filled, and hope strengthened.*

Today will be a good day, I decided. Today *is* a good day.

I showered, dressed, ate hurriedly, poured some tea into a to-go cup and set out for my appointment with Suzie. When I arrived Suzie was finishing up with another client.

"Hey, Marjie, wow your hair has faded. You should have come in sooner."

"It looks okay to me," I replied, looking in the mirror, checking myself.

"Well, believe you me, it has faded." Suzie winked at me and pulled me closer to the mirror.

"If you say so," I said cautiously. The twinkle in her eyes caused my wariness-sensor to kick in, wondering what in the dickens Suzie had on her mind.

"How about if we jazz it up a tad? I have a new line of colors. I have one that is perfect for you!"

Suzie was on ruby slipper cloud nine; she danced to the back room, yelling, "Not many people let me play with red."

She mixed up a color that looked like it came straight off a pumpkin. My apprehension doubled, "That won't look orange on my head, will it?"

Suzie answered, "I don't know. This is a new shade. Let's try it."

Flustered, I said, "What, are you using me as a guinea pig?"

"You don't mind, do you? I can always fix it," laughed Suzie.

"I'll kill you if my head ends up looking like a pumpkin!" I can't believe I said that, but I was just kidding at the time.

"No you won't. You'll still be my friend, besides, it's almost October, you'll fit right in with the autumn colors." Suzie started brushing the dye on my hair with relish.

"If it looks bad, I'll tell all my friends who did my hair." I thought that was a pretty smart threat.

"Stop worrying. Enjoy yourself. You only live once," Suzie said.

I sat there trying to think about the rest of my day, checking my to-do list: After work I was taking Jakie to Bingham Manor for a visit, Henri's mother was arriving tomorrow from France—will I have time to go to Prayer Meeting? I glanced in the mirror and yelled in horror at Suzie who was talking on the phone in the back room.

"Suzie, get this stuff off of me. I'm a pumpkin head!"

Suzie rushed in with a paper towel and wiped a strip of my hair. "OMG! We'd better get you under the faucet."

Suzie rinsed my hair frantically, threw a towel my way, yelling, "Rub it as dry as you can while I mix up something to calm your pumpkin head down."

Heads turned and voices buzzed, everywhere I went the rest of the day—even in the Temple. I collected Jakie as he got off the bus.

He yelled, "Grandma, your hair looks like it's on fire. Razzamatazio!"

"Razzamatazio?" said I, "Where did you learn that word?"

"Nowhere, Grandma. I just made it up. It's a pretty good word, huh, Grandma?"

"It's an excellent word, Jakie. We should submit it to Webster's."

"Who's Webster?"

"A company that writes dictionaries."

"What are dictionaries?" So glad he was asking a lot of questions, taking my mind off my hair, off Suzie and what I might do to her.

"Books with lots of words in them. I'll show you mine when we get inside and we'll look up some words just for fun, okay?"

Jakie nodded his assent and we promenaded side-by-side up the steps, excited about learning new words.

Later that evening Jakie and I went in to start preparing for dinner. Jakie set the table. I asked him where the napkins were, he said, "Right there on the table, Grandma."

"But, honey, I can't see them."

"Of course you can't, Grandma. They are ghost napkins."

He laughed and I joined in, hugging my increasingly intelligent grandson.

After dinner I drove to prayer meeting alone. Jakie preferred to stay home reading the dictionary. Tina and Henri, making preparations for the ensuing arrival of Henri's mother, had barely mentioned my hair. Henri pretended, (I could just tell), to like the outrageous color and Tina merely laughed.

Prayer meeting was wonderful. Eileen was in charge. The Holy Spirit renewed and uplifted me. I didn't think about my pumpkin head until after the service when everyone gathered in the aisles and at the front to visit, I thought someone would mention my hair, but no one did. Feeling foolish, even childish for being disappointed, I began to worry my hair was so hideous that my friends hesitated to mention it. Then Rob came over to me. I might have known.  He loved it. He tousled the orange locks and asked if I would be their front door decoration for Halloween!

That night as I cleaned and moisturized my face, I studied my hair under the light and in the reflection of the mirror. It didn't exactly look like it was on fire, but it was bright, much brighter than I ever intended and orange. "Razzamatazio," Jakie had said. It was brighter than Tina's and that was saying a lot. I decided to wash my Raggedy Ann mop every day with a strong dandruff shampoo. That should tame it down a bit. I would live through this.

*Dear Lord, please help me to stop thinking about my hair and worrying about what other people think.*

My unfettered mind jumped in—what will Al think and when will I see him again. I miss him and the feelings he creates in me.

Cookies fresh from the oven, hot cocoa ready, a plate of home baked bread and some cheeses prepared, I rested with a book of poetry and a cup of tea. The weather had taken a turn to the chilly side and I wanted Laetitia to feel welcomed with warm food and drink. I hadn't seen Henri's mother since the last time I was in France. She'd just lost her husband so I hoped I could be of comfort to her. I know what it's like to lose a husband.

The door opened and Tina came through first, lugging a huge duffel bag. Next, Laetitia, a short, rounded figure, dressed in a long black dress with a heavy dark wool shawl draped around her. Henri brought up the rear with two large rolling bags. Tina and Henri collapsed on the loveseat in the entryway as I hugged Laetitia and welcomed her.

"Let's all go into the family room where we can be comfortable," I suggested. "I've got hot cocoa, coffee and tea to drink and cookies and warm bread. This is your home for as long as you want to stay."

Laetitia looked questioningly to her son, Henri and said, *"Ce qu'elle dit?"*

Surprised that Laetitia didn't speak any English after living with Tina and Henri for several years, who both spoke beautiful English, I laughed at myself, realizing I don't speak French and my whole household speaks perfect French. What an opportunity for Laetitia and me to learn each other's language!

Henri translated and his mother followed him into the family room.

"Please have a seat, Laetitia," I said motioning toward the recliner. This time Tina translated.

Laetitia looked tired, as any seventy-two-year-old or anyone else, for that matter, would be after a trans-Atlantic flight and two plane changes, one in New York and one in Atlanta, before landing at KCI. She sat timidly on the edge of the rocking recliner, nearly falling to the floor as the chair suddenly seemed to have a mind of its own. Henri quickly assisted his mother into the Queen Anne chair, lifting her feet onto the matching ottoman. She nodded her appreciation and sat quietly.

I asked Henri to find out what his mother wanted to drink. Finding that a glass of wine was preferred, that Laetitia had a glass every night before bed, I was at a loss. There had never been any alcohol in my house, except cooking sherry—which is acceptable since the alcohol evaporates when cooked.

Tina and Henri looked at each other. Tina said, "I'll get it." She ran upstairs and was back shortly with a bottle of what looked to my uneducated eye like wine. I felt like a stranger in my own home. Tina knew strong drink was not permitted in this house.

"When did that get here?" I asked Tina as I followed her into the dining room and over to the china cabinet while Henri stayed behind to see to the comforts of his mother.

Tina's face was defiant. "Henri and I drink, Mom. He's French! Laetitia's French! We drink wine with every meal. I thought you knew that. You need to be more cosmopolitan."

Tina poured the wine into my crystal goblet that had heretofore only been used for water, ice tea and lemonade. "Your glasses will finally be used for what they were designed for. Henri and I have been using jelly glasses and rinsing them out so we wouldn't have to go through this very discussion with you."

"You've been drinking? Here in my house?" I felt myself sputtering.

Tina turned and walked away.

When Tina and I returned to the family room, Tina carrying the intoxicating beverage to her mother-in-law, we discovered Laetitia asleep, her head sagging to the right, snoring peacefully to the tick tock of the grandfather clock. The afghan that usually hung on the back of the sofa covered her. Henri was nowhere to be seen, but I heard him, carrying and dragging, his mother's luggage down the basement steps to the converted rec room, now a bedroom for Laetitia.

I met Henri at the top of the stairs. "Are you going to let your mother sleep in that chair all night?" How did my hands get on my hips so frequently anymore? My irritation with Tina fresh, but in truce mode for the time being, putting Laetitia's needs first.

The three of us discussed pros and cons of waking and navigating her down the stairs or leaving her in the chair. Henri came up with the solution. He propped his mother's head up straight, securing pillows on both sides of her head, while Tina gathered a pillow, sheets, and blanket for Henri to sleep on the couch until his mother woke and could be taken to bed.

Tina and I escaped to separate rooms, Tina flouncing upstairs to her Laura Ashley refuge and I wandering to my sea-foam green and pale pink haven at the back of the house. It wouldn't have been so bad if they hadn't been so sneaky. I prayed for illumination on the subject of wine, peace for our growing household and the ability to be nonjudgmental of others.

♥

The next morning I awoke thinking, Jesus drank wine.

He turned water into wine at the wedding at Cana, *good wine* like what is usually served first before people are drunk. So Jesus created wine to give to people that are already drunk? I have read this scripture many times. It does contradict the Word of Wisdom found in the Doctrine and Covenants that it is not good to drink wine or strong drink, or smoke tobacco or even drink hot drinks, which some think means coffee. We, as a church, have pretty much done away with the stigma of drinking coffee, but alcohol causes so many problems, dividing families. It lowers a person's inhibitions. Denise told me how wild she was when she used to drink.

If Tina and Henri have been consuming wine these last four months right here under my roof, why haven't I even noticed? I knew that wine would be sold at the café, wine from vineyards across the Midwest and from France already stocked the bar and wine cellar.

I grabbed my Bible, determined to clarify in my mind whether I should allow alcohol usage in my home. I looked up all the references in the concordance, finding many.

There's the one about putting new wine in old wineskins—Jesus said, *the old is good*. That would be the fermented wine, I guess, hmmm. Numbers 6: *When either men or women make a special vow, the vow of a Nazirite, to separate themselves to the Lord, they shall separate themselves from wine and strong drink...*

Apparently, Samson, Samuel and John the Baptist were all Nazirites, promising God to follow certain rules about cutting their hair and fasting from any grape products.

Isaiah, the Prophet, writes that *the Lord of hosts will make for all peoples a feast of rich food, a feast of well-aged wines...*

Here's a good one from Genesis 9:20, 21: Noah gets drunk and naked, then curses Canaan because he saw him naked and told his brothers.

In Proverbs I found several evil effects of wine: it leads to violence, mocks a man, makes him poor, bites like a serpent, impairs the judgment, inflames the passion and in Hosea *wine takes away the heart*. I certainly don't want anyone's heart taken away.

I continued searching, at last finding Matthew 11:19: *For John came neither eating nor drinking, and they say, 'He has a demon', the Son of Man came eating and drinking, and they say, 'Look, a glutton and a drunkard...' Yet wisdom is vindicated by her deeds."*

That's it. If alcohol does not beget evil, it is wise. If it does beget evil, it is not wise, so it depends on the person and the results. I haven't seen any ill effects from Tina and Henri's drinking wine in their room. And I know from books and movies that it is true that the French drink wine at meals, even the children. Jakie has never asked for it, so maybe they never gave it to him. He's so little. I wonder what age French parents begin offering wine to their children. Something to ask Laetitia, I suppose, if I ever learn to speak French.

In less than a week my family will be serving wine at *La Vie en Rose*. I won't be serving it, I'm a hostess. I already told them I did not feel comfortable serving alcohol and they understood.

*My life is changing so fast, Lord, please help me be wise and keep me close to you. I'm fifty-three years old and have never been around alcohol, until now... I've been sheltered and blessed. Thank you and please keep me that way and help me not to judge other people, just love them.*

# CHAPTER SEVENTEEN

We sat around Eileen and Rob's dining room table for our Friday night dinner. Rob looked at Henri with his casual grin. I knew something was brewing in his witty pit of a brain, as Eileen called it.

"Oh Henri, how are you going to play the traditional snooty French waiter that everyone expects when they go to a French restaurant? You haven't a snooty bone in your head!" Rob raised his eyebrows, his smile radiated good humor, but his tone threw out a dare.

Henri blushed red.

"See what I mean," taunted Rob, his smile turning to smugness. "Who ever saw a Frenchman blush?" He pointed his finger at Henri while looking around at all of us women, Tina, Eileen, Laetitia and me.

"Rob, you've never seen me upset or seen me as a waiter. I can be snooty." Henri's shoulders went back, his chin up.

"I don't mean mad, man. Can you sneer? Let me see your sneer!" Rob challenged Henri with a wonderful sneer of his own.

Henri stood up, his posture soldier-like, he grabbed Rob's napkin from the table, planted it properly on his mocker's lap, all the while leering at him with the most awesome sneer I had ever witnessed.

Rob hooted, "I guess you can sneer with the best of them. Good job. I'm expecting to see that at the rehearsal next week. What about you, Tina, can you walk by your customers and ignore them. Can you stare right through them as if they weren't there?"

"Seriously, Rob, you would ask me that? I've been ignoring people all my life." Tina laughed heartily.

"I can vouch for that," I said, chiming in my two cents worth.

"Me too," stated Henri, losing his sneer.

Jakie joined in adding, "Me three."

Laetitia didn't understand most of what was being said, but she laughed cheerfully along with the rest of us.

I, for once, was glad she didn't understand, thinking Laetitia might be offended at Rob's ribbing Tina and Henri, in actuality, making fun of the French people. After all, Laetitia had just gotten off the plane last night.

I wondered if the people of Independence were ready for a full out sneering French waiter and rude waitress. I needed to talk to Tina and Henri about this. People here expect good service as well as excellent food. This nagging fear that the people of the town I have lived in my whole life would not support *La Vie en Rose*. I prayed they would. Tina and Henri have worked so hard. I was glad that they had decided to have the dry run with our friends a week before the actual opening. That would give us time to overcome any glitches.

♥

Saturday morning I rounded the corner coming from my office into the kitchen where Tina, Henri and Laetitia sat at the table. I thought, what are they talking about now? Will they ever speak English again?

"Hi, everyone, what's going on? I heard you talking, but didn't understand."

Tina looked at me strangely, lined the salt and pepper shakers with the butter dish, and took a deep breath before speaking. "Mom, Laetitia wants to go to Mass tomorrow. She wants to know where the closest church is. I told her St. Mary's. We need to find out the Mass times. Henri, why don't you check the internet?" Henri agreed and took off for my office.

I took Henri's chair. "You know we only have one car and I have responsibilities at Shady Grove tomorrow."

"Yeah, yeah," Tina responded, "You always have responsibilities, but Laetitia will want to go to a Catholic church. She just lost her husband. She needs her own church. I don't think she will like Community of Christ."

"Well, check the schedule. I think they may have a Saturday Mass at five p.m. One of my friends goes to it."

I do understand her wanting to go to her own church. We need to get another car. I think the kids have decided that it is too expensive to have theirs shipped over here.

My friend from Group, Cindy, came to mind. I think she usually attends the five o'clock Mass at St. Mary's. That would be great if Laetitia would attend Mass on Saturday, then if she wants to she can go with us on Sunday morning. I went to my office to pray. Henri was there looking for St. Mary's schedule on my computer.

"You are right, Mère Marjie. They do have a five p.m. Mass. I'll go check with ma mère to see if she wants to go today."

I stayed in my office praying that Laetitia would feel at home with us and God's will be done.

At four o'clock I went to see if Tina was taking Laetitia to Mass at five, but I couldn't find Tina, Henri or Laetitia. Jakie was in his room playing quietly.

"Where are your parents, Jakie?" I asked.

"They went to the café." He barely took his eyes off his construction set, my future engineer!

I can't believe they didn't bother to tell me they were leaving. I hope they left the car here.

"Where is Mamie Titia?"

"She's taking a nap, Grandma. Something about jet lag. Of course, she said it in French."

"Jakie, I am so proud of you for speaking two languages," I gushed and hugged my small grandson.

"Grandma, you'll be prouder to know I can speak some Spanish, *tambien. ¿Como esta usted? Hola, buenas tardes, Abuela.*"

"Jakie, you are really something. I have enough trouble with English."

He had sidetracked me with his linguistics, but I knew it was time for Mass. "Jakie, do you think I should wake Mamie Titia for church. I know she hasn't had enough sleep since she's been here,"

"That's okay Grandma. She won't mind if you wake her for Mass," said Jakie.

"I'm not sure.  I think I'd better call your parents to see what they think."

"OK, Grandma," Jakie said as he went back to his toys.

Tina answered rudely. I never knew what to expect from her. Where was the cute little smiling freckled faced girl? That's right, her teen years ended that. Henri got on the phone and thought that we should let her sleep. Goodness knows, she has been through a lot. They could take her to Mass in the morning if I could get a ride with someone.

I decided on peace in the family. Of course I could get a ride with any number of people, but who should I call first.

While deciding who to call the phone rang. It was Al wondering if he could escort me to church in the morning. What luck, or was it more than that? I accepted. Al agreed to pick me up at eight-thirty so we could join the breakfast crowd. I explained that Eileen and I had been trading off and it was my turn to teach the High School Sunday School class tomorrow, but he could go to one of the adult classes. He bravely wanted to attend the class with the most challenging conversation. I assured him that would be the teenagers' class.

I hung up the phone, puzzling how I could possibly teach my class with Al there. Good thing I wouldn't be eating in the class! But I would have to eat at breakfast. Why does he make me so nervous? Is it his charm and aristocratic looks? Just like Cary Grant, people said.

Laetitia slept until after six. When she awoke she found Jakie and me eating sandwiches in the kitchen. Apparently she was upset that we had let her sleep through Mass. Tina and Henri were still at the café. I asked Jakie to tell Mamie Titia that Henri would take her to Mass in the morning. She could go at eight or eleven.

Jakie translated for me, "Mamie says she will go to the early Mass just like at home."

The three of us finished off the sandwiches and a chocolate cake that Tina had been experimenting on, then worked a jigsaw puzzle. I had found a stack of them in the basement, thinking that Laetitia and I wouldn't have to converse while working a puzzle together. I asked Jakie to ask Mamie to choose the one she wanted. Laetitia selected a five hundred piece wooded scene with a doe and two little fawns. The three of us went to the den and put pieces together for about an hour, when, out of nowhere, Laetitia asked Jakie to start teaching her English.

He began naming things in the puzzle and when she showed enthusiasm he began naming items around the room. I wanted to learn the French words so Jakie had his hands full teaching both his grandmothers to speak a foreign language. He was in his element, jumping from one side of the room to another, "picture," "tableau," "chair," "chaise," et cetera.

When I went to bed that night my thank you prayers included some French words, a new friend in Laetitia, an unbelievably intelligent grandson and wonder at a timely phone call from Al.

♥

On Sunday morning Henri and I reached the kitchen at the same time. He started the coffee, wanting to make sure it would be strong enough. He and Tina had worked at the café until late last night, finding all of us in bed when they returned.

I was already dressed for church in my pale green pants suit with the embroidered jacket. Henri still clad in pajama bottoms and tee shirt. I reminded him his Mère had chosen the early Mass starting at eight.

"It is seven now, should I wake your Mère and shouldn't you get dressed? I asked him.

There was no need to wake her. Laetitia, fully dressed in her long black mourning dress strolled out to the kitchen and used her new English words. "Good morning" and "chair", smiling, she sat down in the aforementioned chair.

Henri poured his mother a cup of coffee and buttered some toast for her.

Laetitia said something in French.

Henri, a thoughtful son-in-law, saw my confusion. He said, "Ma mère reminded me she cannot eat until after communion."

He turned to her and said something in French.

"Where is Jakie?" asked Henri, also in French, but amazingly I understood.

"Henri, tell your mother that I am going to wake Jakie in a little while and see that he dresses in his church clothes, but he can take his time. We won't leave until about eight-forty-five."

Henri did as he was told and explained to his mother that Jakie still had time to get ready because he didn't need to leave for an hour and a half.

Laetitia looked perplexed and once again spewed in French.

Henri explained that she expected Jakie to go to Mass with her.

I asked him to explain that Jakie was used to going to my church and that he really enjoyed Sunday school class and being with his friends there.

Calmly, Henri translated again. Laetitia became more upset by the moment. She said something under her breath that didn't sound very nice, I thought, but wanted to give her the benefit of the doubt.

Laetitia looked me full in the face and said, in French "My grandson is Catholic. He will go to Mass with his father and me."

I didn't understand verbatim, but caught the gist of it. I certainly didn't want any fighting over Jakie. We should think of what was best for him, shouldn't we? It didn't look like Laetitia was in any mood to consider his feelings at this moment.

I was right. Laetitia stomped out of the kitchen, last night's fun and camaraderie all seemingly forgotten.

Five minutes later a sleepy Jakie stood in the kitchen having been towed by his short, plump Mamie in black mourning.

"Jakie will go to Mass with me," Laetitia said in emphatic French and I understood.

I looked at poor Jakie, rubbing sleep out of his eyes. Then I looked at Henri, who looked like a forlorn calf, caught between two fence slats.

Finally, Jakie spoke. "I want to go with Grandma and see my friends at Shady Grove."

I began to talk to Jakie about going to Mass this Sunday and to Shady Grove next Sunday.

Tina entered. "What's going on?"

Henri explained.

Tina's eyes threw darts at me and Laetitia. "I will not have my child fought over by his grandmothers about which church he will go to. He won't go to church today and not any day unless you all can work something out." She grabbed Jakie's hand and took him upstairs to her bedroom.

He balked, "but Mams, I really want to go to Grandma Marjie's church."

"Hush, we'll talk about this later," said his mother with finality. Jakie mournfully followed her up the stairs. "Come on. Let's read Harry Potter or one of your new chapter books," Tina said as she pulled Jakie up the stairs.

Laetitia and I looked at each other. I know I felt chastised and I think she did too, by the look of her mournful face. Actually, I hadn't tried to sway Jakie, but I knew how Laetitia felt. I asked Henri to ask his mother if we could pray together. She agreed. We prayed, then, hugged. Henri took his mother to St. Mary's and I went to Shady Grove with Al.

I missed having Henri and Jakie with me, but Al made the day a true mystery adventure. He was great with my teens, had them laughing about the Royals and Chiefs and joined in the lesson I was teaching that week about the Good Samaritan. He gave a modern day example, telling about a time he had been mugged in San Francisco right in front of a mission. He had to explain what a mission was, but the kids got the message.

I received a message, too, but it was so conflicted. He likes me, teenagers and everyone else it seems, but what is he *thinking*? That was the question. What does he want from me and even more important— what do I want from him? Going to church together used to signify a serious relationship, but this, on again, off again, disappear for weeks at a time, with no phone calls—what was this?

After church Al took Mom and me out to lunch at another wonderful place, this time north of the River in Parkville. We enjoyed our time with him, but he wasn't sure when he would be back in town. Ah well...for the best?

This afternoon at prayer group I asked for prayers that God's will be done in every situation I faced—home front, men friends, and the café. Yes, I asked them to pray that I was spending my time wisely with Mark and Al. The discussion that followed convinced me that I had no idea what I was doing.

Tonight Laetitia was Skyping on my computer when I wanted to use it to chat with Mark. I hated asking her to get off my computer, so I waited until she appeared in the family room, tried to reach Mark, but he was offline. I needed to ask Henri to let his mother know about my appointment with Mark on Sunday evenings.

Later Mark and I connected online and chatted quite a while. He shared news about his kids' activities. His son was in debate now, which was causing conflicts with his football practices. He was going to have to make a decision which activity to pursue. His oldest daughter tried out for the school play and got the lead, Annie Oakley in *Annie Get Your Gun*. His younger daughter made the elite soccer team in St. Paul. He went on and on, thankfully, for I couldn't think of much to say, not wanting to mention Al, who was on my mind frequently. I managed to tell him that Laetitia was staying with us and helping with Jakie and the café, keeping positive while feeling a heavy weight on my shoulders.

❤

We had worked months leading to this day—the dry run for *La Vie en Rose*. The local farmers that we contracted with delivered their goods on time. The acceptance and absolute popularity of their food at Adelaide's party had given Tina and Henri a terrific boost. We had invited fifty of our friends to be guinea pigs tonight, more wanted to come when they heard of it, but Tina insisted we stick to a set number and a schedule of staggered arrival times similar to an actual day of business. The food was on the house for this evening, a tax deductible event.

Rob, Eileen and the whole McNamara clan arrived first, all sixteen of them. It was so good to see Beth and Jerry together, looking happy, seeing that old spark. Beth had decided that she and Susanna would move back in with Jerry the day before Thanksgiving. They were going to have a renewal of their vows that evening before the whole congregation. Praise the Lord things were looking up for them.

Kathleen, Foster, their granddaughter, Carrie, and her family came next.

Another fifteen minutes went by when Adelaide, her sister

Annabelle, and her latest beau, Jack "Slim" Henry arrived with Mary Florence, Anna Jean and Eugene. That made six more, now we had twenty-nine guests. Everything was going like clockwork. The waitresses and waiters did their best to actually give great service, while giving the appropriate sneers. Tina and Henri manned the kitchen, creating scrumptious offerings of food, while hoping that everyone was enjoying themselves.

Al came alone, even though his invitation was for him and a guest. For the first time his Hawaiian shirt was covered by a sport coat necessitated by cooler weather, I suspected. I seated him with Kathleen and Foster's family, since they had met at church already, and I didn't have long to think, because Denise and her family arrived, adding eight more, now thirty- two people sat in gilt chairs around square tables.

No one was leaving, they were enjoying themselves too much, but that was okay because the café seated up to one hundred guests.

Laetitia and I played hostess while Mom popped up every so often to greet friends, sit with them a while, then move to another table. She was in her element.

The liquor license was still a no-go, but as this was a private party, everything on the house, that didn't apply tonight. I wasn't too concerned since Denise's husband, Kenneth, was on the City Council, but was he really an ally in this matter? Wine flowed freely, well, as freely as possible with the majority of the guests members of Community of Christ and teetotalers like me. Tonight most folks drank soft drinks, many enjoying the sparkling non-alcoholic beverages in the graceful, long necked bottles.

I sat for a moment, catching my breath, talking to Al and Foster, my back turned to the door. Laetitia escorted some new guests over to the table behind us. Suddenly arms grabbed me from behind. I recognized the cologne immediately. It was Mark. Living in Minnesota, as he did, I had invited his mother, but not him. My surprise immense and confused, I turned into a full frontal hug.

I felt Al's eyes on me and noticed Mark's eyes on Al. Apparently, Rosalie had decided to bring Mark and his children as her guests as a surprise for me. Mom hurried over to welcome them and chat with Rosalie. The two of them had become fast friends since they met at the picnic, mainly plotting how to get Mark and me together, although Mom told me privately that she favored Al.

It seemed that Mom entertained higher hopes for a more serious relationship between Al and me—*For one thing*, she would say, *he doesn't have children to complicate things, for another, he lives in*

*Independence, at least partially, when he's not gallivanting in California. You could keep him here, Marjie, if you wanted to.* I was convinced that Al's charm and good looks had swayed Mom to his side. I wish she's quit saying he looks like Cary Grant, although I do enjoy watching his old movies with her.

I could see Mark was at an advantage, identifying Al immediately by his shirt and I saw the look between him and his mother. I guessed the gossip game was at its peak with my mother, the veritable blabber-mouth, filling Rosalie's head with my personal information, not that it was a secret, but why did she have to tell Rosalie, who she knew would report my every move to her son. I hadn't revealed Mark's expression of love to me to my mother, but I bet Mark told his mother, who reported directly to mine.

I also knew Al didn't have a clue who this person hugging me was. I saw him lean closer to Kathleen and Foster, but they wouldn't know who Mark was. After all, Mark had never attended our church, he may have attended some of the youth activities, but that was back in the Seventies, over thirty-five years ago.

Rosalie, Elsa and Mark Jr. hugged me, but Greta was a hold out. I was certain that Al took everything in. Mark and his family sat down with Denise and her family.

When Grace and Samuel came in with their new baby, I escaped the Mark versus Al scene to join half the population of the restaurant who crowded around them, oohing and aahing, ignoring the other children until Isaac shouted "Hey, I'm the big brother! Pay attention to me."

Jakie came over and claimed Isaac, his classmate from Kindergarten and church school, and introduced him to his Mamie Titia.

Tina and Henri and their staff worked as fast as they could. The food was wonderful, but they were starting to run out of Beoeuf Bourguignon and Crème Brûlée. They still had plenty of the Boules de Picolat, several chicken dishes and many pastries. They were only expecting about ten more people, so everything should be fine. Some would be disappointed that their menu choices weren't available, but this apprised them what dishes would be the most popular. This was a valuable night.

Our next-door neighbors, Mandy and her parents, arrived at their appointed time, making forty-eight. I began to escort them to a table on the balcony, but Mandy wanted to be with the other children, so they squeezed a few more chairs around the table where Jakie was holding court, exultant that his parents' dry run was a success and he had friends there to impress.

Helen Reed and some of the Bingham Manor residents came in behind Mandy's family, some in wheel chairs, followed by Cindy, her boys and another couple. I seated them, making sure that everyone had menus and water.

I caught sight of Anna Jean waving me over to her table. "Eugene has asked me to be his bride and we want you to perform the nuptials. Will you do that? You can, can't you, aren't you an elder or priest or something?" Anna Jean waited expectantly for my answer while Eugene put his arm around her possessively. She pressed her head against his shoulder.

I contemplated the elderly couple. Their romance had not been a whirlwind, but it certainly had been a roller coaster. I saw Mildred sitting on the other side of Eugene as usual, but she had her eyes on someone else. It was Al. She couldn't take her eyes off him.

I turned my attention back to Anna Jean and Eugene, answering, "What an honor. I would be delighted to perform the ceremony. Can we get together next week to start making plans and I will have to give you some counseling on marriage before the wedding date."

"You've got to be kidding, Marjie. If you add Eugene's and my marriage experience together, we've been married over a hundred years. What are you going to counsel us about?" quipped Anna Jean.

I mulled over their situation. Church tradition, actual policy, stated the necessity of counseling before marriage. True, the possibility existed that I would learn more from them than they would from me, except neither of them had retained all their mental faculties, but they were in love and willing to take the big step, even though, as far as housing was concerned, all it meant was moving to a double room at Bingham Manor. "Well, let's get together anyway to plan the ceremony, okay?" I asked.

We decided to get together next week on Thursday afternoon.

I wondered if I would ever marry again. I looked at Mark, then Al, then ran to see if I could help in the kitchen, wanting to bury my head in a soup tureen.

The dry run for *La Vie en Rose* was a big success. Guests were gone, everything cleaned up, the hired help and the family members savored the moment with a group hug and Henri's toast. Jakie and I toasted with ginger ale then left with Laetitia to get Jakie to bed.

In the car on the way home Jakie said, "I can get my dog now! Papa said everything was a success—I can have my dog." I couldn't see him well, but his voice radiated excitement and yearning.

I stared in the rear view mirror at Laetitia, who shrugged her shoulders. I caught my grandson's eye, "What are you talking about,

Jakie? This is the first I've heard about a dog."

"Oh, yes, Grandma. Papa said I could have a puppy as soon as the café was a success. It was tonight, so when can we get my puppy?"

Startled, I pulled the car over to the side of the street even though we were only a block away from home. I turned around to face Jakie in the back seat.

"I think your Papa and I are going to have a talk about this. Puppies are big responsibilities, Jakie. Who would take care of it?" My stomach began to churn and my sweat glands kicked in.

"I would, Grandma. And don't call him it. It will be a boy dog. I want a dog just like Mamie Titia's. Well, he was Grandpa's dog before he died... unless, we can bring Hugo over here?" he said, turning to his Mamie, "Can we Mamie? Can we bring Hugo over here? I know he misses me and Papa and Mams and you, Mamie Titia. We should have him sent over here." Jakie said in French then translated into English for his language-challenged grandma.

The two of us grandmas looked at each other, sizing up the situation. This was the first I had heard about Jakie wanting Hugo to fly to the U.S.

I like dogs, but I'm not a good dog owner. I don't like slobbering, jumping, muddy dogs. I want dogs to lie still all the time. I prefer stuffed animals that don't shed on my pastel colored furniture. Oh my. A dog would change our lives more than the café or even Laetitia moving in.

While I was off in la-la land thinking about all the reasons I didn't want a dog in my house, Laetitia spoke excitedly to Jakie in French, of course. Jakie listening attentively, cried "Yea!" then turned to me and told me his Mamie Titia said they could not bring Hugo to the United States. He was too old and the trip would be too hard on him.

Silently, I said, thank you, Laetitia, but my gratitude came too soon. Jakie continued:

"Grandma, Mamie Titia said she would buy me a new Hugo. He's a French bulldog, Grandma. You'll love him." Jakie's voice and eyes showed how much he wanted this dog. And now his French ally was promising something that she had no right to promise. This dog would live in my home. I felt certain that I would be the one taking care of it, unless, Laetitia would agree to care for it and who knows how long she will be here.

I directed the Toyota back out on the street without saying anything more. Jakie and Laetitia were laughing and carrying on like two kindergarteners in the back seat. I'll have to take this up with Tina and Henri, but I'm against it. It makes me feel like an old meanie, but I'm not good with dogs. This will require a lot of prayer, patience and possibly the loss of affection from my only grandchild.

♥

I slept little and rose before the sun, hoping to catch Henri and give him my point of view about the puppy situation. I found him in the kitchen opening cabinets. "Henri, so glad to find you alone. I have something to talk with you about."

"Mère Marjie, last night was heaven. Everything went so well, better than I had hoped. Thank you so much for everything. I'm looking for the heating pad. Tina wants it for her back. Do you know where it is?"

"You are welcome. I am glad too. The heating pad should be in the bottom drawer of the upstairs bathroom."

"It's not there. I looked," he said gesturing upward.

"Well, I wasn't in on the heating pad hiding escapade," I said, my tiredness and frustration coming out. I never said things like that. But I was upset about the puppy promised to Jakie. I tried to calm myself.

"Henri, I want to talk to you about something that Jakie said on our way home last night. He told me you said that he could have a puppy. It was the first time I had ever heard anything about a pet, much less a puppy. I am not a good pet owner. I have had some bad experiences. Once when Tina was little, Jake and I bought her a puppy for Christmas. The puppy turned out to be a monster. It chewed my furniture, my slippers, my favorite table cloth—long, story, short—we gave him away. I felt so bad. Tina cried and cried, but I just couldn't take it. Later, when she was older we tried again, a darling older dog, a dachshund. I loved that dog. She got sick, leukemia, who knew that dogs could get leukemia? Anyway, I rocked that dog just like a baby, for weeks. It wouldn't eat. I tried feeding it with an eye dropper. We got it blood transfusions. It died. Then for years I dreamt about starving dogs. Dogs I was supposed to be taking care of, I guess. I always felt so guilty after those dreams. I just don't think I can handle another dog."

Henri put his arms around me. "I understand. I'm sorry that I didn't talk to you about it first. I'm surprised that Tina never told me about your bad luck with dogs. She agreed that a puppy for Jakie would be a good idea. I'll go talk to her and we'll talk to Jakie."

As Henri went upstairs with Tina's coffee and still no heating pad, I felt worse than ever. Now Tina and Henri would have something else to fight about. Everyone in this house, but me, wants a puppy—four other people. Should I be so selfish? But wait a minute. Tina and Henri are busy with the café. Who knows how long Laetitia will be here? I definitely would end up taking care of the mutt. My life is so full now, how can I handle even one more thing—especially a dog!

I filled my mug with hot water from the teakettle, dropping my favorite morning tea in the mug, Ashby's Apricot. After two minutes I pulled the bag out, added a teaspoon of sugar, stirred and while it was still whirling in the cup, added a dash of skim milk. I stood over the cup watching the milk blending, swirling with the tea, thinking how wonderful the color was. I sipped the hot beverage, relishing in the fruity aroma, then walked over to the refrigerator to get the wheat nut bread, made toast, topping it with the elderberry jelly that Grace's mother had given me.

I carried toast and tea to my office where I slipped into my comfy chair to read the Daily Bread, hoping that the Lord would grant me a few minutes of peace and give me some wisdom about this puppy question so I could get on with other matters. After reading today's selection in the Daily Bread, I sat in silence, trying to feel God's presence. Many thoughts popped into my head, but nothing puppy-related. I felt nothing but pure peace and happiness. This lasted about ten minutes I supposed, losing track of time. My remaining tea left untouched, was room temperature when I tasted it, so maybe it had been longer. As much as I love my family, these times alone with the Lord are so precious.

Hearing voices in the kitchen, I rose to join them, but remembered the puppy and sat back down. I picked up my journal and wrote, *Puppy, or no puppy, that is the question.* I drew a line under *no puppy*, but put a question mark after it. I decided to do a Ben Franklin list—pros on one side cons on the other. Let's see: Pro—It will make Jakie happy. Con—dog hair, muddy paws, drool, dog dishes under foot, dog under foot, no fence in the yard, dog walks, pooper scooping. I knew I could go on and on, but making Jakie happy was so important and if Tina and Henri wanted a dog, too. What should I do? Pray. I'll keep praying, but knew Jakie would not leave this alone and I couldn't very well avoid him. I had promised to take him and Mandy to the zoo today. More animals. That should take his mind off the puppy, *right*. I can't believe that Tina and Henri and Laetitia have put me in this position. Making *me* the bad guy—bad grandma, even.

The voices in the kitchen grew louder. Tina and Henri were fighting. I hated to interfere, but heard Jakie crying and Laetitia spouting French and my name shouted in all its various forms, "Grandma, Mom, Mère Marjie", so I mustered the gumption and went in to join the fray and defend myself if necessary.

Henri was upset with Tina for not telling him how I felt about dogs. Tina was mad at me and Henri—me, for not wanting a dog, Henri, for not convincing me to get one. Laetitia couldn't understand anyone not wanting a French bulldog, the best breed that ever was.

I could see that Jakie hated all the yelling by the way he had his hands over his ears and knew he couldn't understand why his Grandma Marjie would deny him anything. He looked at me with such a hang-dog look, I couldn't take it. I just turned around and went back to the serenity of my office, but it was not to be serene anymore. Tina was the first to break the peacefulness of my sanctuary.

"Mom, why can't Jakie have his dog? There are plenty of us to take care of a pet and it will be good for Jakie. Teach him some responsibility." Tina flounced onto the fainting couch in the corner of my office. I felt her staring a hole in the back of my head.

"Tina, I can't believe you put me into this position. You should have talked to me before saying anything to Jakie. We don't have a fenced-in yard, which means someone will have to go out with the dog every time he does his business. Winter will be coming soon and I certainly don't relish standing outside in the cold, do you?"

"We could put up a fence," said Tina, smiling at me, thinking she had me on the ropes already. I do know my daughter.

"This is such a bad time. The café hasn't even opened yet. Am I the only adult in this house?"

"Mom, you know how Jakie feels I don't love him? This would give us a way to bond."

I moved to the fainting couch so I could sit by my daughter, taking her hand. "Tina, I can think of lots of ways that you and Jakie can bond. And why do you think he thinks you don't love him?"

She pulled her hand away. "I'm so moody and he takes it personally."

"He's only five years old. How is he supposed to take it?" My earlier serenity seemed suddenly stolen from me.

Tina swallowed hard and bit her lip. "Are you attacking my mothering skills?"

"You brought it up," I was at my limit and Tina began to cry and naturally, so did I.

Henri knocked gently on the door. I whimpered, "Come in."

He put his arms around his wife and me, his used to be favorite mother-in-law. We remained quiet for a few minutes.

I have no idea where this came from, but I broke the silence with,

"Let's tell Jakie we have to have a fence built and wait for spring when the weather will be better to train a new puppy, then he can have his French bulldog. How does that sound?"

"Sounds good, as long as we can blame you for the delay," laughed Tina, tightening the group hug.

"Why not, your father always said I had broad shoulders for a broad," I smiled at Tina and a special moment of remembrance flashed between us.

"He was a character. A wonderful character. I miss him so much. I wish he were here. He would love helping Jakie train a puppy," sighed Tina.

With that the three of us went looking for a small boy to convince that spring was the best time for a new puppy.

Saturday came again. Laetitia told Henri that she was getting more acclimated to the time change and she thought she would try Saturday mass. Tina and Henri had to work at the café, so I elected myself to drive Laetitia and Jakie to St. Mary's Church and attend Mass with them. I hoped I would see my friend Cindy.

I hadn't been inside a Catholic church for years. When Jake was Fire Chief we attended a lot of firemen weddings and several had been Catholic Nuptial Masses, but never one at St. Mary's.

We arrived early. Awed by the beauty of the structure, I was glad to be there, hoping that sharing worship with Laetitia would create a stronger bond between us.

I looked for Cindy, but didn't see her.

The priest gave a short sermon, only in the order of worship it was called a homily. I was surprised when the Mass only lasted forty-five minutes, but more surprised to see people leaving before the service came to an end. I turned around and seeing Cindy sitting in the back row by herself, hoped she wouldn't leave early. I wanted to talk to my friend, but didn't want to disturb Laetitia who was kneeling, praying with her head down, eyes closed. By the time the Mass ended and the priest announced that we could *go in peace*, I looked to see if Cindy was still there. She was not. I stood and took Jakie's hand. Laetitia was still kneeling in prayer so I asked Jakie to tell his mamie that I wanted to look for someone and would wait for them in the foyer.

Not seeing Cindy in the church, I rushed out the door and looking to the right, spotted Cindy getting into her car but with difficulty, so I caught up with her just as she sat behind the wheel.

Cindy, startled by my appearance, jumped a little, then laughed. "Marjie, what are you doing here?"

"I brought Laetitia and Jakie to Mass. I need to go back in, but I just wanted to say 'Hi' and let you know I'll probably be seeing you at Mass every Saturday for a while."

"Well, to tell the truth. I don't make it every week. If I'm feeling too tired and don't feel like driving. I stay home." Cindy's MS must be getting worse.

"Why don't I start picking you up? You live near here don't you?" I asked.

"I don't want to be any trouble," said Cindy.

"Hush, no trouble at all. I'll be coming anyway."

"Well, that would be wonderful. I don't like to miss Mass, but I am getting afraid to drive when I'm tired."

I reached through Cindy's car window and hugged her. When I stood up I discovered Laetitia and Jakie waiting for me at the top of the steps. I waved them over and introduced them to Cindy. We chatted for a few minutes then Cindy drove away.

That night I had a new thank you. I loved the spirit of the Mass and sharing with Laetitia and Jakie and was glad to have a new connection with Cindy. I fell asleep thinking of the peace that surrounded me.

Sunday evening I chatted on Facebook with Mark as usual. He had gone home on Saturday, so we did not see each other after the dry run.

I told him about the puppy discussion and resolution. He told me about his kid's games. He didn't mention Al and neither did I. We signed off until next Sunday.

### *CHAPTER EIGHTEEN*

The house was quiet. I took my tea out to the front porch to relax and take in the autumn air before taking off for work. My cell phone rang to break the silence. "Marjie, good, I caught you." My supervisor, Helen, sounded relieved and upset in the same breath.

"I was just finishing my tea. How can I help you?" Helen had never called me at home before.

I heard a smirk in her voice. "Can you stop by the police station on your way to work and pick up Mildred?

Now, this is a new one, I thought. "Why is Mildred at the police station?"

"Don't ask. You'll find out when you get there…and, Marjie, thanks. I've got my hands full here." The phone went dead and I knew Helen had hung up.

That Mildred—last time the group from the Manor went to Independence Center she went off by herself and forgot where the designated meeting place was. We're going to have to watch her more closely.

I entered the lobby of the police station and went to the window. The clerk looked up and emitted a guttural drawl of "y-e-s". I tried not to stare, but her decorated breastbone cried out to be noticed, covered with a beautiful blue butterfly tattoo and softly accented by a cowl neck shirt of pink and blue flowers. The butterfly appeared to be resting on the flowers and seemed part of the ensemble. I searched for a name plate and found it. Her name was Mary.

"Mary," I said, "That is the most beautiful tattoo I've ever seen. It's lovely."

Mary smiled.

When I told her I was here to pick up Mildred, she looked at me

229

with sympathy and chuckled, "Is she your mother?"

I explained that she is a resident at the Bingham Manor Senior Living Home where I work.

"She's a pistol, that one." She laughed and picked up the phone. "Bring Sex Shop Mildred up. Her caretaker is here."

I saw no reason to explain my role at the Manor to her. I sat down and waited for Mildred wondering at the label Mary had given her. Ten minutes later Mildred appeared on the arm of a handsome male officer.

"Marjie, the charges have been dropped, but I told them this isn't the first time I've been handcuffed." She turned and batted her eyes at the officer. "Officer Joe has been so helpful."

"What happened?" I asked, feeling totally out of my sphere of reference.

Officer Joe gently unwound her arm from his, unable to hide a grin, "She was arrested for shoplifting at the *Mom and Pop Sex Shop* on 24 Highway just before you cross into Kansas City."

"The what?" I exclaimed.

"Marjie, it was all a misunderstanding. I wanted to get a wedding present for Anna Jean and Eugene, something I thought they would actually use. I went to my favorite toy store. I thought I saw my taxi drive off, so I ran outside."

That answered how she got to the sex shop in the first place.

"I was going to pay for it. These oafs came running after me, hauled me back in to the store, a little rougher than they needed to be. I am almost ninety, you know. Then this nice policeman came and brought me here. Those people at Mom and Pops have changed management. The old owners would not have called the police. It's a chain store now, not an independent. Can you believe it? I'll never shop there again. I can tell you. I told them I would pay, but then I didn't have my billfold. I must have left it in the taxi."

I took a deep breath and thanked Mary and Officer Joe. "We'd better go, Mildred. What taxi company did you call?" I asked.

"I just wanted something for Anna Jean and Eugene. He's almost ninety—thought they could use something to jazz things up a bit. I don't think Viagra is safe for old men." Mildred nodded like she knew what she was talking about, but I didn't want to know any more than she had already told me.

I asked again about the taxi company. She didn't remember, but I found the number on her cell phone, we prayed about finding her billfold, called them and blessings continued to fall on Mildred that day. The driver would deliver her billfold to her at Bingham Manor.

♥

Anna Jean, Eugene and I sat around an interesting desk in Anna Jean's room that served as her kitchen table. The surface was so small that my scriptures, notepad, hymnals and assorted wedding music completely filled it.

"Marjie, I hope you don't mind, but Eugene and I have already done most of the planning," Anna Jean said smugly. "We've both been through this before, you know. Actually, Eugene has been through it a few times."

"Only four, Anna Jean, and this will be my last. I will never love another as much as I love you." Eugene put his arms around Anna Jean and kissed her firmly on the lips."

"Why don't you tell me what you have planned?" I said.

"We want this to be a day that we will never forget, a day that Bingham Manor folks will never forget—a day that you, Marjie, will never forget."

I waited for a lull, "How do you plan to make it special?" I queried, fearful of the response.

"We want to get married on Veterans' Day at your church, all the military that have them can wear their clothes…" began Anna Jean.

"Uniforms, Sweet Pea," said Eugene.

"Don't start correcting me, Eugene. Marjie knows what I mean. But wait till you hear the best part. We get to dance here every week. We don't want a dance for our reception. We want everyone to go bowling with us. We're gonna reserve the bowling alley. I know everyone will love it."

Intrigued with the idea of it, but wondered about the practicality, I uttered, "But how will most of them bowl. Many are on walkers and in wheel chairs. How do you expect them to bowl?"

"Oh Marjie, don't be a stick in the mud. Eugene said they have contraptions…"

"They are called ramps, Sweetie Pie," inserted Eugene.

"Eugene, what did I say about correcting me?" Anna Jean's voice tilted upward.

Ah, love! I thought.

Anna Jean continued, "Anyway, you sit your ball on this contraption, this *ramp*, if you must have the exact word, Eugene, and it flies down the shoot and on to the alley and gets a strike most every time. Don't you think this will be the most fun our guests have ever had!"

I prayed silently for their marriage.

I tried to get them focused on the wedding ceremony itself, but to no avail. Anna Jean wanted to plan the bowling alley pizza reception and all Eugene cared about was wearing his uniform to the ceremony. He had retired after twenty-five years in the Navy and was proud that he could still wear his dress whites.

I decided to enlist Mary Florence's help, so I went to her room, leaving the love birds arguing over whether they should buy matching bowling balls and shoes for the reception. Anna Jean was pro—she wanted a baby blue ball and shoes, Eugene was con—just use house ball and shoes, they would probably only use them one time, he said.

When I got to Mary Florence's room I heard Adelaide's cackle from outside the door. Ah, well, may as well just go in and enjoy myself. I'll plan the ceremony on my own. I can't wait to see what these two are up to.

♥

What a day! It was late. I had scrambled all day, taking the day off work and skipping all my usual activities to help Tina and Henri on opening day. Laetitia and I scurried, scampered, skipped, even skittered to keep pace with the customers. *La Vie en Rose* opened at eleven o'clock for lunch. Tina and Henri were industriously employed in the kitchen, waiters and waitresses engaged with their customers, all of us thrilled that so many people came to try out the new French restaurant on the Square. At dinner time hungry patrons happily waited up to an hour for a table, many glad the bar was stocked with fine wines to sample. I never thought I would be pleased that people like to drink and I wasn't, but I did want happy customers and I reminded myself that I'm trying not to judge. I guess Tina and Henri owe the city council a thank you letter for coming through with the liquor license just in time.

In bed I was so wound up I starting reading *Death Comes for the Archbishop*, hoping it would help me fall asleep. But I heard Tina and Henri's voices. It sounded like they were arguing, but I couldn't be sure because sometimes their fun conversations became so animated and loud. I could tell they were in the family room. Not listening was not possible, they yelled so.

Tina was loud as a child. In fact, Jake and I worried that she might have a hearing problem, so we took her to have her hearing checked. The doctor tested her and determined that Tina was just enthusiastic. So we lived with a loud, wild, emotional child and loved her for it. When I first met Henri, he seemed so quiet, but now living under the same roof, I found that his voice could outdo Tina's at will. His mother, Laetitia, spoke out loudly in French, but when she spoke English she lowered her volume and I had to ask her to speak up. Thinking of Laetitia, I wondered if she could hear them argue from her bedroom in the basement. Because now I was certain they were quarreling. Why would they fight on this of all nights? The café opened as a success. They should be celebrating.

I'll think positive. That's all I can do right now. Everyone raved about the food, especially Tina's desserts.

*Lord, thank you for the blessings we received today. La Vie en Rose was filled to capacity. Please help Tina and Henri to recognize their blessings and not focus so much on their differences. Help me to know if there is anything I can do or say to help them.*

The next morning Tina and Henri were all smiles, no sign of a quarrel, so thankful that their opening had been a success. Several local food critics had been there and they were anxious for the Sunday Star reviews to come out, but they couldn't rest on their laurels, today was another day with another special to promote. I gleefully spotted Henri kissing Tina's hair on their way out the door.

Young love, I thought, so grateful they had made up, whatever bothered them last night put aside for now.

What about old love? What is in the future for me? I can't think about Mark and Al right now. I'll think about them later, much later, I said to my Scarlett O'Hara self.

Soon Jakie was awake and so was Laetitia. We two grandmas fixed his breakfast together. Laetitia prepared the eggs while I made toast and cut up some pears and bananas, adding blueberries for a nice compote. Hard to believe, but we were getting along famously. I was so busy with my job, the café, mom and friends, I relished sharing my kitchen and even my grandson with Laetitia. Her help with Jakie, the house and the café was necessary and extremely appreciated.

I called Cindy to see if she wanted a ride to St. Mary's—she did. We all went to Mass together. Laetitia practiced her English on Cindy, Jakie and me in the car, her vocabulary and pronunciation improving each day, while my efforts with French languished. I must not worry about that either. I'll just be happy for Laetitia.

❤

I woke to the sound of the local weather on NPR. The area had suffered a freeze last night. "Oh, Pickle, why does it have to get cold so early? I dressed and went out on the porch to lean over and look at the plants in the yard. Frost covered the lawn, making it look like a blue lake in the dark morning light. I checked the plants. The mums would be okay and the knock-out roses, but what about the hosta?

Brrr. It was cold. My goodness. What were these doing here? I was dismayed to see my indoor plants on the porch, my peace lilies, begonias, shamrocks, tropical hibiscus—my Agatha, (I had named my hibiscus after the Agatha character on Magnum P.I.), everything was covered with frost. Who could have put these out here? I would never put these outside, because the bugs eat them and you never can tell about Missouri weather. I began carrying them into the house like my long lost babies, tenderly putting them back in the various spots they had occupied for years, many given when Jake died. Oh, I didn't want to lose them. Surely Tina, wouldn't have, or Henri. Jakie couldn't carry them. It had to be Laetitia! She's from southern France where they don't get frost, at least not in October, I don't think. What shall I do? I don't want to upset her, but they are *my* plants. Why in the world would she put them outside?

"Oh, Laetitia. Henri. Good morning." I set the purple shamrock on the counter, its petals frozen, stalks drooping. Laetitia, appropriately in her black mourning, started to cry.

I said, "Ah, yes, the plants. The weather turned cold and zapped them, but hopefully they will come out of it." I tried to smile and act like everything was okay.

Laetitia stammered in broken English. "*Mon Dieu*! Sorry. Forgive please. I know not..."

She turned to Henri, blubbering something in French, undoubtedly asking Henri to translate something.

Henri said, "Mère Marjie, ma mère wants me to tell you she will buy you new plants. She is so sorry. She thought they needed some fresh air."

"Henri, please tell her it is not a problem. Most of them will recover. I know she isn't used to Missouri climate, warm one day, cold the next."

I gave Laetitia a hug and we smiled into each other's eyes.

❤

Mom and I decided to eat at her house today before going to the Prayer for Peace at the Temple. She sat across the table from me grinning like a Cheshire cat, a little devilish sparkle in her eyes.

"Mom, what is going on? You look like you are about to burst. Is there something you want to tell me?"

"Yes, there is, but I'm sworn to secrecy." She darted her eyes to the teapot. "Another cup?"

"Secrecy, who would swear you to secrecy?" I didn't like the thought of this, but Mom seemed happy, not worried, unusually animated.

"Oh, Honey. I just can't tell you." She busied herself by taking a bite of sandwich.

"Well, we've never kept secrets from each other before." This was so unlike my mother.

"Sure we have—the Tooth Fairy, Easter Bunny and Santa Claus." She took a drink of tea.

"Is this something like that? You know I'm over fifty years old. I think you can tell me most anything."

"I'm afraid you'll be really mad." Mom set her teacup down and missed the saucer.

"Mad at whom?" This was the strangest conversation Mom and I had ever had.

"At the person who made me swear." She righted her cup firmly in the saucer.

"Honestly, Mom, how can anyone make you swear?" My life keeps getting more interesting.

"This person is very intelligent and persuasive." Her chin quivered a little bit and I started feeling guilty for causing her to be upset, but she started the whole conversation.

I put my hands in my lap and stared at my mother, who was acting like a child. "Well, either tell me or don't. I don't like playing games and you don't either, by the way."

"Okay. I won't." She finished the last bite of her sandwich and got up to put the dishes in the dishwasher.

I was still eating, chewing my sandwich while my brain chewed on this crazy conversation. Always one for a mystery, my curiosity piqued, I changed my mind. I did want to know. I decided to try some questions that might dig this shrouded secret from her lips.

"Have you been over to Bingham Manor without me? Is it Anna Jean? It sounds like Anna Jean."

"I said she was intelligent and persuasive." Mom played well at this game, not giving me any new clues.

"She can be. It was her idea to have their reception at the bowling alley, you know."

"I can't tell you." Mom firmly screwed the lid back on the mustard jar, opened the frig and stuck it in the side door compartment.

I felt the need for the Prayer for Peace more than usual that day.

♥

It was Halloween. I inhaled the colors of the leaves, red, golden, yellow, some still green, through the senses of sight and smell as I drove, windows down, on the way to Bingham Manor. Every year I believed this autumn more beautiful than any other in my experience. How sorry I felt for people who live in climates with no deciduous trees, the ephemeral beauty catching my breath, denying that this transitory artistry boded the coming of winter.

I bounded up the steps to locate my friends. Mary Florence met me at the door.

"Hi Marjie. Is your grandson still coming to visit in his costume today?"

"I hope so, Mary Florence. Tina said she would bring him, but you know how busy she is with the café."

"They brought in a nursery school class today. We had cookies and punch for them. They were so cute in their little princess and Spiderman outfits and such," commented Anna Jean. "Oh, shush, *Millionaire's* back on. I just love that Meredith Vieira. She's so sassy. Reminds me of myself. She kinda looks like me. Wonder if we could be related?"

Mary Florence let out a huge laugh. "Oh my good Lord, who is that kid coming in here looking like the Grim Reaper. Who would bring a kid to a nursing home dressed as the Grim Reaper? Look at that scythe he's dragging. Ha Ha. It's bigger than he is."

"I don't think it's one bit funny," snarled Anna Jean.

I spotted Tina with this little child with a ski mask pulled down over his face. It had to be Jakie.

"I don't either, Anna Jean, but it just happens to be my grandson." How could Tina bring him to a senior citizen home dressed like that, how embarrassing. Luckily, at least Mary Florence was amused.

"Hey, Grim Reaper, come over here and pose with me," chuckled Mary Florence. Jakie came right over and stood next to her, a big smile on his partially masked face.

"Here, Anna Jean, take our picture" said Mary Florence as she handed Anna Jean her trusty Canon Sure Shot.

"Oh, all right," groaned Anna Jean, "but I'm standing clear over here. I'm not getting anywhere near that Devil of Death!"

"I'm sure he's an angel. This is just for fun. And he is Marjie's grandson. Lighten up, Anna Jean, and use the zoom if you're gonna stand on the other side of the room," directed Mary Florence.

Tina and I looked at each other, laughing—me, in spite of myself.

"Thanks for bringing Jakie today. Even if you did embarrass me almost to death," I said to my mischievous daughter.

After all the hoopla of the party, after all the guests had gone, cake and ice cream devoured, Kathleen and I relaxed on the sofa talking about *the roast* her children had given her to celebrate her ninetieth birthday. I continued the fun, reminding Kathleen about the time she dressed up as a gypsy for one of her daughter's birthday parties.

"Remember, Kathleen, your fortune-telling skills impressed one of guests so much she offered to hire you for her own daughter's party and you accepted. Remember, it was a girl that Charleen didn't particularly like and she was so upset with you."

Kathleen snickered, "I wouldn't take any pay for it. It was too much fun. My reputation grew to where I was reading palms at every kid's party around town."

I held out my hand, face up, "I'm conjuring up a time when you read palms and tea leaves at the Shady Groves Fall Festival. You were the hit of the festival."

Kathleen grinned, "I decided not to wait to get senile to start embarrassing my children. I began at an early age so they would be used to it when I finally lost it completely."

"Did I tell you about Tina and Jakie's visit to Bingham Manor yesterday? Talk about embarrassment! Tina dressed Jakie up as the Grim Reaper and brought him there to see Anna Jean and Mary Florence. In our family the embarrassment shoe is on the other foot. Thank heaven Mary Florence saw the humor in it. We all had a good laugh."

"You've got to laugh as much as you can. It makes life so much more fun. I think I owe my good health and even my eyesight to laughter," said Kathleen.

"Your eyesight?" I wondered where was she going with this train of thought.

"Yes, I spend time looking for the humor in things. It keeps my brain working good and I think my brain is in charge of most everything—even my eyes." Kathleen's bright blue eyes, with a hint of green, twinkled.

I smiled, so glad to have Kathleen as a friend and mentor.

♥

Several times in the last few days I heard the surreal sounds of honking geese flying over the house. This morning they sounded like they were right outside my office window. The radio announcer was interviewing a representative of the Missouri Department of Conservation. Apparently there were hundreds of thousands of snow geese migrating. The conservationist said:

*It could even be over a million—so spectacular, really gets our attention. They are looking for warmer temperatures and improved feeding grounds. These geese are so abundant in Canada; they are ruining their nesting grounds along Hudson's Bay. Boys, get your guns ready. There's no limit on snow geese!*

My thoughts were, Oh dear, the poor geese. They are multiplying too fast. Now the hunters will have to thin them out. *God's in his heaven, all's right with the world* jumped into my mind.

But I didn't feel like everything was all right. The hunters were killing the geese. Tina and Henri weren't happy even though the café was doing well, actually better than expected, but Henri was disgusted by hurried lunches, having to have food ready quickly so people could get back to work. I heard him complain about Americans. Wondering why they couldn't be civilized like the French and take two hours for lunch.

They were fighting more than ever. I heard Tina accuse Henri of flirting with that raven-haired waitress. What was her name? I sat, lost in thought, trying to remember her name. Then I chastised myself—what difference does it make what her name is—why is Henri flirting? Is it just his way of coping with the stress? I know he loves Tina, and she is hard to live with sometimes, but flirting with other women is not the answer. I wondered if there was anything I could do to help.

♥

I walked in to Suzie's shop. I had washed my hair more in the last six weeks than ever before in my life, trying to lighten the pumpkin shade.

"Marjie, your hair looks so good. I love the color." Suzie knew just what to say to get my ire up.

My chin jutted out a bit. "It's not so bad since it has had six weeks to fade. In fact, I would like to keep the color just the way it is in its faded state."

"I think that's doable. Just let me mix up a little bit of magic." Suzie grabbed her mixing cup and headed for the back room.

My dander was up. "Whoa. Let's leave it the color it is now. No magic."

"Just kidding! I'll try to match it as closely as possible, but I do want to get that orange shade out of there. What do you want to do about the style?"

"The style is fine, too. Just trim it up a bit. Make sure the bangs are shorter than you usually cut them. You know I can't stand hair touching my eyebrows."

"We could shave your eyebrows," she joked, at least I think she was joking.

Suzie was close to stepping over the edge with me. "Don't even think about it. I have a wedding to perform tomorrow."

"A wedding! Who's getting married? Anyone I know? We'll have to make your hair extra special." Suzie's practically jumped up and down with delight.

"I don't think you know them—Anna Jean Stokes and Eugene Sylvester. They live at Bingham Manor, and just my regular cut. Nothing unusual."

Suzie continued talking as she mixed my color in the back room. "Oh that really nice nursing home out on the east side of town."

I hated when people called Bingham Manor a nursing home.

When Suzie returned I studied the color in her clear plastic cup. It looked similar to what she used the first time and that turned out all right. It may be a little darker, but no hint of pumpkin orange. I exhaled, relieved and decided to set her straight about Bingham Manor.

"Well, it's more than a nursing home. There are several stages of living there. Some people require no assistance, some a little and some a lot. Anna Jean and Eugene are both pretty healthy physically, but they are becoming more childish as time goes on."

Suzie brushed the color on my roots as we talked. "Do you really think they should get married?"

"About as sure as I was when I was nineteen and married Jake. I think they will both feel more settled having a mate. They've been going steady for several months and for the most part, I think it has been good for them."

"How old are they?" she asked.

She's eighty-three and I think he's about the same age. I've never asked. He's kind of debonair—he probably doesn't want anyone to know his age."

Suzie finished the roots and moved on to the rest of my hair.

"I'd like to be a fly on the wall of the church for this one. I just love weddings. They are so romantic. Are they reciting their own vows?" asked Suzie.

"Not if I can help it. We practiced with the standard vows, but Eugene talked about writing something, then Anna Jean wanted to, but as of yesterday, neither one had come up with anything. I'm hoping they don't."

Suzie finished putting the color on and began on her next customer. I settled in with *Pride and Prejudice*, ready to enjoy Elisabeth Bennett's sense of humor and Mr. Darcy's haughtiness.

Engrossed in the characters' lives, time flew and Suzie called me over to the shampoo chair for my rinse. That done, I sat down in Suzie's cubicle facing a mirror, the color looked fine. What a relief. So I focused in on the story, one of my favorite parts—Jane was sick at Mr. Bingley's estate, so Elisabeth walked over to care for her—through the muddy fields. *What a scandal, thought Miss Bingley.*

In the background I heard Suzie and Jolene talking about something. The latest *Dancing with the Stars* or *American Idol* maybe. Suzie's scissors stopped snipping and she whirled me around to look at the back of my head, but there was no back, my hair so short I could see my scalp.

"Suzie, what have you done to me? Let me see the front!" I was shocked.

"Well, at least you won't be complaining about your bangs getting into your eyebrows for a while." Her voice trembled as she tried to calm me.

My head looked like a newborn baby with just wisps here and there, shorn, I was shorn like a sheep.

Suzie's voice evidenced panic. "It's a pixie. One of the newest things. See right here in this hairdresser book."

"This is not like any pixie I've ever seen. Good grief, Suzie, what were you thinking? I've been coming to you for twenty years and never, ever have I worn my hair this short! I have a wedding to perform tomorrow."

If I didn't believe in peace and love, what would I do at this moment?

Suzie began to cry. "I didn't mean to cut it that short. I must have gotten carried away. Will you ever forgive me?"

"Only if you can find me a wig by tomorrow morning! The wedding is at two o'clock in the afternoon."

I wrote my check without a tip this time and handed it to the wilted Suzie. "It will grow, but do find me a wig, Please. I'm not kidding about that. Call me as soon as you have it. Do you have a scarf I can use for now?"

She found one and I took it, glaring at her. I left the shop, looking straight ahead, trying to compose myself. *Lord, please let me realize that my hair, red, orange, green or gone is of little consequence in the bringing about of your kingdom.*

My family noticed my hair. Tina tried positivity, uncommon for her. "You'll be the talk of the town. A trendsetter. It's kind of like picture's I've seen of Mia Farrow, maybe a tad shorter."

Jakie said nothing. His surprised look said it all. He snuggled into my lap with some papers he brought home from school. I opened the crumpled art work, finding our house, with its wraparound porch, two grandmas seated on the porch swing, one with a long black dress, one with fire engine red hair, but at least there was hair, two parents—his mom and dad and Jakie sitting on the porch steps with a puppy licking him. The tongue was almost as big as the dog.

I smiled and hugged my grandson for putting everything into perspective.

Al called and we talked for an hour. I did miss him. On a whim I invited him to Anna Jean's wedding. Since I was officiating, I asked him to meet me there.

That night my thank you prayers included my family, friends and even Suzie, my non-hair stylist.

♥

Suzie came through with the wig. It was blonder than my hair, but long enough to cover any bald spots, so I accepted it gratefully.

I drove to Bingham Manor early, wanting to meet with Anna Jean and Eugene again before the ceremony. I found the bride in Mary Florence's room dressing for the occasion, her antique white satin gown an empire-style, A-lined from the bodice, overlaid with fine burgundy lace.

I first viewed Anna Jean's reflection in the mirror. She was beautiful. Peace descended on me alleviating my worries about the ceremony.

Anna Jean turned and walked toward me. "Marjie, I'm so glad you are here. I want you to meet my daughters, Lily and Rose, and my granddaughters, Michele, Yvette, Cerise and Crystal."

"What a lovely family you have," I said.

"Oh, these are just the females, wait till you meet the men!" declared Anna Jean.

I examined the faces of Anna Jean's daughters and granddaughters, thinking that their feelings might be hurt, but saw nothing but happiness and, perhaps, a trace of amusement.

Michele spoke next, "She's not kidding, Marjie, our men folk are extraordinary. They all have beautiful wives and daughters."

We all laughed.

I remembered my purpose for coming early. "Anna Jean, I thought you and Eugene and I could get together for one last run-through…"

"Marjie, I can't believe you'd even think that, much less suggest it! You know that Eugene can't see me before the ceremony. It could simply ruin our marriage." Anna Jean was serious.

I concluded there was no way to get them together, so I asked Anna Jean if she had any questions about the ceremony.

"Marjie, you just don't listen. I've told you that Eugene and I have been through this before. Him more times than I would like and it scares me some that his wives keep dying on him, but I don't intend to do that. I intend to stick around and see him ten feet under just like I did with Ralph."

I tried another tack. "Anna Jean, did you write anything to read at the ceremony? Like vows or anything?"

"What have I been telling you? Quit worrying about my part and just get yours right. I thought you were an experienced minister. Do I need to call Rev. Jones from the Baptists?"

I decided to give up with Anna Jean. This was useless. I just did not want to be surprised. I felt the sympathy of Anna Jean's family. I excused myself and went looking for Eugene, determined this wedding would be the joyous celebration that it was meant to be.

I found Eugene watching a football game with a crowd of men— each wearing a red carnation with a blue and red ribbon. The groom certainly stood out in his dress whites. I guessed none of the other men could fit into their uniforms or they didn't own them after all these years.

Eugene welcomed me to the group and made a place for me on the sofa beside him. "Marjie, the Chiefs are ahead. What a special present for our wedding day!"

"Eugene, could we have a few minutes to talk?"

"Just a minute Marjie, wait until this next play is over…go, go, go. What a run! Touchdown!"

My memory bank flooded with the many times I had heard Jake say, *Wait till this next play is over.* The men slapped each other on their backs, some waving their canes in the air.

I wandered away from the riotous football lovers, found a chair in the empty dining room and sat down, forced to wait until time for the wedding to find out if they had written their vows. I relaxed, breathing calmly, deeply. The Lord would take care of it. Everything would be fine.

And it was. The ceremony was short, but beautiful. Eugene recited a lovely poem he had written for Anna Jean, but we used the traditional vows. I felt everything had gone well. They were married in the name of Christ, in sickness and in health, from this day forward, until death…

Al smiled throughout the entire wedding. I had forgotten that I had even invited him.

The high emotions of the football game and wedding ceremony exhausted everyone. We decided to postpone the reception for two days to allow for rest. I called the bowling alley to reschedule. Luckily they were able to accommodate us on such short notice.

It was still early. Al followed me home and we enjoyed some private time, having the house to ourselves—Jakie at my mom's, Tina, Henri and Laetitia at the café.

Al said he felt so at home and that he could get used to this. We drank tea and talked of dancing, setting up a date for a week from Saturday night. He had to be in California until then.

After he left I wondered if I should ask the McNamara's if we could include Al in our Friday night dinners. This is getting serious on my part. I hoped it was on his.

### *CHAPTER NINETEEN*

Al called to tell me he found a place that had ballroom dancing over in Mission, Kansas for our Saturday rendezvous. I know I could have asked him to come to a Bingham Manor dance, but didn't think it would be a good idea. Not sure why. He would pick me up at six o'clock for dinner first. Jakie would stay with Mom because Tina, Henri and Laetitia would not be home in time.

My emotions drifted between giddiness and fear of embarrassment. Dancing can be romantic if you know what you are doing, but in my case, Barbra Streisand on roller skates in the movie *Funny Girl* seemed more likely. Maybe I'll fall into his arms—that would be charming.

He suggested I wear a dress with a full skirt, something long, if I had one. I assured him not to worry. I would find something. I think he was hinting that he wanted to buy me something. Rare for him not to come right out with what he wants to do, though.

I searched the back of my closet for my mother-of-the-bride dress, wondering if it still fit—according to Jake the aquamarine watered silk gown flattered my figure.

I found it and laid it across my bed to inspect it, all the buttons remained, no soiled spots apparent. I slipped the dress over my head and smoothed it in place. It was perfect.

After I hung it in the closet I went out to the porch to watch for Jakie's school bus.

He dismounted and ran up the steps to my open arms for a hug. We sat down on the swing so I could look through all his papers and he began making noises.

"HMMM. HAAA. HOOO. OOOEE. HMMM. HAAA. HOOO. OOOEE."

I had to ask. "Jakie, what are you doing."

"I'm exercising my mouth, Grandma. It's fun."

In this day and age when many children seem to require expensive game devices for entertainment I was glad that Jakie only needed himself and his imagination. How his grandpa would have enjoyed him.

♥

The house to myself, incredible—Jakie at Mom's and everyone else at the café. I leisurely sunk into a deep bubble bath and turned on the whirlpool, realizing this was the first time I had allowed myself this pleasure since my family moved home. I lolled, promising to treat myself more often. There was no reason not to.

As I brushed my teeth to get ready for my big date, a dancing date with Al, I looked at my floral prints on the bathroom walls, their beauty astounding and yet, peaceful—the Pink Sweet Peas, Jimson Weed, and Oriental Poppies. Wait a minute, either Georgia O'Keefe added some white dots on those poppies where I didn't remember them—or there was toothpaste spatter on the glass. I'd have to check this out later when I clean, if I clean. It never seemed to happen anymore.

Moving back to the bedroom, I pulled on panty hose noticing my legs, the veins, dark purple, jagged like mountain roads. What work of art would O'Keeffe have created with these as inspiration? Thankfully my dress was long. I imagined Al's face seeing these veins for the first time. Was I ready to be seen naked by anyone other than my doctor—a woman, by the way? What brought that to mind? We were going dancing not to a motel room.

I dressed and put on makeup, willing my thoughts of nakedness to be replaced by images of dancing instead. That didn't help. The tranquility of my bath began unraveling further. I thought, what if Al is swinging me around and I go off like a projectile-flying nun or Great American Hero. Maybe I should beg off on this evening. But it was too late. The doorbell sounded.

Al stood in the doorway dressed in a gorgeous black tuxedo, the coat a Nehru style with a Mandarin collared shirt, no tie. I almost gasped at his attractiveness, but caught myself. I looked pretty good, too, if his face showed any reflection of what he thought of me.

♥

I leisurely drank my tea after everyone else had gone off to work or school, day-dreaming about being in Al's arms as we waltzed and did other dances that came natural as I followed his lead. How much fun we had. I got to be dipped and twirled. I felt like Ginger Rogers. I felt like *me.*

We went to Jasper's Ristorante after leaving the ballroom and Al declared that he loves me—wants to marry me. The thought of being his wife is alluring, magical even, but we haven't really gotten to know each other. We've never talked about politics, religion—even though he has gone to church with me a few times. I don't know what he believes. I tried to bring this up, but he said it was late and that we would have a lifetime to get to know each other. I did not commit myself to him. I just melted against him, speechless.

But, now he was gone again. He wouldn't be back in town until after the New Year. Over five weeks. He said he would call.

I picked up the Sunday magazine section of the paper to take my mind off Al. I had no idea of what I would find. I discovered a poet with whom I was not familiar. Her name is Wyatt Tinley, unusual name for a girl, Wyatt. She's the Poet Laureate for the state of Kansas. I love poetry, not so much to search for meaning but to enjoy the collection of words, the variety, the cleverness of the turn of phrase, the spurt of an idea.

I enjoyed about fifteen minutes of browsing then remembered— tomorrow is Thanksgiving Day. I didn't have time to read or think about reading right now—must bake pies and nut bread for the church dinner. I had promised six cherry pies and a dozen banana nut breads.

While I baked I looked forward to the ceremony tonight. Beth and Jerry would renew their wedding vows and go on a short honeymoon. Their daughter, Susanna, would stay with her grandparents, Eileen and Rob. I prayed for their happiness and commitment to a solid marriage. Then prayed for wisdom for myself and Al.

I skipped the Prayer for Peace today at the Temple, but managed to read it online while listening for the oven timer. This afternoon after baking I worked several hours at Bingham Manor. I was so glad I did. I would have missed Eugene dressed as a turkey, Anna Jean as Pocahontas and Mary Florence as a proper pilgrim. If only I had had my camera with me.

Beth and Jerry's renewal of vows was beautiful. Not a dry eye in the house.

Tonight my thank you prayers overflowed my cup. And Al would be back in town after the first of the year. Strange he didn't call tonight.

♥

Tina and Henri kept the café open until six p.m. on Thanksgiving, featuring Cornish Game Hen as their special for the day. Laetitia worked with them, but Jakie chose to stay with me so he could attend the dinner at Shady Grove and for once his parents and both grandmothers agreed on something.

Plans for Thanksgiving dinner for the neighborhood and homeless came to fruition. I was so proud of our congregation, everyone pitched in to make this a success. We advertised in every possible way: going door-to-door with flyers, talking to anyone who answered their doorbell, posting notices at the Palmer Center, Sermon Center, Boys and Girls club, grocery store bulletin boards, spreading the word at the Salvation Army shelter, homes for unwed mothers and victims of spousal abuse—anywhere we thought there might be people who wouldn't have an invitation for Thanksgiving Dinner. We had no idea how many would respond, but we trusted God to provide enough food, expecting at least fifty from our congregation, we decided to triple that number and plan for one hundred and fifty. Rob purchased eight twenty-two-plus pound turkeys. We wanted enough to send leftovers home with our guests, which we did. Believe me, everyone took home food. At last count we served seventy-five people here, made up to-go dinners for about twenty homebound congregants, leaving lots of food to send home with people. We salvaged some for the Salvation Army shelter and the Community Services League, sending non-perishable items to them.

Our dinner at church started at one o'clock and ended at five, so Jakie and I stayed to help clean up, took Mom home and delivered meals to Sully and Genevieve, my other meals-on-wheels clients thankfully with family today. We beat Tina, Henri and Laetitia home. Jakie jumped on them when they walked in the door. They reported a full house and pretty good profits for the day. We all gathered in the family room to share our day and to relax, but not for long.

The doorbell rang. Jakie and Henri answered it to find Mark, his mother and children standing on the porch. Rosalie bounced through the door. That woman has more energy than a compact fluorescent light bulb. They were on their way to the Plaza lights and came by to invite us. As tired as I was, their enthusiasm was contagious, so I decided to go along and so did the rest of the gang.

I hadn't been to the lighting ceremony since Jake and I went together, a Yuletide tradition for us, but this year I was coming out of my shell. I think he would approve.

Tina explained the festivities to Laetitia, Henri and Jakie, who naturally wanted to go see all the colors, the concert, the crowds. Mark reminded us we had already missed the pre-show festivities and the flip of the switch that turned on the lights, but he assured them the lights would still be spectacular outlining the Spanish-style buildings in blues, reds, yellows, greens, most buildings monotone in color. My favorite has always been the Time Tower, always in red, or the ones in all blue, I never could decide.

We couldn't all ride together. I rode with Mark, but Greta decided to ride with Tina and Henri. I thought she would want to keep an eye on her dad and me, but she probably thought riding with all the French people would be different, a learning experience, perhaps?

Traffic was terrible, but traditions die hard; those of us who live in the Kansas City Metro love our Plaza Christmas lights. It is a rite of passage to make it through the Plaza on Thanksgiving night. We knew our cars would not be able to stay together, so we arranged to meet after the drive at Winstead's for a warm up hot chocolate or cold malt, but should have known we couldn't get into the parking lot. Thank goodness for cell phones, we decided to get away from the crowd and meet back at my house for warm up drinks or ice cream, whatever suited.

We were all tired but didn't want the evening to end. We sat in the family room with our snacks and drinks—adults on the sofa, love seat and chairs, kids on the floor, except Jakie who sat between Mark and me.

Mark said, "Son, tell everyone about the skink you found."

Mark Jr. roused himself from his horizontal position. "My new pet. I found this skink on a log in our backyard."

I had to stop him. "Excuse me, exactly what is a *skink?*"

Mark Jr. started to speak, but his father beat him to it. "It's skunk with one *I.*"

As tired as I was my imagination flew to picture this skunk with one eye. I said, "It's a skunk with one eye? I've never heard of such a thing." By now, everyone was laughing and they were laughing at me. "You don't keep it in the house, do you?" Their laughter was contagious. I began to laugh.

Mark gently said, "Marjie, a skink is a lizard, a very cosmopolitan creature, so, yes, we keep it in the house."

"A lizard, you say, but does it have just one eye?" I knew I was off base, but I just couldn't get the one-eye thing out of my mind.

Finally Tina said, "Mom—the *I* is a letter. It's how you spell skink—take out the *U* in skunk and replace it with an *I.* Got it?"

We laughed until tears flowed from all of us. I made a spectacle of myself. First, I took a drink of water at an inopportune time .The water went up my nose. I continued laughing and spit the next sip of water clear across the room. It was a good time with family and friends and I didn't mind being the source of all the hilarity.

Every muscle in my body melted into the mattress when I finally got to bed. Thanks to Mark and the homeless dinner, I didn't even have time to miss Al. Sleep took over before my thank you prayers had a chance.

♥

Thank goodness Jakie's school bus came a little early today. I had never seen Henri in an uproar. I had heard him fighting with Tina before, but never actually seen him up close yelling at her. It was all in French so heaven only knows what they were saying, but Laetitia knew. He slammed the door when he left, almost directly in front of screaming Tina. She ran after him, managing to get in the car before he took off.

I looked at Laetitia for illumination, translation, whatever I could get from her. She stammered, "Cherie—Tina wants Cherie gone. Henri, he, what she say, flirt, with Cherie."

"What was Henri yelling at Tina about? Does he realize that he does flirt with Cherie? I've noticed it, haven't you?" I asked, hoping she could understand me.

"Bah. Oui. He flirt with her. Means nothing. His père, my Gregoirie, he flirt. Meant nothing. Still loved me. Henri loves Tina. I know this. Henri yelling about Tina picking up her clothes—all over bedroom. I see it. Just like in my house. Tina is messy."

"But what does her messiness have to do with him flirting?" I wondered aloud.

Laetitia shrugged her shoulders. "Henri upset. First thing…wants his house…neat."

Even with my concern over Tina and Henri's relationship, Laetitia amazed me with her ability to speak English. I still wasn't learning French. She had been attending English as a Second Language classes at the high school whenever she could. I needed French as a Second Language classes, but would probably have to go to France for that.

Jakie was in bed when Tina and Henri came in from a long day at the café. They joined us in the kitchen where Laetitia and I sat drinking our favorite beverages, wine for her and tea for me.

Henri kissed Tina's hair and they went happily to their bedroom to pick up Tina's mess together, wine bottle and glasses in hand. I felt certain that Cherie needed to find a new job. Laetitia and I clicked my cup and her glass together in a celebratory gesture.

Laetitia entered the family room where we were watching a Disney movie with Jakie. She stood in front of the TV set, her black dress adorned with a bright pink scarf. I wondered where that came from.

She spouted off a few short phrases. I didn't understand a word she said, for it was in French, but I saw the shock on Henri's and Tina's faces.

"Translate, sil vou plait!" I said.

"I have news. I must go home. Gerrard wants me for his wife." Strange words coming out of Tina's mouth, but exciting news for Laetitia.

Henri paced. Tina sat, frozen.

I hugged Laetitia, not knowing who Gerrard could be, but she looked happier than I had ever seen her.

Laetitia smiled.

Henri began to grill his mother for information. We found out that Laetitia and Gerrard, who happened to be her late husband's brother, have been connecting on Skype all the while she has been here.

Ah ha, I thought. That's why she spent so much time on my computer.

"I am like Catherine the Great. I must have the love of a man. You understand, Marjie, oui?" Laetitia stood with her arms wrapped around herself, legs spread like a Cossack.

I'm so glad Laetitia learned English while she was here. I wouldn't have missed hearing her say that for the world. I will miss her. Henri will surely accept the marriage of his mother and uncle. He's Henri.

Time flew during the last few days of Laetitia's stay with us. She packed and sang all over the house. I found out that the pink scarf she wore for the announcement of her engagement was bought as a thank you gift for me. She placed it around my neck and wished me an early engagement with Mark or Al, whoever I ended up choosing. She favored Mark because he had children and she thought I should have more children in the family, but Al was so rich and handsome. She, graciously, would leave the choice up to me. I wasn't sure I wanted either one of them. Mark is a friend and Al is the one I feel drawn to romantically, but he is gone so much and there is something mysterious about him. Lately, I have talked to Mark on Facebook more than I have heard from Al.

I took Laetitia to the airport by myself since Tina and Henri needed to be at the café and Jakie was at school. She chattered all the way to KCI about her plans with Gerrard, also asking how soon we could come and visit them. That was a huge question because Tina and Henri probably wouldn't be able to get away for a long time. She knew that, but hoped they could find someone to take care of the business while they were gone. Also, she pressured me to spend my honeymoon in the south of France—the perfect place for lovers.

I told her I'm not sure it's the perfect place for me and, besides, I have no intention of marrying anyone at this time—not Mark or Al, certainly, and thanked her for the invitation.

She said, "Bah—you crazy not to marry one of those handsome men."

I laughed and agreed that I may be crazy. I hadn't told anyone about Al's proposal. With him gone again and only rare short phone calls, I felt confused. Did I want to spend the rest of my life with an enigmatic man?

I dropped her at the curbside check-in and went to park the car, but couldn't find a parking place after circling around four or five times. I pulled over to the curb and called Laetitia to explain.

She said, "No worry, I found friend to talk to until plane comes and we going through security now. Thank you, Marjie, for everything. I love you. Talk to you on Facebook, yes?"

"Yes, we will. Laetitia. Let us know when you get home. Have a wonderful trip and tell Gerrard 'hello' for me. I love you."

I drove home and relaxed with a cup of tea and the dreamy voice of Luciano Pavarotti singing *O Holy Night* until Jakie arrived home needing consoling since his beloved Mamie Titia was gone back to France.

My nerves were on edge when Mom and I pulled up in front of Suzie Do's Salon. Tina and Eileen, well, most everyone I know, could not believe that I was going to allow Suzie to touch my hair again. But Suzie and I go way back. I just couldn't hurt her feelings by going somewhere else, although the thought of Rodolfo did cross my mind.

Suzie's natural glow was up about three notches. She told me she's seeing a weight lifter, Tony, who owns his own gym. Tony is training

Suzie and Jolene in the art of weight lifting.

"Marjie, you should join Tony's gym. You can't believe how firm I'm getting. Check this out." She lifted her shirt to show me her defined abs.

I told her that just thinking about that much exercise wore me out.

Suzie said, "You lift weights every time you stand up. Your body is a weight."

I said, "I'll lift my coffee cup to you. It's about the only weight I feel like lifting right now. Even sleep wears me out."

"Marjie, that doesn't sound like you. You know exercise keeps you young and fit."

I couldn't tell her about Al, that missing him and worrying about what to do when he came back, had me acting like a teenager. Then I got nervous. Suzie was so distracted trying to talk me into joining her new gym before I even sat down. I was torn. Should I just cancel my appointment or take a chance?

I am a coward at heart and I love Suzie, so I stayed. As I sat in the chair, Suzie mixed my color, and I gave her positive feedback on her trim look and congratulations on her new boyfriend, who sounded so nice and…muscular.

Mom and Jolene were having a nice conversation about Mom's condo board's Christmas festivities.

I am proud to report that Suzie got it right today. My hair had grown out enough for her to just feather it a little into a respectable pixie and the color came out perfect—the strawberry blond of my youth. My faith in Suzie was justified—this time.

## CHAPTER TWENTY

I went to pick Mom up for lunch. Her face gave her away.
Something was wrong. Seriously wrong. She asked me to come inside.

"Marjie, sit down," said my mother, looking extremely grave.
"Have you heard from Al lately?"

"We talk on the phone pretty often. What have you heard? Is he
okay?" My mind began to create disasters of every sort, but my mother
wouldn't hear if something was wrong with Al before I would. That
didn't make sense.

"Rosalie called me. She finally got that lazy private investigator to
give her a report on Al."

"What private investigator?" This was taking a turn to the
ridiculous.

"Remember the day I told you there was something I couldn't tell
you?" asked Mom.

"You have got to be kidding. Rosalie hired a private eye to follow
Al? Why in the world would she do that? Has she gone insane? I don't
want to know what she found out."

"Marjie, you do need to hear this." Mom sat quietly giving me time
to think, I supposed. Her countenance underwent a change. I could tell
that she was praying, a peaceful look came over her. Maybe I did want to
hear whatever information she had.

"Okay, I'm ready. Did she find out that Al is a CIA agent?" I
laughed, trying to lighten the mood.

"No. She found out that Al is not divorced like he said. He is still
married and living with his wife in California whenever he's not here
with you. I hope you haven't given your heart totally to him," said Mom.

Her words hit me like a wall of bamboo. I looked at my mother.
"What? You can't mean that. Al is still married! Married—not divorced!

Al. Our Al. My Al! I was starting to care for him. How can he play with my heart like this? He proposed to me. Mother, what should I do? I am, er, was, falling in love—enamored with him. Wait till I get my hands on him. No, I never want to see him again."

Needless to say, I didn't feel like going out to lunch. Mom fixed us some chicken noodle soup and my favorite crackers with pineapple cream cheese—just like when I was sick as a child.

We went to the Prayer for Peace and that helped take my mind off Al for a few minutes. Then I had to go to work, so I put thoughts of the dastardly, dirty, creep on hold until my drive home.

I wondered what you do if you find out that the man you are falling in love with is married to someone else? Do you fight for him? Not for that liar, that rotten *skink!* Do you go hide under the kitchen sink? Talk to your best friend or mother or Anna Jean or Adelaide? Yell. Scream. Beat him up. Beat his wife up?

As soon as I got home I called Al. I couldn't find his phone number so I traced my incoming messages to find it on caller ID. He didn't answer, so I left a message, asking him to call me as soon as possible.

I didn't have to wait long for his call. "Hi Sweetness," cooed the rat skink-lizard.

I didn't feel sweet. I felt angry. I blurted it out. "Why are you courting me while you are married to someone else?" I waited for a response.

"Marjie, what are you talking about? You know I'm divorced. You know I love you. I asked you to marry me."

I wanted to believe him, but Mom seemed pretty certain.

"A friend of mine hired a private detective to follow you." I didn't care what he thought. I just wanted to get to the bottom of this.

"So that's who it was. I had no idea who R. Bryant was. You see, I hired a P.I. to find out who was checking up on me." Now he sounded mad. Then he took a deep breath.

"Okay, to tell you the truth…"

Here was a warning sign. Jake always said: *Whenever someone says, 'to tell you the truth', you'd better watch out, they're lying.*

"You had better tell me the truth," I said. My heart beat faster than a mix-master, my stomach roiled and my head pounded.

"I wanted to wait until after the first of the year when we were together."

"Tell me now." I knew then he was the lying cheat that I hoped he wasn't.

"I love you, Marjie. I cherish you. We have such wonderful times together. I love you very much. This doesn't change anything. I have asked my wife for a divorce. As soon as my divorce is final we can get married. I want to be with you for the rest of my life." He sounded sincere and charming, as always, but not so self-assured.

I had to ask. "Did you ever think that before? How many women have you dated while you've been married?"

"Marjie, I have dated other women. My wife understands me, but I don't want her understanding anymore. I just want you. I feel differently about you. I feel we are soul mates."

"Soulmates. I don't think so. I would never lie to you and to quote my mother: 'The grass will always be greener with someone else.'"

"But my children want to meet you."

"Al, you never even told me you had children." I hung up.

Before I had time to cry, throw something or yell Jakie ran in to my office to show me his knee. He was occupied with his Legos when I went in to call Al. His knee didn't appear to be hurt. I asked him what he wanted to show me.

He said, "Grandma, say hello to my knee to stop the itching."

I said, "Hello, knee, why do you want to itch? Hello, Hello."

Thank heaven for this wonderful child in my life and for his mother and father and my mother and friends. Jakie and I wandered into the family room to enjoy the beauty of the Christmas tree. His Legos were spread in front of the sparsely covered tree skirt. He knelt down to play.

I began musing about Al. What would Christmas have been like with him? Then I remembered he was a skunk, a skink lizard, a lying married rat. As much as I hated the fact that Rosalie hired a private eye, I was blessed to know the truth about Al. My dancing days were over. Romance was history. I was a happy widow with a wonderful family and friends—a rewarding job and volunteer opportunities that made my life interesting and fulfilling. I was satisfied. I must be satisfied.

Christmas was just three days away. Under the tree there were a few presents for Jakie, Tina, Henri and me, but not nearly as many as there used to be when Tina was a child. I was trying to cut back on materialism and so were Tina and Henri. There are earrings for Tina, a tie for Henri and a few handmade wooden toys for Jakie. His parents had bought him mostly clothes because he was growing so fast.

This year I decided to give goats to all my family, to Mom, Tina, Henri and Jakie, not goats for us to keep, but goats for people in, perhaps, Bolivia or Zambia, Haiti, Malawi to help those in need. I wasn't perfect, but I wanted to try to be a better world citizen.

♥

On Facebook that night I asked Mark if he knew Al was married. As soon as he read my message, Mark called me on the phone. He said he didn't know his mother hired a P.I. until yesterday, but was glad she did.

"Marjie, I want you to know that I am truly sorry that you have been hurt, but I can't help hoping that you might find it in your heart to love me."

I couldn't hear this right now. I stopped him. "Mark, let's be friends. I do value your friendship so much. Can't we be friends?"

He answered, "We can be friends, and I will be patient for a time, but I see our friendship growing into more. We both deserve to be happy."

"I am happy and so fortunate to have you in my life, but for now let's keep it simple. Maybe we can spend a little more time together—as friends. Are you going to be in town for Christmas?"

Why did that come out of my mouth? I didn't need complications right now.

Mark said, "We will be in town from Christmas Eve through New Year's Day and I plan to monopolize your time as much as you will let me."

I tried to think clearly, but it was impossible. My feelings were still raw. "Mark, I thought I was in love with Al. I can't just transfer that love from him to you. Let's take one day at a time, okay? How would you like to go to the Christmas Eve service at my church? I won't be able to sit with you because I'm presiding, but we can go back to my house afterward. Tina and Henri are keeping the café open until eight, but they should be home by ten."

"What time shall we pick you up? Oh, and is it okay if I bring the kids and *Mom*? I know you are upset with her right now, but she just wants us to be together. She feels it in her bones and Mom's bones are never wrong. She was hoping to find something about Al's character or background or something to discourage you from seeing him."

"She certainly did that." I paused, trying to focus on what he had just said, "Bring your children? Of course." Then I turned to Laetitia's favorite word, "*Bah.* Rosalie, your mother, my favorite librarian certainly did pull the dirty laundry out of the bag. By all means, bring her, but she is going to get a piece of my mind."

"She just did it because she loves you so much, wants you as her daughter, wants us to be happy."

After we got off the phone I thought about Rosalie and how much she has always meant to me ever since high school. How she instilled a love of reading in me. I knew her intentions were good and I am glad to know Al's dirty little secret, but she has to know that she shouldn't go behind people's backs. I don't know. I believed in always giving people the benefit of the doubt, what does that really mean? Shouldn't it be giving the benefit of *belief.* Figuring that out would drive me crazy, but anything would, I was so close already—short trip.

Rosalie wants me as a daughter. That may be a little scary. What kind of mother-in-law would she be? Always interfering? Well, Mark and I are just friends. She has to accept that.

That night my prayers were jumbled until I relaxed and asked for God's will. That's always the best.

On Christmas Eve Day Mom and Jakie had been playing with the Wii all afternoon. I was taking the holidays off because so many residents were with their families. The café was open tonight so Tina and Henri were working. Mom offered to watch Jakie so I could prepare for the Christmas service. She came to my bedroom door to see if I was ready and to tell me that Mark and his family had just arrived. I grabbed her and pulled her inside my room.

"Mom, what do I say to Rosalie?"

"Honey, I think you should bury the hatchet." Mom said in her most persuasive tone.

"What, in her back?" I joked.

"Better to do that in Al's back, don't you think? Beyond a shadow of a doubt, you should forgive her. It's clear as crystal to me that she meant only the best for you and Mark. She wants you to be her daughter. What a compliment. And I don't mind sharing you with her one little bit."

Heavenly days. I had unleashed Mom's cliché dictionary, but she is right that I should forgive Rosalie.

Thankfully we all fit in Mark's van and seeing his family and my mother sitting all together in the front pew was wonderful. Even Mark's daughter, Greta, smiled and, every once in a while, closed her eyes during the service. She didn't even glare at me once or roll her eyes when we sat around the family room prior to coming to church.

Adelaide brought Mary Florence to the Christmas Eve observance. As I stood in the foyer following the service I could see Adelaide towering over everyone in the receiving line. Her pasty makeup glowed and the broad red lipstick smile exceeded her usual grin. I heard her cackling over the general sound of conversation and was thrilled when she got to the front of the line.

"MARJIE, BEAUTIFUL service. Reminded me of PUCCINI'S TOSCA. The BELL choir. The SINGING. Almost made me forget the NEWS I have for you. My Christmas gift to you, Tina and Henri—the FOOD critics on Walt BODINE'S show want to BROADCAST LIVE from *La Vie en Rose*. Set it up, GIRL. And TV 5 and Fox 4 want to do INTERVIEWS with them. You'd better get busy."

I was amazed at Adelaide's ability to make things happen. She hadn't been living in the KC area for a year and has created a successful accounting business and important contacts. Tina and Henri frequently tout her financial savvy. I could barely wait to tell them about her professionalism in public relations. What a blessing. I knew Tina and Henri would be so pleased and I could quit worrying about being their PR person.

♥

When we arrived home I served hot chocolate and the Christmas cookies Jakie and I made yesterday. He was so proud showing everyone the Santa's sleigh, reindeer and big fat Santa's he decorated. "All by myself," he bragged.

Mark went back out to the van and brought in a huge red plastic bag filled with Christmas gifts. I had not bought anything for his family, but I tried not to feel guilty about that. Christmas is not about presents. It's about love—of God, Jesus and each other, all of us on the planet.

Tina and Henri came in delighted about the successful day the café had. They gave bonuses to all their employees. Tina gushed about their new waitress that replaced Cherie, and using one of her grandmother's favorite expressions, called her "a diamond in the rough."

"Think she's a diamond in the rough. Wait till you hear what Adelaide did for you." I told them to their gleeful response.

Tina said, "Adelaide may be a bit caustic and bossy beyond belief, but worth every penny and insult." She began planning the live broadcast menu on the spot and Henri practiced posing for the camera, even though it would be a radio show, as Rosalie took pictures of everyone all around.

Mark suggested we open the presents.

Greta said, "Me first." She pulled a box out of the bag and carried it across the room giving it to me. I opened it slowly relishing the feelings brought on by her gesture. It was a small ceramic dish, shaped as a red maple leaf, so graceful, a true work of art, an imitation of nature.

"I made it in art class at school, Marjie. I want you to have it," she said smiling a bit shyly.

I was overcome. How, why had her feelings for me changed? Every other time we had been together I saw resentment in her face, her bearing. I stood up, placed the dish carefully on the coffee table, and put my arms around her. She let me hug her. Amazed, I thought, when will I learn not to question God's goodness, his workings in our lives?

Next, Mark Jr. handed out tins of chocolate, peanut butter and vanilla fudge, all from his mother's recipes. He told us that after her death his dad carried on the many traditions that she had begun and now it was his turn to continue them.

My gaze turned to Mark, realizing, not for the first time, but maybe, more intensely what a wonderful father and friend he is.

Young Elsa, not to be outdone, gave out the Rice Krispie Treats she made into shapes of bells, Christmas trees, and wreaths, decorated with red hots, M & M's and marshmallows.

Mark had brought lots of gifts for Jakie, a truck, puzzles, Dr. Seuss books, a fire chief hat. He gave Mom a beautiful scarf and Tina and Henri a CD entitled *Romantic French Music*.

Thankfully, Jakie had taken a long nap earlier today so he enjoyed every minute and so did the rest of us.

Mark and his family got ready to leave. It was almost midnight and we were all winding down. Mom and Rosalie had both nodded off a few times as they sat next to each other on the couch, close as sisters.

While Mark's children and Rosalie gathered their coats and hats from my bed and said their goodbyes to my family, Mark and I found ourselves alone. I asked him about the change in Greta's attitude toward me.

He said, "My mother started the ball rolling. She has been gradually promoting my cause, and hers, ever since the Jacomo picnic and when Greta saw you lose yourself over the skink, spit tea across the room, laughing so hard when you thought a skink was a skunk with one eye, it caused her to rethink her animosity toward you. We had a talk. I told her I love you and someday hope to marry you. I asked her to give you a chance. She's a wonderful girl, Marjie. I know you will both come to love each other. That's my prayer—for our families to become one."

I was afraid to speak, was I still afraid to love? The wounds of Al's deceitfulness were still fresh, but Mark wasn't Al, not at all like him and I had known him since we were kids. I gave him a hug and told him to give me some time. He hugged me back, firmer and longer than ever before, and said, "Please don't take too long, Marjie."

After they left Tina trundled Jakie off to bed, so Santa could come. He went willingly, revved up as a race car driver before the race. And I was, too, but for different reasons.

♥

## New Year's Eve

♥

I woke early, before the birdsong, thanking the Lord for another wonderful year. This year was more than I had ever hoped for. Tina, Henri and Jakie here with me. The café going well. Anna Jean and Eugene happily married. Beth and Jerry back together. Mom's health doing well. New friends: Adelaide, Annabelle. Reconnecting with old friends: Mark, Rosalie. Our prayer support group.

I decided to pull out last year's resolutions to see if I had met all of them:

- Let's see, eat healthier, nope
- Exercise five days per week, nope
- Spend more time with my mother, yes, and it has been wonderful
- One hour a day in prayer and study, most of the time, until Tina and Henri moved in, then I missed a lot of days or shortened the time
- Begin a weekly prayer support group, yes, halleluiah! Our group has become so close to each other.
- Prayer for Peace five days a week, I'd say about fifty/fifty since the Deschamps moved in.
- Become a youth friend or foster grandparent, no, but I have my grandson, Jakie, and Mandy. She's like a youth friend and I am in charge of JAM, that wasn't even on the list, so I'll have to give myself an "A" for that one.
- Lunch program for the homeless, never even got it started—we just did the tea, Thanksgiving Dinner and a few fund raisers
- Recycling program at church, yes, and I believe I shrunk my energy footprint quite a bit and have been a good influence on others.
- Go back to school. I did a semester. That was more than I had before.

*Lord, thank you for all that I accomplished with your help. I believe I have grown a lot this year. Last night Tina, Henri and I decided to trim our resolutions down to five. I believe that will make it easier to focus on what is really important. They are going to share five and have only one personal one.*

I planned to continue the prayer group, working with JAM, working at Bingham Manor, Meals-on-Wheels, recycling, Prayer for Peace, but realistically, perhaps one day a week, spending time with Mom, Jakie, Tina and Henri, and a drooling French bulldog, but what did I want to be my resolutions? Reminding myself how important it is to set goals.

*Lord, I know you have blessed me with lots of energy, good health, and wonderful family and friends. I am so blessed I don't know how I can stand much more goodness. Tina has begun to conquer her grief. You brought Mark into my life again, let me meet Al, so that I would have lots of perplexing moments, get my ego fed and teach me, I'm not sure what yet. My hair is reddish-blond again and I feel wonderfully young for the first time in many years. The café is a success. With all these blessings I am overcome! Thank you.*

Dear Jake, if you hear me. Please understand that I love you and will always love you. I never thought I would want or need another man in my life. What you and I had was so special. You weren't perfect and neither was I, but we had a rare love. We were open with each other. We shared so many things and yet, we loved one another enough to allow for experiences away from each other. Remember, how at the end of every day apart we would cuddle up and talk about the day's events. We laughed so much at Tina's antics all through her growing up and cried when we felt we couldn't reach her. I worried about your safety whenever you went to a fire and you worried I would collapse under the strain of being a fire chief's wife, Tina's mother, an elder and you always said, "a friend to everyone I met."

Jake, I don't know how you feel about me seeing Mark, but I do know you want the best for me, whatever that is. As Mom would say, "Time will tell."

♥

Mark and his family attended the *La Vie en Rose* New Year's Eve party with me. After he took his family back to his mother's house he showed up on my doorstep at ten minutes to midnight. Luckily he warned me ahead of time that he was coming or I would have been fast asleep by then. We talked for hours about our children, our mothers, the possibility of him moving his family back to Independence, about Jake, and about God. The rest of the house sound asleep, I got up off the sofa and motioned him outside.

"Mark, take me dancing."
He waltzed me all the way around our wraparound porch.

*Acknowledgements*

I would like to thank the readers of the lumbering first draft starting with my book club friends, who graciously chose my manuscript as a monthly reading selection, then entitled, ***Margie Goody Two-Shoes***, Betty Bennett, Doris Heath, Gail Miller, Janelle Delk, Julie Anderson, and Maggie Boyd. They gave me much needed confidence while wisely telling me to throw out a third of the book. My sister, Susan Daub Kelly, and my sister-in-law, Shirley French Jester, kindly offered specific ideas to fixing problems. I owe them big-time and don't know how to repay them. I will forever remember the encouragement of my editor and spouse, Walter, and the gentleness with which he red-penned through my *baby*, this book, giving me excellent suggestions and guidance. I do know how to give him recompense. I will reciprocate in kind when he allows me to edit his next book.

Thank you to Andie Paloutzian, Program Manager of the Story Center at the Woodneath Mid-Continent Public Library for providing classes and personnel to assist people like me who yearn to see their work in print. I especially want to thank Cody Croan, Woodneath Press and Expresso Book Machine guru, for your patience and assistance with formatting.

The cover art was created by the talented Alice Oshel of Hudson, Kentucky, whose creativity has exceeded my wildest expectations. Thank you Lisa Dotson for assisting with the cover fonts.

I have dreamed of being a novelist since I was old enough to read ***Little Women***. Yes, Louisa May Alcott's scribbler, Jo March, was my inspiration at age nine and beyond. I've started four novels to date and never finished one until ***Our Wraparound Porch***. I still have my research for each one and every word I've ever written. (That may be a bit of an exaggeration.) I hope you enjoy my story about Marjie and her friends because they will be back in Book Two of the ***Wraparound Series*****."**

# *About the Author*

**Diana Daub French** lives in Independence, Missouri with her husband, Walter. They share eleven children, sixteen grandchildren and thirteen great-grandchildren. She received a Bachelor of Arts in English from the University of Missouri-Kansas City and is a retired Human Resources Specialist. Diana holds the office of priest in Community of Christ.